Joan
Quarry Hall: Book 1

By

Michelle L. Levigne

www.MtZionRidgePress.com

Mt Zion Ridge Press LLC
295 Gum Springs Rd, NW
Georgetown, TN 37366

https://www.mtzionridgepress.com

Published in the United States of America
Print Version Publication Date: September 1, 2023

Editor-In-Chief: Michelle Levigne
Executive Editor: Tamera Lynn Kraft

Chapter One

Dawn caught Joan Archer on the Pennsylvania Turnpike, half an hour from her target. As the headlights in her rearview mirror turned into cars, she decided she had a tail.

"Niobe," she muttered.

Suddenly, everything made sense. All the trouble Matt had been facing lately—the competitors trying to steal and patent his designs out from under him, trying to get Homeland Security and the Pentagon to distrust him after six years of partnership—Niobe's fingerprints were all over it. A classic tactic. Attack Joan's friends, keep her busy helping them, and when she was distracted, sneak up on her for the death blow.

Joan thought she was heading to Pennsylvania to investigate one of Matt's enemies, when actually, Mohammed had tricked the mountain into coming to her.

The problem with studying her enemy in the rearview mirror was that all black SUVs looked alike, and Joan wasn't paying attention to where she was going. She had messed up. After four years of security and obscurity in her new identity, she had actually relaxed.

When are you going to learn? There's no such thing as safety. Not until you're sure she's dead, or you're dead. If you ever had a chance of your prayers being answered, now's the time...

Before Joan laughed aloud at the idiocy of thinking God would ever listen to her prayers, a rest stop sign brought a plan. She pulled over and drove down the long ramp. The black SUV followed. Slowing, she caught the license plate number.

Fury and laughter and fear erupted into a knot that threatened to choke her. This was *worse* than if Niobe had discovered her new identity. Worse than if the vengeful psychotic arrived with an army to destroy Joan's new life, the quiet college town where she had made that new life, and all the friends who didn't know she had killed at age eight.

"Idiot." She slammed her car into a parking spot and nearly forgot to put it in park before jumping out to confront the driver of the black SUV.

He parked on her left, got out and looked over the hood, with the same smug smile he wore when he beat her at *Risk* or solved a crossword puzzle question that stumped her.

"What are you doing here?" She knew better than to ask how he had followed her.

Matt Cameron designed security systems. Including tracking systems that couldn't be detected with the standard radio frequency sweeps. A dozen times over the last week, while they worked on identifying his enemy, he could have planted a homing signal in her car.

His smile changed to scorn and he shook his head. His short cap of ebony curls looked mussed, like he had raked his fingers through it a dozen times in the last two hours. Joan felt a little better, knowing she had inflicted that frustration on him.

"My contacts at the DHS think it's the guy in Denver." He rested his elbows on his hood, stretching his deep emerald polo shirt. "I'm guessing your military contacts think the same. And you disagree."

Usually Joan could come up with a dozen lies without even trying. Her tongue tangled at the idea of lying to Matt. Especially when he had to know — this time at least — that she lied. Which made no sense. Their entire four years of friendship was based on lies. So what if some philosophers argued that if you told a lie enough times it became reality?

"If we're both right," she said, to silence the arguments in the back of her mind, "and Carr is stealing your work, this could be dangerous. As in guns and people who shoot and don't care about questions."

"And you're planning on going in there alone?" he countered. He leaned his weight further into the SUV, rocking it a little. "Not smart."

"Recon only. Get pictures, get proof, and get out of there."

After she sent the evidence to her partner-in-crime, Sophie, and to Col. Sidarkis, their Pentagon contact, to get working on that evidence. That was what her custom-designed computer tucked under the passenger seat of her car was for.

"What a coincidence. My plan exactly." He gestured at the passenger side of his SUV. "Get in."

Joan opened her mouth to refuse. She wanted to accuse him of following her to stop her, not to investigate the man trying to destroy his life. But that was ridiculous. The only person who had ever looked out for her and put her interests first was hundreds of miles away. At least if Niobe had targeted Matt to use him to destroy her, she wasn't gunning for Sophie. Joan calculated what had happened, like a video playing in her head. Matt woke up in the middle of the night with a new brainstorm in the search for his enemy. He had called her and when she didn't answer after repeated tries, he had come to the apartment, saw she was gone, and turned on the homing signal/GPS she theorized he had put in her car.

Knowing Matt, he blamed himself and came running to protect her.

When had anyone ever done that for her, in her entire life?

She complied because she knew if she didn't go with him now, Matt would check out Jonas Carr's warehouse on his own. Despite being a genius with electronics and security programming, he didn't know diddly-squat when it came to keeping alive in tense situations.

By contrast, her infancy and childhood had been one long, tense situation. Complete with guns, plastic explosives, and enough hatred to make the Klan seem like a bunch of Mr. Rogers clones.

"Okay, let's get going." In moments she got her backpack and computer out of her blue sedan, locked up, and got in Matt's SUV.

He didn't start the engine. The silvery light of pre-dawn took on the first peachy tint of true dawn.

"Matt?"

"Why are you making like Joan of Arc, sneaking off to go slay some dragons that are technically my dragons, not yours?"

For the first time since they had met at a Butler-Williams University evening class, he didn't smile when he made the joke with her name. Not that Joan would ever admit she had indeed chosen her most recent name because she admired the Maid of Orleans. Even if she had died in flames. At least St. Joan had stuck to her guns and done the right thing.

"Maybe because…" She rubbed at her dry eyes, prickly with weariness. Why not tell him the truth? She owed him that, after all. If her theory was correct. "Because I'm pretty sure my enemies are behind your enemies, helping them attack you. To get at me."

She watched Matt, his face going impassive, eyes half-hooded. Joan imagined gears whirring and circuits flashing as he put things together, all the cryptic phrases, all the questions she answered with jokes or simply changed the subject.

"Wow, that's the most information you've volunteered about yourself in a long time." He slid the key back into the ignition but didn't turn it. "Makes me wonder what other secrets you're keeping from me, that might actually affect me."

"A secret shared isn't one any longer. You're better off not knowing." She inhaled sharply. "Please, trust me on this."

"Uh huh." Which meant the exact opposite.

"Look, we need to get moving. I planned on coming in from behind Carr's warehouse while there are still plenty of shadows and lots of movement all over the place from one shift starting and one shift ending. The best time to spy on someone—when everything is in shadows, they can't see you. Not at night, when people who have something to hide expect people to target them. And not in daylight, when they can see you."

"If you can see the enemy, they can see you." One corner of his mouth quirked up. That was a favorite line from the evil overlord handbook some friends had passed along as a joke. "If they are in firing range, so are you."

"Exactly."

"We're getting off at the next exit. Twenty minutes. Plenty of time to fill me in on all the extra data you didn't bother sharing with me before."

Joan's phone rang, the opening bars of the Westminster Chimes.

"Hello, Sophie," Matt muttered.

Joan glared at him and slid her phone from her pocket. Sometimes she wondered why she had introduced Matt and Sophie. There were plenty of ways she could have applied Sophie's computer and Internet wizardry to Matt's business needs without the two of them ever hearing each other's voice. She should have known better. They got along like a house on fire. Things just got worse when Matt became a Christian, and he and Sophie teamed up to pray for her.

Didn't they know it was useless? Joan didn't have a soul to be saved.

"Data dump," Sophie reported, when Joan opened the connection. "Bottom feeders, chattering about DHS intel coming through on a new ID program. Whatever this guy got, infiltrating Matt's system, he's ready to start the auction, and then it's bye-bye, Ma-Car Tech, hello, federal prison."

"Duh. We're heading over there to check out Carr. Fiver put something in our back door files yesterday. Check it and give me your view on it?" Joan glanced at Matt. He finally started the engine.

"You think Sidarkis will laugh if you ever tell him you named him for a rabbit?"

"You're the one who read *Watership Down*, not me." She grinned and dug her thumb knuckle into her aching temple to relieve the pressure.

Joan referred to Col. Sidarkis as Fiver, meaning the five sides of the Pentagon. Sophie insisted he got the code name because of the mystical prophet rabbit in the fantasy novel, and because there were many levels and hidden pathways to the Colonel, like a rabbit's warren.

Either one fit, actually.

"When you say we... don't tell me you invited Matt along?"

"I didn't. He bugged my car and followed me." Joan grimaced when Sophie's chiming laughter rang through the phone. "Soph, this isn't funny. If the Colonel is wrong and we're right, Matt and I could be heading into trouble. Even though I swear, all we're doing is recon." She glared at Matt as she said it. He didn't look at her as he backed out of the parking spot. "How soon can you give me your take? And an aerial view of his property? A current one, not Google Earth six months old?"

"I'm on it. Tell Matt I'm praying for the two of you."

"Thanks." Joan swallowed a lump with sharp edges. She wanted all the prayers on her behalf she could get. When she put her phone away, Matt was grinning at her. "What?"

"I was just thinking how comfortable you are with this spy stuff."

"We all have our specialties." Hers was living a lie. Ironic, because she hated lying to Matt. Sophie was the only person she had ever been fully honest with.

Joan watched the horizon as the silver streak turned to gold and pink and wished she could pray. Matt belonged to God. That would have to be enough to guarantee them some safety.

"Ready?" Matt said, as he moved over into the exit lane. Jonas Carr's warehouse sat at the back of an industrial park close to the Turnpike exit.

Their gazes locked. Something fierce and alert in his expression made her throat close up and put hot pressure at the back of her eyes.

"No. But that never stopped me before," she lied.

Navigating the back roads to the industrial parkway took more time than she anticipated. Monday morning traffic was at full speed by the time they found the street with Jonas Carr's warehouse. Matt coasted up to the gate in the tall, rusty, chain link fence and they got their first look at the warehouse. Grass stood tall around it. Taller weeds poked up through the cracked asphalt and gravel pits of the parking lot. No cars were visible between fence and warehouse. Matt nodded when she pointed out the electronic gate and the shiny new barbed wire at the top of the fence.

"I counted four cameras," he offered, once they had driven two hundred yards past the warehouse, and down a street that would take them behind the acres that belonged to Carr.

Two low, sprawling buildings had plenty of traffic on this street. Workers were arriving, others leaving. Joan counted a dozen semis at loading bays. This traffic could cover their presence. She preferred crowded conditions to help her be invisible.

Matt continued down the street and made a right turn, exactly where Joan had planned on going. He had clearly done his own research. Soon, there was nothing but trees and high grass everywhere they looked, with a derelict building in the distance and a gravel drive that led into woods tangled with ivy. Matt pulled the SUV into the thick shadows provided by a tall clump of trees.

"One more check, in case Sophie or my military friends sent something." Joan slid her computer out of its case. Matt stayed silent as she checked her robot search engines in case something new had come in during the last four hours on Jonas Carr. When she closed her computer ten minutes later, she looked up from her screen to tell Matt that nothing had changed and found him sitting with his head bowed and eyes closed. He held that little green leather Bible Xander had given him for Christmas when the three of them first started hanging around together. Xander had given her one just like it. She had read it four times, but it never gave her the peace she saw on Matt's face while he prayed.

Her throat and chest ached. Matt opened his eyes and looked straight into hers. For just two seconds, he looked a little startled, then he smiled, shrugged, and ducked his head.

Joan looked away, swallowing hard. Unwanted memories sprang up, Niobe's voice spewing all the venom the woman had expressed for any religious belief.

Ivy made a shaggy, vibrant carpet from the trees and over the fence separating the abandoned property from Carr's. From the dark green thickness of it over layers of years of dried vines, Joan estimated no one had been back here to inspect the security situation for years. If ever.

"It's a given there's no electricity running through the fence here," Matt said. He grasped the rusty bar of the fence, just above his head, where it showed through the tangle of old and new vines. "Wouldn't be surprised to find out the ivy's holding up the fence by now."

"So is this a new lair for these people, or they just don't care, they figure they're safe here?" Joan grasped handfuls of vines in front of her and pulled, testing how strong they were.

"Let's find out."

She reached the top of the fence just a few seconds ahead of him, and paused, holding onto the vines and just poking her head above the top. The back of Carr's property seemed to be in pretty much the same condition as its neighbor: vines and trees and nearly half a dozen outbuildings. Rusty corrugated metal roofs and cinderblock walls, pitted and stained by weather and age and pollution, and weeds growing in the cracks in the mortar. The only difference was tire tracks that had crushed weeds and dug ruts the last time it rained.

They investigated the closest outbuilding and found the inside very different from the outside. Bright lights, metal shelving without a speck of dust or rust, and crates with bright red stenciled codes, stacked up to the ceiling. Joan and Matt both took pictures with their cell phones. Before they got out of the SUV, she had programmed them both to automatically send pictures to her computer and his, and not leave anything in the cell phone memory. Just in case their cell phones fell into the wrong hands, there would be no evidence of what they had seen.

The next building brought them closer to the warehouse, where men's voices and the sounds of truck engines and heavy objects being dragged and dropped filtered faintly through the morning air. Joan stayed outside, watching the warehouse while Matt looked inside.

"More of the same," he said as he shut the door behind him.

A loud creaking followed by low rumbles of metal wheels on cement came from the warehouse. One side of the door that stretched up to the roof, two stories high, slid across the other. Inside was darkness, and a handful of men stepped out into the daylight.

Joan pushed Matt to go right as she ducked to the left. She scrambled behind the building, bent over to try to hide among the hip-high weeds. Another building, smaller, sat in a thick puddle of shadow from the warehouse. She aimed for it.

Her right foot came down on empty air. She tried to throw herself backward. Her left foot slipped downward. The long patch of darkness changed from shadows to a weed-fringed rectangular pit. The darkness swallowed her. She hit hard on her right foot and pitched forward, slamming her forehead into a wall.

Joan saw stars. Fire radiated up through her leg, making her collapse to the ground. She swallowed down the need to shriek as she struggled against the grayness that collected around the edges of her vision. Biting her bottom lip hard and using the pain and the taste of her blood to hold onto consciousness, she scrambled backward, seeking shelter.

Rule one: Get invisible.

Rule two: Get silent.

Rule three: Get out of there as soon as you can.

She pressed a scraped and bleeding hand over her mouth and nose to muffle the sound of her gasping, pain-filled breaths. Joan felt around with her other hand, willing the shadows to be real shadows, and not fading consciousness. She felt slightly damp concrete walls and tucked herself into a corner. The pain in her forehead and ankle kept sending gray sparkles around the edges of her vision.

Gradually, her vision cleared. Joan studied the straight lines among the shadows and decided she had fallen into some sort of maintenance pit. Long abandoned, judging by the weeds hanging down over the sides. That darker, rectangular blot in the shadows at the other end of the pit was probably an access door. Did it lead into the building she had planned to hide behind, or somewhere else?

Her phone buzzed between her hip and the wall and she muffled a sob as she shifted around to pull it out, making more sharp streaks race up her ankle. Matt. She flipped it open.

"Where are you?" Matt whispered, before she could even speak.

"Some sort of maintenance pit. Where are you?"

"Back over the fence. Hold on and I'll —"

"No. They'll see you." She glared at her ankle. "I'm fine. Just let me catch my breath and find my way out of here."

"They have guns."

Joan muffled a choked giggle. Usually, she could detect guns from a mile away. Four years of safety and peace in Tabor Heights had certainly dulled her survival instincts.

"Guess we were right about this guy, huh?" She leaned back against the wall and looked around the pit. Why couldn't she have landed next to the door?

"Too right. You call your friends and I'll call mine. Then I'm coming in for you."

"No. The less movement, the less chance of getting caught."

"Joan —"

"Stay there." She cut the connection, then scrolled down through her menu to "Fiver." Sidarkis would laugh. They hadn't talked so much in the last five months as they did in the last three days, when he called to tell her one of her friends was being framed for treason.

He didn't pick up his phone. She left a message and wondered if he could hear her whisper on his voicemail. Then she called up a map of the area on her cell phone and pinpointed the coordinates, sending them via email to both Sophie and Sidarkis. Her phone buzzed in her hand as she finished sending. Matt. She ignored him, knowing what he would say.

Her ankle and the arch of her foot hurt. She tried to distract herself by planning an icily vicious letter of complaint for the manufacturer of her cross-trainer. It promised support and protection across all terrains. She would have to depend on the high sides of her shoe to keep down the swelling, because she couldn't risk taking her shoe off to examine her foot and then not being able to get it back on again. Besides, she didn't have ice, and she didn't have anything to wrap her ankle.

Now to get out of here.

Joan pulled herself to her feet and hobbled around the edge of the pit to the darkness of the possible door. Every other step, she paused and held her breath and listened, and looked up at the rectangle of increasing sunlight overhead.

Twigs, bones of assorted animals that had fallen in here over the years, dirt, and blown leaves littered the floor of the pit. Nothing to help her climb out or to use as a weapon.

She called Matt, to tell him to go away and wait until dark, then come back for her. He didn't pick up. Joan supposed that was fair, since she had ignored him before.

A chill crept up her back. Matt wasn't the kind of guy to play childish games at a time like this. So why didn't he answer his phone?

She checked her email. Sophie had acknowledged receipt of the information and passed on new data about Carr. At the bottom of the message, she noted that she had forwarded the information to Sidarkis but hadn't heard from him.

Of course not. Joan grunted softly and leaned against the wall to take the weight off her foot. Why did this pit have to be a mile long? *He's busy, probably overseeing the raid on the Denver guy.*

She called Matt. No answer.

Sweat beaded her forehead by the time Joan limped up to the big, rusty, dirt-crusted metal door at the other end of the pit. She felt nauseous from the regular stabs of pain through her ankle. She took it as a good sign that her ankle didn't fold on her, meaning it was only strained, sprained, no broken bones. Maybe her shoe was living up to the manufacturer's promises after all?

"Straighten up, stupid," she muttered, teeth clenched. Was thinking about totally useless things part of having a concussion?

Chapter Two

It was almost an anti-climax to dig at the protrusion crusted with dirt, at the spot where a doorknob or latch belonged, and find a simple lever and handle. Joan honestly expected to find no way to open it from inside the pit.

"Please," she whispered, and pressed down on the latch.

It didn't move. She pressed until her thumb ached. Did she imagine that little bit of give, like it fought against dirt inside the mechanism? She made a fist and pounded on the latch. It gave with a dull click.

More sweat beaded her forehead and trickled down her temples. It wasn't that hot already, was it? How long had she been in this pit? Joan glanced behind herself and considered the length of the shadows. Maybe twenty minutes, half an hour at the most.

She pulled out her cell phone and called Matt. No answer.

One last check of her email. Nothing further from Sophie. No response from Sidarkis.

When are you going to learn not to depend on anyone?

Home means trust, she responded to the voice in her head that sounded a little too much like Niobe.

Joan pulled on the door, using action, effort, to keep the voices in her head from resuming the argument that continued ad infinitum, ad nauseum, waking or sleeping.

It took all her strength to pull the door open, heavy and stiff on dirt-caked hinges. With a groan, it swung open. Losing her balance, she barely avoided knocking herself on the other side of her forehead with the door. But it was open. The angle of the light falling into the pit behind her didn't touch the dark behind the door. She braced herself on the doorframe and leaned forward and sniffed, ready for the thick stench of mold and damp and dirt from enclosed places.

It smelled of dirt and oil and engine exhaust. It was in use.

Where did this dark hole go? Only one way to find out. Joan hesitated before stepping all the way into the room, and that didn't make any sense.

She liked the darkness. She had always felt safest in shadows.

Not because Niobe had trained her to walk in shadows, but because she had made darkness her friend. When she was thirteen, a year after Niobe had left the baby in a stolen car in a river, Joan failed an important assignment. Niobe made her carry a backpack full of explosives into an Allen Michaels crusade, to put under the speaker's platform when the children came forward for the story. The explosion never happened, Allen

Michaels didn't die, and Niobe locked Joan in a bug-infested closet for two days. Joan preferred the darkness. She couldn't see Niobe, and Niobe couldn't see her. The longing to run away had crystallized into a plan during those two days of silence, thirst, stench, and darkness.

First step: Escape.

Second step: Find out what happened to the baby.

Third step: Find out who her father was and get his help to get revenge.

Joan had learned revenge was never worth the planning and effort, and justice never paid back the pain. While she still wondered about her nameless father, she had given up trying to find clues, mostly because it meant going into Niobe's sphere of influence to find information. She had learned to find satisfaction in living quietly, in safety, in the shadows, and wait patiently for her enemies to trip up and punish themselves.

Matt, however, hadn't learned patience and the benefits of shadows. Joan punched in his speed dial number.

"Look, right now isn't a good time," he said, answering on the second ring. "We'll talk when I get back into town, okay?"

"Ah... sure. Where are you, anyway?" Joan held her breath, trying to figure out what was different about the reception between their phones. Something was wrong. Did it sound tinny? Was he somewhere that interfered with the reception?

She nearly banged her head back against the wall when his words suddenly made sense. Why pretend she was bothering him, unless he didn't want anyone to know she had come to Pennsylvania with him?

He had company, unfriendly people listening in on this call. Even if it turned out Jonas Carr really was a legitimate businessman, and not trying to destroy Matt, he wouldn't be inclined to be friendly. Matt had refused to do business with him, and now he had been caught trespassing.

And he wouldn't have been caught trespassing if she hadn't given him Sidarkis's information, if she hadn't helped him identify his enemy, and if she hadn't fallen into this maintenance pit. Knowing Matt, he had gotten caught when he tried to come back for her.

Why hadn't she heard any ruckus when he was caught?

Silence usually meant trouble.

"It doesn't matter," Matt said, after only a few seconds of hesitation, while the realization of their situation swirled through her brain. "I'll talk to you later." He cut the connection.

"I have to get out of here," Joan murmured. If she could get to Matt's SUV, then she could take leverage out of their enemy's hands.

One last attempt to reach Sidarkis yielded another request to leave a message. She switched to email and briefly outlined Matt's theoretical situation. Then she stepped into the darkness.

Micro-steps took her across gritty-crunchy cement. She tried to rein in her imagination, insisting it was just crumbling cement and not tiny animal bones and insect carcasses. If this was a former maintenance pit, logic said the entrance was through the nearest building. Joan reached to her right and immediately found a railing. Two steps, and she banged her injured foot against the riser of the first step.

She was sweating, breathing in gasps through her nose and trembling by the time she dragged herself to the top of the steps. Into more darkness. She waited a few moments with her leg bent, leaning against the cinderblock wall, taking the weight off her ankle. Her first step smacked her into more crates. She choked on a cloud of dust brought down by the impact. No one had disturbed anything in this room in a long time.

Eight steps took her around the pile of crates and revealed a line of daylight coming under a door. Joan grinned and hobbled to the door. In her experience, storage sheds rarely were made to lock anyone in, only lock intruders and thieves out. She still held her breath as she found the doorknob and turned it. For three frustrating heartbeats, it stuck. Then it let out a crack and jerk and moved in toward her. Joan opened it an inch and pressed her face against the opening to look out.

No movement. She couldn't see much of the yard, and the door faced the warehouse, which meant as soon as she stepped out, she would be visible to anyone looking her way. She contemplated taking the time to wrap her ankle with strips from her t-shirt to brace it for fast movement, but could she afford that much time, especially when she didn't have anything but her teeth to tear her shirt? She had a vision of the search for Matt's accomplice leading someone to this outbuilding, and the door being flung open while she was sitting there in her bra, her torn shirt in her hands. Not a good situation.

Bottom line: time was running out.

"Not for me, God," she whispered. "I have to get out of here to get help for Matt. He belongs to You. Please?"

She pulled the door open just enough to let her tip her head out and look further around. Still no movement in the yard between the outbuilding and the warehouse. No signs of movement or sounds in the warehouse itself.

Joan pulled the door open a few more inches, to let her slide out. Her ankle wobbled on the edge of the crumbling step. She caught herself on the doorframe and swallowed down the yelp of pain. The best she could do was muffle it into a grunt that ended in a whimper and gasp. She almost forgot to close the door behind her. The smallest anomalies could attract the worst kind of attention. The tension bowing her shoulders eased as she moved around the side of the building, keeping it between her and the pit she had originally fallen into, away from the warehouse.

Her phone buzzed in her pocket, startling her. Joan pulled it out. Matt. Swallowing hard, she flipped it open.

"Hey, Matt." She kept her voice soft. The silence filling this acreage behind the warehouse made her uneasy. People without things to hide or defend were free to make noise.

"Peekaboo," an unfamiliar male voice said.

"Who is this?" She muffled a groan. *Not a smooth move at all, Archer.*

"The man who has a gun pointed at your back," he said from behind her.

Joan closed the phone. Pressing the tiny pressure-sensitive inserts on the end, she locked down the phone's access and slipped it into her pocket. When — not if — these people took her phone from her, they wouldn't be able to access any of her files. Holding onto the building for support, she turned around.

Three men. With big, glossy, nasty-looking guns straight out of the latest destroying-the-terrorists-to-protect-our-future movie.

~~~~~

Exhaustion and heat worked together against the pain in her ankle and fiery thirst. After two hours sitting in the darkness of a filthy storage shed that smelled of oil and grime, Joan slept sitting up, her back tucked into a corner of the shed furthest from the door.

When the nightmare struck, she almost wasn't surprised. Joan knew she was dreaming as *she followed the taillights of the stolen car through the rainy darkness of Tabor Heights in a summer night storm. The wind pushed her sideways and rain drenched and blinded her, but she felt nothing, heard nothing, as she chased the car, trying to beat it to the river like she did every time the nightmare attacked.*

Again, she reached the river to see the car in the water. Joan stood on the riverbank and watched until the sound of a baby crying in terror filled her ears, drowning out the drumming of her heart. The car rode the racing current and sank deeper into the water until only the top half of the windows and the roof still showed. When the face appeared in the rear window of the car, it wasn't the baby, or Nikki, the girl the baby had grown up to be...but Matt.

Joan jerked awake, gasping, nearly blinded by the salty, rancid pain-filled sweat spilling down her face. She sat up, leaning forward to rest her face on her bent knees, and pressed her hands over her mouth to muffle the sound of her breathing.

It didn't take a degree in psychology to understand the dream. Despite knowing the baby condemned to die in that stolen car had been rescued and raised in Tabor Heights by foster parents who couldn't have loved her more if she was their own flesh and blood, Joan still worried about Nikki. There was always the chance that Niobe would find her, see the resemblance between Joan and Nikki, and realize they were sisters. And in her twisted reasoning that made her keep one daughter and try to kill the other, Niobe would decide to finish the job.

That was why Joan dreamed of Nikki drowning in the car.

Matt was now in the dream because her subconscious agreed: his
~~~~~

present trouble was Joan's fault. Niobe knew about him, and before she punished Joan for escaping her so many years ago, she would destroy everyone who mattered to her.

"Please, God, I know You don't want me," Joan whispered, "but please, don't let them hurt Matt because of me?"

~~~~~

What kind of villain used twine to tie up his victims?

Joan's wrists itched from the fibers as she hobbled down the aisle between tall metal shelves full of grimy crates and packing boxes and gave another testing tug with her wrists bound behind her back. A sharp sensation flashed up her arm, followed by warm wet. Sweat, or she had cut herself with the effort. She was betting on blood, because she had sat for four hours in that dark, grimy storage shed, sweating. All the time she sat there, no one had asked her any questions. She could have been another crate, for all the attention her captors paid her.

That was about to end, obviously. She would have preferred that they had put a hood over her head, but maybe that was a waste of time, since she had seen three of them. They didn't care what she saw, meaning they could keep her quiet and unable to use what she knew against them.

The man leading the way opened a door at the end of the shadowy aisle. Joan guessed the room was a prefabricated module, meant for dividing up large spaces to make them usable. This room sat near the center of the warehouse. The man walking behind her grabbed her shoulder and half-guided, half-shoved her into the room. She stumbled, but the man who went in first, the beardless, taller one of the two, caught her. He copped a feel before pivoting her around, shoving her into a chair in the corner.

Matt sat in the other corner, hands bound behind him, his ankles tied to the battered wood-and-metal-tube chair with the same brown twine her captors had used on Joan. From the sweat and grime marking his face, darkening his clothes, matting his hair, he had been given the same temporary storage shed treatment. He had some bruises on his face and his bared arms, but no other signs of rough treatment. What was happening now, that they were brought together?

His eyes asked a thousand questions, but he didn't say anything.

"So this is Joan. Otherwise known as Nobody." The beardless man settled down at a table on the far side of the room, maybe fifteen by fifteen.

Joan's computer sat on the table, open, and from the blue light reflected on the man's neat green Oxford shirt, turned on.

He couldn't get into it, though. Joan fought a smile as she pictured their captors' frustration.

Of course, if they had her computer, that meant they had the SUV. She and Matt weren't going to escape while their backs were turned, climb over the ivy-covered fence, and drive away.

"Nobody, as in Cameron said nobody was with him. But he had a hard
~~~~~

time backing up that story, when he couldn't open his own computer," the man continued, when Joan just looked at him.

She wanted to remark that she didn't think he was referring to the scene in *The Odyssey*, where Odysseus faced down the Cyclops in his cave. She wouldn't help matters any by being a smart mouth.

"Just what did the two of you find, when you were sneaking around back there, hmm?" He turned the computer around so the password screen faced Joan. "Maybe the better question is, what were you two looking for?"

"You know what we were looking for." Matt's voice was quiet and thin, a bad sign of just how far he had been pushed, how angry he had grown since he had been caught. Joan had only heard him use that voice once before, only a few months after they had become friends. He had been in a courtroom, facing three high school boys who had tried to drag Tris, his cousin, into the woods to punish her for not being "friendly." Their attorney had claimed Tris, thirteen years old, had been the instigator, using language more appropriate to a porn star.

"Maybe I do, and maybe I don't," their captor said, with a slow grin better suited to a crocodile. He nodded to the bearded man, who looked enough like him to be a brother. The bearded man tossed him his gun, and their captor stood guard while he tied Joan to her chair and searched her. He didn't find anything, just like the last two times he searched her, other than her cell phone. That already sat on the table next to her computer, which the first man now closed with a hard slap that got a sharp cracking sound from the case.

Then the two left them alone, in the dark.

"So that's Jonas Carr?" Joan said, when their retreating footsteps faded to silence.

"Just as nasty in person as his bio says." Matt grunted, and a scraping sound told Joan he was trying to adjust his chair. "You were limping."

"Fell into some kind of service pit."

"How'd they find you?"

"If I'd stayed in that pit, they wouldn't have." She couldn't decide if she should laugh at herself, or waste energy being angry. "I figured if I got free, that'd take a bargaining chip out of their hands. Did you get any response from your friends?"

"I left a message. You?"

"Same." Joan closed her eyes and tipped her head back, trying to stretch muscles that ached from her exertions and fall.

"Sorry."

"For what?"

"Getting you involved in this." Matt's voice came out a low, tense rumble with some growing heat.

"You're forgetting something. Most of our info came from my sources. So it's my fault we came here, if you really want to get picky."

"No, I really don't." He sighed, followed by that scraping sound again.

They stayed alone, in the dark. From banging and dragging and thumping sounds out in the warehouse, on all sides, something big was happening. The only place without movement was in their prison. That included the ventilation system. The still air grew warmer, staler.

Joan tried several times to adjust the twine tied around her wrists, to find the end, but only succeeded in tangling it tighter, cutting into her skin and cutting off circulation. Matt reported the same results. He managed to work his way across the little room, shuffling his chair over until his knee rubbed up against Joan's. That little bit of contact made a world of difference for her.

At first, they tried to pass the time by talking, careful to avoid mentioning their quest for information and their government contacts, in case someone was listening. They discussed the schedule of summer concerts on the lawn at the Blossom outdoor music venue near Akron. They debated the Guardians' chances for making it to the division finals this season, and how well they were doing so far that summer. Matt, Joan and Xander had invested in a six-pack of tickets for the season and still had three more games to go. They talked about how the twins, Rocky and Tris, were doing in their inter-church sports league.

The air grew warmer, closer, staler. Their conversation trailed off when they discussed the possible evening classes that Butler-Williams University would offer that fall. That was how they had met four years ago, when Joan first settled in Tabor Heights. Matt, Joan and Xander had taken an evening class in literature. Matt and Xander had taken the class just to learn something new. Joan had taken it because the teacher, Dr. Holwood, was Nikki's foster-father. Her plan to get to know her half-sister by insinuating herself into the community around her had given Joan her first real friends, other than Sophie.

Please, God, don't let Matt get hurt. He means too much to me.

Joan swallowed, wincing at the ache in her dry throat, and fought not to let out bitter laughter. What made her think God would take care of Matt because *she* asked?

The sounds of activity in the warehouse petered out. With a little maneuvering of the chair, making the twine cut deeper, Joan pivoted herself behind Matt enough to see his watch. He twisted his hands around enough to press the button that lit up the face of it.

"Almost three," she reported, and muffled a hiss when a drop of sweat rolled into her eye.

She nearly twisted around to rub her face against her shoulder and clear her eyes. She couldn't waste that moisture. There was no telling when or even if Carr or any of his men would come back to the room and give them something to eat or even drink. For all she knew, their captors were going to leave her and Matt in that room to die of thirst.

The silence changed. Joan wasn't sure what she heard, but she thought it came from Matt. She leaned forward as far as her bindings would let her, until she felt blood collecting along the twine and wicking down to her fingertips. Any other time, she would have been frightened to realize she didn't feel it cutting into her hands anymore. Just how quickly did someone start suffering delusions from dehydration, anyway?

Matt was whispering, little more than sub-vocalized breaths. Joan shivered, afraid for him... until she heard him whisper, "Lord."

Matt was praying.

She shivered, chilled down to her guts in a way that made her want to get up and run. But she couldn't. Joan closed her eyes, though it didn't make any difference, and thought about Nikki to block out the softly breathed words as Matt prayed.

She should have told Nikki they were sisters, but when? Certainly not that first day they came face-to-face, when she saw the thirteen-year-old using the cut-through behind the optician's shop to go to Heinke's Grocery. And not the first time she was invited to the Holwoods' house with the other students who had Dr. Holwood as their advisor. After they became friends, but when, exactly?

If she died here, Nikki would never know who had put her in that car when she was a baby. Maybe Nikki didn't need to know all that. What good would it do her, anyway?

"Joan?" Matt hopped his chair enough to let him nudge her knee with his. "Are you okay?"

"And if I said yes?" She wanted to scream at him, demand to know how he could ask such a stupid question, but she feared sounding like Niobe. Joan refused to die with angry words on her lips.

"Where did you go?" He pressed his knee against hers and kept the pressure up. "I've been trying to talk to you, but you're totally spaced out."

"Thinking."

"I don't suppose you remembered you had a blade in the sole of your shoe? Maybe a remote-control gizmo that'll fly down through the roof and break us free?"

"That's a *deus ex machina*. Dr. Holwood would be really disappointed in you, expecting a *deus ex machina*, after you aced his class." She grinned at him through the hot darkness.

"I got an idea. They left your phone and computer on the table."

"Because they don't need whatever we found. Which wasn't anything."

Chapter Three

"I'm thinking if I tip the chair over, maybe I can wiggle myself over to the table, get your phone and call for help."

"Problem. Security codes to lock down my phone."

"And you don't trust your good friend with the codes for your phone at a time like this?" His voice sounded thick. Joan hoped it was because he was trying to joke with her.

"It's not numbers, it's a sequence on tiny pressure plates in the case of the phone." She sighed. Now was not the time to explain all the security precautions she and Sophie used. Joan had monsters in her past, and Sophie had hers, and they tried to keep the big uglies of their lives from meeting or using either of them to get to the other. "Sophie and I do a lot of beta testing for developers, so we get prototypes, okay? That's the simple explanation."

"Very simple." He sighed. His chair creaked and the pressure of his knee against hers left. Joan missed it. "Okay, if I can get over there and get your phone, I should be able to get it back to you. Here goes."

His chair creaked. Matt grunted with the effort. The smell of blood came stronger through the thick darkness and Joan imagined that twine cutting deeper channels into his wrists. Metal groaned against wood. The groans went up a few notes. The thumps of the chair legs gained a rhythm, and she felt a faint movement in the air, generated by Matt's efforts.

Please, God...

"There!" Matt's yelp ended with a crash-thud and the sound of metal shrieking and wood groaning, and the sound of a sweaty man hitting the floor. He grunted and then there was a silence that was too complete.

Joan imagined he had fallen face-first and knocked himself out. With the smell of sweat and blood in the air, she couldn't tell if he had hurt himself. She couldn't hear him breathing.

Matt groaned, and she choked, fighting back a sob of relief. She sat still, listening, trying to find his location by the sounds. She flinched when she heard wood clatter and hit the cement floor. Then he laughed, the sound turning into a groan.

"Thank You, Lord." He gasped, and more wood clattered.

"Matt?"

"I broke the chair. If I can get my hands free of the pieces, there might be enough slack to untie them. Then we're home free."

"I'm going to start calling you Houdini."

"Not quite." The next few minutes were filled with the sounds of Matt struggling to break free of the remains of the chair. He provided a running progress report as he maneuvered around, trying to slam the pieces of the chair against the floor to break them. They both laughed when he reported that he got his feet free first and could stand. Joan suspected they were going loopy from thirst. Matt separated the back of the chair from the seat. He now could bring his bound hands and the chair back under himself and slide his legs through the loop of his arms. Then he banged the chair back against the floor until it splintered and set his hands free.

All the time he banged and struggled, no one came running to investigate. Joan mentioned that little detail as he struggled to untie the knots in the blood-soaked twine.

"Makes me wonder where everybody is," Matt said. "Either they've abandoned this place, or they're busy somewhere else, or they're waiting to spring something a lot worse on us the moment we step out the door."

"Then let's not step out the door."

"Uh huh. And just what do you suggest?" He grunted. "And we're on our way."

Joan jumped when his feet shuffled toward her and he touched her shoulder, then followed the line of her arm down to her hands.

"What were you saying about not using the door?" Matt prompted, when he had settled down behind her and got to work on her wrists.

"This room is a module. Prefab pieces brought into the warehouse. I bet we can climb up through the ceiling, and from there work our way along the shelves. Nobody ever looks up anymore. Even if we can't walk the shelves all the way to the door, we'll see them coming."

"If they leave the lights on in here."

"Pessimist."

"Not on your life. We are proof that God answers prayers." He slapped her shoulder. "Done. How does that feel?"

"I'm not sure I want to." Joan blinked hard, fighting tears, as she brought her freed hands in front of herself. Her arms felt stiff and tingly-prickly from being held in the same position for so long. Her shoulders and elbows felt like they had been frozen in place. She rubbed her wrists and palms, wincing at the swollen flesh, the fresh blood that made everything she touched sticky.

Matt made short work of the ties on her ankles. Then he laughed.

"What?" Something in the sound made her shiver, despite the heavy heat of the stale air.

Matt didn't answer, but she heard him get up and walk away from her. A moment later, light flooded the room. She muffled a hiss from the sharp pain in her eyes.

"Should have done that first." He hobbled over to the table to pick up her phone. He made a move to toss it to her, then shook his head and crossed the room to hand it to her.

Joan pressed the sequence and powered up her phone. She wasn't surprised to see five emails from Sophie in her inbox and pulled up the last one first.

"Sophie says to sit tight, the cavalry is on its way."

"What cavalry?" Matt had climbed up on the table to investigate the ceiling tiles while she worked on her phone. He paused with his arms raised, lifting a tile out of the frame.

"Hopefully not the kind that shoots anything that moves." She got up, groaning when her hips didn't want to move.

"Joan..." Matt grinned and shook his head.

"What?"

"You know I love you, but there are times I want to just shake you until your eyeballs rattle."

"You have to catch me first." She stuck her tongue out at him, grateful that he turned back to the ceiling tiles before her eyes filled with tears.

"Cavalry?"

"My military contacts."

"Duh," he muttered, followed by a clatter as he shoved the ceiling tile out of the way. Matt grabbed hold of the support bars for the ceiling and rested his weight on them. They didn't make a sound, but Joan saw dust come sifting down, indicating movement.

"Safe to climb up? Matt?" she said, when he didn't answer.

He waved his hand, shushing her, and the next moment pulled himself up into the ceiling. Joan held her breath, watching him struggle to get up, and imagined what the last six or seven hours of immobility and thirst had done to his body. She waited until his legs vanished into the darkness of the ceiling. Was he on top of the module, or was there another layer to get through before he was out into the warehouse? She couldn't tell, everything was dark above the hole Matt had climbed through.

There was a time for sitting still, but that had passed. Joan filled up her waiting by bringing her chair over and putting it up on the table, so she could climb up. Every step was a dull ache, like molars rather than canine teeth digging into her ankle, so she sat on the table to wait. She checked her notebook to make sure Carr hadn't damaged it while trying to get into it. Matt still hadn't come back, though by her phone he had been gone ten minutes. She slid her notebook inside her t-shirt and tucked it into her jeans, then tied her sweatshirt around her abdomen by its arms, to hold everything secure.

A rattle at the door sent her stumbling across the room, snatching up a leg from Matt's broken chair for a club. Joan looked back at the table with the chair under the hole in the ceiling and wished she had taken it down. Too late. The door was opening.

She crouched down, wishing for some furniture to hide behind. The door creaked softly as it swung open.

"Clear," a man said.

Three men in black jeans and long-sleeve t-shirts, rifles slung over their shoulders and handguns at their belts, stepped into the room. The last man inside turned to face out the door. The second stepped over to look up at the gap in the ceiling. The first man in crossed the room halfway and held out a hand to her.

"Joan Archer?" His mouth tipped up in a one-sided grin when she nodded and adjusted her grip on her makeshift club. "Colonel Sidarkis sends his compliments."

"Where's your friend?" the second man said.

"Finding a way out." She set the club down and let the nominal leader reach down to help her to her feet. He whistled and shook his head and turned her wrists to see the damage the twine had done.

"How bad off is he?"

"Other than some bruises and his wrists..." She shrugged.

"We have most of the warehouse secure, but not all the tangos are accounted for," the third man said. "It might be touch-and-go, and we don't want to shoot your friend."

"Cap?" The man at the door looked over his shoulder at them, then gestured with his rifle out into the darkness. He stepped out. Matt came through the door, his hands raised to shoulder height, with another man escorting him from behind, a gun pointed at the middle of his back.

"Your friend?" Cap said. When Joan nodded, the man holding a gun on Matt stepped out of sight again, down the hallway.

"You okay?" Matt said.

"For now." She tried to smile, but suddenly everything inside her skin ached.

He looked back and forth between the two men in the office with them. "Cavalry?"

~~~~~

A fire broke out before their rescuers got them to the door of the warehouse. Cap sent them to an outbuilding they had taken over as a command center, under the care of Lindstrom, a woman who seemed to rise up from the ground when they emerged into daylight. Joan and Matt sat in a corner of the command center, listening to the chatter on Lindstrom's radio, and waited for the news that Carr and his people had been captured.

Joan learned Col. Sidarkis had sent teams to investigate both men that her and Matt's search had pinpointed as suspects, but he had led the larger team to the other target. Carr and his men had been distracted for a short time, dealing with Matt and then looking for Joan, which allowed Cap's team to get into position, observe, infiltrate, and obtain the last pieces of incriminating evidence. While the two of them had sat in the dark office, Carr and his men had been loading up trucks and dismantling equipment, preparing to abandon their operations in the warehouse. By the trails of
~~~~~

gasoline spilled around the foundations, they intended to burn it to the ground, presumably with Matt and Joan still inside.

They listened and stayed quiet as Hunter, the team medic worked on their wrists, iced and bound up her ankle, gave them salt pills and water, checked their vitals, and fed them. As the afternoon turned to evening, the rest of Cap's team reported on rounding up the last of Carr's men. In simple terms, Carr and his network of specialists were mercenaries; the kind who enjoyed destruction and pain. They made a profitable living stealing identities and destroying reputations to cover their tracks. Matt was only the latest decoy to distract the authorities by investigating him, while Carr and his men finished up their work and moved on.

When it was safe for them to leave, Joan was half-asleep, compliments of the pain pill the medic had slipped in among her salt tablets. Matt supported her on the short walk to one of the team's vans. Lindstrom drove them to a small, clean little motel seemingly in the middle of nowhere. She found them a few pieces of clean clothes: sweatpants and t-shirt for Matt, a t-shirt three sizes too big and gym shorts for Joan. Their room was straight out of a movie from the forties. Lindstrom took up guard in front of their door.

Matt's SUV had been emptied and the seat covers had been slashed. Joan knew it was ridiculous to worry about her few credit cards and her driver's license, because they could be replaced. It was just proof of how the day's stress had drained her, that she focused on such small details. After all, she had her phone and her computer. Her secrets were safe.

Joan used the shower first, with her wrists and ankle wrapped in plastic bags to keep the bandages dry. When she came out, another meal was waiting, burgers and salads in plastic containers from the little diner attached to the motel. She could only eat half her burger, giving in to the exhaustion that made her dizzy. Joan was asleep before Matt got out of the shower.

She dreamed of Matt falling into the river of fire that surrounded Nikki's sinking car. Joan tried to dive in after him, and woke, falling across Matt's bed. She shrieked when big, warm hands came out of the darkness and grabbed her.

"Hey, it's okay," Matt said, when she struggled and kicked. He twisted her around in his grip, pinning her arms to her side when she punched at him. "It's me. It's Matt. You're okay. It's just a nightmare."

"Matt—" Joan thought she would vomit, but the thickness in her throat and the cannonball in her stomach burst out as tears. She dug her fingers into his t-shirt and sobbed until she thought she would suffocate.

Vaguely, she was aware of Lindstrom poking her head in the door and Matt responding to her questions, but ninety-nine percent of her awareness centered on his warmth and scent and the hardness of his arms tight around her. She stiffened when she thought he was letting go of her. Then Matt slid an arm under her legs and swung her around so she curled up on his lap with her head tucked under his chin. Her tears stopped immediately, with an almost audible click inside her head and heart.

"Hey, you okay?" Matt leaned back.

Joan opened her eyes. The nightstand light between their two beds had been turned on. She blinked the tears out of her eyes and took an experimental breath.

"Just a stupid nightmare," she managed to croak.

"Anything that scares you can't be all that stupid." He stared into her eyes for a long moment. It took all her self-control to meet his gaze. Matt broke the eye-lock first, guiding her head down onto his shoulder. "You want to talk about scared... you realize, if your friends hadn't shown up, we'd be dead. They planned to burn the place down, with us in it."

"But we're not and they didn't." She let herself smile, liking the buzzing sensation of his voice in his chest, under her cheek. If she could spend the rest of her life like this, wrapped in Matt's warmth and scent and strength, that would be more than she could ever have hoped.

"I almost got you killed. Dragging you into this—"

"And what do you think I would have done if you tried to go do this alone? You were chasing me down the Turnpike, remember?"

"Hey, don't interrupt my guilt-trip, okay?" He tightened his arms around her, revealing a number of spots where she was bruised. "Joan... we are in big trouble."

"They're wiping up the last of Carr's goons. By morning, we can head home and we don't have to worry about the twins getting any fallout from jerks taking revenge."

"That's not what I was talking about," he said, his words a little softer, a little slower. "You know what I was thinking about when I fell asleep?"

"Eating the other half of my burger?" She yipped, laughing despite the soreness in her throat, when Matt yanked on a handful of her hair. The sound died in her throat when his other hand cupped her chin and he guided her to sit up. Joan didn't want to open her eyes. She didn't want Matt to put her back in bed and go back to his own bed. Why couldn't he just hold her, like this, until—

Matt kissed her.

All her thoughts crashed into a jumble of white noise in her head.

When Matt lifted his lips off hers, she clutched blindly at him, grabbing handfuls of his shirt.

"Okay." His breath was warm on her cheek. "I'm guessing that doesn't mean you're going to punch my lights out for ambushing you like that?"

"Ambush—yes." Her voice didn't sound like her own, though she felt the roughness of it in her throat. She couldn't seem to get her eyes open. "More?"

Matt groaned her name, the sound ending in laughter, then muffled as he kissed her again. She let him lead and released all her inclination to analyze and plan. All that mattered was reacting, and letting everything that was good and warm and strong and clean in Matt feed that bottomless chasm in the center of her being.

~~~~~

Joan didn't want to wake up. The warmth stayed with her as she rose to waking, and Matt's scent grew stronger, but she was alone in the narrow bed with the scratchy sheets that provided a reassuring background scent of bleach. She rolled onto her side. In the sliver of the light from the not-quite-long-enough curtains, she saw his bed was empty.

The *whoosh-clank* of the toilet flushing made her flinch. She held her breath, listening through the thudding of her heart, as water ran. The bathroom door creaked open. Light flashed across the room from behind her. The light went out.

Matt slid into the bed and stretched out behind her. She let out her breath in an aching sigh as he wrapped his arm around her and drew her back against him.

"Sorry," he whispered, his breath warm against the back of her neck.

"For what?" She chose to laugh, to hold back the sweet, aching relief.

"Didn't want to wake you."

"I'm a light sleeper." Joan dug her fingers into the side of the mattress. Survival instincts screamed to get out, get on her feet, get away.

"Crazy day, huh? We should both be comatose after... everything that happened." He tightened his arm around her, fitting himself against her.

Joan thought she had never felt more alive.

That meant she was in more trouble than she had ever known, even while she still traveled with Niobe and carried bombs into crusade arenas.

"Don't ever scare me like that again, okay?" Matt whispered.

"Scare?" Joan stayed still, trying to keep her body limp.

She felt like every circuit in her head had been hit with an EM pulse. At the same time, she was warm and drowsy and happy to be curled up with him.

"Yeah, scare." Matt nuzzled the curve of her neck and tightened his arm around her waist. "I've never seen you cry before. I thought you were sick."

"Stupid nightmare." Joan wished he would shut up. He was pulling her out of the drowsy, languid state and making her think.

"What about?"

"You, hurt."

His chuckle woke her a little more, but she grinned into the darkness. There was something very good for her ego in knowing she could put that heavy, satisfied note in his laughter.

"Since we're handing out ultimatums, don't you ever take stupid risks for me. You had a chance to get away—two chances—and you messed up both of them, coming back for me."
~~~~~

"That's not the way I see it." Matt pressed a kiss against her shoulder. "I've got my ticket stamped for Heaven. You don't. Makes me expendable. Worth anything to make sure you don't go before it's your time."

"Idiot." Joan blinked away the tears and forced herself to smile into the darkness so he wouldn't hear the aching in her voice. "I resigned myself to a reservation in Hell a long time ago. There's nothing and no one who can get me through the other door. I just figure I'm getting some brownie points helping the good guys, you know?" She stopped when her voice broke. She thought she had cried herself dry. She had been wrong.

"That's exactly why I'm never letting you out of my sight again. Besides straightening out that totally wrong thinking of yours—"

"Which you should take as a warning. Get out while you can." She gasped when he levered himself up on one arm and leaned over her.

"I learned something important today." Matt pressed on her shoulder until she lay flat and he leaned over her, caging her between his arm and his body. He was just a dark shadow against the streak of light coming under the curtain from the parking lot.

"You're a lousy spy, so leave it to the pros?"

"Besides that." He leaned down until his lips barely touched hers, and his voice vibrated in the center of her head, despite being a whisper. "You and me, together forever and always, Joan Archer. That's the way it's got to be. Understand?"

He kissed her before she could think of an argument. Matt might be a Christian, but he was a new one. Joan knew more than him, had studied and read every book she could get her hands on, and listened to Sophie talk about the Lord she loved with all her heart. There was no way in this world and the next that Matt Cameron could drag her into Heaven with him, when God wouldn't let her through the door.

<div align="center">~~~~~</div>

Joan woke with the echoes of Niobe's shrieks injecting ice into her marrow. She slid out of the sanctuary of Matt's arms, the warm cocoon of the blankets. She shivered as she pulled on her discarded borrowed clothes and curled up in Matt's empty bed. The scent of him wasn't as strong in the cold sheets, but still made it hard for her to sleep. That was a good thing, when every descent into sleep brought dreams of Niobe's anti-men diatribes. Venom, spewed at Joan's father, the lover who had fathered Nikki, all the men she had worked with, used, fought, admired and then hated through the years. Joan thought about her recurring nightmare, how Matt had entered it recently. If she let it play out to its end, she would find Niobe waiting to kill Nikki and Matt if they escaped the sinking car.

She drowsed away the last few hours, fighting sleep, keeping watch over Matt. The moment he stirred and started to wake, she was up and in the bathroom to take another shower.

Chapter Four

Cap's team retrieved all of Joan and Matt's personal items. Some time during the night, someone had washed their bloody, sweaty clothes. Cap delivered them, showing up in time for breakfast and to debrief them while they ate in the cramped hotel room. The operation being led by Col. Sidarkis in Denver didn't have anything to report just yet, since they were still setting up and observing the target and gathering more information before acting.

"Meaning the amateurs pushed up the timetable for you, and they should keep their hands out of your work from now on?" Joan offered.

Cap just offered her a crooked grin.

Despite what Joan considered a monumental mess of her and Matt's attempt to discretely gather information, Cap admitted they had been helpful, both as a distraction and a justification for breaking into the facility. Most of his team would stay there at the warehouse, investigating Carr's operation and equipment. Two of Cap's team would escort Joan and Matt home, with a side trip to a facility in Aurora to get their injuries tended. Along the way, one member of his team would retrieve Joan's car from the rest stop along the Turnpike and deliver it to her apartment in Tabor Heights.

"How come you aren't arguing about it?" Joan had to ask, when she and Matt were settled in the back seat of a dark red Jeep driven by Lindstrom and Phillips. "Aren't you in a hurry to get home?"

Matt had called the twins last night to let them know he was all right, detained on business, and would be home late the next day. Knowing how the Cameron cousins took care of each other, ever since the deaths of both sets of their parents, she had a good idea how itchy Matt was to get home, just so Tris and Rocky would stop worrying.

"I figure if we go to Southeast General to have our wrists taken care of, there are about a dozen people from my church who work there. We'll run into at least one of them, and before I get home, Tris and Rocky will know. Bandages are easier to hide under long sleeves if they don't know we were hurt in the first place."

"If it's any comfort," Lindstrom offered, glancing over her shoulder at them as she drove onto the on-ramp for the Turnpike, "you're going to be busy and out of town for a while, helping us clear your name. Yesterday's operation went a long way, but there are reams of paperwork to work on."

"That's what I get for having a government contract," Matt said with a groan. He offered Joan a crooked smile. Then he lifted his arm, silent invitation for her to spend the trip curled up next to him, wrapped in his warmth.

She wanted it so badly, she ached.

Anything she wanted that badly could never be good for her.

"I think we should get as much work done as we can, clearing up things, before we get home." Joan bent to pick up her computer from the floor of the SUV.

On the drive home, she concentrated on gathering up all the evidence they had found about Carr's operation, preparing it to be used in the effort to clear Matt's record. Despite that, she still felt his gaze focused on her.

The discrete clinic in Aurora looked like an expensive spa facility on the outside. Joan suspected part of it did indeed cater to the upper spectrum of society with massages, relaxation and cleansing treatments, saunas and whirlpools. All she cared about was that she had time away from Matt while Dr. Malkin took care of her torn wrists, x-rayed her ankle, and gave her medication for the swelling and pain. She also gave Joan her phone number, with instructions from Col. Sidarkis that if she had any medical needs in the future, she was to come to her first.

"Very impressive connections, you have," Matt remarked, four hours later.

They stood alone in the back parking lot of the clinic/spa, looking at his SUV. One of Cap's very efficient team members had driven it back to Ohio and had the seats fixed. It smelled faintly of a mix of chemicals Joan couldn't identify. She assumed Sidarkis's people had been over Matt's vehicle to gather all the evidence they could use against Carr.

"I think the less said about those connections, the happier we'll all be." Joan pulled open the passenger side door. "Let's go home."

"That's what I need to talk to you about." He slid into the driver's seat and waited until she was settled, her door closed, before he started the engine. "What we were talking about before, in the hotel—"

"We were both under a lot of stress."

"I'm not using that as an excuse." He crossed the empty back parking lot and headed for the long driveway out to the street.

"Matt, don't ruin it, okay?" Joan flipped open her computer. "We have about forty minutes to wrap up this report. Why don't we concentrate on this work we need to do, and leave... well, leave what happened between us for later, when we're both a little more relaxed and we've caught up on our sleep and... when we've put some time between us and it, okay?"

He was silent so long, ice infiltrated her veins again. But when she finally got up the courage to look at him, he looked serene as he concentrated on the road in front of them.

"Okay," Matt finally said. "Doesn't matter how long we wait, because I'm not changing my mind."

Yes, you will.

~~~~~

"Do something for me, will you?" Matt said, as he pulled off of Main into the dead-end street next to her apartment over the optician's shop.

"Depends." Joan offered him a smile, hoping he would take it as teasing. She felt like she had forgotten how to breathe until he grinned back at her.

Matt made her wait while he did a three-point turn and came back to face Main, with the passenger door next to the sidewalk, right in front of the enclosed staircase leading up to her apartment.

"Think about what I said last night."

"You said a lot of things last night." She slipped her computer case over her shoulder and grabbed the canvas bag with her change of clothes and the ointment and medication the doctor had given her.

"About you and me, together."

"Matt..." Joan looked away as she hit the latch for the door. She met the gaze of a tall, lean Black man with a shaved head and pencil-thin goatee, who lounged against the building on the other side of the street. He tipped his bottle of iced tea to her and lifted it to his mouth.

"I want you to marry me."

"No, what you want is to get a good night's sleep and put some distance between you and what happened to us. It's just stress." She slid out to the ground a little too quickly and hit on her bad foot. Joan choked back one of Niobe's profanities. She took a deep breath and turned, forcing herself to meet his gaze. "Everything that happened last night was just stress. Coming close to death. Being scared."

"No, it wasn't. You wouldn't have let me...we made love, Joan. Not sex. There's a difference." He leaned over the console, his hand resting on her empty seat. "I love you, and maybe you've forgotten, but you said you loved me."

"I did not." She stumbled back a few steps, and fumbled at her computer bag as it slid off her shoulder. "You're delusional."

"Hmm, maybe. But maybe not." Matt gave her his teeth-bared grin that always signaled trouble for someone in the near future. "Just think about it, okay?"

She wanted to tell him that thinking about marriage would be a waste of time, because it would never happen. Joan swallowed down a dozen other retorts and settled for nodding. She limped to the base of the stairs and watched as Matt drove away. Her gaze landed on the stranger on the other side of the street, who still leaned against the building, enjoying his drink and the balmy summer evening.

When she entered her apartment, two of the six speakers hooked up to her security system were silent, no longer filling the air with crystalline chimes. Someone had tried to get in and gave up quickly, only triggering some of the sensors. It could have been her landlord, checking up on her.
~~~~~

Or it could have been someone with entirely different motivations.

Joan made sure the alarm system was re-armed. Before she turned on any lights, she looked out the side window. No one lounged against the building across the street.

~~~~~

She needed another shower, for the warmth and to get the antiseptic smell of the clinic off her. Joan stood under the scalding spray, her plastic-wrapped wrists braced on the walls of the stall and out of the water, and let the heat soak in. For two seconds, she flashed back to the hotel, the glorious relief of washing away her ordeal, then coming out into the neat, shabby little room and seeing Matt there, knowing he was safe.

The heat of this shower turned into the heat of Matt's arms around her, driving away the ice that sometimes seemed like a permanent resident in her marrow.

"Stop it," she snapped, and slammed the swivel control for the shower to turn off the water. She could stand under the hot water until her skin burned and peeled off, but she wouldn't feel as warm and safe as she had felt curled up next to Matt.

He wouldn't marry her. Not after he had taken enough time to sit back and think. Matt was smart, a genius in his own way. Once life was back to normal, he would see nothing but stress and their close brush with death made him think they had to get married. That and a heavy load of guilt for having sex outside of marriage.

If this had happened a year ago, before he became a Christian, would Matt still want to marry her? He hadn't been promiscuous, but he had had his share of warmer-than-casual girlfriends, all discretely handled to protect his much-younger cousins. Joan knew because she had checked him out, and Xander, when she started hanging around with them.

Joan let herself play with the idea of spending the rest of her life with Matt. She snorted, spattering the last few drops dripping down her face. The picture painted by her hungry imagination included Tris and Rocky. Even the four of them sharing a home. Why not? Becoming a Cameron, having a real name for the first time in her life, was a tempting reason to marry Matt.

Dressed, her hair wrapped in a towel, she put the kettle on the stove for a big pot of black cherry tea, and braced herself to called Sophie, to report before her partner-in-crime called her.

It went without saying, or even thinking, that she wouldn't tell Sophie about her nightmares, or landing in Matt's arms.

Joan settled on her back on her futon sofa and looked up at the unframed print of a painting of Joan of Arc. She held her cell phone in her fist and studied her namesake, facing into the sunset, all alone in the forest clearing.

"At least for all your mistakes, you knew who you belonged to," she
~~~~~

whispered. "Is it worth dying for?"

Blinking against a sudden burst of heat and wet in her eyes, Joan flipped open her cell phone and punched Sophie's listing in her directory.

~~~~~

Joan was a firm believer that dreams were messages from the subconscious, reassembling fragments of data gathered up during the waking hours. Whenever she had her recurring dream about Nikki in the sinking car, she had to check on her sister. Just in case that sense of threat came from something she hadn't noticed. When she rang the doorbell at the Holwoods' house, she claimed she was checking on the schedule for next fall's classes, wanted the reading list for Dr. Holwood's classes, so she could spend her summer preparing.

Doria Holwood was alone in the house, because her husband had taken the current gaggle of foster children for a long walk to get ice cream cones. She welcomed Joan and invited her in, to sit while she searched her husband's office for the list. Joan liked coming to the Holwoods' big, white Century house, four stories tall, with plenty of room for foster children and all the students Dr. Holwood brought home for social gatherings.

"Here you go. Rance will be sorry he missed you," Doria said, coming back into the living room with three sheets of paper stapled together. She chuckled when Joan's eyebrows rose at the long list. "Oh, don't worry, you won't be required to read every single one next fall."

"I like to read." Joan stood, folding the papers to put in her pocket. "Did Nikki go for ice cream, too? I haven't seen her in a couple weeks, how's she doing?"

"Sometimes I wonder myself." Doria's dusky face lost its usual cheerful glow.

"What's wrong?" Joan headed for the door, when she really wanted to stay and put her sister's foster-mother through the third degree.

"Our little girl is growing up, I suppose. We just never expected her to turn into a rebel right under our noses." She patted Joan's shoulder. "With enough time and prayer, it'll end up being nothing to worry about."

Joan hated the unspoken words, *We hope*, that seemed to echo against the doorframe as she pulled the heavy front door open and stepped out onto the wraparound porch.

"Nikki's always been such a good kid. What's she doing?"

"Well..." Doria studied her face for a few moments. Joan could almost hear the older woman assessing her, considering her relationship with their family. "We just found out Nikki has been seeing a young man since the winter. He has some sort of traveling job, and whenever he passes through Tabor he calls her... He's at least twenty-five."

Like mother, like daughter. Joan immediately shoved that thought to the back of her mind. Nikki would never be like Niobe. She was a firm believer in nurture over nature.
~~~~~

"I bet you had a big fight with her," Joan offered.

"She wouldn't stand still long enough to have a fight." She wrapped her arms around herself and offered up a brave smile. "I'm sure that if we don't push too hard, if we let it go, show her that we trust her, Nikki will get tired of him eventually and break it off."

"Reverse psychology. If you push, she'll hold onto him."

"With all the children who pass through our house, all the different types of minds and hearts, we do have a few things figured out." Doria's smile looked closer to normal.

"Nikki's smart and she's a good kid," she offered as she stepped down from the porch. "I'm sure she'll be okay."

Joan passed Dr. Holwood and the four foster-children on their way back home. They exchanged greetings, and she obliged the youngest boy, Aaron, by stopping, listening, and groaning when he had to try his latest joke on her. She blamed the stress of the last two days for the jittery sensation in her chest and her feet, urging her to hurry away, to run through the center of town, searching for Nikki. Common sense and experience said to act as if nothing was wrong. Just in case someone was watching.

The best way to step back from a problem was to think about the little details of ordinary life. Joan made up a shopping list as she walked down Church Street to the cut-through behind her apartment. She decided she could get by with just picking up some cartons of juice and milk and any of the day-old bakery that would be available at the end of the day at Rick's Bakery. That would take care of breakfast. She could buy more groceries tomorrow after she visited her landlord, Mandy Gordon, with the rent money for the month.

Nikki and a man Joan had never seen before were sitting at one of the little wrought iron cafe tables inside Rick's when she stepped inside. Her half-sister didn't even look up, all her attention on the man who held her hand and leaned so close to her their foreheads touched. He spoke in a low voice, but whatever he said made Nikki's eyes shine.

Joan thought about Matt, how close he had held her in the dark. She shoved the memories away and concentrated on the day-old bakery rack. Her ears ached with the strain of listening for whatever Nikki and her boyfriend were talking about.

There was a time for stealth, a time for discretion, and a time for facing the enemy. Ignorance was dangerous.

"Hey, Nikki. How's it going?" Joan said, crossing from the register once she had made her purchase.

Ten minutes later, she walked out the door and studied the car with out-of-state plates parked at the curb of the side street next to Rick's Bakery. Joan pulled out her cell phone and snapped a picture through the front window of the bakery, of dark-haired, square-featured Brock Pierson smiling at Nikki. Then she headed home. Whatever she was up to, Nikki wasn't embarrassed or afraid to introduce her boyfriend to anyone. Joan took that as a good sign. Her sister was too happy to be completely rebelling against the upright principles her foster-parents had raised her to follow.

As for Brock Pierson, dressed in expensive casual style, dark good looks, and the wary, assessing look of a predator... Joan hoped he was a few years younger than he looked. Otherwise, there was only one thing a man could be looking for in a girl who was at least ten years younger than him.

If he hurt Nikki, if he used her, destroyed her innocence, Joan had many options she was more than willing to use, to punish him. Even if they were tactics Niobe would use.

For now, she would give his name and picture and license plate number to Sophie and start an investigation of her own.

~~~~~

"You know, usually the only people who insist on paying in cash are either the men Open Doors sends to me, to help them get on their feet after prison. Or people who are in trouble." Mandy Gordon dunked her fresh chocolate chip cookie in a mug of milk and took a bite.

Joan just smiled at her landlady and dunked her own cookie. She had never learned the habit of milk and cookies before she settled in Tabor.

"I've turned down a lot of people who wanted to pay cash, but when you showed up four years ago..." Mandy took another bite of her cookie and sat back, folding her hands in her violent orange and purple caftan-clad lap. "My gut told me you weren't trouble." She patted her ample belly. "The bigger the gut, the louder it is, but it's never wrong." She chuckled.

Mandy was one of the few people in town who didn't make her itchy and eager to pick up and run when she started in with her half-spoken questions about Joan's past. The big, pillowy, always-cheerful woman had taken Joan under her wing since the day she knocked on her door, asking about renting the apartment. Joan hoped she never had to leave Tabor Heights, because she didn't want to disappoint Mandy. That would definitely happen if the woman ever discovered all the security measures she had installed in her apartment without permission.

Joan had decided, after only two months in Tabor, Mandy was what mothers were supposed to be like. Slightly nosy, always there with advice, glad to see her, armed with milk and cookies and an amusing or touching story, and a penchant for caftans in eye-watering shades and dizzying patterns.

Even more important, Mandy didn't gossip. She enjoyed a juicy story just like anyone, and she might talk a little too much, but Joan had learned quickly that Mandy never broke a trust. She was a pillar of her church—a loudly dressed, jolly pillar—and her observations of people were spot-on. Joan had no hesitation to share with her what she had learned the day before about Nikki, Brock Pierson, and the Holwoods' concerns for their foster-daughter.
~~~~~

"Well, I hate to say it, but it's probably about time. That Nikki is a sweetheart, but she's about due for some stupidity in her life. After what that Rich Thomas did to her, I'm not surprised she took up with someone who doesn't live in town."

"Oh, yeah. Him." Joan broke a cookie in half and dunked it into her mug hard enough to slop over the edge.

Rich Thomas had been the golden boy at Tabor Christian Church. Head of the youth group, an example to the younger children, aiming toward a sports-related teaching job. He and Nikki had been an item for almost two years. Then he went away to college last fall and from all reports, turned his back on everything he believed in and broke Nikki's heart. Joan had fought the temptation on several occasions to mess up Rich's financial standing and transfer all his scholarship money and savings to someone more deserving.

"Consider Nikki surrounded by prayer. I'll contact my prayer chain — no names, of course—and we'll get to work on protecting her." Mandy patted Joan's hand. "You're a good girl, Joanie, looking out for her."

"We have a lot in common," she offered.

~~~~~

Matt was in and out of town for more than three weeks, meeting with his contacts in Homeland Security and other government officials, as they all worked to untangle the mess caused by Jonas Carr. Joan was careful to check on Matt's activities with his cousin, Tris, and she didn't talk directly with him. The longer the silence between them, the better the odds Matt would think clearly again and realize they were better off as good friends.

When she couldn't avoid it any longer without awkward questions, she agreed to meet Matt and Xander for their monthly Saturday morning breakfast at Stay-a-While. They briefly discussed the trip and the fallout from their bungled investigation. Xander knew what had happened, not just because he was a friend, but as Matt's lawyer. While they discussed their plans for going to Blossom for concerts, and upcoming Guardians games at Progressive Field, Matt watched Joan. The intensity in his eyes made her uneasy. It combined with the queasiness that had been a background complaint for the last three or four days.

He accompanied her down the street when the three of them left the cafe. Instead of continuing up the street to the municipal parking lot, when Joan turned onto Main, he stayed with her. She said nothing, waiting for him to speak. If he was going to be smart and admit they could never be anything more than friends, he had to say it in his own time.
~~~~~

Chapter Five

"Thanks for all your help, all your connections," Matt said, after they had crossed Main at the corner by Rick's Bakery. "If not for your friends..." He grinned, shaking his head.

"I've been thinking about those friends. Sidarkis has this need to protect his resources—meaning me and Sophie—so he checked you out. That's probably how you got your first contact for government work. So essentially, it might be my fault, all the trouble you've been having."

"Maybe. I'd rather look on the positive side." He followed her down the side street to the stairway behind the optician's shop. "When are you going to invite me up to your place?"

"You don't want to see what I have up there." Joan grinned up at him, hoping he took her words as teasing.

"Now, see? That's the kind of stuff that just makes me more curious. And after what happened... well, it kind of feels wrong, not trusting me enough."

"Matt—"Her brain froze up, refusing to supply her with the words to get out of this situation.

"Marry me, Joan." He reached for her and she backed up, until her shoulders hit the wall of the optician's shop.

"You don't get it, do you?"

"I love you, and you said you loved me."

"If I did, I was delirious. Exhausted. In pain. One night of celebrating not getting killed. Stress sex. It didn't mean anything."

"You're scared, aren't you?"

"I'm realistic." She slid sideways when he reached for her again and skipped three steps up her stairs. "Matt, don't ruin things. We don't belong together."

"Yeah? Then what's been going on the last three, four years?" He jammed his fists into his hips and took a step toward her. She went up two more steps, so he had to tip his head back to see her.

"That's friendship. Not... not lifetime. Besides, you have the golden ticket, I don't. That means we shouldn't be together."

"All you have to do is ask!"

"It's not that easy."

"Yes, it is. Look, let me call Xander—"

"If you sic Xander on me, I'll never talk to either of you again." Joan wanted to run up to her apartment, but if Matt chased her up the stairs, he would catch her before she could get her door open. Taking a deep breath, she plunged down the steps. By some miracle, Matt stepped aside instead of trying to catch her.

Joan ran, crossing the street against the light, and down the street leading to Heinke's Grocery. The queasy feeling grew stronger. Her lungs labored and her muscles felt weak, bruised deep inside. She slowed as she reached Aspect and looked back. Matt wasn't following her. Joan stepped into the grass and braced herself against a tree while she struggled to breathe.

Queasy turned into cramp. Joan grabbed hold of the tree with both hands to hold herself upright. She refused to collapse here, on the side of the access road by Heinke's. More than half of Tabor Heights came to this little shopping plaza during the day and might see her.

Joan walked slowly, keeping her steps soft, one hand pressed hard into her belly to fight the cramp. Matt was nowhere to be seen when she reached her apartment again. She heated up her herbal neck therapy pillow in the microwave, put it on her stomach, and curled up on the futon under the painting of Joan of Arc until the pain faded back into queasy.

When she slept, she dreamed *she was thirteen, aching with cramps from her first period, lying on a bare mattress in the closet that served as her bedroom. In the flat in Liverpool where she had stayed during the entire visit to England. Joan had read, managed the cooking and cleaning, and stayed in the shadows whenever Niobe and her "associates" returned to the flat to talk and plan and argue. She didn't want those big, sweaty, angry, grimy men to notice her.*

In her dream memory, Joan shivered, hearing Niobe raging. She had managed to rinse the blood from her underwear three days before she had been caught, and then the woman had exploded. Somehow it was Joan's fault that she had hit puberty right at that moment. It was her fault that men would come sniffing around like cats in heat.

"I won't have it! Do you understand me?" Niobe had screamed.

Joan woke, rolling off the futon, her arms raised to ward off the blows as Niobe burst through the door of the closet with the bottle of whiskey she had been forced to drink until she passed out. Even through that drunken, nauseous haze, Joan had felt the big, rough hands on her, and saw the light flash off something long and pointed.

Those memories had stayed with her until she came to Tabor and learned what happened to her baby sister, and then the nightmare of the car and the river and Nikki had replaced them.

Why had that dream returned?

She was awake now. The nightmares couldn't hurt her. And the queasy, cramped feeling had gone away.

But it came back. Joan endured in silence, trying herbal remedies and over-the-counter analgesics until Wednesday. Then she went to her recourse of last resort: she called Sophie.

"You dummy," her friend sighed.

"Oh, thanks much." Joan laughed, then whimpered when the mere movement of laughing irritated her insides. If Sophie called her a dummy, that meant there was an answer, something she hadn't thought to do.

"Correct me if I'm wrong, Joanie-gal, but don't you have your own personal doctor now?"

"My own doctor?" She started to sit up, then stopped, pressing her hand into her aching abdomen.

"The Colonel's people? The clinic in Aurora?" Sophie sighed, then her voice lost its teasing note. "Joanie, honey, you are definitely not yourself. Get your sorry butt to that clinic and let somebody help you for a change."

"I'm going." Joan inhaled to muffle a sob. "Thanks, Soph."

She closed her phone and waited a dozen heartbeats before she got to her feet, moving slowly, breathing shallowly to avoid aggravating the queasies. The next moment, she staggered across her apartment to her bathroom and barely got the lid of the toilet up in time before she emptied her breakfast into the bowl.

Joan leaned back against the tiled wall and fumbled her phone out of her pocket while she caught her breath. When she got the doctor's answering machine, she listed her symptoms, how long she had been having discomfort, what she had been using to treat herself, and said she was on her way to the clinic.

Just before she got on I-71, Joan wondered if she had made a mistake, and programmed the wrong number into her phone. Meaning she had just left the details of her physical health on a total stranger's answering machine.

The next thing she knew, she was blinking gray haze from her eyes and heading toward the divider wall. Fortunately, no one was within five car lengths of her. She managed not to overcompensate and jerk the car across three lanes. She wiped sweat from her forehead and barely got over in time to the ramp taking her to another highway.

Five miles of her trip vanished. Joan took deep breaths and gripped the wheel tightly enough to dig holes in the vinyl. And blinked, to see she was on a side road and had no idea how she got there.

"Please... please, God... help," she whispered. Joan drove, watching for traffic behind her, until she got to an intersection and could identify the road. She had gotten off an exit early. She knew where she was.

Her vision turned gray, but she didn't go off into ditches or hit anyone before she reached the clinic and parked in the back lot. A door opened as she pulled up to the awning extending out from the entryway, and a woman in a white lab coat came out to meet her. Joan's hands shook as she put her car into park, and it took two tries before she could grip the key hard enough to turn off the ignition.

Dr. Lena Malkin gave her one of those cool, efficient smiles she had probably learned in a special class in medical school. "We have some theories based on your symptoms. The first thing we need to..." Her eyes widened and her gaze dropped down as Joan got out of the car.

Gripping the door, Joan looked down. It took her several moments to realize the darkness across her lap was blood. She turned, losing her grip on the door, and saw the puddle of blood sitting in her driver's seat.

"Well, that makes sense." She tried to laugh, but the sound escaped in a sigh.

Then the gray met the queasies and she sank through the pavement.

~~~~~

"What kind of periods have you been having?" Dr. Malkin settled back in the padded chair between the window and Joan's hospital bed.

"Never the same twice in a row," Joan finally answered. After three days of lying in a haze, she found it hard to think and to talk. It was as if several unfamiliar, uncooperative firewalls stood between her conscious mind, her memories, and her tongue. Fortunately, the staff here at the discrete clinic didn't push when she couldn't communicate as quickly as she wanted.

"The simplified answer to your problem starts with your uterus. It was scarred. I've seen damage like this before, but only in some horrific third world country that resorts to such barbaric tactics to ensure prostitutes don't get pregnant." She reached and caught hold of Joan's hand, which gripped the bed rail hard enough to turn her fingers white, with the red of trapped blood in the tips. "What?"

"I was just remembering... when I was... puberty..." Joan pulled on the bed rails, trying to sit up without irritating her abused abdomen. The words caught in her throat, along with her breath, until the doctor pressed the button on the bed controls to help her sit up. "She said she'd make sure I wouldn't bring any brats home," she finished on a gushing whisper.

"Unfortunately, where such an operation doesn't kill the victim, it *doesn't* prevent conception." Dr. Malkin held onto Joan's hand and met her gaze.

"I don't..." Joan swallowed, anticipating an upsurge of nausea. "Tell me?"

"We estimate you were about four weeks pregnant. The changes in the uterus, the development of the sac, the adjustments in the blood vessels in preparation for supporting the growing fetus, it all combined to make you susceptible to hemorrhaging. You didn't miscarry right away. Much of your discomfort was from pressure, from your body fighting to keep the baby, and warning signs. If you hadn't come down here when you did, you could have passed out in your apartment and bled to death."

She felt as if the bed were about to collapse under her and she would drop through the floor, at the same time someone yanked the ceiling up and all the oxygen with it.
~~~~~

Matt's baby.

She could never tell him. It would destroy him.

"So, since it's so damaged... did you take it out?"

"No, we did a great deal of repair. I'm an advocate for repair rather than removing a damaged organ. The body is an amazing mechanism, and if you give it a chance, it will heal itself. Removing the scar tissue could conceivably solve the problem. Time will tell."

"Wouldn't it be safer just to take it out?"

She hadn't even known she was pregnant before she lost her baby.

"I don't recommend that. You're a healthy young woman. You don't need to have to worry about hormone replacement therapy and all the attendant problems. Besides, you might still want to have children." Dr. Malkin stood up, giving Joan's hand one final squeeze before letting go. "Once you know what to look for, what help you'll need, you could carry full-term."

Never happen.

Joan managed to nod and offer a weak, thin-lipped smile, and was glad to close her eyes and fall back into drugged, dreamless sleep.

<p style="text-align:center">~~~~~</p>

At the end of two weeks, Joan needed to leave. She had brought her computer with her but couldn't focus enough to do more than check her email until the second-to-last day. When she was able to stay awake the entire day, she knew it was time to leave. Dr. Malkin affirmed she was safe from hemorrhaging. Thanks to transfusions, the surgery, and the rest of her treatments, she was nearly as good as new. Several prescriptions to put her hormones back in balance would take care of the rest. As long as she followed doctor's orders and took it easy and made sure she ate properly.

The drive home took far less time than the drive to the clinic. That made her laugh when she realized it, because Joan knew she had been semi-conscious for a good portion of it, thanks to blood loss. She let her brain go into neutral, to avoid thinking, while still aware of every mile that passed, every exit. When she got off the highway, she considered a dozen different stops: see Nikki, get groceries, or just buy the most greasy, sugary, gooey thing sitting in the display case at Rick's Bakery?

She was still debating that last option and delighted to feel hungry for the first time, as she parked, got out of her car, and headed for the stairs to her apartment.

A box sat on the top step in front of her door.

"Bomb squad."

Joan flinched and nearly looked around to see who had spoken. Her throat ached from speaking, after days of silent convalescence. Her voice echoed a little in the enclosed stairwell.

A ten-ream-sized box wrapped in brown paper sat on the landing at the top of the stairs.

It didn't belong there. She had all her mail delivered to the Tabor Heights Post Office, just a short walk of a few blocks south of her apartment.

Joan licked her lips and put one foot on the bottom step, then the other, moving up so someone walking on Main past the side street wouldn't see her there.

The temptation to call Col. Sidarkis and ask him to send a bomb squad over almost drove away the surprise she felt that she would ask anyone for help.

Bad enough she had been forced to rely on his help for the past two weeks.

Really, what were the chances someone had left a bomb on her doorstep?

Yes, bombs were Niobe's favorite tool, but not when she wanted to punish someone. When or if the woman caught up with her, Joan knew she would be made to suffer a long time.

"It's not a bomb," she muttered, and climbed the steps. The effort pulled in her much-abused abdomen.

Logic said if Sidarkis wanted to get her out of the way permanently, he could have had her put to sleep while she was helpless, delirious and bleeding in that clinic. He had good reasons to want to shut her up, but even better reasons to keep her alive to provide discrete, quick, secretive services the next time national security came under attack.

"It's not a bomb," Joan repeated as she reached the step that put her shoulders even with the box. She reached out and shoved it against the heavy, metal fire door.

It didn't explode.

A single shuddering sigh threatened her balance. She supposed she had almost hoped for a bomb. Almost, but not quite. She believed quite sincerely in Heaven and Hell, and preferred to stay on Earth, in this body, and avoid either destination right now, thanks very much. Joan took a deep breath, straightened her shoulders, and dug in her purse for the tiny, key chain fob control for her alarm system.

Then she took the last few steps, so she stood over the box. It took several minutes to make sense of the writing on the heavy brown paper, even though her name was clearly spelled in big block letters across the top.

H. Carter at the Arc Foundation, Portage Trail, Akron, had brought her a package.

There were no labels on the box, nothing to indicate UPS or FedEx or any other courier company had handled it.

H. Carter knew where she lived.

Joan looked down the steps, but no one on the street or in the parking lot behind the optician's building could see her in the shadows of the stairwell. Was someone sitting in hiding, watching, waiting for her to take the box inside? How long had the box, and that watching person, been waiting?

With ginger, soft movements, Joan picked up one end. The box wasn't heavy. She shook it a little and something slid inside, sounding well-padded. Maybe she still had some medication in her bloodstream, affecting her common sense, but Joan decided to take the risk, and picked up the box. She cradled it against her chest and thumbed the code for the alarm system control. Her door buzzed and swung gently open.

As she stepped into her studio apartment, she wracked her brains, trying to decipher some link leading to H. Carter. She couldn't think of anyone she and Sophie had done security work for, who might have been working for or with someone named Carter, or any organization in Akron. One of their first steps when considering freelance work was to check out all the collateral connections, to discover any potential source of trouble. The practice had saved their necks on more than a dozen occasions, including discovering a trap before it could spring on them.

Nothing came to her. She shoved the door closed with her foot in frustrated punctuation. She couldn't remember if she had heard anything about an Arc Foundation. Akron was only an hour or so south/southeast of Tabor Heights, after all.

No answers, no memories, not one clue arose to the front of her brain as she crossed the tiny strip of living room. She put the box down on the floor, sprawled carefully across the futon on her back, and stretched out her legs.

The soft crystalline chimes of her white noise machine, left running night and day, sent a reassuring shimmer through the air. Joan closed her eyes and let out a long, sighing breath. She hadn't been able to sleep well at the clinic. Too many unfamiliar sounds, and even unconscious she couldn't trust anyone else's security measures.

Joan of Arc silently welcomed her home. The bookshelves lining the apartment walls enclosed her in security. Joan had made this her nest, the one safe place in the entire world for her, other than the safe house in Ithaca, New York, that she and Sophie laughingly referred to as "the summer place."

She sighed, opened her eyes, and turned to roll gingerly off the sofa, onto the floor. Lying there and vegetating would not get her mysterious box opened. At the last moment, she remembered to press one hand to her abdomen, to brace it.

Joan snagged her purse, which she had dropped next to the box, and pulled out her pocketknife. In short order, she had the brown paper and packaging tape slit. She lifted the lid slowly, holding her breath, poised to leap away, waiting for the first *ping* of a wire snapping or hiss of released gas or some other booby trap.

Nothing happened, other than a crinkling of brown paper crumpled up inside the top of the box to cushion the contents.

She lifted the first wad of paper. It fell to the floor from her suddenly limp hand. She stared until her eyes watered, because those couldn't be tears in her eyes. Could they?

"Fuppy," she said on a sigh, and then winced, because she hadn't intended to speak.

Her hand trembled as she reached to pick up the pale blue, threadbare, half-deflated Teddy bear lying on top of another layer of crumpled packing paper.

She sniffed, half-expecting the odor of dusty flannel, foam stuffing, cornflakes, spilled milk, and the strawberry lip gloss she had used to draw a mouth on the bear when she was only three years old. Niobe had thrown away Fuppy Bear when Joan was four. Her latest scheme had gone sour and they had to leave town in a hurry. A toy, even as threadbare and thin as Fuppy Bear, took room away from the bare essentials.

It didn't matter that Joan would have carried the bear, rather than put him in the duffel bag almost too large for a four-year-old to carry. Niobe threw it away, and smiled, as if she hated anything that got more love than she did. Joan had wailed until she got slapped hard enough to make her ears ring. She had cried silently after that, and obeyed when Niobe told her to run, even though she wanted to go back and dig through the garbage to find Fuppy Bear.

He had been a present from a social worker when Niobe had infiltrated a woman's shelter to find the runaway wife of an associate. Joan couldn't remember what Niobe had done or said, but the woman had hung herself by the next morning. Niobe had been so pleased with her success she had let Joan keep the bear. For a while, at least.

Someone had found him and kept him all these years. Why? Did this person know how much the threadbare old toy meant to her?

She cuddled the bear, tucking him under her chin, and let a few tears fall, thick with memories. He smelled of soap and a taint of plastic. Probably the bag he had been stored in all these years.

Who had saved Fuppy Bear, and why had they sent him to her *now*?

Chapter Six

Her hand didn't shake as she lifted out more crumpled packing paper. Her shoes came next; white running shoes with blue stripes and glittery laces. Joan remembered how long she had saved up to buy those shoes, so she could be on the track team in middle school. Niobe had slapped Joan's face with the shoes, then made her toss them down the garbage chute of their tenement building. That night, they fled their home of nearly six months. She blamed Joan for the ten-hour drive to another state, another identity, another life. Participating on the track team at school might have earned attention, a mention in the local paper, some kind of notice that could be deadly.

Joan grimaced, choking on something that might have been laughter. Niobe had obviously been justified in her paranoia. Someone had been watching them, closely enough to retrieve the things she threw out. Close enough to know what had been precious to Joan.

That frightened and angered her. Why had the unseen watchers simply *watched*? Why hadn't they stepped in, done something about the unhealthy situation she lived in, and taken Joan from the woman who birthed her? Or didn't they care about her paranoid delusions?

Joan lifted out more paper and found a long white envelope with her name written on it in neat block letters.

Dear Joan, the single sheet of paper inside read.

Yes, as you've already surmised, I have been watching you from a distance for many years. Always able to watch, but never possessing the strength, the reach, to interfere and make a difference. I lost track of you when you fled Elaine. That is the name your mother used when we had our affair so many years ago. I'm proud of your quick wit and stealth, and your choice to flee, even if I was unable to contribute to your upbringing.

Who am I? I have been many things in my life, and few would make you proud of me. But perhaps I can be your Oracle, a far more genuine Oracle now than I ever pretended to be when I thought I held the world in my hands and uncovered every secret I set out to find.

Joan inhaled sharply and re-read the last few sentences. Capitalizing *Oracle* had to mean something. Perhaps... naming himself *the* Oracle? She had heard about the Oracle during her years of searching for the truth of Niobe's past, and her father's identity. If this man writing to her claimed to be the information broker known as the Oracle, he was one of the most powerful men in the world, with no political boundaries. Or loyalties.

The Oracle had vanished from the international scene perhaps fifteen years ago. Joan knew the stories, unsure what was truth and what was based on fear or hatred. No one had ever been able to uncover the Oracle's true identity. Anyone who wanted to live didn't try to find out. He held too many secrets, too much influence over too many powerful people and organizations, corporations and governments. It was in everyone's best interests to let him live and protect the secrets he knew.

If this man who had written to her was the Oracle, then why hadn't he used his considerable power to thwart, even destroy Niobe?

Joan couldn't remember Niobe ever using the name Elaine. Then again, she had never called herself Niobe, either. That was the name Joan chose, from mythology, because she refused to even think of that psychotic as her mother. What if Elaine was her real name? Had she been so hurt, so infuriated by the betrayal from Joan's father, she left that part of her past, her personality, perhaps her sanity behind?

Joan shook her head and resumed reading the letter.

> *Please come see me at your earliest possible convenience. It's time we meet. I doubt you would be willing to be anything more than friends, but I hope we have enough in common that you will be interested in the proposition I want to make to you.*
>
> *Enclosed is a cashier's check for immediate expenses, and if you trust me enough, a credit card in your name, from the Arc Foundation, to take care of your needs from now on.*
>
> *I look forward to meeting you at last.*
>
> *Your father, Harrison Carter, III.*
> *P.S.: Col. Sidarkis sends his regards.*

Joan closed her eyes and leaned back against the futon. The clearest response among all the roiling emotions and questions was anger. Col. Sidarkis had promised to keep her and Sophie's existence secret. Despite all his help in her most recent troubles, he had just proven he couldn't be trusted. Next time he needed something done quickly and discretely, he could just go to the CIA. If he needed to leave the CIA out of the equation, that was just his tough luck.

The problem was, now that he knew about her miscarriage, could she ever dare say no to him again?

Her anger faded under the cascade of calculations and implications and fragments of information that snapped together in her mind.

Why would this Harrison Carter imply he was Oracle, unless he was? Why risk being found out? Why write his secret identity on a piece of paper?

The Oracle had enemies with long memories. If this letter was truth and not a trap, Joan held in her hands the Oracle's true identity and his address. The key to his instant destruction.

Why would he claim her, why would he have sent her shoes and Fuppy Bear — why did he hold onto them all these years — if he hadn't been watching her all along?

The whirlpool of tangled speculations made her head hurt. For distraction, Joan looked through the remainder of the box, the few things still hiding under the crumpled brown paper.

First printing, pristine copies of three of her favorite science fiction authors. A five-pound bag of her favorite fruit and nut mix; the hard-to-find variety with dried strawberries, cherries and blueberries. Two bags of chai mix; chocolate and vanilla.

These simple things didn't mean much on their own. Combined, they sent the message that Carter had been watching her, closely enough to know the things she liked. She wondered if he had sent the little treats to soothe her, maybe as provisions while she holed up and thought hard and came to a decision.

Joan only had two choices. Either she went to see her supposed father to learn what he really wanted from her, or she fled. Ignoring the Oracle would be useless. If he wanted to see her, he would eventually see her, whether she wanted to meet him or not.

If she fled, she would have to shed her comfortable identity, the life she loved, her first real friends, and vanish. And if she ran, she would have to keep running.

"I am so sick of running," she whispered, and looked around her cozy apartment. A snort of shaky laughter escaped as she looked at all her books. There was no way she could take her books with her. The last time Sophie had come to visit, she had joked that Joan would survive a nuclear blast because of the insulation of all her paperbacks piled up along the walls.

One of the few positive things she had learned from Niobe, besides the ability to change her face, mannerisms, and identity, was to let go of possessions in favor of speed and invisibility and staying alive.

And yet, hadn't she spent the last fifteen years of her life trying to erase that woman's influence and lessons from her mind and soul? Hadn't she collected treasures — her library, her few friends — because Niobe pounded the message into her body and her soul not to ever value anything, anyone, ever?

Fuppy Bear sat on her futon, staring at her with the worn holes where his button eyes had been. He had come back into her life, so maybe ...

Maybe what?

She couldn't think, here in her sanctuary. The air felt thick and close. Sitting still was always a trap. Waiting for anything or anyone was always a danger. She grabbed her remote control and shoved it and her wallet into her jeans pockets, tapped the wall control for her door, and slid out through the narrow opening while it still swung open.

The automatic door closed and locked with a comforting series of clicks as she descended the stairs. What would Mandy Gordon think if she vanished in the night and her landlord discovered all the subtle little security precautions installed in the apartment? Joan hoped the woman would feel sorry for her, and sad, not disillusioned and angry.

"Don't run. Don't let anyone make you run," Joan softly scolded herself as she turned right at the bottom of the stairs, with a vague plan of getting in her car and picking up some groceries, then maybe going to the Metroparks and taking a long walk in the woods.

Taking a walk, she insisted silently, was not running away.

It wouldn't be running away unless she had a couple changes of clothes and her computer in her car. She was just getting groceries.

Matt perched on the nose of her car, arms crossed, head bowed, facing the back of the building. His ebony vintage Corvette sat parked across the back bumper of her car, blocking her into the tiny parking lot behind the optician's shop. He only drove his Corvette for special occasions. Was he celebrating something?

Joan pressed her hand unconsciously over her empty belly and stared at him. Matt was the last person she wanted to see, with the lingering scent of the clinic still in her clothes and skin. With his dark, curly head bowed, she knew he didn't see her. Not yet. She played with the idea of turning quickly and heading down the street the other way, crossing Main and going to Heinke's on foot for her grocery shopping. It wasn't that long a walk, despite how achy and empty she had been feeling lately.

She could stay away, walking all over town until Matt gave up.

Or could she? Matt knew all her favorite haunts. Becoming a Christian had softened him in some ways, made him reckless and more determined in others. It was ironic that Joan liked Matt even more now.

He looked exhausted, just like he had after that ordeal in Carr's warehouse. That bowed head meant he was praying. Sophie looked that way when she prayed.

The idea of Matt praying for her filled her with warmth that marginally soothed that aching emptiness in her belly. Sophie prayed for her constantly, and Joan was grateful. If anyone and anything could get her into Heaven despite all the horrid things she had done in her life, it would be Sophie and her prayers. If she could ever make up for her crimes and truly become the person she pretended to be, Joan wanted to be just like Sophie someday. Her adopted sister knew her ugly secrets. They had been a team for years, protecting each other, sharing the same enemies and adventures. Sophie knew most of the truth, of Joan's psychotic mother, her abandoned baby sister, the reason she had chosen to settle in Tabor Heights four years ago. She knew these things, had held Joan when she woke up with her chronic nightmares, and still loved her. Joan wasn't quite sure how that was possible, except maybe Sophie was one of the few people on the entire planet who came close to being like Jesus.

Matt only knew the Joan Archer she had created four years ago. She had finally become the person she had always wanted to be. Outwardly, at least.

"Hi." Joan silently scolded herself not to run when Matt's head snapped up and his big, dark eyes focused on her.

"Where have you been?" He stood up, taking a step away from her car, and jammed his hands into the back pockets of his jeans.

"Out of town. Emergency."

Queasy pain shot through her as her thoughts flashed to the cause of that emergency.

"We need to talk."

"The answer is still no." She wanted to say *yes* so badly, it made her dizzy.

"Joan, I love you. Doesn't that mean anything?"

"No, you don't." Panic made her angry. "You feel guilt, not love. So we had sex. Purely a stress reaction. It's not going to cancel your ticket to Heaven, so what's the fuss?"

"This has nothing to do with me being a Christian."

"It has everything to do with it."

"I nearly got you killed."

"No, Jonas Carr and his creeps are to blame. Not you." She licked her lips. "Look, one sweaty roll in the hay —"

"It wasn't a roll in the hay!" His voice rang off the cinderblock wall behind her.

"Okay, it was one crazy, terrified night. A stress reaction. Celebrating coming out of that whole mess with our hides intact. Stress sex. Nothing more."

"It was more than that for me. I'm positive it was more than that for you — or why did you run away as soon as I got home again?"

"I said, an emergency."

If she told him she had been pregnant and miscarried, would that drive him away, or make him more determined than ever?

Maybe she should tell him she had *aborted* their baby?

No, that would drive him away forever.

"Look, one night doesn't equal eternity, you know? You had to be Galahad and ask me to marry you. I said no. That should have been the end of it. If you won't listen —" She swallowed, feeling as sick as two weeks ago, when the baby she didn't know existed died inside her. "Either accept my *no* and go back to the way we were or go away forever."

"We're best friends."

"That doesn't mean we have to get married." That thick, choking feeling in her throat was laughter or nausea. How could Matt claim they were best friends when he didn't know a single truthful detail about her?

"Can't think of a better choice for marriage than your best friend." He tried to smile, and the pain in his eyes almost cracked her resolve. Joan imagined flinging herself into his arms and surrendering.

"Yeah, well, what about what your Bible says about being unequally yoked?" She choked on bitter laughter at the confusion that put that endearing wrinkle between his brows. "I know more about the Bible and what Christians are supposed to believe than you do, and I know it's wrong for you to marry someone who doesn't believe like you do."

"With all you know, why don't you believe?" A tired smile lit his face.

"I should, after all the things I've seen, all the things Sophie has told me and showed me and…" She shook her head. "I can't."

I can't come in. I'm not welcome.

Matt stared at her, his face lit by the afternoon sun coming down between the century-old buildings, the wrinkles of hurt slowly smoothing out. That determined light she knew so well came into his eyes. A chill of premonition went up her back. Matt was one of the most determined, creative, and patient people she had ever known. Those qualities had made him independently wealthy, with two doctoral degrees under his belt at the ripe old age of thirty-four. It made him a valuable ally and best friend. And the worst opponent she had ever faced.

Oh please, God, I know You'll never listen to me, but please make him give up before he ruins what we've got. Why can't he leave things the way they are?

Joan yanked her thoughts out of that track. Praying was Sophie's territory. She left prayer to the ones who had souls.

"For now." Matt nodded for emphasis. "Your way for now. Just friends." His crooked, determined smile made her shiver in apprehension, but strangely warmed her at the same time. He glanced past her, toward Main Street. "I'll see you around, Joan."

"Yeah. Around." She waited until he got in his car and pulled out onto the dead-end street. Then she let herself breathe. She waited until she heard the distinctive rumble of his engine fade away down Main.

Joan stopped with the key inserted in the lock of her car, staring at the new fabric covering the driver's seat. She could still see the puddle of blood she had left behind. Her knees wobbled. She stepped back, tucked the keys in her pocket, and headed for the street.

Maybe she should give up on groceries and walking. She would go back to her apartment and curl up and think about the box and Harrison Carter's communication. And then call Sophie. She needed Sophie's advice, but only in the matter of the Oracle. There was no way Joan could confide in her about Matt's insistence on marriage, because she had never confessed to Sophie about that night in the hotel. She certainly couldn't tell her about the baby she had miscarried before she even realized she was pregnant.

What would Sophie tell her about her baby? Did something that small and new have a soul? Was her baby in Heaven?

She snorted, the closest she had come to laughter in weeks, and walked past the stairwell, heading down the street to the intersection.

Ironic: She thought of the baby as a *baby*. A living being. Not an 'it,' but a person. Would Sophie point out that if she ever wanted to see her child, she would have to surrender to God and secure a place in Heaven?

Joan believed in God, but she doubted God believed in her. There were some lines that couldn't be re-crossed. After all, she hadn't read anywhere in the Bible about Satan getting a second chance, and she had read it cover to cover, in many translations and multiple languages.

The light to get across the street was green, but the crosswalk warning flashed. Joan hurried across Main and tried to focus on what comfort food she would buy, to stop wondering if the baby would have looked more like her or Matt.

Nikki came up the slope of the bridge where the street crossed the branch of the Rocky River and gave access to the small shopping center. The sixteen-year-old walked arm-in-arm with Brock Pierson, heading away from Heinke's.

"Hey, Joan." Nikki rolled her eyes in exasperation when Brock immediately disengaged his arm from hers. She skipped down the sidewalk a few steps to meet Joan, swinging the big green cotton bag her foster-mother used for shopping.

Joan supposed Nikki had gone shopping and ran into Brock. Or more likely, Nikki had let Brock know she was going out and he had come to meet her.

He walked away down Main toward his car parked in front of the Bucking Bronco Tavern, swaggering a little as if he knew Joan watched him. What did a guy in a Lexus, with a cell phone and a big gold watch, see in a teenager in a quiet college town?

"Grocery shopping?" Joan glanced at the bulge in the cotton bag, the heavy swing, and calculated a gallon jug of milk and some smaller items. "Shouldn't you get that home before it gets warm? Kind of hot out here."

"Oh, yeah, really hot." Nikki giggled. That little smirk, that cat-in-the-cream satisfied look, jolted Joan just like it did every time she saw it. That was Niobe's expression, but with an innocent mischievousness the grown woman had never worn.

"You're not—" Joan glanced down the street toward Brock, in time to see his dark head vanish as he slid into his metallic blue car.

"Not what?" Her sister straightened her shoulders and that smirk dropped off her face as her eyes widened a little.

No, Nikki wasn't having sex with Brock, and Joan was more relieved than she liked to admit. The problem was, the word "yet" silently finished that sentence. It was only a matter of time. And that disappointed Joan. She knew the Holwoods were strong Christians, deeply involved in Xander and

Matt's church, Tabor Christian. She knew they had brought Nikki up right, from the day the police rescued the baby from the flooded Rocky River.

Please, God, don't let her make the same stupid mistakes...

Would telling Nikki the truth—sisters, illegitimate daughters of a psychotic woman who slept around to punish men—put some fear and common sense into the girl?

But why ruin her life with the truth?

"Men aren't worth it," she said, and looped her arm through Nikki's, turning them both so they faced Main Street again, ready to cross back.

"How would you know?" Nikki stiffened, but she let Joan lead her across the street when the light turned green. "Matt Cameron follows you around like you're the only woman in the world, but do you notice?"

"I notice. I just don't want to mess up my life that way."

"Men don't mess up your life. They make it... incredible." She sighed.

"He's too old for you. Nikki, listen to your folks."

"They don't understand!" Nikki yanked her arm free as they reached the curb and fled up the street, to the cut-through to the next street.

Joan leaned against the cinderblock wall at the base of her stairs and watched Nikki vanish around the side of the conservatory building. She flashed back to that first glimpse of her sister since that night when Niobe tried to kill her. It had been right here on this dead-end street, using the cut-through. There had been no doubt who that bubblegum-blowing girl in the basketball uniform was, despite her immaturity. Joan had seen the same squared cheekbones, tangle of dark, red-tinted hair, snub nose, and muddy hazel eyes in the mirror when she had been twelve. It startled her, seeing that glimpse of their mother in Nikki's face, even though Joan had been hoping for some resemblance between them.

She had come to Tabor, intending to take English classes and get Dr. Holwood as her student advisor at BWU, just so she could have opportunities to get close to her half-sister. Joan had nowhere else to go. She had rented this specific apartment because the location guaranteed she would run into Nikki as she ran errands and went to school.

"I'm not leaving," she whispered, as aching weariness settled into her bones. "You're going to need me, Nikki. Nobody but Sophie has ever been there for me, but I'll make sure I'm here for you."

Chapter Seven

Joan went back up her stairs. The door didn't open quickly enough and she banged her nose against it as she tried to slide through the too-narrow opening. She sighed and curled up on the futon before the door finished closing and locking. She cuddled Fuppy Bear under her chin, closed her eyes, and fell asleep on her third breath.

And woke with a scream caught in her throat. The nightmare had returned and changed yet again.

Matt dove off the riverbank to swim against the raging current to the car, to rescue Nikki. Joan dove in after him, the paralysis of helplessness shattered by her heart-stopping fear for him. The moment she touched the water, the river turned into a wall of flames and they were back in the warehouse where Jonas Carr had planned to let them die.

Joan curled into a sweating, shuddering ball. She spied Fuppy Bear on the floor and snatched him up to hug close. She should have expected the dream, after the emotional roller coaster of the last two weeks.

"So what if I'm alone?" she told the bear and her nightmare. "I'm not helpless. I'm strong. I have knowledge and connections and… the Oracle is my father," she said slowly, testing the words. The Oracle, even retired, was more security than she could have imagined in her wildest dreams. "Maybe I'm not alone."

If she made contact with Harrison Carter III and the Arc Foundation.

Time to call Sophie.

~~~~~

"You sound a little ticked," Sophie said, her voice coming soft and smooth through the cell phone.

"A little." Joan snorted and slouched lower on the futon. "Try a lot. You know what I realized when I was dialing you? I'm more angry that he found me before I could find him, than about any other part of this."

"You wanted to show up on his doorstep and shock the life out of him?"

"Maybe after a few years of watching him, getting to know all about him. Deciding if I would want to be friends or if I could use him. Or trust him. Or if I should just pull the rug out from under him when I ambushed him with my existence." She sighed and closed her eyes and wished her cell phone was large enough to tuck between shoulder and ear without getting a cramp in her neck. "There was a little part of me that wanted some evidence that he turned Niobe so warped and vicious. That she was a nice, balanced person before he came into her life. From the tirades she spewed
~~~~~

when I was little, I realized I either had to hate him or love him. No neutral ground."

"You're not ready to give love to someone who watched you all this time and didn't do anything to swoop down and play the superhero?"

"Partly that." Joan smiled at the hint of teasing in her voice. What would she have ever done without Sophie to speak sense to her and tease her back into balance? "Carter could be just as much a victim as me."

"Kind of an odd coincidence, that he's been in Akron all this time, and you decided to settle just a few miles away."

"I figured that one out. No coincidence at all. We were here in the area for a few days, when I was twelve. I remember being dumped at the Akron Zoo for about five hours, just walking around pushing the baby carriage she stole that morning and..."

She sighed and closed her eyes, fighting a sudden urge for tears. What if she had told the truth to the old lady who asked her where her mother was? Would she and Nikki have been taken by Child Protective Services that day?

"She came back in a raging fury and just drove until we ended up in Tabor in a storm."

"Your mother went there, specifically looking for your father? Maybe to get revenge?"

"Probably. And whatever she found out, it wasn't what she wanted. Whatever she learned, she decided he wasn't there. If it's just a matter of waiting, she gets cold and she hunkers down to wait until the time is right. It's when she doesn't get what she wants that she blows up and blames the whole world." She shuddered a little and rubbed at her belly, even though it wasn't bothering her. "It was the tipping point for Nikki, at least. Niobe was grumbling about her being a burden for weeks. She had to punish someone."

"So she thinks your father isn't in Akron. So if he *is* there, you're pretty safe, because she won't be hanging around, still looking for revenge after all these years."

"Yeah, but if she thought the man she was looking at wasn't him, what are my chances this guy who contacted me is the same guy and he really is him?" Joan could almost laugh at her twisted reasoning.

"And why, oh mistress of the web, are you asking me to work some of my magic and gather up everything there is to know about the man, and then some? Why can't you do it yourself, and ten times faster?" Sophie laughed, making a lie of her aggrieved tone. Joan heard the tinkling of crystal and metal beads as her friend's multiple, waist-length braids swayed with her movement.

"Because I need the data right away, and I don't dare do any searches on my computer until I've checked it for bugs and stolen information. I figure, I was out of it from that fever that took me to the clinic." Her tongue tangled for a moment and Joan cringed at the lie. She couldn't tell Sophie she had had a miscarriage and nearly bled to death. That would mean telling her about sleeping with Matt and his marriage proposal. "Sidarkis has enough tech wizards under his command, they could have broken into my computer, searched the files, hacked through all my security, and put it back without being caught."

"Joanie..." She sighed. "I'd trust the Colonel with my life."

A dozen sour, sharp, sarcastic remarks caught in her throat, making it impossible to respond to her best friend, her sister-in-all-but-skin.

"He's a believer," Sophie added, her voice a little softer.

"He said the right things, wore the right expressions, to make you think he believes like you do." Joan winced but refused to apologize or undo what she had said.

"I trust him. If you trust me..." She trailed off, leaving the words unspoken but clear and obvious: *If you trust me, you'll trust my judgment, and trust him.*

"Soph, he broke his word and told this Harrison Carter about me."

"Hmph. Maybe."

"Maybe?" The force of her word jarred Joan's sore abdomen.

"Okay. I'll do it while you go through your paranoid routine."

Joan swallowed down a dozen teasing retorts, mostly out of fear the teasing would turn bitter. "Thanks." She opened her eyes, sat up and pulled the envelope with the letter, check, and credit card off the box. She read off the address and account and bank information. Sophie's keyboard hummed with the speed of her typing.

"Foundation, huh? Scientific or medical research, maybe. Some kind of cover identity? Government, but not admitting it," Sophie mused, her voice going soft and slow.

Joan smiled. She could almost hear the circuits in Sophie's head buzzing as she processed the information, nearly as quickly as the Web search program they had created churned through the data available.

"Might be a government affiliate," Sophie continued. "If Sidarkis sold us out—"

"If?" Joan barked laughter, harsh enough to make her throat hurt.

"What if your father has something on him? If he's the Oracle and he's been watching you, then he knew when Sidarkis drafted us for the last job. Heck, he probably knew what was going on the first time we ran into Sidarkis and his geeks and realized we were untangling the same mess. Ha!" A long sigh ended on a chuckle. "Oh, you're gonna love this."

"What did you find?" Joan braced for something disappointing.

"The Arc Foundation is a recent creation. Based in Akron. Set up in Quarry Hall—"

"You're kidding." Joan choked on the bit of laughter, remembering the tour she took last Christmas with Matt and Xander and some friends from

Butler-Williams. Quarry Hall was a historic home, on the list of "America's Castles," a remnant from Akron's heyday. What was wrong with her that she couldn't remember that link between Quarry Hall and the Arc Foundation when her little surprise package showed up?

"You know the place, I assume. Carter bought the estate from the city, when a few economic downturns put the place in a bind. There was a historical preservation group that tried to take it over. Sounds like there's been wrangling over it for the last twenty-odd years. Carter moved in and started renovations nine years ago." Sophie snorted. "Arc is a philanthropic foundation and right now supports an even dozen women's shelters and homes for unwed mothers, plus sponsors fifteen scholarships every year for students at a few Christian schools in the Akron area. Well, at least we know what your father's doing with his money."

"If he really is my father."

"Seems he provides the money and connections, and Mrs. Carter — Elizabeth Witherspoon-Carter of the Boston and Chicago Witherspoons — does all the front work and administration. Got the feeling she's your step-mamma."

Joan snorted loudly, knowing it was expected of her. Of course, Carter had to be married. Hadn't she suspected there was a wife all along? Hadn't Niobe raved enough times about some mysterious "she" and "her" who had come between her and her paramour?

"Her name is on the original deed — no changes or additions. Looks like she's been there since he moved in, and she's been running the foundation the whole time." A few more clicks of keys. "Funny, didn't really have a name until three or so years ago."

Joan didn't like that feeling of a connection and a solid "click" in her mental processes.

She was an intuitive genius, making logical leaps, reaching conclusions and seeing answers without a path of connections and facts that could be immediately traced. Just because she trusted what her talent told her didn't mean she had to like it. Or act on it before she went through more mundane methods of verification. This was one of those times.

She had chosen her current name, intending it to be permanent, four years ago, when she came to Tabor and found Nikki. Why did it feel like more than a coincidence that Carter had given his foundation a name *after* she put down roots? Was she just being paranoid, seeing a connection between Joan of Arc, her namesake, and the Arc Foundation?

Besides the fact it meant Carter had known about her, her new life and location, in intimate detail, for at least that long?

Did his wife know about her? Did his wife know he had an affair with an amoral, psychotic genius that resulted in Joan Archer, emotionally stunted fugitive? If so, why had she stayed with her husband? And how could a man who courted and married a high society woman have fallen for someone as vicious and crude as Niobe?

"Hey, Earth to Crusader Rabbit," Sophie sing-songed. "You must be thinking pretty hard. Is there smoke coming out of your ears?"

"Close." Joan related what she had just been thinking.

"Ouch. Still, you've told me Niobe can be pretty charming when she wants to be. How do you know she didn't hoodwink your father?"

"We're talking the legendary Oracle. The Ice Man. Mr. Omniscient. Can you imagine anyone deceiving him like that?"

"Hmm. True. Maybe he was ticked at his wife and had an affair."

"I just can't see Niobe wanting a man that badly. I remember her ranting about a so-called friend letting a man mess up her mind."

"People change. She decided she was in love, justified everything she did, and then when she didn't get her happy ending, she cracked," Sophie offered. "The thing is, your father stayed with his wife all this time. Has to be some big, important backstory to all this. See, Mrs. Carter is one heavily spiritual, committed lady. I'm reading through these published precepts and ground rules for the shelters she's set up. Nuns have it easier."

"She's religious." Joan knew she should have suspected that little complication a long time ago. After all, the one thing certain to make Niobe foam at the mouth was Christianity.

"Washed in the blood of the Lamb and walking the straight and narrow," she murmured.

"Fine, then you go in my place. You'll fit in just fine with all the other holy rollers."

Joan couldn't muster up the usual energy and zing that she got from lightly teasing Sophie about her life of faith. Maybe because her hunger for that serenity had grown painful over the last few weeks? If she had known about her baby, if she had prayed, would God have listened to Joan Archer, professional liar and former juvenile murderer?

The "ifs" were smothering her.

Sophie chuckled. "Other than the fact that I'm Swiss mocha and you're white chocolate latte... won't work. I'm in the middle of a big project that can't be put down. Not for another week, anyway."

"I can wait two weeks."

"For you, I can do the research while I'm waiting for this new program to process. Joanie-doll, this is the answer to your prayers. Even if you didn't know you were praying. Go meet your father. I'll join you when I'm free and clear, if that'll help. But you have to go first. Alone."

"Give me all the info you can on Arc. Then I'll think about it."

"Coward."

"Cautious and alive."

"Yeah, there's that to consider."

"And consider this." Joan slid to the floor again and picked up Fuppy. "Niobe hates my father. If Harrison Carter was the Oracle, that means he's gone public with the foundation. So he might show up on her radar screen again. What if she's watching him? We've already had two close calls, close enough for her to strike at your shadow, the last time she went after me. Do we want to risk another close encounter of the nuclear fallout kind?"

"You got a point." Sophie exhaled loudly. More keys tapped at deafening speed. "Go clear up things so you can take off for a long visit with Daddy, and I'll get you the info in four days, tops. Pack your prettiest dress and leave behind those Scooby-Doo boxers you sleep in. Pull out that nice nightgown-and-robe set you got, when we were pretending to be suit-and-pocket-protector geeks at that conference."

"He's an hour away. If I go. Why should I stay overnight?"

"Why should you take a chance on being followed home if somebody nasty is watching the front gate?"

"You got a point, too." She tucked the threadbare toy under her chin and closed her eyes. "If she finds out I've found my father, made contact with him… be careful. I don't want her backtracking you for a little collateral damage. She could know about that bounty the Oligarc has on your head, and money is a close second to revenge on her list of favorite things. That Idi Amin wannabe won't give you a chance to say no a second time if she gives you to him."

"Hey, we're talking the Wizard of the Web, here. I'm always careful."

When Joan hung up ten minutes later, she couldn't sit still. None of the treats Carter had sent tempted her. She could only work so long on checking and verifying the security of her notebook computer before hunger intruded, to the point of making her nauseous. Her head ached and her abdomen still felt abused, though the doctor at the clinic assured her it was more psychosomatic than any real damage, and what discomfort she would feel was all healing. It was almost time for her next dose, and Joan didn't want to take her medication on an empty stomach. Tea wouldn't do to buffer her insides. Despite the weary ache in her legs, another attempt to go to Heinke's was in order.

Her cautious peek around the edge of the stairwell irritated her. What was wrong with her, to be so timid? Caution was one thing, but acting like she expected to be ambushed the moment she stuck her nose outside of her sanctuary reeked of a defeatist attitude. Fury at herself propelled her across Main Street, across the bridge over the river, and through the long parking lot to Heinke's. Milk, bread, bananas went into her basket quickly enough. She wasted twenty minutes in the home cooking section, picking over the freshly prepared meals. Nothing appealed to her, but she knew she had to eat.

Susan Reichman stood at the flower shop section of Heinke's, near the door, when Joan completed her purchase and walked out. The sound of the local fashion plate's laughter made her temples throb. Joan thought of her latest run-in with Matt, and tears pressed at the backs of her eyes. Susan wanted Matt, had all but hung a sign around his neck, to warn all the other women in their church away from him. If Susan knew that Matt had asked Joan to marry him, she might just lose her sugary public mask and reveal to the world the sanctimonious, self-righteous shrew Joan knew lived inside her.

"You can't have him," Joan muttered as she ducked out the door and hurried home. Even if Matt and the twins hadn't given her a taste of what it meant to have a family, to belong, she would have attached herself to his life just to irritate self-appointed-saint Susan. "You can't have him," she repeated. "All you can have is being friends, nothing more."

Joan remembered her post office box, detoured up Main Street, and turned up the slight hill to the side street. Not that she expected anything except a few bills and junk mail, but survival and staying under the radar meant cleaning out the mailbox regularly, so someone wouldn't become concerned that something was wrong and start asking questions.

Exhaustion took over again by the time she trudged up the stairs to her apartment, but on the good side, she hadn't run into anyone she knew while she was out. Her brain wasn't up to answering questions, fending off invitations to sit and talk at the Perk & Perch, or explaining why she hadn't been around for the last week or two.

Her answering machine blinked and a "1" flashed on the readout. Joan guessed who would be calling before she pressed the button.

"Hey, Joan." The smile in Xander's voice came clear through the message. "Matt says you're back. We've both been praying for you. What'd you do to get him so tense? Don't forget I'm a lawyer, so I'm going to get my answers eventually. Stop on by and check out my new offices and make your confession before I wear you down. How about we meet after my Bible study tonight, since I'll be just down the street from you?"

Involuntarily, Joan glanced over her shoulder, as if she could see through the wall, up the street and several blocks over, to where Tabor Christian perched next to the Post Office. If she didn't respond, Xander wouldn't stop by. Still, she couldn't resist the urge to fly down the stairs, get into her car, and just drive until midnight.

That was running away. She refused to run away. Hadn't she been doing that ever since she fled Niobe?

"I'm not you," she told her reflection, when she got out of the shower an hour later. In the steam filling the little cabinet-sized bathroom, she could almost see Niobe's face looking out of the mirror, drained and lined and aged by thirty years of fury and frustration and hatred. "I'm not you, and Nikki won't be you. And you'll never find us."

For the first time in years, the vow, "I'll kill you to keep her safe," stuck in her throat.

When she went to bed, sleep came quickly, despite her empty stomach and aching head. She still hadn't taken her prescription. Joan wasn't surprised that the nightmare returned. Three times. Each time, she woke up and shuddered and wiped sweat off her face, and immediately fell asleep again. Morning came as a relief and a reprieve.

~~~~~

As a student at BWU, Joan had access to the exercise equipment at the Student Center. She needed to work off the tension winding her insides into a tight knot that Thursday morning, a residue of her nightmares, sleepless night, and all the decisions demanding her action. Besides, Fuppy Bear seemed to stare with forlorn accusation at her, despite the lack of button eyes. She couldn't put him back in the box, and she couldn't have him sitting there, silently demanding to know what she was going to do. In her efficiency apartment, there was nowhere to go to get away from his silent question, except out.

Maybe this was her way of going psycho, just like Niobe?

Joan peeled out of her sleeping shorts and tee, reeking of medicines and antiseptic sweated out of her tissues, and grabbed the first pieces of workout clothes her fingers found on her closet shelves. By some miracle, they matched. In minutes, she slid down the stairs, keys crunching quietly in her pocket. At the bottom of the stairs, she paused for a moment, half-afraid and half-hoping that despite the early hour, Matt waited in the little parking lot behind the optician's shop.

"Definitely losing it," she muttered, and broke into a lope, taking the back way behind the shops and cutting through a backyard to the next street. What was the use of going to a gym if she drove there, after all? It was only half a mile away. The exercise would do her good.

Joan couldn't remember if Dr. Malkin told her to take it easy or if she could go back to her regular routine. She had probably told her, but she hadn't been up to listening.

"Don't think about it. Can't change the past," she told herself as she approached the side door of the Student Center facing Sackley Road.

Nikki stepped away furiously on the elliptical when Joan entered the sparsely populated equipment room. That was the nice thing about BWU in the summer. All the facilities were open, even if the student population dropped to one-fifth. Family of faculty and staff had full access to everything on campus. Joan headed across the room, to climb onto the elliptical next to Nikki. Then she remembered: her sister only used the fitness equipment when she was upset and needed to sweat away her frustrations.
~~~~~

Chapter Eight

Joan just didn't know if she could handle one of Nikki's seething sessions, today of all days. The girl unconsciously mirrored Niobe just before one of her volcanic rages burst through, although Nikki wasn't the violent type. Niobe always struck out to punish someone, whether innocent or guilty, it didn't matter. Nikki in a fury made rash decisions that usually ended up hurting her more than anyone else.

That decided Joan. Even if she could never take the risk of telling Nikki they were sisters, she had a responsibility to look after her.

What kind of a coward are you today? she silently scolded herself as she climbed up onto the elliptical and grasped the moving handlebars. *You* need *to interfere in her life. Because you don't have one of your own.*

"Hey." Nikki flicked a glance at Joan and tapped the panel to increase the resistance of the elliptical.

"You must be pissed." Joan grinned when the younger girl frowned at her and slowed down for a few rotations. "Two miles in less than thirty minutes? Must be a new record."

"Yeah, well..." Nikki groaned when the display panel scrolled horizontally, telling her to start pedaling backwards. She came to a stop and started pedaling backwards.

Joan wondered if Nikki ever considered she *didn't* have to do everything the machine's program told her to do.

"Who hacked you off?" She decided to be prudent and start out slowly. Low resistance, low angle on the pedals, two miles per hour.

"Everybody." Nikki lost her rhythm and slowed for a few rotations.

"Sorry about yesterday."

"That wasn't anything." She offered a crooked grin, eyes sparkling like Niobe's eyes had never done.

"Well, not a good thing to do when I haven't been around much."

"Maybe I'm ticked at you for not being around when I wanted to hit a movie?"

"Yeah, like you'd go to a movie with me when Brock is practically glued to you." Joan muffled a groan when Nikki scowled and pedaled faster. "Let me guess. You finally got into it with your folks over Brock."

"I don't see why—"

"Besides the fact that you're sixteen and he's going on thirty?"

"I'll be seventeen in October," Nikki grumbled, and slowed to match Joan's pace.

Nikki was actually seventeen now. Joan remembered clearly the summer storm that blacked out the free clinic where Niobe had given birth. She had sat on the hard metal chair in the corner and read every months-old magazine in the waiting room. She had dared to hope Niobe would die, so she could be a "normal" orphan. Joan had been twelve, going on forty. She wasn't about to confess those memories to Nikki, and she definitely wasn't going to tell her she was seventeen now. That would only lessen the little bit of inhibition that kept Nikki in check now, in her relationship with Brock Pierson.

"My folks are so prehistoric," the younger girl continued.

"Be grateful you have them." Joan had to laugh when Nikki snorted and rolled her eyes. "They're good to you. Have you ever really fought with them over anything before Brock?"

"No," was the grudging, almost whispered response.

"Ever think maybe they're right?"

"Brock loves me."

"Yeah, well…" Joan sighed, flashing back to waking up curled up with Matt. She knew what Nikki felt. Or at least, what Nikki *thought* she felt. "That gooey stuff doesn't last."

"It's not gooey!" Nikki flinched when her voice echoed back to them. "I bet your parents never ragged on you over your boyfriends."

"I never had any boyfriends, and it was just my mother and me, and she was psycho. I'm talking about a woman who plotted the bombing of churches and government buildings for fun."

"You're kidding me." Nikki smiled, but the left side of her mouth drooped with uncertainty.

Joan pulled back her hair, showing the scar along her hairline above her left eyebrow. "She threw me against the toilet because I messed up my part, when she tried to kill Allen Michaels during a big crusade down in Cincinnati. I was thirteen."

"They caught her, right? The police rescued you, right?"

"I ran away when I was fourteen. I knew I had to, before she got me killed." *Or killed me with her bare hands,* Joan added silently.

"Is it hard, running away?" Nikki turned back to the display on her machine and pedaled a little harder.

"When your only choice is to die, you do what you have to do."

"How? If she was as bad as you said," Nikki hurried to say, "how did you get away?"

"Learn patience. Plan. Don't do anything different. And don't think about what you want to do when anyone can see you." Joan sighed. "Yeah, like you'll ever need to know that kind of stuff. You have it good, Nikki."

"Hmph. That's what you think."

"You're—" She bit her lip, knowing that if she told Nikki, *you're just a kid,* she might ruin any chance she had of talking sense into the younger girl.

"Be grateful you have someone who cares about you as more than a tool. Your folks love you like you were their own, not a foster kid. Somebody ought to slap some sense into you." She reached across the gap between the machines and grasped Nikki's forearm, shaking her a little. To her relief, the other girl grinned crookedly and nodded.

~~~~~

Another message waited on her answering machine when she got home, stinking even more of the medication and poisons seeping out of her flesh. Joan hoped she had purged her system and she could settle down to normal again. She peeled off everything, stuffed it into her laundry bag, and had one foot in the shower stall when she remembered the blinking light on the answering machine. Growling softly at her shattered attention span, she wrapped a towel around herself and went out to check the machine. The opening bars of the *William Tell Overture* burst out of the machine in Sophie's distinctive off-key whistle. Despite the signal that something might be ready to tip over the edge into trouble, Joan grinned. Only Sophie would insist on James Bond-style gizmos and signals and passwords.

Sophie wouldn't use that signal unless there was something time-critical. Joan called her , still wearing her towel and sweat.

"So, who do you want to be today, Tonto or the Lone Ranger?" Sophie greeted her in the middle of the second ring of her phone.

"You're in an awfully good mood for playing the red alert."

"Red alert for me, but not for you. I'm going to go mobile, just in case."

"Sophie—"

"Got data on all the millions and billions of bucks your father is probably eager to dump on you."

"Billions?" Joan hated the little lurch in her chest. Her need for some security, to constantly invest to secure her future, formed her largest weakness, a place where the enemy could track her. "I seriously doubt—"

"Lots of investments. All across the board. No matter how bad the economy, no matter what companies fold, he's secure. And that money seems to be tied up in such a way that it goes through every loophole and escape clause possible without participating in some pretty shady money-laundering schemes. Everything funnels into the Arc Foundation and out to the folks who really need help." Sophie whistled appreciatively. "Imagine all the good we could do with that kind of backing. And the Oracle's security system to keep us invisible."

"That's not a good enough reason to go find out what—" Joan's tongue seemed to thicken and choke her. Why couldn't she decide what to call Carter? "Whatever my alleged father wants," she finished after struggling a moment.

"Yeah, but it is a good reason, all the same."

"If you're trying to guilt-trip me into going..." She sighed. "Give me some more time to think, okay?"
~~~~~

"And who said there was a time to think and a time to move your butt before you got it kicked sky-high?"

"What sort of problem is making you go mobile?" Joan retorted.

"I've had one too many attempts to penetrate my search threads and backtrack me to a physical site. Nobody has broken through the outer defenses, but I want to muddle the trail, just in case. I might just go cold turkey from the Web, hit the summer place for a few days and catch up on my reading." Sophie's breathy little bit of laughter told Joan just how much it worried her that someone threatened the solidity of six layers of false ISP addresses.

"Give the word, and I'll be up there with you. Ithaca is beautiful this time of year."

"Yeah, steamy and in a coma." Her snort sounded more like her normal humor. "Joanie-doll, go meet your father. I know you've been wondering about him like forever."

"I never said word one about him."

"That's how I know. When you don't talk about things a normal girl would wonder—"

"Since when do either of us approach 'normal'?" Joan demanded, nearly letting go of the towel still tightly clutched around her.

"True. Go. I'm going right now. You need to be mobile, for different reasons. I'll check back in three days. I'm going to try one more thing before I shut down completely. I hope I'm wrong, but I'm going to check out that back door we created for Sidarkis. If the trouble is coming through there, I'll contact you and let you take care of contacting him and sending that last resort patch we whipped up. Keep your phone powered up and turned on. Love ya. Praying for ya." The connection broke.

Joan sat for nearly ten minutes, staring at the screen of her cell phone, clutching the towel, and thinking. It startled her to realize she was listing all the things she needed to do to before she went away for a few days. Sighing loudly, she hitched her towel tighter around herself, got up off the futon, and finally headed into the bathroom for her long-overdue shower. It looked like she was going to Akron to visit Quarry Hall.

~~~~~

Joan had a stack of library books, DVDs and books on CD to return to the library. It bothered her that she hadn't returned them yet. The ingrained need to never leave a trail, even something as trivial as late fees at the library, stayed with her. She held onto many of the habits she had learned in childhood because they kept her safe… ironically, safe from the one who taught her those survival techniques.

Coming out of the Tabor Heights Library, she reached the sidewalk and stood a few moments, looking across the municipal parking lot at Poe Lake and the gazebo, and considered taking a walk. Or she could go home, throw a change of clothes into a bag and head to Akron to get this
~~~~~

confrontation with her alleged father over and done with. With any luck, she would stop in Fairlawn and get a very late lunch or early dinner on the way home.

"Joan!" Xander Finley's rich voice contrasted sharply with the homely face that met her gaze when she turned around to face him.

The sidewalk curved around the library, leading to the city hall/municipal court/police department complex. Judging from the briefcase dangling from one hand and the stack of folders clutched in one arm, she guessed he had just come from meeting with a judge or defending yet another too-poor-to-pay-for-a-lawyer client. Xander got a little funding from several Christian organizations that believed in his vision of a string of legal clinics across the country devoted to justice for those who couldn't afford it. So far, Common Grounds Legal Clinic was a dilapidated collection of third- and fourth-hand office furniture and a rented space in a former furniture store on Pearl Road in Greenbriar.

"I was just thinking about you. How are you doing?" Xander's caring grin was crooked and mischief sparked in his big brown eyes. "What have you done to tie Matt into knots?"

"He keeps asking—" Joan choked, refusing to admit Matt was pressuring her to marry him. Maybe she should blame pain medication residue? "He keeps pushing me about church and giving God a chance. I ... I got nasty."

"You? Since when? Not that I blame Matt for pushing. Anybody can tell he cares about you a lot, so yeah, he's worried."

"Well, he shouldn't be. I've just got some ... things going on in my life. Like I said, I got nasty. I'm avoiding him." She managed a shrug. "It's hard to apologize. You know how Matt gets when you admit he was right."

"Oh, yeah." His grin softened, warmed a little more. "Anything I can do to help?" He shifted his armful of folders into the arm holding his briefcase and gripped her arm with his newly freed hand. "I'm praying for you, like always."

"Yeah, and my life would be a lot less complicated if you'd lay off for a while. Stop reminding God I'm around, would you?" She tried to grin, to match the smart-alec tone of her voice, but her mouth trembled a little.

"Hate to tell you, but He doesn't need reminding. You think I'm bad? You might as well give up, because He's not giving up."

"Yeah, well, I could give some lessons on stubbornness."

"Joan..." Xander let out a strangled groan as three folders slipped out of his grip.

She leaped and caught most of the paperwork before it fell into the mercies of the gentle summer breeze. Laughing, they struggled to get the folders back into his secure grip.

"You need a new briefcase. Or an assistant."

"Yeah, well, find me somebody who'll work for next to nothing, would you?"

"Honestly, Xander, if I had a million bucks, I'd give them to you. How's the new place?" She considered, for about two seconds, confessing Matt's insistence on marrying her, just to get Xander's opinion and advice. That moment of considering the idea was just a sign of her fraying grip on her sanity. Then again, this was Xander, just as trustworthy as Sophie, in his own way. Joan knew he cared about her, to the point that she almost believed he wouldn't stop caring if he knew all her ugly, dirty secrets.

"It's getting there. A church down in Cincinnati is donating some tile they didn't need for their new sanctuary. We're having a flooring party next week. Join us?"

"I might. If I get some personal business taken care of." She bit her lip, then went with her gut instinct. "I… I never knew my father, but there's a chance I might have found him. I don't go in for praying, but—"

"I'm always praying for you. You know that. And I bet you like it, even if you gripe all the time," he added with a chuckle.

When they parted a few minutes later, Joan was amused and a little stunned to realize she felt just a little lighter, a little more energized.

That energy coalesced into a tight, sharp-edged ball sitting heavily in the pit of her stomach when she returned to her apartment and found Sophie's message on her answering machine.

"Make that delivery for me, would you, Joanie-gal?"

Col. Sidarkis had an email address devoted to high-security deliveries and messages. The only way anything could get through to him via that email address was if the sender contacted him ahead of time and told him so. Then he would set up a limited time access for the sender's email address. The last thing Joan wanted to do was call Sidarkis before she had a chance to check out Harrison Carter and the Arc Foundation. Unfortunately, as she had learned long ago, "necessary" trumped "don't want to."

"Well, Joan Archer, how are you doing?" Sidarkis's voice sounded a little too pleasant. She had called on his secure line, so he had to know business was grim.

"Just peachy. But you aren't. I'm sending a patch to your system that my partner and I devised after our little job for you. She's gone mobile to shake a tail that might be trying to get to us through our back door into your system. Please install it ASAP."

"High quality service. You are definitely your father's daughter."

She nearly hung up—proof Sidarkis not only knew about Carter's claim on her, but that the two men were in communication. For all she knew, Sidarkis had told Carter she was going home, and that was why the package was waiting for her yesterday.

"How fast can you open up the door? I'm ready to send the package as soon as I get off the line."

"Doing it as we speak." A faint tapping in the background, his fingers on his keyboard. "So, what did you think of that surprise package?"

"I suppose it was exactly that." She bit her tongue against telling him to mind his own business. And asking what part he played in the delivery.

"He's a good friend."

"Obviously good friends mean more to you than keeping your word."

"He asked me to look after you."

The hurting words tangled in her brain and caught in her throat, burning, so she had to swallow hard before she could speak.

"Why does he have to contact me now, rather than ten years from now, or two years ago?" she said instead.

"I don't know, but it has to be serious." He sighed. "Archer... I'm sorry about your loss."

"Don't I have any privacy?" She refused to ask him, afraid it would turn into begging, not to tell Carter about her miscarriage.

"I owe you and your father more than I and this country can repay in a dozen lifetimes."

"Then leave me alone!" She thumbed the "off" button before he could respond. For two seconds, she played with the idea of not sending that program patch, but she would be cutting her own throat by doing so.

Half an hour later, with the morning rush hour traffic down to a trickle, Joan got in her carefully nondescript, ten-year-old pale blue sedan, drove down to Sackley and then to I-71, to go south to Akron. She slid her cassette of wind chimes into the tape player to drown out the rumble of the highway and soothe her thoughts into a semblance of order. Silence was her sanctuary and her sentinel, but in this case she needed a barrier, no matter how fragile, between her and her immanent future. Joan envied people who could put music on, lose themselves in a song and work out their frustration or jubilation by singing along. As far as she could remember, she had never sung. Not even Christmas carols. Her mother had never played music, never sang, never even hummed. Her life had been hemmed by silence and cacophony. Wind chimes and nature sounds recordings had been a conscious decision, a step to break out of the pattern set in her childhood. Since she had come to Tabor, she had discovered Blossom, the outdoor music venue down by Akron, and had grown to love orchestral music performed against the backdrop of nature. She had gone by herself the first year, until Matt and Xander discovered that she had a book of lawn tickets. Then they had become a threesome, sometimes with Tris and Rocky tagging along.

They hadn't gone to any concerts this summer, so far. Joan had ordered her book of lawn tickets just before the Matt discovered someone was trying to steal his identity, his latest invention, and frame him for treason. The tickets were in the mail the day after she and Matt returned from their close brush with death. Joan wondered now if their comfortable threesome would do anything together ever again.

What would stop Xander from asking Matt for the true story of their current argument? Those two had a connection she didn't share. Was their spiritual link strong enough for Matt to confess how they had ended up in bed together? Matt had been the leader of their threesome, until Xander took him to an Allen Michaels crusade. He came home changed and looked to Xander as his spiritual guide. Joan would have broken off their friendship altogether... except the move felt hypocritical. Sophie was her sister in all but blood, and Sophie was a Christian the way Joan thought Christians should be. Real and solid and logical, practicing before she preached.

What would Xander say if he knew about the hotel? Matt had held her after the nightmare and kissed away her tears. The first person in her life who had held her when she cried. It seemed so natural, so right, when the clinging and kissing turned to something else entirely. She had fallen asleep curled up against him, feeling safe and content and wanted for the first time in her life. When Matt had said he wanted the two of them to be together forever, she had been happy, eager, hungry for the future that promised. Until the memories rose up through her sleep, terrifying her, warning her. If she truly cared about Matt, the worst thing she could ever do was share her life with him.

If she told Xander, could he explain to her what was going through Matt's mind and heart? Could Xander explain to Matt why she refused to marry him?

"He'd probably tell me he's been praying for us all this time," Joan muttered as she got off the highway and turned onto Market Street. "And he'll pray some more. Wouldn't hurt, would it?" She sighed. "God, I know I'm not even on Your radar, but please, it sure looks like my... my maybe father and his wife belong to You. Don't let me totally wreck things? For their sake?"

She shook her head and gripped the steering wheel a little tighter. It was getting to be a bad habit, trying to pray when she knew it was useless. What did it say about her grasp on sanity, that she kept trying?

Chapter Nine

Joan made mental notes of her surroundings as her route took her through a long commercial district, full of restaurants and stores. She rarely ventured south for shopping, preferring to limit her buying to the stores in Tabor and Padua or on the Internet. She imagined offering to take Nikki on a shopping trip down here in Montrose and Fairlawn.

"Yeah, right, and as a topper to the day, you'll casually slip into the conversation that you're sisters." Joan caught the old woman in the car next to her staring, probably wondering who she was talking to. She stuck her tongue out at the woman, whose eyes bugged. She said something to the driver and the car pulled away. Joan laughed, her voice cracking.

No one yet had noticed the strong resemblance between her and her half-sister, but she was grateful. If she never had to face Nikki with the truth, that would suit her just fine. There was enough of Niobe in Nikki's expressions and her mood swings, Joan imagined the violent explosion that would occur when the younger girl found out they were sisters, and all that went with that relationship.

The long strip of shopping plazas gave way to hospital facilities and churches and municipal buildings, and back to older residential districts. This used to be the wealthy neighborhood of Akron, back when the rubber industry had just gotten started. The big, old houses had deep lawns crowded with enormous trees covered in craggy, dark bark.

She was responsible for Nikki, so that meant Joan had to do something about Brock Pierson, figure out just who he worked for and what exactly he did for a living. When she finished up this little problem with her father, Joan decided she would approach the Holwoods about her concerns regarding Brock and Nikki's relationship. She would have to get Sophie to do a more in-depth data search, so she had something concrete to work with. If she had to, she might just confide in them the real reason why she was so concerned about the girl. The Holwoods were such wonderful people, maybe they wouldn't hate her too much?

Then she turned onto Portage Trail and her heartbeats raced for a few seconds. Not much longer now and she would be there. All the glib lines she had practiced, the scenarios she had imagined on the drive down to Akron, evaporated. She wasn't even sure how she would get through the gates, let alone what she would say when she met her father. *Calm down, stupid. He knows you're coming, he invited you down here, let him carry the ball.* She drove down the street, noting the rolling lawns, golf course, tennis courts, swimming pool and other facilities of the country club on her left, and the increasingly larger and more elaborate homes on both sides of the street.

She nearly missed her turn when she got to the gates of Quarry Hall, situated on one corner of the T-intersection. Joan pulled into the neat, asphalt-paved apron in front of the closed, wrought iron gates, and put her car into park. Her heart thudded loudly. She felt her pulse in her fingertips. After counting to ten, she didn't see a security camera or a speaker, and the gates didn't automatically swing open, even though her bumper was just about a foot from the elaborate fleur-de-lis pattern.

"Okay, so how do I get in?"

She got out of the car, leaving the door open and the engine running. First rule of survival: have as many avenues of escape as possible. Joan walked up to the gate, looking for a call button, a speaker grill, security cameras, something that would let her communicate to the main house and ask for permission to come in. Maybe she should have gone to the back entrance? Maybe this gate setup was just for show? But this was the address on the envelope, not a side entrance for deliveries on another street, half a mile away.

A Tudor-style two-story stone cottage sat to the right of the gates, a dozen yards back in the shadows of enormous pines. Before Joan could look for wiring, in case the gate was electrified, the front door of the house swung open and a tall, lean, broad-shouldered Black man stepped out. He wore black jeans, black boots, and a dark green Oxford-style shirt that shimmered in the morning sunshine like silk. His head was shaved, his goatee narrow and sharp. His long, lean face broke into a smug grin when he saw Joan looking at him from the other side of the gate.

"Hello, Joan Archer." He stopped in front of the gate where the two halves came together.

Joan suppressed a whimper at hearing him speak her name. Was it very good that he knew her name, or very bad?

"It's about time you got here." He nodded, looking her up and down.

That made Joan bristle and stopped the frantic racing of her thoughts. She jammed her fists into her hips, and swallowed the first dozen caustic responses that came to mind.

"Who are you?"

"Vincent." He bowed his head briefly, giving her a tiny salute, first two fingers tipped off his eyebrow. "I'm in charge of security here."

"That makes sense. I guess." Joan took a deep breath, finally able to breathe normally. "Do I go around the back, to get in?"

"Oh, no. Everybody comes through the front. Only enemies and thieves come in the back or over the walls," he added, with a widening of his smug grin.

Joan muffled a groan. She knew she had heard that line somewhere before, but she wasn't sure if that came from the Bible, which fit in with what Sophie told her about this place. She suspected the answer would give her some insight into how Vincent thought.

He stepped back, reached into his pocket, and drew out a flat device a little larger than an index card. She suspected it was either a remote control or a cell phone. She saw his thumb glide over the surface, then a buzzing ran through the gate and it swung inward and open.

"Just follow the drive on up to where it branches. You need to go to the right and park at the carriage house."

"And then what?"

"We'll go on up to the house." He gestured for her to get back in the car.

When she slid behind the wheel again, Joan realized she had seen him before. Vincent had been waiting across the street from her apartment when she and Matt had returned from Aurora.

For two seconds, the urge to head back to Tabor overwhelmed everything inside her. But right now, Harrison Carter knew far more about Joan Archer than she knew about him. She hated an imbalance, and the only way she could rectify that was to drive through those gates, park at the carriage house, and do whatever it took to meet her father.

Then, if she didn't like the place or the people or the situation, she could run back to Tabor Heights. No, not run. She refused to run. Strategically retreat to consider her options, yes, but never run.

She drove slowly, noting the long, sloping lawn, the apple trees lining the driveway, and the Tudor Revival house that sat at the top of the rise in the landscape, serenely surveying the countryside.

The carriage house was actually two buildings, connected by a covered walkway. One side looked like a stable. Joan caught a whiff of hay and horse through the open window of her car, just before she put it into park and turned off the engine. She stayed outside, though the sliding doors into the garage-like second building were open and she could see plenty of space inside. Parking inside would indicate a willingness to stay for a long time. Joan wasn't about to commit to anything like that, even if she had brought her sleeping shorts and tee, and a change of clothes. She rolled up the window, slung her purse into place, pocketed her keys, and got out of the car, leaving her overnight bag behind. No sense in letting them know she was willing to stay until she got a sense of the situation and people here at Quarry Hall.

Her second step nearly landed her on top of a bear-like dog covered in lush, dark gray fur.

Joan froze in the open door of her car, staring down at the dog. There was something almost roly-poly about the beast, but she prayed this wasn't a puppy. Its back was halfway up her thigh, just standing on all fours. She didn't want to know how big the dog would be full-grown. Judging by those oversized paws, this dog would indeed be a bear.

"Ulysses!" Vincent strode up behind her before she could finish her assessment of the beast. He clapped his hands together twice. "Go on. Back to your kennel."

The dog tipped his head to one side, surveying Joan and then Vincent. With a seeming shrug, he turned around and sauntered away, his bushy tail curved up slightly over his hindquarters.

"Is he yours?" Joan fought the grin of relief she felt at the sight of the man.

"Ulysses?" He shook his head. "Nope. He doesn't belong to anybody. In fact... he usually ignores people. Even at dinnertime. Must be something about you he likes."

"Please tell me he's not a puppy."

"Nope. He'll be full-grown in another four months, probably. He's an Akita. Smart breed. Loyal. That's why I use them and a few other breeds for security."

"What if they bite someone? Animal laws—"

"My dogs don't bite." Vincent grinned even wider, with a nasty, mischievous light in his eyes. "When they're through with you, though, you'll wish they had."

"Are you trying to frighten me?" She kept her voice quiet.

"You? Why?" He gestured down the blacktop path that led to the main house. "You belong here, Joan Archer. No, I only want to frighten the folks who don't belong, but who try to get in anyway."

Joan bit her lip to keep from asking who he meant. She could easily imagine all the enemies Oracle had earned in his highly lucrative, damaging career in the Information Underground. Could a bunch of big, silent dogs who didn't bite keep this vast estate safe? Maybe they were only window dressing, to distract from the real security measures.

"Who's watching the gate while you're here with me?"

"I am." He brought out the remote she had seen him use before.

Now Joan saw it was a tablet, with half the surface devoted to a video screen that changed images every few seconds. She saw several sections of road, forest, manicured gardens, and a raw stone wall, before he put it back in his pocket. In two images, Joan glimpsed a big dog lying in the shadows. She didn't doubt one wrong movement or sound would have the dogs springing into action. Still, high-tech gadgets and big dogs weren't enough.

She decided to use her energy to study her surroundings as she followed Vincent to the recessed front door of the mansion. Graceful lines, curtains of clinging ivy, leaded glass windows and a sense of great age all combined to give a sense of permanence and solidity to the house and grounds.

"*Non Nobis Solum,*" Vincent read, pointing to the words carved into the stone coat of arms over the door.

"Not for us alone," Joan said, and couldn't repress a smug little smile of her own.

"You did your research."

"I read Latin."

"And four other languages." He pulled the front door open.

"You did your research." She didn't feel that chill she usually got when an unknown quantity revealed too much knowledge of her.

"Not research. Your folks know so little about you, every little bit of information they get is like gold. They share it with everybody involved in finding you."

"My folks?" Joan stopped short with one foot over the threshold.

For one arctic, paralyzing moment, she had an image of Niobe standing next to Harrison Carter, their faces bright with vicious triumph, their arms open like the jaws of a bear trap, ready to snap closed on her.

"Your father and stepmother." Vincent guided her through the cool, gray stone foyer, to the left, down a short hall paneled in dark wood, into a room furnished in gold and white French Provincial, the walls swathed in scarlet and gold brocade. "Didn't you do your research?"

"Elizabeth Witherspoon Carter. I can give you the addresses and phone numbers of the shelters the Arc Foundation sponsors."

"No need to prove anything." He gestured around the room. "Have a seat. Somebody'll be in to meet you." He nodded and strode out of the room, back the way they had come.

Joan heard the heavy front door creak open, and then close. She settled down in one delicate chair and studied the furnishings. She wondered how many came with the estate when Harrison Carter bought it. From the little she had read of Sophie's report, Elizabeth Carter didn't have much time to spend on decorating or a social life.

Then again, the size of this estate probably required a full staff just for around-the-clock cleaning and decorating. By the time the Christmas decorations came down, Easter neared; then they had to think about Fourth of July and then Thanksgiving. She wondered what it would be like to live in this museum and never have to lift a finger to keep it clean and orderly. She would hate the lack of privacy. It was too high a price to pay for luxury.

A shadow moved at the edge of her vision. Something warm touched her hand and she looked down to see Ulysses settling down at her feet. Something about his big, gray-green eyes bothered her, but she couldn't decide what it was.

"What do you want?" Joan tried to look away, but the somber regard of those not-quite-canine eyes kept drawing her back. "How did you get into the house, anyway?"

She couldn't picture a dog door flap violating the style of this grand old house. She didn't know the floor plan yet, but it seemed a long way from the logical location for a dog entrance, the servants' quarters, to this waiting room at the main entrance.

"I suspect there's no lock or closed door in the world that could keep these dogs out of the house if they want to get in," a warm, honey-colored, female voice said.

It took all Joan's self-control to only turn her head toward the second door at the other end of the room, rather than jump to her feet. The dog stood up and walked over to the woman, nudged her fingers with the side of his head, then came back to sit in front of Joan again.

"Well, it seems he's adopted you." The woman smiled, adding more wrinkles to the laugh lines around her mouth and eyes. "Welcome, Joan. It's good to finally have you here. Your father and I have waited a long time." She plaited her long, elegant fingers together in front of her and took two steps into the room. "You've no doubt guessed, I'm Elizabeth Carter." One corner of her mouth quirked up. "Your wicked stepmother."

Joan rarely made snap judgments, but she had learned long ago to trust her gut reaction to people and situations. She decided she was going to like Elizabeth Carter, even if the rest of the day was a disaster. Would liking this woman be a problem, or a help?

She stood up and was relieved when Ulysses moved out of her way. She hadn't looked forward to nudging him or tripping over him.

"All I have is the word of Harrison Carter that he's my father. What if you made a mistake and I'm not his daughter after all?"

"He knew you'd say that." Elizabeth nodded, her gaze never leaving Joan's face. "There's not much of him in your features, but from what we know of your actions, your reputation and your mind, you are your father's daughter."

Joan knew already she didn't look much like her father, simply because she and Nikki looked so much like Niobe.

"Well, you're here at last, and that's what matters." Elizabeth crossed the small reception room and sat down on the sofa, smoothing her pale gray skirts under herself.

Now that she was closer, Joan could see the silver and white strands mixed with the blonde of the woman's loose chignon. A light dusting of pale, rosy powder and a touch of warm pink lipstick were her only concessions to makeup. From the slight sagging in her jaw line and around her eyes, Joan guessed this face had never come anywhere near plastic surgery or Botox injections. Tiny gold hoops, an unadorned gold wedding ring and a gold chain around her neck with a small watch for a pendant were her only decorations.

"Did I come from an affair, or did my mother pull some nasty tricks to get me?" Joan had intended to ask Carter that question, but a flash of insight told her she would learn more from someone who stood to the side of the events, rather than in the middle of them. She sat again.

"An affair. Yes, your father and I were married when he became involved with your mother." Elizabeth's warm, pleasant expression never changed.

"What's it like, facing the daughter of the 'other woman'?"

"There are always two sides to every story, Joan. Remember that in the future. In this case, however, I think there are four."

"Did you know Ni—my mother?" slipped out before Joan knew she wanted that information. That frightened her. Speaking before thinking usually led down paths she was later sorry she had followed. The only way to stay safe was to plan ahead and stick to those plans.

"Your father kept me separate from his business affairs before we were married." Elizabeth shrugged in a genteel manner. "Something like the Mafia dons, who kept their families separate from their criminal activities. He learned differently, once we were married. That was part of the problem that gave your mother her edge, her opportunity."

"You influenced him, pushed him into considering ethics."

"Perhaps. I like to think the Holy Spirit influenced him more."

"Not enough to keep him faithful." She winced. "That wasn't what I meant to say."

"Hmm, perhaps not. But it needed to be said." Elizabeth's eyes narrowed for a moment. "Don't ever assume the injured party is innocent. We all make choices and some are bound to be wrong, or to hurt those we love even if they are the right choices. If a man breaks his wedding vows less than a year after making them, there has to be a reason."

"So you're saying you drove him into that psychotic's arms?"

Joan felt slightly breathless, surprised at herself. As a rule, she tried never to attack. She considered it a waste of energy, and rude. It was far easier to let the enemy come to her, expend energy and emotion and resources, then simply sidestep and use her enemies' weapons against them. Yet in the space of a few moments, she had been rude and attacked an innocent woman.

She nearly laughed when she realized she considered Elizabeth Carter innocent, even after what she had just said.

"This is starting to feel like a soap opera, but you're not acting like a soap opera wife."

"Be sure, I was wounded when I found out about Elaine and about you, later." Elizabeth tipped her head to the side and studied Joan's face again. "No matter how strong our marriage became through our struggles, there are scars. But you are innocent, Joan. No matter what your mother might have told you. I'm not innocent, so what right do I have to punish you for your parents' sins? You are Harrison's daughter, so you will always be welcome here."

"Welcome here," Joan echoed. That choking, breathless sensation returned. "Why am I here? Why did he send for me now? You've been here all these years. Your Arc Foundation has been going strong as long as I've been in Tabor, an hour away. Why contact me now?"

"Time is no longer an unlimited resource." She stood and beckoned for Joan to follow.

"Oh, that tells me a lot," she muttered, and got up.

Ulysses stayed close on her heels as they left by the second door of the reception room and went left down the wood-paneled hallway. Elizabeth tugged open one panel, revealing a hidden staircase.

"Your father called in quite a few favors to obtain this estate when it went on the market. I'm afraid he manipulated circumstances in his favor... but considering the alternative, what could have happened to this wonderful old house if other hands had gotten hold of it, I'm no longer ashamed of the methods."

She paused a moment longer, looking around at the carved wood paneling, the closely fitted, smooth stone paving, as if they stood inside an ancient castle. Sunlight streamed in from other rooms, filtered through high windows of wavy glass. With a sigh and lightly weary smile, she gestured for Joan to follow her up the stairs. Ulysses stayed at their heels.

"We had planned to retire here. Retreat from the dark, dangerous world your father lived in. We thought he was free of Elaine at last. Then we learned that you existed, more than a year old. It changed our entire perspective on Harrison's connections, his influence throughout the world, the resources still lying in his hands. Our hands."

Elizabeth paused as they came out into a hallway on the second floor. She gestured at a door on the right, which led into a room on the front of the house. Sunlight streamed through the wide windows.

The man sitting with his back to the windows still wore the vestiges of physical power; wide shoulders, muscular arms evident despite the draping of the thick, chocolate brown velour robe. The hair capping his square, rugged face was glossy and thick, but stark white, and lines of pain circled his eyes and mouth. Pallor betrayed the healthy tan that still lingered, indicating this illness was fairly recent. The thin oxygen tube clipped to his nose and the tank sitting on the floor, discretely tucked in the folds of his robe, hinted at awful possibilities.

Chapter Ten

Harrison Carter smiled slowly as he watched his wife and Joan walk into the room. His eyes brightened and his gaze raked Joan from head to foot several times in the few seconds of silence. Then the dog darted past Joan, went up to the man and put a paw on his knee.

"Ulysses, isn't it?" he rumbled, with a rattle of phlegm at the back of his voice.

In that voice, Joan heard a man who was used to speaking with power and confidence. What was it like to be betrayed by his body? She understood now what Elizabeth had meant by saying time was no longer an unlimited resource.

Her father was dying. Would he have ever sent for her if he wasn't? Or had his illness simply pushed up a plan that must have been years in the making? Why else would he have been keeping watch over her?

"He's adopted you, has he?" he continued, and leaned forward to rough up the dog's fur. He nodded, his smile widening a little bit, when Ulysses let out a soft whine and darted back to Joan's side.

"I don't know about adopted. I mean, I live in an apartment. Where would I put a dog?" Joan bit her lip before she started babbling.

"You could live here. Eventually. When you feel comfortable. Until then, Ulysses would stay here." Elizabeth settled down on the long sofa next to her husband.

"Live here." Joan could see herself moving into the mansion and never running into these people for days at a time.

"If that's what you want to do," Carter said, nodding. "Please, Joan, sit. Make yourself comfortable. As comfortable as you can, considering how much a strain this must be for you."

"Not for you?" She chose a chair that faced them both and yet didn't put her back to the door. Ulysses settled next to her and rested his head across her feet. Joan resisted the urge to twist her foot around and shove the dog away. She felt anchored to the floor, unable to leap to her feet and run at need. That was not a good feeling.

"We've had most of your life to prepare for this meeting."

"Yeah, most of my life."

"I imagine you're angry with Col. Sidarkis," he continued.

"Since when does a politician keep his word, anyway?" She tried to shrug, as if it didn't matter.

Actually, she was surprised her father brought up the subject. Joan had taught herself to trust practically no one, but she had trusted Sidarkis. Enough to do repeat work for him. She thought he was a man who meant what he said and kept promises, no matter what. Obviously, he counted his loyalty to Carter more important than his promises to her.

"He's no politician. He will never rise any higher in the ranks, because he refuses to play political games." Carter leaned forward a little, resting his elbows on his knees. "He's an old friend. He didn't know who you were to me until he asked my help in destroying all traces of your work and your association with him."

"But old friendship still won out over promises."

"Some concern for you, I think. It took quite some convincing before he believed you are my daughter."

"You still have to convince me."

"Of course." A twinkle flared briefly in his shadowed eyes.

"Convince me that you won't sell me out, just like Sidarkis sold me out to you."

"Believe us, Joan," Elizabeth said, "you haven't been sold out. Your father and I worked for years just to find your trail."

"Why?" shot from her lips on a harsh whisper. Joan gripped the arms of the chair and didn't care if they saw or not.

"I'm your father. I have a responsibility toward you. More than just throwing money at you. More than trying to free you from Elaine," Carter added, his voice strained. As if he might run out of breath if he used too much force.

"I'm free of her."

"You'll never be free of her. You're constantly looking over your shoulder."

"Moving in with Daddy isn't going to make me any safer. Did she know your real name all those years ago, or were you just the Oracle? Does she know who you are now?" A ragged, bitter laugh burst from her and Joan raked the fingers of one hand through her hair. "We were in Akron sixteen years ago, most probably looking for you. She left in a spitting fury, so I assumed she didn't find what she wanted, or your shields made her think you weren't you. But that could change. It might have changed already. If she knows who you are, then she's watching for her chance to follow up on her threats. Which means she'll eventually learn I'm here. I signed my death warrant, just coming through your gates."

"Yes, you could have. And no, she didn't know my true name."

"She's tried to penetrate the illusions and barriers the Oracle erected at the height of his power," Elizabeth said. "As far as we know, she hasn't succeeded. There's safety in numbers, Joan. Together, you and your father are too powerful, have too many connections and friends, for her to strike at either of you."

"Like a big, fat, poisonous spider sitting in the middle of a web that goes on forever." Joan nodded. "All it takes is one really big rock, thrown from a safe distance, to squash the spider flat. If she finds us together, that might push her over the edge. She bombed churches when I was a kid, just for the fun of it. What's to stop her from climbing over your little iron fences and getting past your guard dogs?"

"My few links with my past exist solely to keep track of her movements. She was dealt a very serious blow with that work you and your friend did for Sidarkis, and she's in no condition to hurt either of us right now." A little color returned to Carter's face when Joan caught her breath at the news. "Together, we can make up for some of the evil she's done in the world. That is why you named yourself after Joan of Arc, isn't it? To pay back the world for the evil she's done?" He held out his hand. "Join forces with me, Joan. Let me be your friend, if it's too late to be your father. Make a difference for good in the world."

"There are only two sides in the conflict," Elizabeth said softly. "Choosing to sit on the sidelines only helps the side of evil. All it takes for evil to triumph is for good men to do nothing."

"What makes you think I'm good?" She flinched when Ulysses whined, sat up, and put his head on her knee.

"You're not working with her right this moment." Her father nodded. That sparkle came back into his eyes. "I've been backtracking you, learning about you through the things you've done. Your friend, Sophie, is quite a maestro when it comes to computers and programs and the Internet. The two of you have redirected dirty funds into innocent hands, and foiled efforts to defraud the innocent. Is she Robin Hood to your Joan of Arc?"

"Nope. She's just a religious fanatic." Joan shrugged. Despite herself, she responded to the widening smiles from her two hosts. "Sophie'd fit in just fine here with all your morality and charity and all that."

"I think you'd fit in just fine here, too," Carter said.

~~~~~

Joan walked down a path paved with uneven slabs of stone, between two rows of slim, elegant birch trees. Ulysses walked beside her, silent but for the occasional scraping of his claws on the stones. At the end of her first interview with Carter, Elizabeth had gestured out the door from the two-story-tall Great Hall and suggested Joan take a walk while she digested everything they had talked about. At the end of the lane, Joan saw a stone railing and then a sweeping vista that seemed to go on forever. How could this landscape be possible in the middle of Akron? She supposed good planning over a century ago, and lots of money, could make anything possible.

A tiny snort escaped her when she considered Elizabeth's words. Yes, there was a lot to digest. She felt as if she had eaten a heavy meal far too quickly, and wasn't quite sure yet of half the things she had taken in.

Like Sophie had said once, an ant could eat an elephant, one bite at a
~~~~~

time. She wasn't going to get any of her thoughts organized unless she took one detail at a time. Common sense said to pull out the things that were clear, the things she did believe, and put them aside so the rest of it wasn't quite a jumble.

First, she did believe Harrison Carter was her father. She had his hands, long and lean, with that odd bump on the longest finger on both hands and the extra-large knuckle in both thumbs. They also had the same arrowhead-shaped mark on the inside of their right calves. Joan trembled now, just remembering. Carter had tugged up the leg of the dark green sweatsuit he wore under his robe and turned his leg to show her the mark. Then he smiled that crooked smile and invited her to touch it.

"To assure yourself it's not a fake, painted on to trick you."

The mark was just a little larger than her thumb, raised, dark reddish, the skin rougher and thicker than the skin around it. Just like the one on her leg. Not a birthmark, but essentially a clump of thicker, darker skin, like a clot of moles. When she was a child, she had imagined it was clay that got stuck to her skin and just needed extra scrubbing to remove it.

"A friend got close enough to see it when you were ten," Carter had said, when Joan returned to her chair and he had pulled his pant leg down in place again. "Until that point, I couldn't be quite sure Elaine hadn't simply claimed you were my daughter to punish me."

"So, it's more a genetic thing than an actual birthmark."

"I suppose. The mark has bred true for the past three hundred years. Some families have a tuft of white hair at the back of the head, others have a cowlick, others have a bald spot, a blotch of pigment in a specific shape. Our family, on my mother's side, has that arrowhead somewhere on the leg." A sigh that sounded like a chuckle escaped him. "That mark helped get back some children who were taken captive by Indians, before the Revolutionary War."

And now it's helping get another child back.

Joan came to the end of the path and stood looking at the flagstone apron and the small structures on either side of the waist-high stone railing, like sentry houses with gabled roofs.

Why had he gone to so much effort and expense, before he was sure she was his? She had asked him that about halfway through their conversation.

Because, her father explained, he had a responsibility. He had harmed her through his sinful actions, his wrong choices, and he was duty-bound to make up for it.

Joan had laughed when he said that. "What? You're not going to claim you've always loved me?" That was a line she would have expected from someone trying to use her, for profit or to get to her mother. The lack of that line convinced her before Carter answered her mocking question.

"Let's be honest, Joan. I don't know you, only what people have told me about you. I admire you. I respect you. I'm proud of your intelligence and resourcefulness, and I'm vain enough to believe you inherited some of that from me. But I have no idea how much you're influenced by your mother's upbringing, her bitterness, her warped view of the world, her cruelty. It's hard to love an image, and I'm honest enough to admit I hesitate to offer love to Elaine's mirror image."

"Yeah," Joan muttered now, staring unseeing at the vista sprawling away from her as she crossed the stone apron to the railing, "but what about her negative image?"

Sophie had accused her of working hard to do everything Niobe wouldn't do, or to choose a path she would disapprove. Joan had never thought of her choices and values having that motivation, but she realized her friend was right. It frightened her. Could she really consider herself free of Niobe's poison, if she used her as her *negative* measuring rod?

Her head hurt. Joan needed to not think for a while. She rested her arms on the flat stones topping the railing and looked down. A series of ponds lay in front of her, connected by wide channels, with narrow bridges arching over the water at several spots. The history of the house, which Sophie had sent her, said Quarry Hall got its name from the stone quarries that used to be on the property. Most of the stone used to build the house had come from those quarries. The family who had built this house during Akron's heyday had lined the old pits with clay and turned them into an area for swimming, fishing, canoeing, and skating in the winter.

The bright sunshine, the gentle breeze that ruffled the leaves of the surrounding trees, the birds that fluttered down to the water's edge or perched on the railing of the nearest bridge, and above all the silence, combined to create a sense of serenity. Peace. Distant from the rumbling, dirty, busy world. Joan envied the family who had built this sanctuary, and she found she envied her father for having this place to hide in.

Did he hide here? There was a difference between a fortress and a castle. Had Carter come here to rest, to retire from being the Oracle, or to hide? She couldn't imagine he simply let go all his ties to the Information Underground. How could he stay safe, otherwise? So, was this quiet sanctuary a hiding place, or was it a staging area, a stronghold to support whatever actions Harrison Carter, the Oracle, was still involved in?

Clunking, uneven footsteps snapped her out of her thoughts. Joan glanced at Ulysses, who patiently sat at her feet, watching her. She would have felt more comfortable with the dog if he had acted like a dog, dashing off to investigate every sound and movement. He just walked with her, like a short, furry friend who was content to let her think in peace, without demanding any of her attention. She didn't know if she liked it or not.

Right now, the dog pricked up his ears and turned his head to the left, looking through the carved stone posts of the railing. Joan followed his lead. After a few more seconds of waiting, she saw a woman come up from the shadows beyond the farthest pond. She carried an armload of what looked like wildflowers and lots of leaves. Sunlight glinted off something on her left foot. A few more steps closer gave Joan more details. She had long, reddish-brown hair, pulled back in a ponytail high on her head. She wore jeans, a green polo shirt, and clunky hiking boots.

Mismatched hiking boots.

Joan snorted. That wasn't a hiking boot on the woman's left foot, but a plastic walking cast. A shadow separated from the others and followed the woman out into the sunlight as she crossed the bridge closest to Joan. That shadow was a big, black dog. Probably the same breed as Ulysses.

"Your sister?" Joan said, glancing down at him. He blinked at her and waited, watching the two through the gap in the railing.

The other dog let out a low, whuffing sound. Not quite a bark. Joan suspected these dogs were too dignified to bark. She rather liked that. Too much of her childhood had been spent in places where dogs were kept as alarms and had high, yapping voices that made her ears ache. The woman paused, just at the bottom of the bridge, glanced back at the dog, then around, until her gaze met Joan's. She tipped her head to one side for a moment, then continued walking.

"This ought to be interesting," Joan muttered. She put her back to the railing when the woman started up the slope, on what was probably a hidden staircase. The stranger coming toward her hadn't smiled, but she didn't seem surprised to see her there, either.

The black dog darted out from behind some tall, flowering bushes that had masked the stairs at the top. The woman appeared a moment later, limping a little, her face flushed as if with strain. She stopped at the stone bench in the shadow of the first guardhouse and put down her armful of flowers and leafy, thin branches. Then she looked at Joan as she straightened and raked sweaty strands of hair out of her face.

"We're not expecting anyone today... you wouldn't happen to be Joan, would you?"

Joan laughed. Now that she really thought about it, the overall impression since she arrived was that everyone here had been waiting for her. It was a relief to meet someone who didn't know what she looked like.

"I get the feeling you don't laugh often enough." The woman held out her hand, looked at it, grimaced, and wiped her palm on the seat of her pants before holding it out again. "I'm Kathryn."

"I'm Joan. Of course. How many Joans were you expecting, anyway?" She approved of what she sensed about Kathryn in her handshake. Very few people nowadays offered their hands when meeting someone; it implied openness, trust as well as being trustworthy. Joan felt strength under the sharply delineated tendons and bones in this woman's hands.

"Only you. And only because we've been praying so much more than usual for you." Kathryn tipped her head to one side and frowned a little, her gaze intensifying.

"Praying. For me." That made her shiver, though she wasn't quite sure why. "What's wrong? Do I have mud on my face or something?"

"Hmm? No. Nothing like that." Her thoughtful expression shifted to a smile that was almost rueful. "This is going to seem rather strange but… do you get a lot of flat tires when you go to the library?"

"What?" Joan took a step backward, nearly stepping on Ulysses. She bent to stroke the big dog's head to apologize, using it as a cover to collect herself and guard her reaction.

The truth was, she had experienced a flat tire every time she drove to the Tabor Library. Most of that was because she rarely drove there, but when the weather was unfriendly or she was in a hurry, Joan had driven her car instead of walking. Every time she spent more than half an hour inside, she came out to find at least one tire flattened. Sometimes two. Usually when she realized the problem, she had looked around and found broken glass nearby. She had taken to walking to the library, no matter how bad the weather, just to avoid the hassle.

"I had a dream, and you were in these clothes. You were coming out of a building with your arms full of books… and your car had a flat tire."

"Oh. Makes sense."

"No, it doesn't." Now it was Kathryn's turn to laugh. "You're polite, but you think I'm strange and I'll bet you're going to make up some excuse to get out of here as fast as you can."

"Well, you don't run into prophets every day."

"I'm no prophet." Her humor fled as quickly as it came. "I simply have very truthful dreams, that's all. I saw a bottle break and spread all over the ground, and a woman's hand picked up the biggest piece and stabbed your tire." She shrugged. "You can believe me, or you can shrug it off as someone who needs her medication adjusted."

"What medication are you on?"

"Fresh air and sunshine and plenty of bed rest." Kathryn stepped back and held out a hand. Her big black dog leaned against her leg, whining softly as she stroked the furry head.

"Okay." Joan fought two conflicting urges: run or get more information. "Suppose I have had flat tires lately. What's to prove that you haven't been doing it, just to set me up?"

"Why would I do that?"

"I have no idea."

"Don't be silly. You have lots of ideas. You think anybody who's given her life to Christ is a religious fanatic in need of some heavy-duty counseling and medication. Don't you?" A smile hovered at the corners of Kathryn's mouth.

In that moment, Joan decided she liked her. A lot.

"My whole world is under the microscope now. Who knows what I'll believe tomorrow?"

"You don't work that way, Joan. I've heard Uncle Harrison talk about you, all the bits and pieces and reports he's gleaned over the years."

"Uncle? We're cousins?" Joan's voice nearly cracked from the force of shock that cut through her chest and stole her breath.

"I guess we are. Isn't that funny? I never thought about it, until now." Her somber expression softened, and a brief shadow across her face gave Joan the impression Kathryn had suffered a serious illness recently.

Of course, judging by that walking cast on her foot, a major accident was the more logical explanation.

"Anyway, I've seen the reports on you, the things you've done, the people you've helped. You're not changeable unless there's a need. You have to be proven wrong before you'll relinquish anything you believe in. Probably because you don't believe in very much, I'd guess."

"Dr. Kathryn, I presume?"

"Hardly." A sparkle lit her dark eyes. "You're a good person. We could use you on our side."

"The good guys?"

"Oh, most definitely. You're staying for dinner, aren't you?"

"I haven't thought that far."

"Stay. And stay overnight, too."

"To avoid the library parking lot slasher?"

"Hmm. Maybe." Kathryn nodded, and her gaze grew hazy for a moment. "Brooklyn made apricot carrot muffins, and they're heavenly for breakfast, warm, with slathers of butter and honey. And the sunrise is gorgeous from here. You really should stay and see it. And let the place kind of… soak in."

"Brooklyn is the cook?"

"Oh, we all take turns cooking. Brooklyn is Uncle Harrison's nurse, officially. But she's a friend from the old days, and she's signed on for the long term. You'll like her."

"I guess."

"Besides, she makes a wicked lasagna, and that's what's for dinner."

"Uh huh." Joan had to grin. "Is that listed in my files? That I'd sell my soul for a good lasagna?"

"No. *I* would, and that kind of refined taste creates a visible bond between like-minded individuals. Besides, Uncle Harrison breaks down in tears when Brooklyn makes her lasagna, so I figure it's genetic." She stepped back and scooped up her wildflowers. "Let me put these away, and I'll take you on the grand tour, if you'd like."

Chapter Eleven

"Sounds good." Joan settled down on the edge of the stone railing. "Will your foot be okay with all that walking?"

"Nothing to worry about. Thanks for asking." Kathryn turned toward the path that led to the peaked glass rooftops Joan had seen earlier, and assumed were greenhouses. Her big dog got up and started to follow her. "No, Bea. You stay and rest. I'll be right back."

The dog whined, but she settled down again. Ulysses moved over next to her, and the two dogs rubbed muzzles. Joan pulled her gaze away as soon as she realized she was staring.

"Nobody has warned you yet, about the dogs around here?" Kathryn's voice turned rich with repressed laughter.

"A little bit. Just that they go where they want. Bee? As in... buzz?"

"Bea as in Beatrice."

"Dante's guide in the *Divine Comedy*?" Joan guessed.

"I certainly hope your knowledge of the classics goes beyond that." Kathryn shook her head when Joan opened her mouth to respond. "Later. We have plenty of time to get to know each other. Relax and think about what you want to see, when I get back." She hurried down the path and was soon out of sight, hidden by bushes and the drop in the landscape.

"How do I know what I want to see, when I don't know anything much about this place?" Joan muttered. She settled herself more securely on the thick stone railing and swung her legs just enough to bang her heels against the stone posts underneath her. The two dogs sat in companionable silence, watching her.

She had glimpsed a stone walkway, extending out directly opposite the door from the Great Hall, with an amazing view of the rolling valleys beyond. She had a general idea of the surrounding landscape and thought the Cuyahoga Valley Park system lay in that general direction. She decided she wanted to walk in that direction when Kathryn returned, and maybe through the shadows of what looked like a long grape arbor. It was green and thickly grown, and she wondered if any grapes were growing there yet. Simple questions about things like the growing season for grapes struck her with her lack of a well-rounded education, perhaps even a well-rounded life. Traveling with Niobe had left her lopsided in her experiences and emotional development. The effort to stay free and healthy once she had escaped hadn't done much for her balance, either.

Wouldn't it be nice, she thought for just a few unguarded moments, if she could stay here and pretend the outside world didn't exist? If she could live in this big house and explore the gardens? If she could ride one of those horses in the stable every day? If she could learn about trees and flowers and growing cycles, and play with the dogs? Maybe then she could learn what it was like not to live looking over her shoulder.

She could learn what it felt like to belong, to be not only welcome, but wanted. And not wanted just for the things she could do, but because people knew her and liked her. It was possible, wasn't it? After all, these people seemed to know a lot about her already, and they accepted her and wanted her there. It wasn't like with Matt and the other people in Tabor Heights, who only knew the mask she had worn for four years.

Joan snorted, closed her eyes, and willed away the headache that always seemed to strike when she let her guard down and dreamed of a normal life. Normal was letting Matt Cameron talk her into marrying him, living in his big house, and raising a few kids. Normal was becoming a soccer mom and working for the PTA.

Normal wasn't debugging computers and security systems and getting calls from military and scientific bigwigs, owing them favors and getting favors from them. Normal wasn't worrying her multi-layered identity would shred and Niobe would rise out of a big gap in the ground and slaughter her. Normal wasn't making friends with her half-sister, letting her live as a foster child, and never telling her what they were to each other.

Normal, for all intents and purposes, had nothing to do with Joan Archer.

"Nice dream while it lasted," Joan whispered.

A touch on her knee had her gasping and jerking upright. Not a smart thing to do when she sat with her back to a thirty-foot drop.

Ulysses sat up on his haunches, one massive paw resting lightly on her knee. With his head cocked to one side, his eyes big with inquiry, Joan could have sworn he was… worried about her. Which made absolutely no sense. He was just a dog.

"What is with you?" She slid down off the railing, just to dislodge that paw.

Both dogs watched her as she moved into the shadow of the left-hand shelter, but neither one followed her. Joan pressed her forehead against the cool stone pillar and concentrated on her breathing, slow and deep, to enforce a sense of calm and clear her thoughts.

What was she doing here? She thought she had come to this mansion to meet her father, to find out what he really wanted. Period.

Wandering around in the sunshine, playing word games with someone who foresaw the future in dreams, and making a half-serious commitment to stay for supper had been no part of her plan when she left Tabor that morning.

"You look like you have some pretty big problems weighing on your shoulders," a rich, alto voice said from behind her.

Joan turned slowly, wondering what resident she would meet next. First glance stamped the woman as the gardener. A tangle of blond hair nearly to her shoulders and deep blue eyes that seemed to turn green then gray when she turned her head, were the only features that stayed in Joan's mind. The stranger wore faded jeans, grubby work gloves, a sweat-stained khaki shirt, and dirt-crusted work boots. She had a rake in one hand and a grubby canvas bag tied to her belt and hanging past her knees. She had one of those weathered, healthy faces that made pinpointing her age impossible.

"Nothing is as bad as you can make it seem," the stranger added, when Joan's mind stayed uncharacteristically blank a few seconds longer.

"Are you going to tell me you read minds, just like she sees the future in dreams?" Joan gestured in the general direction of the greenhouses.

"You must mean Kathryn." She grinned, her eyes sparkling. Joan wavered between thinking she laughed at her or invited her to laugh. "Nobody sees the future in dreams. Just bits and pieces of warnings. Even choosing to ignore a warning can change what happens next."

"Are you a philosopher, or a gardener?"

"You can call me Messenger." She plucked a weed from the tine of the rake and tucked it into the bag hanging from her belt.

"You didn't answer my question."

"I did." A twinkle brightened those changeable eyes. She nodded up toward the house. "I'll be seeing you around, whenever you need someone to get you angry."

"What do you do around here besides pull up weeds and talk like the guru on the mountain?" Joan forced herself to relax, rather than clench her fists. Maybe she really was losing her mind, thanks to the stresses and hormonal changes of the last few weeks. Or maybe she was turning into Niobe, despite her best efforts.

"I'm Messenger." She shrugged and gestured back toward the greenhouse. In the momentary silence, Kathryn's uneven footsteps came through loud and clear. "Sometimes the best plan is to flow with the moment." She winked and crossed the pavement, heading toward the birch tree walkway and the shadows. Joan watched her go, until she heard Kathryn call her.

"Ready for that tour?"

"Yeah. Sure." Joan stepped out into the sunshine. It had weight and solidity, like heavy, warm hands pressing down on her shoulders, squeezing just enough to nudge some tension out of her muscles. She glanced toward the birch path but didn't see Messenger anymore. Then she heard the clatter of dog nails on the stone pavement and sighed, the sound turning into a chuckle. "What's with the dogs?"

"The dogs?" Kathryn slowed her steps and glanced at the dogs, who had run ahead of them a good five yards. "What do you mean?"

"Why is Ulysses sticking to me, for one thing? And why isn't anyone surprised? What's with the 'adopted you' line?" She tried to rein in her frustration and not take it out on Kathryn, but her encounter with Messenger made her feel like she had grabbed high voltage wires.

"It's not a line." The other woman shrugged and kept walking, heading down the line of birch trees. "The dogs here are a little different, if you haven't noticed yet."

"I have no idea how dogs are supposed to act. There was no room for pets when I was growing up."

No room, she reflected, for anything but Niobe's personal vendettas and punishing the world for the pain she had brought on herself.

"The dogs are smarter here. They have personalities, I guess you'd say. And Vincent trains them to protect."

"So… Ulysses is keeping an eye on me so I don't pull out a knife and start slicing everybody's throat?" Joan offered a weak smile as she said it.

Just when she had started to think she might like the dog's constant company, that bit of information from Kathryn changed everything. She thought she felt a little sick, on top of the aching in her empty stomach that reminded her she hadn't eaten much of anything for breakfast.

"No. He's guarding you."

"Why? What's dangerous here?"

"Doesn't matter if there's danger around or not. That's the way the dogs are here. Ulysses chose you as his, forevermore. That means he guards you."

"I live in a studio apartment. There is no room for a dog, even if my landlord would let me have one." The truth was, Joan had no idea what the rules were about pets.

What frightened her was the realization that it felt perfectly natural to consider taking Ulysses home with her. She had never had a pet in her life. After Niobe threw out Fuppy Bear, Joan had sensed pets weren't a subject to bring up. It was hard enough knowing her beloved bear had ended up in a trash bin somewhere. What would Niobe have done to a living creature, if it got in her way? If she could deposit her infant daughter in a car in a flooding river, what cruelty would she have done to an animal?

Joan shuddered and pulled her thoughts back to the present.

"Hmm." Kathryn gnawed on her bottom lip for a few seconds. "The truth is, we were all sort of hoping you'd come to stay here."

"Stay?" Joan turned, instinctively looking for the peaked roofs of the house beyond the tops of the trees.

"Just for a few days, at first. We all know you have a life of your own, but… well, Uncle Harrison is your father. Don't you want to get to know him?"

"It's not that easy." She thought of the man she had watched while they talked, the signs of pain, the illness eating him from the inside. He hadn't mentioned his illness at all.

Elizabeth had said that time was no longer a limitless resource. That had to mean something, didn't it?

Until she met Sophie and they connected as if they had known each other all their lives, Joan had lived without friends. She could be friendly, but she knew better than to let anyone past whatever mask she had created for the current situation. Her regular pattern was to travel lightly and settle lightly, ready to pull up stakes and re-invent herself as soon as people started to suspect she wasn't as she appeared to be. Friends meant roots, and tearing up roots was painful. Roots were only for people who belonged.

She and Sophie "clicked" from the moment they met because they had so much in common, always on the move, looking over their shoulders. Mutual protection pact, like minds. It made for the first freedom she had ever felt to share even a glimpse of the real person inside.

Her relationship with Sophie fed some of her hunger, but what she had with Sophie was a totally different proposition from getting to know her father, sending down roots, and belonging, with the threat of death in the background.

"We're all going to die eventually," Kathryn said, when the silence between them stretched out a few seconds longer. "It's just that some of us have the information stamped on our foreheads, rather than just whispering from the darkness. Why should that stop you from getting to know him?"

"Do you do that all the time?"

Strange, how it didn't bother her as much as it should have. Maybe she had simply gone past her weirdness quotient for the day, and nothing else could really bother her?

"Do what?"

"Know what people are thinking."

"It's what we all think about." Her smile was gentle, touched with sadness. She looked around, until her gaze landed on the dogs, who paused a few steps ahead of them. "Lunch. Go tell Brooklyn. Kitchen." She made a gesture toward the house. Bea let out a soft *whuff* and darted through the trees.

"Your dog talks to people?"

"Not really. But it's almost time for lunch, and if Bea comes in without me, Brooklyn knows that means I'm on my way."

"Does everybody have a dog around here?"

"Just those of us working on the outside." Kathryn led the way out of the trees, across the lawn, toward the raised back patio of the house.

"On the outside." Joan didn't think that meant security or yard work.

"For the foundation. We each get a bodyguard who can't be bribed or distracted. Vincent trains all the dogs. Once they've bonded with someone, they won't take food from anyone but their person, or Vincent. You wouldn't believe how many people think they're safe with dogs as guards, and never think of the enemy hitting them with poison in a doggy treat."

She shook her head and made a *tsk* noise.

"So… Vincent is a dog trainer?"

"Among other things." Kathryn paused on the patio and glanced through the big glass door into the Great Hall. "Let's go in the side." She turned left, going back along the house, down the steps, into the brick-lined yard Joan had noticed earlier. "This used to be the drying yard. For laundry. And this is the servants' porch and dining room," she added, leading the way up a short set of steps to a door. "When we have meals together, we eat in the morning room, but when it's just one or two of us, the servants' dining room."

"Then what do you use that big dining room for, with the Canterbury Tales tapestries?"

"You like that room? That's for impressing the bigwigs, and for meetings with the advisory board." Kathryn grinned and gestured for Joan to go in ahead of her.

"Advisory board?" Joan stopped a few steps into the long, homey-looking room. The oak table and the dishes set up on display in the hutch along the wall looked like they might have been original furnishings. "Mighty nice for servants."

"Do not muzzle the ox as he threshes your grain." She laughed when Joan frowned. "It means, take good care of your servants, because they're taking care of you. And if you think about it, we're all servants here."

"Uh huh."

Kathryn led Joan out another door, and a few short steps down the hallway to a long, green-tiled kitchen, with the biggest, blackest old-fashioned stove Joan had ever seen. A tall, elegantly thin, white-haired black woman presided over the stainless-steel work counter in the middle of the kitchen. She wore pristine white leggings and a white muslin shirt with short sleeves. She glanced up from the sandwiches she arranged on a clear glass platter and nodded to the two.

"It's about time you got here, Joannie-girl," she said in a clipped British accent. Handing the platter to Kathryn, she gestured at the double-wide refrigerator. "Salads and dressing and tea in the first door. Anne called and should be here in another hour."

"Great. Thanks." Kathryn took the platter in one hand and stepped over to the refrigerator. "This is Brooklyn."

"Uh. Yeah. Thanks." Joan had to mentally shake herself to keep from staring at the woman. "Nice to meet you. Brooklyn?"

The woman tipped back her head and laughed, the sound chiming off the ceiling. "You wonder why I'm called Brooklyn when I sound a thousand miles away from it? I knew your father, back in the bad old days. He helped save my life, and hid me in Brooklyn, where I had to learn the accent and mannerisms right quick to fit in. It's a joke, and a reminder of how far the Good Lord has brought us all." She gestured again at the refrigerator, where

Kathryn took out a glass pitcher of iced tea. "You take the salads, will you? I'm upstairs to check on something right now. We'll have a nice talk later, all right?"

"Sure." Joan kept the smile on her face until Brooklyn glided out of the kitchen. She fetched the single serving bowls of salad from the refrigerator, nudged it closed with her heel, and followed Kathryn back down the hall to the dining room.

That was when she realized the dogs had stayed in the dining room, rather than following them to the kitchen. She didn't comment on it, but Kathryn must have seen her look at the dogs. She waited until they were both seated, then snapped her fingers. Bea and Ulysses settled down on the floor along the wall by the outside door, where no one would trip over them.

"Those are well-trained dogs," Joan murmured.

"Vincent's a good trainer. He won't say, and it's better if you don't ask... but from what he's let drop, he was in some kind of ultra-secret, Black Ops group. Nasty and deadly. He trained dogs to kill, to sniff out bombs and drugs, that sort of stuff. Now, he trains them to protect... and never give anyone a single excuse to protest our dogs being with us," she added with a grin.

"Sounds good." She reached for a half-sandwich that looked like it had slices of chicken and Swiss cheese and put it on her plate. Then she held her breath, bracing for a few seconds of discomfort. After all this time working with Sophie, she knew what would come next.

To Joan's surprise, Kathryn bowed her head, covered her eyes with her fingers, and didn't pray aloud. Her lips moved, and Joan looked away so she wouldn't be caught eavesdropping on Kathryn's conversation with God. A few seconds later, her companion let out a little giggle, making Joan jump.

"I kind of figured it might make you uncomfortable, me praying aloud," she offered, when Joan turned back to face her. "I have to warn you, if Uncle Harrison is up to sitting at the table tonight, you'll get a nice, long, out-loud prayer. But not so long it threatens all that lasagna."

"Thanks for the warning," Joan said, grinning and feeling a little dazed. "I've been meaning to ask you—"

"Are we blood relatives, or just cousins by marriage? Blood. Uncle Harrison is my mother's older brother." Kathryn grinned wider. "I wasn't reading your mind. I just figured that was one of my first questions, when I learned you existed, so it's probably yours, too."

"It's going to take some getting used to. Having family," she admitted, and picked up her sandwich again just to smooth over the awkwardness she felt.

"You're stuck with us, you know. No returns allowed. Now, what I was saying, about the advisory board?" Kathryn took a tiny bite, chewed quickly and swallowed. "It's hard getting the charitable community to trust a newcomer. Arc has only been functioning publicly for three, four years now. So, Uncle Harrison put together an advisory board from local church and civic leaders, to give us connections and some instant validity. They have no real power."

She paused to sip the iced tea Joan poured for them, nodding her thanks. From her slight frown, Joan guessed what she would say next contained something unpleasant.

"Some of the original members have left because of problems. Disagreements. Mostly caused by their own stubbornness and stupidity. I mean, if you're told from the outset you have no power, no authority, what makes you think you can make big promises and public announcements without getting into trouble? They give advice, not make decisions. But these ex-members of the board decided something should be done and made promises to people. That was bad enough, but then they decided Arc needed publicity, so they told the press something was being done when Uncle Harrison had no intention of taking the first step."

"They promised help when... when those with authority didn't want to go in?"

"They sidestepped Arc's basic operating rules. Always investigate every request for involvement, whether it's a one-time injection of money or long-term support. And we always work quietly. No big public relations announcements, no fanfare, no getting listed in the programs at graduation." Kathryn shook her head. "Some folks never learn."

"Why are you telling me all this?"

"You help people, don't you?"

"Yes." Joan nodded slowly. Why did people simply assume she would go along with their plans for her before she even heard them? And why hadn't she jumped in her car and headed back to Tabor already? That question bothered her more than anything else. What had happened to her well-honed sense of self-preservation and invisibility?

"Wouldn't you be able to help more people with the power and resources of the foundation behind you?"

"Come here to work for... my father." She fought the temptation to shrug or grin or laugh or push away from the table and run.

It made sense. It felt right. As if she had been working up to this all her life. But the sense that the decision had been taken from her hands made her balk.

"Do you want to do this because it will irritate your mother?" Kathryn mused, her head tipped to one side. "Or because your father wants it and you want to make nice until you figure him out? Hard decision, huh?"

Chapter Twelve

"You do read minds." Joan couldn't manage any humor in her voice and the joke fell flat.

Then again, she really hadn't been joking.

"No. It's how I'd feel, if all this was dumped on me." Kathryn reached across the table and rested her hand on Joan's. "Don't make a run for the gate or anything, but they did tell you why they named it the Arc Foundation, didn't they?"

"I can guess." She reached for her glass of tea, when the last bite of her sandwich stuck in her throat.

"It was right after Uncle Harrison found you in Tabor."

"Joan of Arc," Joan whispered. She bent her head and hid her face in her hands. She didn't know if she should laugh or cry or start screaming. Part of her had been hoping that idea was just a bit of arrogant wishful thinking in her paranoid, over-active imagination.

A whimper warned her, just before Ulysses rested his muzzle and then one massive paw on her knee. Joan uncovered her face and looked down at the big, half-grown dog. The sympathy shining in his strangely light eyes made her feel protected.

What kind of a pitiful state had she fallen into, when she was delighted to have the unwavering support of a dog she hadn't seen before today?

Joan took a deep breath, braced herself, and rested a hand on Ulysses' head, just behind his ears. Tentatively, she stroked down his muscled neck. There was something soothing in the feel of the thick, silken-coarse fur under her hand. Maybe having a dog for a confidant and support wasn't such a bad thing?

"Okay." Joan sighed and finally looked at Kathryn again. The sympathy in her eyes didn't feel like such a heavy blow now. "So I'm supposed to just walk in and… what?"

"If you stay — when Uncle Harrison is gone — you'll *be* the foundation." Kathryn offered a shrug and a crooked smile. "To get back to the subject… Some former members of the Advisory Board ignored the word 'advisory' in their title and claimed authority they never had. When they were told their services were no longer wanted, they refused to step down."

"Hey, just don't invite them to any more meetings." Joan toyed with the crust of her sandwich, fascinated by this information and the problems it presented, even though it implied responsibilities she hadn't consciously agreed to take. Yet.

"If only it were that simple. Anne and Vincent and I have been traveling to the shelters and other places Arc has either established or is a major sponsor for, to tell them in person what's going on. They've dealt with us before, face-to-face, so they're taking our word over whatever the dethroned advisors have been trying to tell them."

"But the snakes aren't going away, no matter how many times you stomp on them?" Joan guessed. "Why do they insist on breaking the rules?"

"They don't see it as breaking the rules. These particular troublemakers like making a big stink over how much time we supposedly waste, and how many people supposedly slip through the cracks while we insist on our intensive background searches. They want to paint themselves as heroes, problem-solvers, while we're the time-wasters and cynics. One of the biggest flaps we just cleaned up was over a women's shelter that specialized in runaway girls. Our loudest ex-advisor threatened to expose us to the evangelical world as frauds. He threatened us with a complete loss of support if publicity got bad enough. Which just showed how much attention he paid when he was first asked to join the board."

"Meaning?" Joan prompted, when Kathryn grinned and rolled her eyes and took another big bite of her sandwich.

"We don't take donations." She momentarily tucked her mouthful into her cheek. Her eyes sparkled when Joan frowned and shook her head. What charitable organization didn't take donations? "Everything we do is funded solely through the foundation's extensive investments. So it doesn't bother us at all when someone threatens bad publicity to make people stop donating. We don't take the money people do try to send us. The other half of those threats do affect us, though."

"You don't want any publicity, so bad publicity can still do damage," she filled in, letting Kathryn take another bite and nod while she chewed.

"With Uncle Harrison, the more pressure someone puts on him, the more he resists. The shelter was a complete unknown in the charitable and social work world. That raised a red flag for us. The fact that they tried to put pressure on us, along with the loud-mouth ex-advisor who shall remain nameless, just irritated him. His first impulse is to say no when someone wants an answer right away."

"If people don't want to give you time to think, that usually means they have something to hide," Joan murmured.

"Exactly." Kathryn took a gulp of her tea. "Something smelled fishy. Vincent went with me to give it an in-person inspection." She took a bite of sandwich and gestured at the plastic cast on her foot. "We found out it was a front for a prostitution pipeline, in and out of the country. The ones profiting from it all, and laughing up their sleeves at the do-gooders, didn't like having their secrets exposed."

"Ouch." She winced. A dozen possibilities for how Kathryn got her foot injured flashed through her mind. "I can bet the loud-mouth didn't like that when his pet charity got exposed."

"And that's exactly why we insist on thorough examinations before we get involved. To be sure we aren't throwing money at something that looks good but is a cover for the same filth we're trying to stop."

"And that's where I come in." Joan took another bite of sandwich and chewed while she thought. She liked the idea, actually. She knew Sophie would be ecstatic to get involved in something that more actively helped people in need.

"You'd be researching and acting as the face and voice for the foundation."

Joan nearly choked on the mouthful she had just taken. An immediate vision of being seen on television or having her picture in newspapers or magazines flashed through her mind.

If Niobe ever saw her... the possibilities were too chilling to consider without growing nauseous.

"Consider the story of the purloined letter," Elizabeth said, from the doorway of the dining room. She leaned against the frame and her gaze flicked back and forth between the two at the table. How long she might have been there, listening, Joan had no idea. She had been too involved in Kathryn's narration.

"Edgar Allen Poe?" Joan guessed, after swallowing quickly.

"Hide in plain sight. Would Elaine ever expect you to let your face be seen by the media?"

"No."

"If you agree to become part of the foundation, you would have a very carefully cultivated image to present to the media and to the scrutiny of the public." Her faint, warm smile took on a mischievous gleam. "A very different face from your daily, working face and mannerisms and voice."

"Ah." Joan nodded, relaxing again.

The cold filling her stomach partially dissipated. She imagined herself dressed in a severe, elegant navy business suit, her hair pulled back, pearl earrings, elegant makeup, glasses, maybe a slight accent hinting at foreign education and culture. And then spending all her non-public time in jeans and t-shirt, sans makeup or jewelry, total antithesis to the face of a multi-million-dollar philanthropic foundation.

"It's the cloak and dagger aspect that makes up for all the boring parts," Kathryn offered.

"You, young lady, are incorrigible." Elizabeth sighed. "I'm sorry, Joan. We're throwing so much at you, so quickly, not giving you time to think. I suppose Kathryn has told you we want you to stay for dinner?"

"And overnight. And for a couple days, from the sound of it."

"Your father wants you to stay forever," she said, her voice softening to a near-whisper.

"Why?" Joan didn't feel the anger she expected. There was something about this place, these people, all the hints and strangeness that intrigued her, that drove away the fight-or-flight reaction so deeply embedded in her. The certainty she usually felt that she would eventually be ejected with rancor wasn't there at all. "Why does he want me involved? Why did he name the foundation after me? Why watch me all these years? Why not write me off as a loss, from the beginning? Why does he want to hand everything over to me someday, when he hardly knows me?"

To her amusement, Joan heard a plaintive note in her voice, like someone who had been left out of the game for so long and couldn't understand why she was finally being included.

Maybe that was it, she theorized in a split second, while Elizabeth licked her lips and prepared to answer. The reason she didn't burst out in anger was because she *wanted* to be included, despite training herself to never, ever want to be on the inside. Wasn't it safer on the outside, hiding in the shadows, free to run, not boxed in somewhere?

These people seemed to want her, need her, and knew more about her than anyone else in the entire world. It was no longer enough to play superhero with Sophie, helping people and foiling the enemy through their wits and computer skills. A gang of two wasn't all that much company or fun. An entire foundation to work with and play with, to wrap around her, to talk with as she had with Kathryn and Vincent, Elizabeth and her father, awakened a hunger and ache she had managed to shove out of her consciousness for years.

"He's your father. He loves you. He's seen evidence of your work, and he believes you'd do well carrying his duties." Elizabeth's voice caught for a moment. She smiled a little wider and blinked rapidly, and Joan realized she fought tears. "Let's just hope you have plenty of years to work with him, get to know him, and get all the training you'll ever need." She nodded to Joan and Kathryn and turned quickly to leave.

"What's killing him?" Joan said, pitching her voice so only Kathryn could hear.

"We're not quite sure."

Kathryn wouldn't look at her as she answered, which always spelled evasion, for Joan. She didn't push, reasoning she would get the answers eventually. After all, whatever was killing Harrison Carter was part of the reason why she had been invited to Quarry Hall.

Brooklyn offered them apple pie pockets for dessert and shooed them out onto the patio to eat in the sunshine. She muttered something about children not getting enough fresh air and sunshine, and Joan nearly laughed with a mouthful of pie. That would have been a crime and a waste of flaky crust and apples cooked into a tender, nut-and-honey flavored mass that melted in her mouth.

They went down to the lowest level of the house and examined the gymnasium. The antique exercise equipment was still there, pushed to one side to preserve it and let future generations admire and laugh at what was once thought the height of physical fitness and science. Exercise mats and a compact weight station sat tucked into one corner of the room. This was Vincent's territory, Kathryn explained.

"Hand-to-hand combat?" Joan remembered what her guide had said about the security man earlier.

"Basically. It's not safe out there. That's why we have our friends here." Kathryn bent to ruffle Bea's fur. The dog whined, her tongue lolling out and eyes closing in momentary ecstasy over the caress.

Joan looked down at Ulysses, who walked on her right, as Bea walked on Kathryn's left. The big dog didn't whine or give her a pleading look, but Joan still felt guilty not indulging in that loving touch.

"Vincent trains us to defend ourselves. Never attack. But we need to know how to resist anyone who would try to hurt us, and to defend others. The Bible never said to run away." She shrugged, giving Joan a crooked smile and a studying glance. "If you think about it, the armor Paul describes in Ephesians doesn't imply having armor on your back, only on your front. Paul said to make a stand. He didn't say anything about attacking. Just… stand. Resist."

"Paul who?" Joan knew who Kathryn referred to, thanks to Sophie and all her studies. Her momentary blip of humor surprised her, and she barely managed to keep a straight face.

Kathryn gave her a "You've got to be kidding" look. A heartbeat later, they grinned at each other. Joan liked the easy, unspoken communication and understanding between them. This was the same bond that had formed almost immediately when she first met Sophie. She liked being with people who sensed the unspoken words.

She was in trouble already. If she decided she couldn't become part of Arc and fit in with these people, it would be very hard to leave this place behind.

"Vincent probably knows a dozen ways to kill without leaving a mark, without using what other people would consider a weapon. He teaches us what we need to know to defend ourselves. If we have to take it that far to defend others," Kathryn added, her voice dropping nearly to a whisper, "we can kill." She shook her head, took a deep breath. "We never use weapons. One of our basic rules is to never give anyone any reason, any excuse, to accuse us of doing something wrong."

"Sounds kind of paranoid."

"Hmm. Maybe." She gave the brightly lit gymnasium one more look, then turned to lead the way back up the steps from the sub-basement, to the center corridor that ran through the lower level of the house.

They explored the boiler room and furnace room. The octopus of the old-fashioned heating system sat in quiet, dark, dusty splendor, thanks to the small, efficient heating system installed in one corner. The antique equipment of the laundry room had been pushed aside, just like in the gymnasium, so the modern, efficient washing machine and dryer and sorting tables could be used.

"This place doesn't go to waste, does it?" Joan mused, after they explored the wine cellar, the coal room, the photography dark room, and others, all of which were still being used, either in their original function or adapted.

"Good stewardship. Uncle Harrison has opened up the place for pastors' conferences and retreats, and Sunday school picnics. And holiday tours and civic and church group activities. When there are missionary conferences and revivals at the different churches in the area, he's invited the guest speakers to stay here, instead of the church putting them up at a hotel." She grinned. "It just ticks off the Pharisees, who want him to declare allegiance to one denomination. They can't stand it when he looks at people and only sees God's servants, not the artificial lines that religion makes."

"So if I stay on here, I get to hack off a bunch of hypocrites on a regular basis?"

Kathryn frowned for a moment, then her expression melted into a grin. The two shared a look of complete understanding.

"And this is the best part. At least, in the winter." Kathryn pushed open one last door.

The room they stepped into looked like a locker room, without the lockers. Joan glanced around at the changing stalls with green gingham curtains pushed aside, the hot tub sitting on a raised platform in one corner of the room, and the doorway beyond, where greenish light filtered through. A whiff of chlorine hinted what was there. At Kathryn's gesture, she stepped through the changing room to the open door.

A small built-in pool sat under dimmed green lights, the surface of the water rippling softly in a few places, evidence of the filtration jets at work.

"The original owners called it the Plunge, and we kept the name. So… elegant." Kathryn tossed her head and took on a momentary languid pose, pressing the back of her hand to her forehead. "The water level can be raised and lowered to suit the swimmers, and it's heated, but we keep it chilly most of the time, to wake us up. Care for a dip?"

Joan hesitated, when what she wanted was to pull off her shoes and leap in right that moment. There was nothing more relaxing, to her point of view, than floating in total silence and solitude. Water blocked all sound and softened all sensations. She could rarely indulge, though, because the pool at BWU was never empty. Swimming outdoors was too dangerous, simply through being exposed to all comers, and she had a phobia about not being able to see what was in the water with her. This indoor pool, however, seemed made to order.

Kathryn opened a closet and showed Joan a selection of bathing suits in a wide range of sizes. Most of them looked brand new, all of them clean and dry and sealed in plastic zipper bags. After pointing out where the towels were kept, the swim caps, and the soap for showering afterward, she headed for the door.

"You aren't—" Joan floundered for a moment, caught between the certainty she was being rude, and her hunger to be utterly alone.

"You heard Brooklyn, before? Anne is probably here by now. I have to help with her debriefing. Besides, this thing would drag me down to the bottom." She lifted her foot enough to tap the heel of the cast on the tile floor. "Enjoy your swim." Kathryn smiled and pulled the door shut, leaving Joan utterly alone.

Except for Ulysses' company, of course.

"Why do I have the feeling I'm never going to be alone again?" Joan muttered. She reached out to lightly stroke the dog's head. He closed his eyes, tipping his head up to take full advantage of the caress. "Well, dog, what are we going to do, huh?"

Ulysses opened his eyes, regarded her for a moment, then with his nose nudged the suit she had taken off the shelf. Joan laughed. She couldn't have had a clearer answer.

The water wasn't so much chilly as slightly below room temperature. Refreshing without being shocking. She supposed it was cooler in the morning. Joan swam ten laps of the short pool until her abdomen started to ache, then allowed herself to do what she liked best: floating on her back, water in her ears, eyes closed, relaxing.

Thinking.

Everything came down to survival. Would it be safe, a smart move, to align herself with her father, get involved in his charitable work, take up the role that waited for her?

Was it dangerous to have anything to do with him?

The thing is, she acknowledged, after her thoughts had tangled and untangled and tensed her body so she nearly started to sink. *The thing is, this place feels right. It's kind of weird, with everybody 'in' with God. And the dogs. And the problems with bureaucrats and self-righteous jerks that I'll have to deal with. But I like it here.*

Was comfort a strong enough reason to stay?

Then Joan realized the water felt warmer.

She turned onto her stomach, paddled the short distance to the edge, and pulled herself up to sit. Water dripped and some spattered onto the tile. When she first got into the water, it was cooler than the air. Now, her legs were definitely warmer, in the water, than the rest of her body. Not all of it could be blamed on being soaking wet, or evaporation.

"What the heck is going on?" she muttered.

Ulysses, sitting in the corner where he faced the door, raised his head. His tail thumped twice on the tiles, then he lowered his head again and closed his eyes.

"If you're relaxed, that means it's okay?" Joan shook her head. Maybe the problem wasn't this household, but her.

The door from the changing room swung silently open. Joan drew one leg up, poised to leap and run. But where could she go?

Carter paused, braced in the doorway. He wore net deck shoes, loose blue trunks, and a thick blue terrycloth robe that hung open. His chest was pale, somewhere between the pallor of illness and the pasty look of a man who never went without a shirt. Joan saw the long lines of scars crisscrossing his chest. The telltale centipede scar over his breastbone looked well healed. Joan wondered how long ago his heart surgery had been, and why he needed it. She saved that question for later.

"Relaxing, isn't it?" Carter nodded, pulled his shoulders back, took a deep breath, and pushed off the doorframe.

He didn't totter like an old man about to fall off his legs, but some unaccustomed emotion ached inside Joan's chest as she watched him walk slowly across the tile floor to the ladder at the pool's edge.

"Kathryn suggested it." Joan didn't know if she should offer to help.

"Sorry I interrupted."

"You're not. I was thinking of getting out."

"Getting warm?" He gestured at a device on the wall that Joan had simply assumed was part of the pool filtration system. "A heater on a timer. Warm water therapy. It takes the weight off my legs, improves circulation. What's the use of having all this if you don't use it?" He slowly lowered himself into the water, holding onto the ladder tightly enough Joan saw his knuckles whiten.

"Sophie would call it good stewardship," she offered, and settled down again, letting her legs dangle in the water.

"Do I make you uncomfortable?" He held onto the side and turned his body so his legs floated. A soft sigh escaped him, magnified by the acoustics of the small room.

"What do I call you? How am I supposed to feel about you? I believe you are my father, even without the blood test and all those other proofs we talked about."

"But a label is different from a relationship." He nodded, dipping his chin into the water. "Forget about what should be, Joan. I've learned it's a waste of time and energy and keeps me from enjoying what I do have. What we could have, from this day forward."

She bowed her head, studying her foot, her toes peeking up above the surface of the water. Questions tangled on her tongue. She wasn't sure what she wanted to know, what she could ask. Still, awkward questions were better than this silence.

"What's killing you?"

Chapter Thirteen

He opened his mouth as if to answer, then closed his eyes, smiled a little, and shook his head. Joan waited while he settled into the support of the ladder, hooking an arm through the bar and letting his body drift.

"My past, I suppose," he finally said, and opened his eyes. Despite their gazes meeting, Joan sensed he looked beyond her, seeing someone else, perhaps another time and place.

She waited, trying to guess from his expression what he would say. Studying his face was easier here in the strange half-light of the pool. Even with his scars and pallor, he seemed stronger, more alive.

"We're still not sure what it is, only what it's doing to me. Genetic warfare at its worst, I suppose."

"Genetic?"

"You didn't think Oracle's reputation and the weight of all my accumulated knowledge would keep me inviolate, did you?"

"Well… yeah."

"So did I. Until this happened." He ran his index finger down the scar blazed along his breastbone. "We realized later, the bomb wasn't meant to kill me, only to put me in a position where I would need medical care. It isn't enough for my enemies to kill me. They want me to suffer. Vincent was already working with us, and he was a true gift from God that day. He pulled strings and had me flown to a high-security facility under the care of some people who owed him quite a few favors. They kept me alive for two weeks, until it was safe to perform the surgery that saved my life. Unfortunately, I have an extremely rare blood type."

"I don't."

"For which I thank God. Especially after this happened." He shook his head. His face wrinkled in momentary pain, but Joan sensed it was in his spirit, his memories, rather than in his body. "Sometimes, I wish Vincent hadn't been quite so skilled or fast, or the doctors had written me off as a lost cause and let me die."

"Why?" burst from her lips before she could censor herself.

"Kathryn has the same blood type." He shrugged, offering up that rueful smile that Joan realized she had seen on her newfound cousin. "Kathryn offered her blood before anyone could even ask. The facility she went to for the blood draw had faulty security. When they gave her a glucose feed, to make up for the large quantity of blood they were taking, over the course of several days, our enemy struck. A genetic time bomb, fed into her blood, to pass on to me."

"She looks fine," Joan whispered.

"Her youth protects her, gives her more resilience, and the lion's share of the attack did pass straight on to me. We theorized that someone got enough of my blood when the bomb went off to do a slapdash job of genetic engineering. They took the opportunity to feed the genetic time bomb to Kathryn when they weren't able to get to me. Their work was tailored to me, but we have enough genetic similarities that the disease did partially bind to her. Just enough to send down roots, so to speak. You could liken it to a man-made cancer, finding nesting spots in the nervous system, the liver, the lungs, the bones. It steals oxygen from the blood, blocks neural impulses, and stores toxins in vital organs."

"Dialysis—"

"It's not in the blood, to be filtered out, but in the marrow. We've considered radiation and bone marrow replacement, but the problem is that our extremely rare blood makes that a difficult proposition at best. Kill all our bone marrow, but we need a new source to replace it. As things stand now, the only cure is to rewrite the genetic code and trick our bodies into healing themselves, just like they were tricked into killing themselves slowly."

"Do you have people working on it?" Joan shivered and slid down into the warm water, but that didn't help drive away the chill that started in the pit of her stomach.

"Even Oracle has a limit to the favors people owe him. For Kathryn's sake, we keep trying." He shook his head. "Don't feel sorry for me. I've earned every evil thing that has ever happened to me."

"But you're—it's not fair—you've reformed."

"Just because I've repented and turned my riches to charity doesn't mean I can escape the consequences of my past."

"It's not right." She held onto the side of the pool until her knuckles turned white.

"What's not right is that I waited so long to make contact with you. What's not right is that I had an affair with Elaine, ignoring her warped soul because of her brilliant mind and her sensuality. You've suffered for my sins. What's right about that?"

He spoke calmly, nothing in his voice and face but weariness and a hint of a solid, underlying peace. An indefinable quality in his gaze made her ache, deep inside. Joan wanted something, sensed she had the answer she needed within her grasp, but she had no idea how to actually reach out and take it. Or even what she was grasping.

Not knowing, not being able to understand, irritated her. It always had. She hated this blankness where she expected a smooth flow of data and comprehension. She couldn't quite tamp down the anger rumbling against her heart and tightening the vise that made her head ache.

"This is really crazy." Despite the coolness in the air and the soothing warmth of the water, she heaved herself out again. This time, instead of sitting on the side, she got to her feet and staggered a few steps away from the pool's edge. "I've just met you. I should be furious with you for ripping up my nice, quiet, safe life. At the very least."

"What's safe about constantly looking over your shoulder, with no one to depend on?" he asked calmly. "It's not peaceful quiet. It's the waiting quiet that tears at your nerves."

"So it's better to put yourself in the public eye and paint a target on yourself?"

Carter laughed. It wasn't very deep or long or hearty, but in that sound, Joan heard a hint of the rich laughter he had once enjoyed before illness ate away at him.

"You'd be amazed how eagerly the world ignores you when you do good works and avoid publicity and praise."

"There's always a scandalmonger trying to see under the wholesome mask," she shot back.

"True. If it's a mask." He nodded, studying her across the pool, with the gentle light bouncing off the rippling water and striping his face. "But we don't wear masks here. We don't carry weapons. Not weapons as the world sees them, anyway."

Joan glanced at Ulysses, who waited by the door, watching her. She thought of the damage a big dog like him could do, just jumping on someone. No need for claws or fangs. Just bruises and broken bones, and an obstacle to slow down her enemy.

"You don't need my money, and I doubt you need the training I can give you. You can take care of yourself. All I can give you is purpose and a place that will always be your home, and the family you've never had."

"I don't believe what you believe," she whispered. "I can't."

"I won't demand that you fake a spiritual life. I can point you in the direction you need to go, but only you can walk that path and make that choice. I can't buy your way into heaven. But I can share what I've learned and try to spare you some of the pain and mistakes that nearly destroyed my life." Carter heaved himself up the ladder and perched on the edge of the pool, shoulders hunched, dripping water. "I'm glad you're honest enough to admit you don't believe. That's half the battle. You know the difference between us. If you played along and smiled and jumped eagerly on board… then I'd be worried. I'd see your mother in you."

"She hated churches," Joan whispered. "Was that because of you?"

"Most likely."

"I remember her spending weeks watching a church that was really active, really making a difference, helping people. She'd work herself into a fit, until she was almost foaming at the mouth. She'd follow different people, watching them, tapping their phones and stealing their mail, just to find something wrong with their lives. And she'd be so happy when she found someone cheating or stealing or... whatever." Joan reached for the enormous towel she had brought from the changing room. Despite the humidity, she felt more chilled than ever.

"And sometimes she would set a church on fire, or bomb the pastor's car, or just indulge in some vicious, juvenile vandalism. I know. I knew her style, her signature, and that let me follow her trail, no matter what she did to go invisible. If she hadn't made a habit of destroying churches and Christian organizations, I never would have been able to find you at all. Ironic, isn't it?" Carter smiled wearily.

"She always got nasty with the churches where she couldn't find fakes." She shuddered and tugged the towel tighter. "Sophie says I try to do whatever she *wouldn't*. Whatever would make her angry. How come I'm not a holy roller?" She offered him a smile.

"Because you're honest." He held out his hand. "I'm not asking you to devote your life to the foundation. I'm not asking you to decide now, right this moment. Any decision that someone pushes you to make without giving you time to think, that's a decision that's bad for you. I don't want to put a guilt trip on you. All I'm asking for is time. Your mother had you for fourteen years before you escaped her. You learned from her, gained the tools you needed to escape. Now, all I'm asking is that you give me time, learn from me, let me give you the tools I think are important for life. Maybe it's too late to be your father. All I'm asking is time, and a chance."

"I do owe you that much," she said, nodding.

"No, Joan. You don't owe me anything. I owe you everything." His face grew stern, and she saw in his eyes a dim reflection of the implacable, unstoppable force of the Oracle.

"Drafting me into a life of charity work and fighting those jerks on the Advisory Board doesn't sound like paying back that debt."

"You enjoy a challenge, don't you?" A sparkle touched those eyes again, and she was glad to see it. "Who wants to be bored?"

~~~~~

Joan heard Kathryn's voice and turned down the winding garden path to look for her. The hand-drawn map Brooklyn gave her said she was headed toward the Oriental garden. She stopped short, heart in her throat, when a blur of brown and black leaped from the shadows of the overhanging trees and bushes and became the biggest German Shepherd she had ever seen. Joan knew better than to look into an aggressive animal's eyes. Especially when said animal could knock her flat on her back. Those jaws looked big enough to take her throat in one bite. She tried to look away, but she couldn't yank her gaze free of the dog.

"Argus!" Kathryn called.

"So that's your name?" Joan started to smile, then wondered how the big dog would react to her showing her teeth.
~~~~~

Ulysses stepped up next to her. He made no sound, but Joan could have sworn she felt something flicker through the air between the two dogs. Argus bowed his head, touched noses with Ulysses, then wagged his tail twice and turned to go back through the archway of trees sheltering the entrance to the Oriental garden.

"Sorry about that," a new voice said. A girl who looked like she was in college stepped into the stray beams of sunlight that penetrated the tall canopy of trees in this part of the estate. Adolescent slim, she had perfectly straight, honey-colored hair hanging to her waist, a green gingham short-sleeved top, new jeans, and white sandals. The big dog whined like a puppy until she put her hand on his head.

"Anne, this is Joan," Kathryn said, still out of sight. "Come on in."

"I'm not interrupting, am I?" Joan rested a hand on Ulysses' head, grateful for his presence once again. She could see how useful the big dogs could be, as comfort and protector and passport through difficult situations.

"Argus is just a little touchy around strangers right now," Anne said. She shrugged, offered a bright smile, and turned so swiftly her hair flew back behind her like a cloak.

Inside the Oriental garden, Joan found benches and Japanese-style statuary, moss everywhere, and a fountain that tinkled softly; a soothing, cooling sound.

"Anne Hachworth, Joan Archer." Kathryn stayed seated on her bench, peeling an orange.

"Gee, a lot has happened since I left." Anne settled down on the mossy paving stones, legs crossed. Argus lay down so he could put his head in her lap. She stroked down his back and his tail thumped up and down three times.

Joan made a guess that whatever errand Anne had been running for the foundation, it had involved some sort of trouble and her big, furry bodyguard was still touchy about her safety. Funny, but she felt a little jealous.

Ulysses nudged her leg and whined a little. She looked down at the half-grown dog, and silently laughed at herself. What did she have to be jealous of, with him attached to her by an invisible umbilical?

Silence. Joan looked at Anne, who studied her with her head tipped to one side, her face partially hidden in shadows. Somebody had to say something. She felt that prickling sensation she hated, which had always signaled to her that everybody else here knew a whole lot more than she did. Right now, everybody knew about her, but she knew very little about anyone.

Except maybe her father. That encounter in the warm pool room had filled some gaps and settled questions she had only sensed and not been able to put into words yet.

"So." Joan settled on a bench on the other side of the squared little garden area. "Did you say we were having lasagna for dinner?"

Kathryn laughed. She tried to stop, but ended up snorting, when Anne gave her a questioning glance.

"Joan wasn't sure if she was staying or not," she explained. "Feeling more comfortable?"

"There's still a lot I need to learn."

"We're always learning." Anne continued to slowly stroke down Argus' back as they talked.

"Anne was just telling me about her last trip, so we can write up the report," Kathryn said.

"Report? As in, paperwork?"

"Self-defense. If nothing is kept hidden, then nobody can accuse us of playing games and keeping secrets and ulterior motives. If we keep meticulous records, we won't be caught with our pants down, figuratively, when the attack comes."

"Attack?" Joan smiled. Instead of irritating her, such talk felt like a challenge. That swim in the pool had done more for relaxing her than she had thought.

"Once you dedicate your life to Christ," Anne said slowly, "don't you know it's like painting a target on your forehead?"

Joan thought about the harassment Xander already received from the legal community for the work he was doing, the ethical stand he had taken. Common Grounds Legal Clinic had barely begun its work. She nodded and waited for Anne to go on.

"We have a rule that basically covers everything," Anne said after a few moments of studying Joan's face again. "Always have witnesses, and never go solo on anything important. If you're dealing with a child, always have another adult around. A police officer or minister or someone important in the community is always best. Never go into any situation without telling someone what you're doing, even if you think you're wasting time. You always need a lifeline."

"Even if it's just someone praying for you," Kathryn added.

"Makes sense." Joan offered them both a shrug and a smile. "I have a friend, Sophie—" It felt strange just speaking her soul-sister's name aloud to people who didn't know her. "She's like you. Faith. She prays for me all the time. I'm convinced it's kept us both out of a lot of trouble."

"Imagine how much more effective you two would be if you were praying for her, too," Anne whispered.

Again, that silence filled the garden. Joan felt as if she stood at the corner of a turning point, heavy with longing to the point of pain. She held her breath, waiting for a clue, and then the moment passed. She felt that empty, dropping sensation that came when something wonderful was expected, but never materialized.

"Anne was playing escort to a mother and three children, running away from the mother's husband, who didn't happen to be the father of the children," Kathryn said.

"He didn't want to let them go?" Joan guessed.

"He was abusing the girls and intimidating them into keeping it secret. When the mother accused him, he blew up. When he took off on a two-day bender after beating all of them bloody, she decided it was time to get out," Anne said, studying the mossy stones in front of her.

To Joan's questioning look, Kathryn answered, "Anne's... specialty... is abused children. She's been able to point out instances where the children were lying to get a stepparent or guardian in trouble, or lying because one parent told them to, to get revenge on the other."

"Ah. Useful."

"Not like that," Anne said, with a snort and a shake of her head. "I don't look into people's heads, like Kathryn sees things in dreams. I have experience." She met Joan's eyes on the final word, giving emphasis to it.

Joan shuddered, understanding in that instant what Anne meant.

Who better to determine if a child was truly being abused, sexually or emotionally or both, than someone who had gone through it herself?

"How did you come to work here?" Joan asked, hoping to steer the conversation around, if not away from that painful area.

"The Black Prince." Anne smiled. A snort escaped her, touched with laughter, when Joan cast another confused look at Kathryn.

"Someone Uncle Harrison used to know, in the bad old days. He brought Anne to us and asked Uncle to watch out for her," Kathryn explained.

"Is that his code name?" Joan had to ask. She stopped short of saying, *Like my father used to be Oracle*, because she wasn't sure just how much anyone here knew. Just because she seemed to be in the dark didn't mean she could leak secrets that others were trying to keep.

"That's what I call him. I never learned his real name." Anne bent her head and stroked Argus a little faster. The big dog whined and nuzzled her other hand but didn't get up or react in any other way.

"Once upon a time," she continued, after a ringing pause, "there was a king and a queen and a princess. They let a kind, wise old man live in the rooms under their castle. They didn't know he was an ogre, because he used magic to trick everyone. He became very good friends with the king and queen, so they trusted him and they laughed at his stories. And when the princess was bad, he would tell stories so the king and queen didn't know what she had done.

"But at night—" Anne closed her eyes and her voice caught. "At night, the ogre climbed into the window of the princess' bedroom and he hurt her. When she cried, he told her she was a bad girl. He told her she deserved to be hurt. She got sick, and the king called in doctors, but nobody could help her. The ogre told her that if anyone ever found out what he did to her at night, he would kill the king and queen, and it would be all her fault, because she was a bad girl. So the princess didn't tell anyone. And she got sicker. And the queen worried. And one night she thought she heard the princess crying, so she came to see her. And the queen saw the ogre, without his mask. So the ogre killed the queen. The king heard the noise and came to see what had happened, and the ogre killed him."

Joan opened her mouth to tell Anne to stop, she didn't have to say anything more. Kathryn stopped her with a stern look. Joan wrapped her arms tight around herself and held her breath and waited.

"The ogre put on his mask again, so the soldiers thought he was a good, kind, wise man. He told the king's ministers that the king had hurt the princess, and when the queen caught him, the king killed her. He told them the king tried to kill the princess, but he, the ogre, stopped him. And everyone believed him, so when the princess cried and told them the ogre had killed her parents, no one believed her. They said she was sick in her mind, and they wanted to lock her in the highest tower and hide her, so no one would ever hear her. But the Black Prince came. He had been hunting the ogre, from far away and long ago. He proved the ogre had lied and he had hurt the princess and killed her parents. He proved the princess wasn't sick and she didn't lie. He took the ogre away and promised he would never hurt any more princesses. And he took the princess to see wise men who healed her."

"And the princess came here?" Joan asked, pitching her voice low and soft.

"Oh, no." Anne opened her eyes. They glistened with tears, but she smiled. "The princess thought she was well and strong, and she grew up. Her old wounds opened up again, slowly, so she didn't know she was sick. The Black Prince came back and stopped the princess from doing bad things, and he brought her to a wise man who told her a wonderful secret. The only way to be well and stay well is to help others get well. The only way to stay safe is to protect others." She knuckled the tears out of her eyes before they fell and took a deep breath. Her shoulders slumped as she exhaled loudly. "The end."

Anne, Joan decided in that aching pause, was far stronger than she would ever be.

"Will she live happily ever after?"

Chapter Fourteen

"I think so." Anne bent over Argus at the same moment the dog raised his head. He licked her face. She sat up straight, gasping, and a weak giggle escaped her.

Joan and Kathryn grinned at each other but neither said a word. Anne struggled to her feet. She left, mumbling something about seeing if Brooklyn had made oatmeal cookies as she had promised.

"How old is she?" Joan asked.

"Twenty. Halfway through her freshman year at Princeton, everything just broke open. Fell in with the wrong crowd, started sleeping around, looking for trouble. Self-destructive." Kathryn's usually amiable expression hardened. "The cretins in charge of her trust fund decided to throw her in a mental hospital where patients are kept sedated, rather than trying to heal them. It's a lot cheaper to pay for a bed and drugs, than to fix her. And if she's not using her money, well, somebody should get some benefit from it, right?"

"Who's the Black Prince?"

"Who knows?" She shrugged and slid off the bench to stand up. Bea and Ulysses got to their feet, and Joan followed suit without thinking. "Uncle Harrison never introduced me. I don't think anyone met him. Just one day, he called me into his office and there was Anne, with nothing but a hospital gown and a blanket, still dopey from her last round of medication. Argus was just a puppy, and the first time they saw each other, it was love at first sight. He pulled her out of the darkness in her head. When there's someone depending on you, it's amazing how your thinking straightens out. Then Vincent taught her to defend herself. You can't know how strengthening it is to be able to break someone's arm with your bare hands if you need to, until you've been helpless and furious and unable to do anything about it."

"What did you do for Anne?"

"I pounded her with a fifty-pound Bible. She knew the basics, she just wandered off the path and couldn't see the use in getting back onto it." Kathryn flashed a grin at her. "Come on, before she eats all those cookies."

After learning what she had from her father, Joan wondered what pain hid in Kathryn's past. It seemed everybody here had some great wound to heal or dark past to escape. Was Kathryn's wound her slowly encroaching death sentence, or had something else brought her to work for Harrison Carter and the Arc Foundation?

"I think she's right, though," she muttered as she started down the path after Kathryn. Ulysses' ears pricked up, silent query. Joan laughed at herself, realizing how much she appreciated the dog's company. She refused to even consider how it would feel to leave him behind when she went back to Tabor and her tiny apartment. "It's definitely useful and strengthening to know you can break somebody's arm. Just in self-defense. I need to get to know Vincent a little better."

She caught up with Anne and Kathryn in the kitchen, munching on cookies and drinking big glasses of chocolate milk. Something jolted inside Joan's chest when she saw the glass and napkin piled with cookies on the end of Brooklyn's stainless-steel countertop, waiting for her. How long had it been since someone just naturally assumed she would be there, joining in and doing perfectly ordinary, normal things? She thanked the woman and leaned against the counter, in a row with the other two. And she listened while Brooklyn cooked and talked.

Later, as she helped set the big round table in the cozy, glass-walled breakfast room where the household took most of their meals, Joan reflected that listening to Brooklyn had been like listening to a major cable news channel. The woman seemed to know everything going on in the world. What had she been before she had to flee for her life, before she came to live at Quarry Hall and work as cook and part-time nurse for Carter? Maybe more important, who had she been, and who had she known, and who had turned against her?

~~~~~

Joan wandered downstairs again, when Anne and Kathryn both excused themselves to clean up and take care of foundation office work before dinner. She found Vincent in the gymnasium, going through what looked like Tai Chi steps.

"Care for some self-defense lessons?" he said in the middle of a graceful swinging step, while his back was to her.

"I guess." She bit her tongue to keep from asking how he knew she was there. She prided herself on moving with as little noise and disturbance as possible. It was a survival skill. If Vincent knew she was there, she obviously had something to learn.

"You'd better make up your mind fast," he said, turning to face her.

"Okay, how much can you throw me around before dinner?" Joan stopped on the second step from the bottom and crossed her arms.

Vincent laughed at her and directed her to a storage room off the changing room for the pool, where she could get some exercise clothes.

"Who needs self-defense lessons if you can learn to see through the back of your head?" she grumbled to Ulysses as she slid into gray sweatpants and an olive green, sleeveless t-shirt. Because Vincent was in his stocking feet, she left her shoes in the changing room when she went out to face him.
~~~~~

"Self-defense." Vincent stepped up onto the first of three mats spread on the floor. "First rule: do whatever it takes to get out alive. Run as soon as you can. Don't be a hero unless there are other lives at stake."

Tell me something I don't already know. Joan didn't say it aloud.

Vincent had changed. She had sensed it as soon as she reached the doorway into the gym. He hadn't become different, so much as the background intensity and danger she had sensed in him from the beginning had come to the foreground. She had believed him when he said he was head of security for Arc, even though he smiled when he said it. Now, no one had to tell her that Vincent would do whatever it took to keep Arc safe. Even if that meant beating her bloody black and blue to ensure she knew how to take care of herself.

"Isn't it smarter to just avoid situations where you have to go hand-to-hand?" she asked instead.

"True. But resisting evil implies getting in the face of some pretty nasty characters. Even if you don't go around waving a sword, the fact that you're wearing armor kind of puts the bad guys on the defensive. Know what I mean?"

"Uh... not exactly. I thought Kevlar and all that stuff was made to be worn under the clothes." Joan bit her lip. Smart-alec responses weren't going to get her in Vincent's good graces. Not that she wanted to be buddy-buddy with him, but hacking off the guy who would likely be throwing her across the floor in a few minutes wasn't smart.

"We don't wear weapons and we don't advertise that we're ready for trouble." Vincent's smile was a tight, cold thing that made Joan think of Hannibal Lecter, so calm and dignified and able to kill with a paperclip.

It occurred to Joan that if Vincent had gone with her and Matt to spy on Jonas Carr, the confrontation would have ended with the opposition peeing their pants in terror and promising to be good boys from now on.

Should she tell Vincent that?

No. She would have to explain what incident she referred to, and she didn't want to relive that world-shaking twenty-four hours.

"Our dogs are bred and trained here, or we get them from the government after they've been trained," Vincent said, while Joan tried to come up with a response to his last statement. "Drug dogs, bomb dogs, guard dogs. We teach them a lot of other skills, depending on the personality and talents of the girl they pair up with."

"So you sent Ulysses—" Joan glanced over her shoulder at the dog, who had settled down next to the stairs, looking ready for a nap.

"Nope." Vincent's grin widened and warmed. "He's not quite trained yet, but he's been watching me put the other dogs through their paces, and I'll just bet he knows everything they know." He shook his head. "And then some."

"Why am I scared by that?" she murmured.

"Because you're smart." He gestured for her to step up onto the mat facing him. "Most important thing is to be aware of your opponent's whole body. He'll telegraph his next move, if you know how to look for the signs. Look for patterns in how he attacks, but pray you don't have to fight long enough to detect a pattern."

He lunged on the last word, caught Joan around the knees, flipped her legs up in the air and held her up long enough her back didn't quite slam into the mat. She lay for two seconds, not quite sure she could breathe.

"Next lesson?" she offered when Vincent stepped back and didn't follow up the attack. "Don't let your opponent distract you?"

"Smart girl." He grinned and nodded, amused but still cold. She supposed he wouldn't put his friendly face back on until after the lesson. When he held out his hand to help her to her feet, Joan started to lift her hand to respond, then shook her head.

"I learned that in the movies." She scooted back out of his reach before getting to her feet. "Nobody's going to help you in a fight unless it gives them the advantage."

"Now see? That's where you and I have a lot in common. The other girls, they still believe in the innate goodness of people. They want to trust. You and me...we know better than to trust anyone."

"Especially the guy who just body-slammed you." Joan nodded and spread her arms. "Let's get this over with."

It warmed her more than she wanted to admit when Vincent slapped her on the back at the end of half an hour of bruising and getting the breath knocked out of her, and said she was a natural. His approval meant more to her than she was quite willing to admit.

~~~~~

"Does everyone have dogs?" Joan asked, when the household assembled in the breakfast room for dinner that evening.

Sunset splashed across the estate gardens, creating a bright background for the meal. The windows hung open, allowing the soft splashing sounds of the little fountain just outside to filter in. Vincent, Brooklyn, Kathryn, Anne, Elizabeth and Carter settled down around the table. Kathryn and Anne had kept a seat open between them, and Joan appreciated that thoughtfulness. It was easier sitting between them than next to her father or Elizabeth.

Bea, Argus and Ulysses settled down against the wall, directly behind their respective persons' chairs. There was just enough room for walking around the table without treading on the dogs. Joan wondered if Kathryn and Anne had chosen those seats for that reason.

"The dogs that patrol the estate take care of all of us," Elizabeth said, after glancing at Carter, then at Vincent, who were both occupied with stirring sweetener or squeezing lemons into their tall glasses of iced tea.

"But nobody else got adopted?" Joan offered a shrug and a crooked
~~~~~

smile. She had the sneaking suspicion she had just asked an uncomfortable question. Maybe she should change her half-formed plan to stay overnight?

"Nobody else *needs* to be adopted." Carter met her gaze, his expression grave. "Not yet, anyway."

"What do you mean, not yet?"

"You're aware of Kathryn's dreams?"

"Uh, yeah." Joan glanced to her right. Kathryn poured water from one of the sweating crystal pitchers into a rectangular pan on the floor, big enough for all three dogs to drink from.

"I had a dream, long ago. When I first began assembling the plan for the foundation." Her father nodded. "Not a vision, per se. Not something with specific directions and details. But I had a dream of you working for the foundation, leading it, and sending out workers. Each one would go alone, handling the foundation's missions and problems personally, seeing the people we helped face-to-face. Each one accompanied by a dog raised and trained here, as their companion and guardian."

"And babysitter," Anne offered, giving Joan a wink. That earned smiles around the table and lightened the atmosphere.

"You're so sure I'm going to say yes." Joan snagged her napkin off her plate. "Do you think you know me so well?"

"I know you're a good person, despite what Elaine tried to make you. I know you're driven to help. I think your motivation is purer than mine."

"Don't be too sure."

"I'm sure." He nodded for emphasis, and rested his hand on Elizabeth's, lying on the table between them. "You have Joan of Arc as your role model. You care about what's right and fair. I, on the other hand, am trying to make up for decades of refusing to face the responsibilities that came with my power and resources."

Silence filled the room. Joan thought she could hear the salad wilting in the big, gaudily painted ceramic bowl. She wanted to protest that it was all happening too quickly. Then she met Carter's eyes again, and knew, as if she had Kathryn's gift, what he would say in response.

He had been waiting for this for years. With the genetic time bomb digging deeper into his flesh, merging her life into the Arc Foundation couldn't happen quickly enough.

"So..." She inhaled deeply and reached for her iced tea. The glass jiggled just enough to make the ice cubes chime. "What exactly is involved in this foundation? Do you just hand out money and help people hide from trouble?"

Elizabeth didn't smile, but the joy in her eyes took Joan's breath away. Her cooperation meant so much to so many people. If she stayed and learned more, it would be wrong to abandon it all. If she dug in and learned all they wanted to teach her, she would have made this place part of her. The question was if she could become a part of this place, these people.

~~~~~

When Joan closed the door of the Tudor-style guest room that night, she breathed a sigh of relief. And the next moment nearly tripped over Ulysses. He had never been underfoot the entire day, no matter how closely he kept to her side. So why tangle her up now?

"Sorry." Joan sank down to the floor with her back to the foot of the bed and ruffled the dog's fur around his neck. "I don't know why you glued yourself to me. Do I thank you, or just get paranoid and wonder if I'm losing my mind?"

It didn't seem silly to talk to the dog as if he could understand. From what she had seen today, Joan was willing to believe the Arc Foundation dogs were superior specimens. It couldn't be only the training Vincent gave them. There was something in their eyes she had noticed. As if something besides a dog looked out at the world.

"And if I start believing stuff like that, maybe I really should get my head examined," she said, ending on a long, weary sigh. Ulysses rested his head on her thigh and echoed the sound, pure doggy contentment. "Don't get too comfortable, you monster." She continued stroking down his back, earning a few leisurely thumps of his tail. "I need a bath, for one thing."

The dog just seemed to flatten a little more across the floor. Joan closed her eyes and tipped her head back against the high footboard of the antique canopy bed. She liked the style, which belonged in a museum, but she hoped the mattress was modern.

Talk at dinner had been enlightening. Joan didn't sense that it had been planned ahead of time, to further indoctrinate and convince her to join them.

Two scholarships each at a dozen Christian schools in the area. Four women's shelters. Four food cupboards that also distributed clothes, bedding, hygiene and cleaning supplies. Two clinics that charged for medical services on a graduated scale, depending on the financial situation of the patient. Plans to establish three more by the end of the year. The foundation was ready to expand, but workers were needed. They hired by recruiting, contacting people recommended to them, and by observing the people they met during the course of their work. No applications were ever accepted. Despite the heavy hours, sometimes squalid conditions, and the risk of danger from belligerent, often drugged or intoxicated opponents, those who worked for Arc were taken care of and people wanted to work for the foundation. Elizabeth spent some time every morning sending out letters that thanked applicants for their interest but never promised to consider their qualifications. Then she put aside a tiny percentage for further investigation.

Joan wondered if the numbers would drop if the applicants ever learned the high moral, ethical, and faith standards of the foundation. From what Sophie had dug up already, she supposed applicants knew already,
~~~~~

but like a lot of people, they only heard what they wanted to hear, ignored the warnings, and tried to sue anyone who expected them to follow rules and regulations they didn't want to follow. It made sense for the foundation not to accept any applications but seek out the people who fit the standards and goals. The discussion of the screening process reminded her of problems Xander had with his legal clinic and people trying to force him to act outside his high standards. He would be a good fit with the Arc Foundation.

"He'd probably like my father a lot," she murmured, thinking aloud now. Ulysses whined softly, as if he agreed with her.

Carter admitted to using some of his contacts from his former life as the Oracle. The foundation had connections with the military and intelligence organizations, trading information for services. Vincent hinted at former connections when he talked about working within and outside the Witness Protection Program, hiding people, teaching them to walk and act and talk differently, and creating new identities for them. Joan was proud of what her father had chosen to do. That was probably the strangest part of the evening.

Down in the Great Hall, a clock chimed eleven. Joan listened to the sound echo through the two-story-tall chamber. The house seemed to take a deep breath, like someone rousing slightly in her sleep and preparing to roll over. She liked the feeling of solidity and peace here.

Did she dare reach out and take the gift offered to her? How could she relax her guard and let herself want this as much as she did, after only one day spent absorbing the spirit, the physical presence of this house and inhabitants?

Sophie had always been Joan's grounding point, helping her find balance with a few wisely chosen, sometimes biting, always caring words. With a muttered apology to Ulysses, Joan nudged his head off her leg and crawled to the chair in front of the fireplace, where she had dropped her purse. She pulled out her cell phone.

"Yo, sister, speak to me," Sophie said, answering after the second ring.

"Shielded?"

"As always. Don't teach your granny to suck eggs," she added with a chuckle.

Joan almost laughed at herself for her caution but knew better than to relax here. Maybe *especially* here, in Oracle's house. She rubbed her finger along the side of the phone, feeling the invisible crack where the security chip lay. She and Sophie had designed it with Col. Sidarkis' 'ghost team,' to shield the phone's signal from outside tapping.

If any listening devices had been installed in this antique guest room, they would only pick up static, and constantly changing, high-pitched modulations. Joan's stomach burned at the thought of not being able to trust her father or his household. Then again, she hadn't managed to live this long by trusting everybody who made her feel wanted and welcome.

"So, how's Daddy?" Sophie drawled.

Joan laughed, hitched herself up into the chair, and stretched her legs out. Ulysses came over and curled up under the incline of her legs. When he lifted his head, she felt the muscles of his back against her calves. It was a strangely comforting sensation.

"Right now," she said, keeping her voice soft, "I'm sitting in a guest bedroom full of antiques, trying to decide if I want a deluxe shower or a long soak in a tub bigger than your entire bathroom."

"Staying overnight is a good sign." A horn that sounded like it belonged on a semi-truck or a tugboat blared in the distance.

"Where are you?" The safe house was in a quiet residential neighborhood, so Sophie hadn't made it to Ithaca yet. Joan didn't like that. She wanted Sophie to be safe.

"Tell me your news, first."

Joan sat up, careful to lift her legs as she pulled them in. Ulysses sat up and rested his head on her knee, watching her as she talked. She stroked his head slowly, taking comfort from the warmth.

As they always did when one or the other had experienced something new or had done something beyond their safe, constructed lives, Joan went through her day in chronological order. Sophie asked no questions, but Joan heard the tapping of the keys of her ever-present computer as her friend made notes.

"You definitely have to stay at least a week," Sophie said, when Joan finished.

"I don't know. Everything is so simple and straight here."

"That means it's really complicated and deep below the surface."

"I know that." She tipped her head to one side and looked deep into Ulysses' eyes. The big dog's ears pricked up and he snuffled. "I should be scared, you know? I should feel uncomfortable with how easily everything has happened. I should at least be ticked off at how much they know about me, how they assume I'll just step up and take the reins."

"You will, won't you? Sister-gal, this is a gift from God. This is the kind of place you and I have dreamed about for years, when we wanted to help someone and didn't have the big guns to back us up."

"I know that, too."

"You know what your problem is?"

Chapter Fifteen

"Which one is it this week?" Joan smiled and stroked the tip of her index finger down Ulysses' nose. His eyes closed. If a dog could purr, she thought he might have.

"You could believe, if you let yourself."

"It's not that simple."

"Yes, it is. You want to get involved and go out and fight the bad guys with your daddy's big guns backing you up, but you're afraid because you won't walk through that door God keeps holding open for you."

Sophie waited, but Joan couldn't respond. She kept stroking Ulysses' head until even the sound of her fingers moving through his fur grew too loud to bear. She stopped stroking and Ulysses shifted around, pressing between her legs, and put one paw up on her knee.

"How come it's easier for you to trust people, who will let you down even when they don't want to, but you won't trust God?" Sophie finally asked on a sigh rich with teasing laughter.

"I need proof, I guess," slipped from between Joan's lips before she could stop herself. "Assurance."

Sophie did laugh now. "Joanie-love, don't ever challenge God. Don't make Him prove He's real, because He will and you won't like it."

"I'm not challenging. I know He's real." Words she couldn't say, nebulous ideas that made her chest ache, thickened and caught in her throat. "Stop pushing me, okay?"

"Oh yes, you challenged Him." Only the laughter thickening Sophie's voice made this umpteenth repetition of this conversation bearable. "You know what He'll do now?"

"Something close to what the Greek gods always did to mere mortals who defied them, I suppose." Joan looked down at Ulysses, who regarded her with widened eyes, as if he understood exactly what she said and couldn't believe it had come out of her mouth.

"Worse. And a whole lot better for you. Because God knows exactly what you need to get your attention. And believe me, I speak from experience. When God hobbles you and turns you upside down and shakes you by your ankles until your brains rattle, you listen! And if you have any brains, you change." She sighed, the laughter coming clearer through the sound. "Don't ever dare God to prove He's real. Because He'll stake a claim in your life and never let go."

"That might not be so bad," Joan whispered. If God pulled her in through the door, then she couldn't get thrown out again, could she?

"Then do it. Surrender."

Silence. Joan hunched forward, resting her elbows on the arms of the wingback chair, feeling the old tapestry threads dig into her skin. Ulysses whined and nuzzled her free hand. She liked the feeling of caring, of being watched over, of never being alone. What was she going to do when she had to leave Ulysses behind?

"Joan, what's better? Wade into a cold pool, and take hours to get over the misery, or jump in all at once?"

She thought of her private swim in the Plunge that afternoon, and how refreshingly cool it had been, and then how it had gradually warmed up around her. Why couldn't God just sneak up and overwhelm her gradually, like that?

He could, she knew. But He wouldn't. Just like He wouldn't listen when she prayed. Why did she keep praying, hoping, when she knew it was useless?

Another blat of a truck's horn cut through the waiting silence that buzzed through the phones. Joan gave Ulysses a gentle shove and leaned back in the chair again. The dog settled down on the floor at her feet, no more touching. She felt strangely abandoned.

"Tell me why you're not at the safe house yet."

Sophie sighed, ending on a groan. "I am not giving up on this."

"I'm counting on it."

"You can be such a brat, you know that?"

"I never had a childhood. Excuse me if I catch up on my developmental phases." Joan sat forward again. "Spill."

"Sidarkis called me. One of his whiz kids found concrete evidence someone is backwards trailing us through our last job for him."

"Someone followed you to the safe house?"

"I'm taking the long way, going serpentine to throw them off my trail and see if I can get a good look at them. Ether tracking as well as physical. Along the way, I set up some of those booby-traps Sidarkis gave us as party favors. Let's see if his geniuses are as good as he thinks."

"If they found you, they might have been sitting still and waiting for you to run for it."

"I know. That's why I let the good Colonel send an escort for me at a halfway spot, and then sent them on with half my luggage to act as decoy. My mamma didn't raise no sitting duck."

"Are you okay?"

"The neighbors are kind of noisy. I would kill for a Cobb salad and I could really use a puppy like yours to cuddle right about now. Does he follow you around like you're tied together?"

"He's right here, watching me like I make the sun come up. I'll ask Vincent if I can bring you a puppy."

"Ha! As if I could handle a dog in my circuit board and LCD world."

"Sophie... you'd fit in great here. They could use someone with your skills."

"With the goons I have on my tail, I wouldn't be doing them any favors. No."

"If anybody can protect you, Oracle can."

"Honey, we thought the U.S. Marines were able to protect me. We were wrong, and I don't ever intend to put anybody else in danger just to test and find out if I'm wrong a second time," she added, her voice dropping to a whisper.

"Give me the address of the data on this shadow coming after us. I'm going to ask —" She swallowed hard, shocked at how easily she reached for a solution that had never been there before. "I'm going to ask my father if he'll have his people look into things from his side."

"That might not be so smart. Even for Oracle."

"Sophie. What aren't you telling me?"

"There's something hinky about the data trail. Someone piggybacked in on a probe from an outside user with a legitimate password. Sidarkis went all 'need to know' on me, but I think Oracle is working for the Pentagon, not just as old buddies with Sidarkis, and our enemy is his enemy, too."

Joan closed her eyes, nausea taking over all other reactions. She hadn't felt this sick since that children's crusade, when she wanted to stay and listen to Allen Michaels speak but knew the bomb her mother put in her backpack would kill her, too, if she didn't stash it under the platform and leave. She moaned and lurched forward, feeling an almost physical stab of pain as certainty lashed through her.

"Joan? What are you thinking?"

"Imagine you found the man you hated more than anybody in the world. Imagine you found out he's looking for the daughter you need to destroy. Wouldn't it be fun to sit back and let him do all the work?"

"I hope like crazy you're wrong."

"Get to work and prove I'm wrong."

"You can't stay there, and you can't leave. If you're right, she could be watching right now. The minute you take off, she could be on you like stink in a swamp."

"No." Joan opened her eyes and looked at Ulysses as he sat up and rested both forepaws on her knees, almost on eye-level with her. "No, I don't think so. I think I'm safe here. I've got no proof, just a gut feeling."

Sophie was silent for so long, Joan wondered if the connection had died. She heard a few more distant blats of truck horns, the grumble of engines and the low-pitched whining of enormous tires racing past.

"Your gut has gotten us out of more trouble than I can keep track of."

"That and your praying."

"Believe me, I'm praying." Sophie sighed, loudly. "Okay. I'll get to work on things from my end. If I run into trouble, I'll head for the safe house and give you a holler."

"I'll come running with the Marines and the Cavalry."

"Better than that, learn to pray. Later, sister."

Joan waited until the connection died, then took a deep breath.

Learn to pray? She had learned how to pray years ago. The problem was that no matter how good the telephone was, if there wasn't anyone on the other end, listening, it was all a waste.

~~~~~

Morning came slowly, with frequent bouts of wakefulness through the night, lying on her back, staring up at the canopy of her bed. Joan listened to the house, wondering about the secrets of those who had built it, and those who now used it for so many purposes, and several she suspected she hadn't learned yet. Ulysses spent the night curled up at her feet. Several times when she woke up, she reached down and patted the foot or muzzle she found in the darkness.

Niobe had hurt her more than she could ever have guessed, denying Joan a pet.

"What kind of person would I be today?" she asked Ulysses in one of those quiet pockets in the night. "If she had been halfway near a normal mother, if she let me have a dog or even keep Fuppy Bear, what would I be right now?"

Joan tried to imagine, but she couldn't, and that was strange, because her hyperactive imagination was what had kept her alive and relatively undamaged. She had always been able to weave twenty scenarios branching out from every major obstacle or event or decision she met along her life's path. Removing some of the changing points in her life, such as losing Fuppy Bear or the first time she created a new identity, or watching Niobe drive away with baby Nikki and return on foot, or the first night she agreed to go with Matt and Xander for coffee after class — she could imagine only vaguely how different she would be as a person.

"Guess I can only imagine forward, but never backward, huh?" she whispered. Ulysses wriggled around until he could lick her fingertips. She snorted and discretely wiped her fingers on the sheets before curling up and trying to sleep.

After her restless night, she was surprised to open her eyes to sunshine streaming through the window. A glance at the clock showed she had slept until nearly eight.

She chose a cold shower to get her blood moving, rather than indulging in another hot, deep, scented bath. Joan smiled as she put on her one fresh top with yesterday's jeans. Sophie had been right to insist she pack several changes of clothes, even though Akron was only an hour away from Tabor. Joan had no idea how long she would be staying here. Yesterday's clothes
~~~~~

weren't exactly stale, and she had used body odor on more than one occasion as a defensive move, but that wouldn't be necessary here. She wasn't ready to fully relax and sink into the atmosphere of the house, but neither did she feel the need to be completely on the defensive. What was it about this place?

The guestroom door didn't creak when she pulled it open and stepped down into the gallery that ran along one side of the upper story of the Great Hall. Still, Joan had the sense that a signal had been heard somewhere and the house had paused to listen. Ulysses scampered out past her, turned right, and headed for the main stairs. With nothing else to do, and hungry for the first time in several days, Joan followed him.

Vincent was alone in the breakfast room, which surprised her. She had thought he would be either a rabid morning person who got by on nothing but coffee, or someone who stayed up until dawn and slept until noon. He glanced up from his paper and a half-eaten omelet and toast, and nodded to her when she came into the room.

"Help yourself," he said, and gestured through a side door that Joan had noticed the day before. "Breakfast is everybody's own taste and schedule around here."

"Thanks." She sniffed quietly, to check that she actually had smelled hot chocolate, and followed the scent through the door.

Joan stepped into a long, narrow room, with a two-burner stove over a small warming oven, a long counter with hot plates holding carafes of coffee, tea and chocolate, cupboards full of dishes, and a glass-fronted cooler full of eggs, cheese, bread, butter, milk and other ingredients for almost any breakfast food she could want. A quick search of the lower cupboards revealed an assortment of pans and cooking utensils, spices and boxes of cereal.

She settled on fruit salad, a peanut butter and raspberry jam sandwich, and a cup of hot chocolate. Joan looked with longing at the can of whipped cream and decided against it. Indulging felt like giving in, somehow. Like making a commitment to stay, just by making herself more comfortable.

"Paper?" Vincent tapped the sections he had apparently finished already, neatly folded on the table next to him.

"No, thanks." She refrained from adding that she preferred to get her news from three different gathering sources on the Internet. Sources she trusted to get the whole story, not just the slant preferred by that particular network and its political or economic affiliations. Joan filled her mouth with fruit to keep from talking.

"You're like the wolf that got released from its cage and forgot what it was like outside."

Joan nearly choked. She managed to swallow without coughing, blinked hard to fight tears, and looked at him. Vincent grinned, pushed his empty plate away, and slouched a little.

"It's going to take a while to realize you're safe here, isn't it?" His voice turned into something near a purr.

"Safe? Sitting across the table from a man who could kill me with a toothpick if he wanted to?" She snorted. "Hardly."

"You've been reading too many comic books." He laughed. "But that's a good point. Yesterday's lesson was just a taste. You need to learn self-defense. Any time you're ready for the next lesson, just ask. Even better, let's set up a regular schedule. I think you could be a pretty potent weapon, with a little training."

Joan froze as she picked up her sandwich, arrested by the mental image of learning to throw hulks around, or perform moves better suited to skinny blondes fighting TV vampires.

"Think about it." He stood and scooped up his empty plate and utensils. "Ulysses is a good start. Learn to use his senses and his judgment of people and situations. But don't ever think you can get by just on his help."

"I did just fine taking care of myself before I came here." She put down her sandwich before she squeezed it and got peanut butter all over.

"Fine isn't good enough anymore. If it was safe before, don't you think the Boss Man would have made contact? He knew it was dangerous if you two ever got together. He took a big risk, and he's risking all of us, bringing you here. But it's the right thing to do and we'll all support him because we all owe him. Big time. Our lives and our sanity. Get the picture?"

"So the minute I drive out through the gates, I'll get a target painted on my back?"

"You've had a target ready to land on you all your life, kid."

Joan snorted. Standing in the shadow of thirty, she didn't think she qualified for the label of "kid." Then again, she wondered if she had ever been a kid.

"It's time to stop playing Lone Ranger and join the Cavalry."

"Vincent." Elizabeth stood in the doorway. How long she had been standing there, listening, there was no telling. She seemed to have a talent for it.

"Just think about it. You're a good kid. I don't want to see you with a bullet in your head."

"Then don't look," Joan muttered.

Vincent gave her a withering look before he stepped into the little kitchen. Joan heard him pick up a few things; probably the frying pan and turner he had used. Then he walked out the other door into the hall. She and Elizabeth stayed silent until he was gone.

"He's right, you know."

"Maybe." Joan picked up her cup of chocolate.

"You knew you were taking a risk coming here. Meeting your father was worth it. At least, you thought so when you got in your car yesterday morning." Elizabeth stepped into the kitchen for a moment and came back with her own cup of chocolate, heaped high with whipped cream. "What's your assessment now?"

Joan could doubletalk with the best, saying nothing, making no commitment, even sneaking insults in to release some steam, and all the while giving people exactly what they wanted to hear. It was a survival skill she had perfected even as she loathed it. Like stealing rolls and fruit and other portable food from tables in restaurants and outdoor markets, when she was a child and her mother had more important things to do than feed her. Necessary. Not something she enjoyed. Always used to a minimum.

Looking at Elizabeth, Joan didn't want to play the nice-nice games. If she signed on with the Arc Foundation, she knew she not only could be honest without repercussions, it would be demanded of her. Should she start here? Could she?

"I don't know," she finally said, and raised her gaze from her half-empty cup. She wished she had indulged in that whipped cream.

"You probably won't for a while. It's going to take longer than the time you gave yourself for this first trip."

"I guess."

"Kathryn and Anne are spending the morning at our newest clinic, helping set up and getting their checkups. You can spend the morning exploring, or I could show you the business side of the foundation."

Joan considered that Elizabeth had said nothing about Carter. Either he was busy and not to be disturbed, or not awake yet. No matter the choice, he wasn't available. It amused her a little to realize she felt disappointed.

"You really don't know how much time he has left, do you?" she asked, pitching her voice so no one could hear out in the hall.

"Only God knows, and He isn't telling."

"I've never let emotions… no, that isn't true." Joan thought of Nikki and her wavering feelings toward her half-sister. The fear and hatred and resentment she felt toward Niobe. Her curiosity and hunger for belonging that had pushed her to accept friendship from Matt and Xander. "I'm not going to let guilt push me into something that won't be smart."

"What do you do when *smart* conflicts with *right*?" Elizabeth smiled gently as she said it, not mocking, but sympathetic.

~~~~~

Elizabeth, Joan discovered in short order, had more than enough research and negotiating and business savvy to run the Arc Foundation in every aspect, public and hidden. Her blue-blood Boston background hadn't kept her from dirtying her hands with finances and legal and administrative landmines that stood in Arc's way. Joan studied the documents and records that Elizabeth had sitting out on her desk in the room where she had first met Carter, and her admiration and respect for the woman grew.

Carter might have provided the money and the contacts, but Elizabeth
~~~~~

kept everything running smoothly. Joan had played with the idea that her father had gone into philanthropic work to soothe his conscience and pay for his sins, and perhaps to please his wife. She forgot those ideas as the morning flew by and she dove into records and pictures and files showing the good the foundation had done. All guided by Elizabeth.

Sometimes Joan laughed, when she followed the notations of phone calls and copies of business letters and realized that Elizabeth knew how to put pressure on recalcitrant officials. She could and did make sure that anyone who tried to get in Arc's way didn't do it to anyone else in the future. There were the usual government officials and suppliers and inspectors who wanted to make a deal, hinted after bribes or outright threatened the future of the clinic or shelter the foundation wanted to establish. Elizabeth recorded each instance, who made the threat or hint or outright demand, who it was made to, the date and time, and what was done to deal with the problem.

"You're getting a bad reputation. You know that, don't you?" Joan said, shutting another envelope folder and sliding the elastic band back into place.

"Reputation?" Elizabeth pushed her glasses up off her nose, so they rested on top of her hair. She frowned, visibly reading the label on the folder upside down. "Oh. You mean for refusing to play along?"

"For slapping their wrists so hard they make enough noise to get themselves in trouble."

"That's one of our rules around here. Never be the whistle blower, but always stir things up enough that they either hang themselves, or someone else with more authority takes care of it. If you accept your father's offer, always remember that we are not the law. We are emissaries for the highest power there is. Our job is to bring help and comfort and light. We defend, but we do not attack."

"Sounds like what Kathryn was saying, about Vincent's self-defense classes."

"Have you ever read the Bible? The book of Ephesians?" Elizabeth put aside the stack of papers she had been sorting and leaned forward, resting her elbows on the paper-covered top of the desk.

"I've had enough of it quoted at me. That's about putting on armor?" Joan didn't know why she refused to admit that she had read the Bible enough times to have large portions of scripture memorized. If she were going to spend any amount of time with these people, she wouldn't be able to keep up the pretense of ignorance.

Of course, if she ended up staying at Quarry Hall, she wouldn't need to hold onto quite so many masks anymore, would she?

Chapter Sixteen

"We're living in a state of war. Every time we choose to do the right thing, rather than the easy or convenient or profitable thing, we're striking a blow against the darkness." Elizabeth slid her glasses off her head and toyed with them as she spoke. "We can do great damage to the enemy without ever taking the battle to his territory, just by resisting. Imagine how much more damage we can do if we help the wounded and encourage others to resist? Just resist. Standing firm and holding the line."

"So I take it you're against the abortion clinic bombers and the ones who smuggle weapons into foreign countries and hide illegal aliens, claiming to be obeying special instructions from God?"

"The Bible says to obey the government and to live in peace with our fellow man as much as we are able. It also says to obey God, not man."

"Render unto Caesar?" Joan guessed.

"Always obey the law, except where it specifically forces you to disobey God."

"So we work with the law and do a little housecleaning on the side, whenever we can?" She gestured at the piles of files she had been examining, the paperwork Elizabeth had been handling, and all the unseen records inside the computer sitting on the big desk.

"Basically." Elizabeth's eyes sparkled. "Am I pushing things to assume that when you say 'we,' it's not a slip of the tongue?"

"I don't know."

~~~~~

"Canadian Brass are at Blossom tonight," Kathryn said, coming into the office just moments after Elizabeth left to go to a meeting at her church.

Joan and Elizabeth had worked through lunch, which Brooklyn had brought upstairs, accompanied by broad hints to get outside and forget about papers and reports for a while. Joan had pushed the tray of empty dishes aside to finish up reading one more fascinating report on a doctor who was looking for help to set up a clinic in a tiny mountain village, and fully intended to take them downstairs. Eventually.

"Canadian... Oh. Yeah. I was thinking about going..." Joan trailed off as she adjusted her thoughts to take in the outside world again. It was Friday, wasn't it? Matt loved the Canadian Brass. He would be at Blossom tonight.

"Want to go?" Kathryn leaned against the doorframe and waved a familiar yellow-and-green ticket booklet.
~~~~~

"Umm..." Joan tried to calculate the odds of running into Matt among the thousand or so people spread out across the wide bowl of lawn around the performance pavilion. She knew where Matt liked to sit, so it wouldn't be hard guiding Kathryn to another part of the lawn. "That'd be fun. Thanks."

On the way down the stairs, they discussed when they would leave and were covering the important detail of snacks to take with them when they walked into the kitchen so Joan could deposit the tray of dirty dishes. Brooklyn scolded them for even considering stopping at a grocery store, when she could provide a feast. Joan wasn't about to argue, trading shrimp cocktail and homemade buckeyes, freshly made lemonade and brownies, for the pretzels and ginger ale she had planned to buy. Her mouth watered, thinking of the menu, until something new occurred to her, derailing her train of thought.

"What?" Kathryn laughed when Joan gave her a confused look. "Something just went wrong. I could tell from your eyes."

"Oh. Yeah." Joan shrugged, feeling foolish. It gave her an odd feeling, having someone besides Sophie almost reading her thoughts. "I don't have any more clean clothes, for tomorrow."

"Well then, go on home and pack a bigger suitcase. I don't care that we're only an hour from your apartment, with all the things you have to do, you know it's going to take a long stay." Brooklyn waved them out of her kitchen. "Get out and run your errands and let me get my work done." She sniffed in mock pique. Joan and Kathryn grinned at each other and hurried to leave.

Joan still wore a grin, but crooked, feeling a little breathless when she found herself in her car with Kathryn in the front seat and Bea and Ulysses in the back seat. She had no clear recollection of how they got from the kitchen to her car.

"Something wrong?" Kathryn asked, when Joan paused, the key just an inch from the ignition.

"I don't do this. Stay with people I hardly know. Feel so relaxed. Want—" Joan shook her head.

"Want to belong?" Her voice was soft, no smile quirking her lips.

"Not exactly... but close enough."

"Your mother put you through the wringer, didn't she?"

"Not just that." Joan wasn't about to confess, after such a short acquaintance, the multiple identities and church bombings and other "ordinary" aspects of her childhood. Not even to this cousin whom she liked so much, so quickly. Fighting not to grit her teeth, she shoved the key into the ignition.

Halfway through the gates onto the main road, she nearly slammed on the brakes, but caught herself in time. Joan's heart raced like it hadn't in days, as she tried to look in every direction without appearing to be looking.

Last night's conversation with Sophie came back to her. What if the enemy tracking them through their connection with Sidarkis was Niobe? What if she had discovered that Harrison Carter was the Oracle, and she watched at the gates right this moment, gathering information and waiting for her chance for revenge? What if she saw Joan, recognized her, and realized she had a chance to destroy them both with one blow?

Nothing I can do about it now, is there? Joan knew already that the seeming openness and lack of security around the estate grounds was an illusion. Between security cameras, alarms, Vincent and the dogs, there were few places safer for a hundred miles in any direction. The problem was, those other places didn't have her psychotic, vengeful mother, with years of destructive experience behind her, preparing to storm the gates.

All she could do was warn her father. A moment of thought made Joan feel like a fool. If the Oracle didn't know that his former paramour was looking for him, if some alarm system among his spider's web of contacts hadn't alerted him already to the approaching danger... then he had toppled far from a lofty height. Joan decided he didn't need any warning. Maybe she should feel some security that he wanted to take her under his wing?

We aren't under his wing right now, are we?

"You're worried about something," Kathryn said, when they were halfway through the shopping district, aiming for the highway entrance. "Don't. Our dogs will protect us."

"I hope we don't need it," Joan returned. *Fat lot of good a big, angry dog will do against a sniper's bullet or a bomb.* Still, she felt better with that reminder. Even if God didn't owe her anything, Kathryn was with her, and she belonged to Him, right? "Hey, how did you —"

"Uncle Harrison warned us that contacting you might stir up trouble, no matter what precautions we took. It's natural to assume you're worried about someone spotting you leaving." She turned sideways in the seat to look at Joan. "Did you think I read your mind or something?"

"For all I know, you've got angels following you around, whispering secrets to you all day." Joan grinned at her own words, despite her sour tone and the sour feeling in her gut.

Then something cold and wet touched the side of her neck and she barely swallowed a yelp. Ulysses was nosing her. She glanced at Kathryn, red-faced from trying not to laugh.

"Keep it up, fur ball," she muttered, which got snorts from Kathryn. The atmosphere in the car relaxed enough that they could both grin at each other as Joan passed the entrance ramp for I-77, heading for I-71.

~~~~~

Joan considered asking Kathryn to wait in the car while she ran upstairs to her apartment to pack more clothes. It felt wrong. She gnawed on the conundrum between asking more questions about Arc. Even getting
~~~~~

a good idea of future plans, projects she might be involved in, couldn't help distract her. Joan thought about asking Matt or Xander or even Nikki up to her apartment, when she had never let anyone but Sophie inside before, and something like terror tied her insides into knots. Yet that sensation didn't strike when she considered asking Kathryn upstairs. What was wrong with her?

By the time she parked in the small lot behind the optician's office, Joan was still undecided. She got out of the car, turned, and saw Brock Pierson peering around the corner of the building. He smiled and came around the corner, heading straight for her. The last thing she wanted was a confrontation with Mr. Jet-Set, with his too-perfect smile, suave manners, and expensive clothes.

"Come on up," she said, turning back to the car. "Might as well let Ulysses see what's ahead of him if he insists on following me around."

Kathryn burst out laughing and pushed the door open. Both dogs leaped out and raced around the car, putting themselves between Joan and Brock so fast, he nearly tripped over Beatrice.

"Uh…hi." Brock slid his designer sunglasses off and hooked the earpiece into the front of his shirt. "Did Nikki find you?"

"I've been out of town." Joan hunched her shoulders, feeling that uneasy warning sensation prickling down her back. "Why? Do you know what she wants?"

"We're—well, she wants to talk something over with you." He shrugged and looked Kathryn over, his gaze lingering on her walking cast. "If I find Nikki, I'll tell her you're home."

"I'd rather you didn't find Nikki ever again."

"None of your business." He laughed, sounding charming and amused, rather than angry, which Joan would have preferred. She wished she could crack his perfect veneer. Just once. Preferably when Nikki was there to see.

"It's more her business than you could ever guess," Kathryn said, with a sweet tone that made the hairs stand up on Joan's arms and the back of her neck.

What did Kathryn know? Was it possible, with all the research Carter had done to find her, he knew about Nikki?

"I know what you are," Joan said.

"What am I?" He jammed his fists into his hips and smiled, challenging her with humor. Joan would have preferred some anger, even threats.

"A lie."

"Oh, that's really deep. Insightful. How about I ask around about you, Joan Archer? What'll I find out about you if I start digging? Something weird about you taking such an interest in Nikki. Who's straight, if you haven't noticed. She likes guys." Brock waggled his eyebrows suggestively.

"She's a little girl."

"Yeah, that's what the Holwoods want her to keep thinking. Something wrong about a cute little White girl living with two Black —"

Joan stared at her fist, hanging in mid-air where it had impacted with Brock's mouth. He staggered backward, pressing his hand against his bleeding lip. Something ugly flashed in his beautiful eyes. He groped with his free hand at his pants pocket, and Joan was sure he had something big and dangerous in that pocket.

She didn't care. She admired and respected the Holwoods, and for the love and security they had given Nikki, she loved them. What did it matter that they weren't the same race as their foster daughter? Joan refused to let Brock talk down about them.

"Hey, what's up!" a cracked voice boomed, and Maggie strolled around the corner in all her summer bits-and-pieces glory. Today she wore a battered straw hat on her tangle of salt-and-pepper hair. Purple Popsicle dripped down her hand and she paused to lick the side of her hand clean while she studied the three people standing in the parking lot. She wore grubby white tennis shoes, and her oversized green plaid shorts hung down to her knees and revealed she probably hadn't shaved her legs since January. Her sunflower-print shirt flapped in the breeze, revealing a neon purple muscle shirt underneath.

Ulysses and Bea let out squeals like puppies and ran to frisk around her legs, chasing each other and banging into her. Maggie chuckled and bent down, offering the rest of her melting icy treat to the dogs.

"This whole town is full of freaks," Brock muttered into the handkerchief he took from his pocket and backed away toward the street.

"You okay?" Maggie said, as soon as Brock vanished around the corner. She cocked her head to one side to study Joan.

"Yeah. Great." Joan swallowed hard. "Thanks."

"That's what I'm here for." She nodded to Kathryn. "Family reunion?"

"What?" Kathryn shook her head, blinking rapidly as if coming out of a trance.

"This is Maggie. She's…" Joan was stumped. What could she say about Maggie, standing there smiling at them, that wasn't insulting?

She wasn't a bag lady or homeless. The people of Tabor Heights were fairly certain she had a home, they just didn't know where. "Resident eccentric" was a tame enough label, but just didn't cover the phenomenon of Maggie, who always had pockets full of change for treats for the children in the summer, and who had an uncanny knack for showing up when a situation needed defusing, like she had done just now. Joan had heard one story about the rescue of Nikki from the sinking car, where Maggie was credited with alerting the police officers who found the abandoned baby. The general consensus in town was that anyone Maggie liked was okay, but if she took a dislike to someone, or they took a dislike to her, as opposed to feeling uneasy or just plain unsettled by her, that was someone bound to make trouble.

"I'm the town crier," Maggie said with a rusty chuckle. She stepped over to the big trash barrel with the Tabor Heights tree-and-grindstone logo painted on it, and tossed her Popsicle stick into it. "I look out for the town. People think I'm strange, but they know I'm harmless." She hunched her shoulders and cupped her hands around her mouth, and whispered, "I got 'em fooled good, y'know?"

Kathryn laughed, to Joan's relief. It wasn't that she considered Maggie a friend, but Joan trusted her gut, and her gut said to trust the eccentric old woman. She didn't realize how much, until she worried that Kathryn wouldn't pass the Maggie test.

"Better watch out for that one. Don't go running off to the ends of the world until you know he's gone, and gone alone, know what I mean?" Maggie hooked her thumb over her shoulder, in the general direction Brock had gone. "Gotta run. Need to see an ice cream truck about some kids." She winked at them, bent to ruffle the fur on both dogs' backs as she passed, and continued up the dead-end street to the cut-through to the next street.

"Pretty cool," Kathryn said, grinning.

"She doesn't freak you?" Joan wasn't sure if she should feel disgruntled or worried.

"The dogs like her. That's good enough for me."

"Yeah… they do."

"Want to tell me more about this Nikki you and the creep were talking about?"

It was on the tip of Joan's tongue to spill the entire story about Nikki. She swallowed hard and gestured at the enclosed stairs leading to her apartment, instead. The dogs raced ahead of her and Kathryn.

"You don't know, so why did you tell Brock what you did?"

"I could see you're defensive of her, and the guy set off my creep alarm. Psychological warfare, that's all. So, who is she to you?"

"Nikki …" Joan tried not to swallow or pause too long. She felt as if a huge lump lodged in her throat. "She's the foster-daughter of my faculty advisor. We hang around together sometimes. And the creep is way too old for her. She's only sixteen."

"Ouch. Maybe you should get a restraining order against him."

"How, without being family? Without getting Dr. Holwood all upset? He's good friends with half the football team and half the baseball team, and those guys would go after Brock with an entire gym full of equipment if he only mentioned he was worried about…" Joan paused at the top of the stairs and clamped her jaw shut, to physically stop the flood of words. What was wrong with her?

"Maybe you should ask a lawyer if you have any standing, first. Know any?" Kathryn said, waiting for Joan to unlock the door.

"Yeah, I do." She found it easier to breathe, as Xander's homely face filled her mind.

Kathryn's gaze immediately went to the painting of Joan of Arc as soon as they stepped into the apartment. She looked away a moment later, without any visible reaction, and surveyed the compact apartment.

"I bet it's great in the winter, when all you can see is snow from these windows and you just curl up and read all day."

"Yeah..." Joan gestured vaguely at the shelves lining the walls. "I like books." She flinched as the thought occurred to her that it would take several trips to get all her books down to Quarry Hall when she moved.

When had she decided she would move down there? Akron wasn't so far away she couldn't commute if she decided to work for her father — and she hadn't decided to do that yet, either.

I am losing my mind.

"Have a seat. It'll only take a minute." She gasped, ending on a chuckle when both dogs hopped up onto her futon sofa. Fortunately, there was one more chair Kathryn could take, besides the swivel chair at the computer desk.

Think about Nikki and getting that creep away from her. She stepped behind the Chinese screen that separated her sleeping area from the rest of the apartment, and yanked the top dresser drawer open.

Ten minutes had her stepping out again, to see Kathryn standing in front of her built-in bookshelves. The bookshelves full of her Bible study books, floor to ceiling. Joan held her breath, waiting for an accusation, a stream of questions.

"You've got a couple books here Uncle Harrison would love to borrow," Kathryn said, glancing over her shoulder once, and then bending down to look at the bottom shelf.

Joan let herself exhale. She checked her answering machine. Tris Cameron wanted Joan to go to Blossom that evening with her. She said nothing about Matt going to the concert, so Joan considered herself safe to attend without running into him.

"You're one of the fastest packers I've ever seen," Kathryn said as they headed down the stairs again.

"When you live on the road most of your life..." Joan shrugged and reached into her bag to pull out her cell phone.

Xander's message system gave her several options to choose from. Joan chose an option not listed, only known to a handful of Xander's associates. She knew because she and Sophie had created the program that linked his phone to his computer. With the right password, she could obtain his schedule for the day, displayed right on her phone. Right now, he was at Tabor Municipal Court, finishing up a routine hearing. She and Kathryn and the dogs wouldn't even have to hurry down Main Street to meet him before he left.

Kathryn said nothing when Joan led their little party of four back to her car, popped the trunk to throw her case in, and headed back down the street on foot. She looked around the pleasantly busy center of town, studying the old buildings, the houses turned into offices and shops, the grassy Triangle with its Civil War statue and cannon and gazebo. The dogs' claws clicked pleasantly on the sidewalk. Joan thought about the Tabor leash law, but hesitated asking Kathryn about putting a leash on the dogs. They seemed very well trained. She shuddered at the thought of leashing Ulysses. There was just something about him that made her think there was more than dog looking out through his eyes.

They crossed Span, staying on Main, and walked past the cluster of shops on one side, the park entrance on the other, to the City Hall complex. Inside was a central lobby leading to the municipal court, the city offices, council chamber, and the front desk of the police department. Joan didn't think about the dogs until they had all crossed the threshold and the big, tinted glass doors closed behind them. She didn't consider the dogs just because she normally didn't have a dog with her. Were animals, besides guide dogs, allowed inside here?

"Funny thing about our dogs," Kathryn said under her breath, as she looked around the vast, bustling lobby. "A lot of times, they just seem to be invisible."

"You know, you really bug me, the way you seem to read minds."

"I read people, not minds." Kathryn hooked an arm through Joan's and guided her over to a grouping of chairs in the waiting area for all the facilities that opened into the lobby.

Joan saw Xander step through the doors of the court building just before she turned to sit down. Tugging her arm free of Kathryn's hold, she started to gesture toward him, when a tall, graying man in a charcoal pinstripe suit strode past her, close enough to brush against her. Ulysses growled, his ears went back, and he turned to watch the man, who approached Xander with his shoes echoing on the tile floor.

"Finley, you haven't returned my calls."

"That's not true." Xander shifted his battered brown briefcase from his left hand to his right and took half a step sideways to get out of the doorway. The man, who still had his back to Joan, stayed where he was, in the exact center of the doorway. "I returned your calls the last three times you called me. The answer was no each time, and the answer hasn't changed and won't change, no matter how many times you call me."

"You're making a mistake."

Chapter Seventeen

"I don't think so." Xander shook his head, a cool, polite smile firmly in place. Joan knew that smile, from when he faced unreasonable classmates and professors in college classes.

"Someone with your talent shouldn't waste his time and energy trying to go it alone, fresh out of law school," the man said, his voice growing louder and colder.

"I'm not 'fresh' out of law school, Mr. Montgomery."

"You're a fool."

"Then you don't really want a fool working for you, do you?"

"That kind of attitude, your determination to waste your time on the incompetent and indigent, the fools who walk into trouble with their eyes wide open—you're condemning yourself to failure."

"In the eyes of the world, maybe." Xander leaned back against the doorjamb a little. His gaze flicked away from Montgomery for a moment and he locked glances with Joan.

She couldn't help it—she mimed strangling. Xander choked, pushed off the doorjamb and rubbed at his mouth, only partially hiding the grin twisting his lips.

"You're living in an ivory tower," Montgomery sneered. "No one will fund you to run a charity disguised as a law firm."

"Legal clinic," Xander corrected him.

"You're dealing in the law, Finley, not practicing medicine."

"I have come to help the sick, not the healthy. Sound familiar?"

"Don't you try throwing the Bible in my face," Montgomery growled.

"Standing on the promises, not using the Bible to bludgeon people into doing my will, falsely labeled as God's will. There is a difference. Sir," he added after a perceptible pause.

Montgomery took a step back from Xander and his shoulders straightened, visibly going rigid. "I offered you the opportunity to be part of something fine and upstanding, and you've mocked me for the last time." He turned, just enough to reveal his cold, square face to Joan for the first time in the conversation. Not that she didn't know what he looked like, from previous unpleasant encounters she had witnessed between Xander and the elder lawyer. "Your failure will blacken the eye of all lawyers who claim to be Christians," he threw over his shoulder as he stomped through the doors into the court building.

"That's the problem, isn't it?" Xander muttered, turning to Joan with a brittle smile as she approached him. "Claiming, but not being."

"If I had a million dollars, I'd give it to you for your clinic," Joan offered.

"Yeah, yeah, you keep saying that." He shrugged and grinned and jammed his one free hand into his pocket. "Put your non-existent money where your mouth is, Archer."

Joan choked on laughter. If Xander only knew how much money she might have at her disposal. It was on the tip of her tongue to counter that she could throw a large wad of money at him if she wanted, but her morning of studying the foundation's procedures and records stopped her. She doubted that her vouching for Common Grounds would be enough for the Arc Foundation to release thousands of dollars to Xander's use. But the thought of finally being able to help her friend with his dream of a legal clinic to help those who couldn't afford expensive lawyers or even the filing fees, put an excited, hollow feeling in her chest.

"How about earning your keep?" she said instead, after only a few seconds of hesitation. "Oh, sorry. This is my cousin, Kathryn." Joan snorted when she realized she had never learned her last name.

"Chapman," Kathryn supplied, holding out a hand to shake Xander's. "Joan and I just discovered each other existed, so we're getting to know each other. We were discussing a little problem, and when I asked her if she knew a lawyer, she brought me down here to meet you. Kind of handy, having a lawyer in your back pocket."

"Not exactly," she said, rolling her eyes.

"And especially nice knowing that lawyer is a dedicated Christian," she added. "Joan needs to find out about getting a restraining order. Against someone named Brock Pierson."

"To keep him away from Nikki James," Joan said, as one of Xander's thick, crooked eyebrows rose in question.

"A restraining order?" He tipped his head to one side and frowned a few moments. "Come into my office." He led them outside and up the sidewalk, heading toward the parking lot, before he continued talking. "I have to come up with something solid before a judge would even consider such a thing. And you're not a relative. Just being an interested bystander won't carry much weight. Unless you could get the Holwoods to make the complaint."

"Yeah, and things are touchy enough at home right now." Joan bit the inside of her lip, almost afraid she would blurt that Nikki was her sister.

Xander was trustworthy, but she didn't feel like offering proof, or going into even an abbreviated explanation of why she hadn't revealed her identity to her sister in the four years since she had moved to Tabor.

"I've done some research," she said, after Xander just watched her, his homely face calm and patient. "I don't want Nikki hurt." She snorted. "I don't want her mad at me, either, but I'll risk it."

"Okay… is this information something I could hand over to Chief

Cooper, and ask him to investigate?"

"I don't know." Joan glanced at Kathryn. She envied her new cousin's ability to look mildly, politely interested, covering up whether she was bored or avidly curious or confused. "It's complicated."

"Yeah, I noticed that where you're concerned." Xander rested a hand on her shoulder. "What's really going on with you and Matt?"

Joan stepped back so quickly she almost tripped over her own feet. Ulysses whined and rubbed against her thigh.

"Matt?" She didn't even care that she sounded a little panicked.

"He hasn't told me anything. Tris called and asked me to talk to you."

"About what?" She glanced at Kathryn, who made an admirable effort not to look interested.

"Well, from things she's said, it doesn't sound like what you told me." Xander glanced at Kathryn. "If Matt's pressuring you about your soul, Tris doesn't know, and considering how close you are to her and Rocky ... She just says Matt is miserable and she's positive it has to do with you. If you're not careful, she'll come hunt you down."

"I'm out of town for a few days."

"Oh, yeah, I can see that." He looked around the municipal lot, taking in the city hall complex and the library. "How far are you from your place? Half a mile, max?"

Despite the panic tying her insides into knots, Joan laughed.

"I'm getting to know my family, down in Akron. Kathryn rode up with me to get some clothes so I can stay longer." She resisted the urge to stick her tongue out at him.

"Okay, so you have a legitimate reason for being out of touch. For a while. But you can't run away from how Matt feels about you." He waggled his eyebrows and Joan wanted to sink through a crack in the sidewalk. Matt might not have confessed that he wanted to marry her, but he had given away enough for Xander to guess. "And I hate to break it to you, but a lot of us think the two of you are perfect for each other."

"It won't work."

Xander smiled, irritating her enough to nudge her out of incipient panic. "Don't underestimate the power of prayer. I had a lot of people praying for you and Matt. Now that he's seen the light, there's even more focus on you than before."

"So that's what my problem is. Should have known you'd be to blame." Joan scowled, but Xander and Kathryn both burst out laughing.

He had an appointment to get to, so after promising to look into the limits and requirements of swearing out a restraining order on Brock Pierson, and after Joan promised to get more information on Brock to Xander, they parted. She and Kathryn stopped at the Perk & Perch to get cold drinks for the ride back to Quarry Hall.

Kathryn took the tall paper cup of iced chai from the clerk, thanking her, and waited for Joan to get her order. She took a plastic cup from the self-service counter in the middle of the seating area and poured some ice water into it. Joan realized she was getting water for Bea. Both dogs waited outside, again without orders or any kind of signal. She thought about the warm weather and kicked herself for neglecting Ulysses. She got a cup of water for him, and both dogs proceeded to lap water out of the cups. Funny, but she didn't feel any irritation over this new responsibility.

"Thanks, by the way," Kathryn said, when both dogs had finished and the foursome started down the sidewalk toward the apartment. "You didn't have to do that."

"Do what?" Joan looked at her cup, pretty sure Kathryn didn't mean the drink she had bought for her.

"Introducing me to your friend as your cousin."

"Well, that's what you are."

"True, but he didn't need to know that. And how are you going to explain my not showing up anymore if you decide to have nothing to do with Quarry Hall or Arc or your father?"

"Just because I *might* choose not to work for Arc..." Joan swallowed hard, feeling a little unbalanced and breathless. "Well, this feels right, you know? I don't want to lose everything, even though it's way too soon to make any decisions. Does that make sense?"

"I think so." She took a long pull from her straw. "A word of advice, though. If you've got a lot of people praying for you, you might as well give up. Prayer warriors, especially if they're lawyers, don't know how to shut up, so you might as well give up."

"That's what Xander says. I should just surrender."

"Smart guy."

"Don't tell him that. He's already impossible."

Kathryn smirked and concentrated on her drink. A humming sound escaped her, and she blew bubbles in her drink, fighting not to laugh.

~~~~~

When they returned to the house, Carter and Elizabeth sat on the flagstone patio off the Great Hall, enjoying the cool breeze and sunshine. Joan felt so encouraged by the sign of good, healthy color in her father's face, when he and Elizabeth expressed interest in the concert at Blossom, she wanted to invite them to come along. She stumbled through the conversation and was grateful when Kathryn carried most of it, talking about their trip to Tabor. That gave Joan time to collect her thoughts, and her courage.

"Do we have enough tickets?" she said, when Kathryn turned to continue into the house. "For more than just us? If you're strong enough to go?" she added, turning to her father.

"We order about ten booklets every year, and give tickets away to friends of the foundation," Elizabeth said. "Are you sure? It's quite all right
~~~~~

if the two of you take the time to get to know each other."

"I would like to spend some social time with Joan," Carter said, his voice sounding a little richer, his eyes a little brighter. "I don't care if I have to take a wheelchair with me, I'm going."

An hour later, they were packed up and ready to go, and the party had expanded to include Anne, Brooklyn, and Vincent. The girls took charge of the baskets and coolers full of "siege provisions," as Vincent called them. Brooklyn carried the blankets and a basket of citronella tin pots to put around their seating area. Vincent had charge of a collapsible, wheeled cart full of folding canvas chairs. That left Elizabeth to walk arm-in-arm with Carter and make sure he didn't push himself. They would be at the outdoor music arena nearly two hours before the concert was due to start, but Anne blithely explained that meant they would get prime parking, the best seating, and enough time to eat all of Brooklyn's food.

The seven of them fit into one vehicle that Joan thought could double as VIP transportation. She remembered Kathryn telling her how the foundation's facilities were made available to visiting preachers and local church functions. The only thing that surprised her was the way Bea, Argus and Ulysses followed them to the carriage house when they loaded up to leave, then sat down in the grass along the driveway. No whining, no attempts to get into the car with them.

"Those are not normal dogs," she muttered, looking back at the three furry bodies sprawled in the late afternoon sunshine, as Vincent drove down the long driveway to the gates.

"Thank the Lord they aren't," Anne said, just as softly. She sat between Kathryn and Joan in the far back seat. "It's not fair we can't take our dogs into Blossom with us."

"Bea likes strings, but not horns. She'd be miserable," Kathryn said.

"What kind of music does Ulysses like?" Joan asked, pitching her voice so Vincent in the front seat could hear.

"That is the most contrary mutt I've ever trained," Vincent called, looking into the rearview mirror. "He likes Third Day turned up to chop-and-liquefy volume, mixed with old tapes of the Blackwood Brothers, early Petra, and the Rambos."

Their party reached the main gates to Blossom before the conversation could get very far into a discussion of the history of contemporary Christian music. Joan just listened, only recognizing a few names from artists she had heard Nikki and Tris Cameron discussing. Their car had sole possession of the long, winding driveway and surprised at least five of the parking lot attendants who seemed to be just coming on duty. Only two cars were there ahead of them, and Anne pretended to be disgusted at someone having beaten them there. The parking spot put them in sight of the lawn seat ticket booth and the arch of the bridge that would take them over the main road, to the plaza and gates leading into the amphitheater area. Vincent ran to flag down a golf cart, so Carter didn't have to walk the entire distance, while the rest of them unloaded.

They had their pick of the entire bowl of the lawn sloping down to the shell of the music pavilion. Joan had never arrived so early, and marveled at how big Blossom's grounds were when there were just a dozen people and lots of green grass and a few trees on the far sides. Usually when she, Matt, Xander, and whoever else they brought with them came for a concert, they arrived with little more than an hour until the concert, meaning the prime spots were already claimed, making it difficult to find a patch of open ground large enough for everyone, their blankets and chairs, picnic baskets and coolers.

Even better than having all the room they wanted was the feast Brooklyn had provided. Deviled eggs, frozen grapes, brownies with cream cheese filling, shrimp cocktail, cheese spread and savory crackers, topped by an insulated container full of meatballs and mini sausage links swimming in a sweet-sour sauce.

"We are going to be half asleep and stuffed before the music starts," Anne declared, rubbing her hands together in anticipation. That earned a smug grin from Brooklyn and laughter from the others.

They people-watched and helped Vincent work a crossword puzzle as the other concertgoers trickled in and found their spots for the evening. Elizabeth brought out a canvas bag that turned out to have six decks of cards and a score pad in it, earning groans and laughter from Brooklyn and Kathryn. She insisted that Joan needed to learn a game they called 'Hand and Foot.' Carter explained the rules, enthroned in his chair above everyone else, while Elizabeth set up the game. The object was to discard and gather up cards to build up three or more of a number or face card. Seven or more were called a meld and earned extra points. The object was for a player to get rid of all the cards in her hand before the others, penalizing them with un-played cards. Joan thought it was easy enough, until Elizabeth pulled out the four printed sheets of rules and points that made everything more complicated and challenging. There was as much strategy as luck of the draw in the game.

Half an hour before the concert was to start, Anne finished tallying up the points from the third round that she had closed out and got to her feet. "I need to make a pit stop. Anyone coming?"

"If you need a bodyguard, you should have brought Argus," Vincent said, not even raising his head from the crossword puzzle book. He snorted when Anne stuck her tongue out at him. Joan suspected he knew the expression on her face from old habit and didn't have to see it.

She opened her mouth to say she would walk down to the restrooms at the bottom of the hill, when she saw Matt's face among the crowd, as if someone had shone a spotlight on it. Panic stole her breath and she froze in place. Just for a few heartbeats that felt like forever.

"Joan." Carter beckoned her over to the clear spot next to his chair. She scooted across the blanket and knelt, looking up at him.

She couldn't see Matt or the others who had been following him. She glimpsed the neon purple sneakers she had seen Tris buy on an outlet mall shopping trip last summer, and the BWU football blanket Rocky always carried to these concerts, but no other details to show her who was with Matt. If she couldn't see them, they couldn't see her.

Joan tipped her head back and found her father watching her. He had that crooked little smile, just one corner of his mouth, and a warmth in his eyes that made her think he had seen her moment of fear, and he understood.

"Who are they?" he asked in an undertone, so someone even two feet away from them wouldn't have heard. That settled that question.

Joan knew she could have shrugged it off and just said they were people from Tabor she didn't want to get into a conversation with. But something inside her screamed abruptly to break all the rules she had made for survival even before she had escaped Niobe.

"Matt, Tris and Rocky Cameron." An increase in Carter's smile made her add, "Patrice and Peter, but nobody calls them by their real names. Rocky got his nickname at church —"

"From Simon Peter, I assume." He nodded, that warmth in his eyes turning to a sparkle. "I know a little about Matt Cameron, just because you spend time with him and that lawyer, Alexander Finley."

"You've been watching me for a long time, huh?"

"Not long enough. You're good friends with the younger cousins, too? How did they come to live with Matt? He's several years older than them, isn't he?"

"Fifteen. And they're twins." Joan adjusted her seating to get more comfortable. It warmed her a little to realize her father wanted personal details about the people who were important to her, and not just rely on the cold facts an investigator could provide him.

"Their fathers were in business together. Inventors and investors, just like Matt. They had a prototype plane they were testing and flew up into the Canadian Rockies with their wives and just vanished. No warning signs, no radio signals, nothing. That was maybe nine years ago. Matt chucked everything to rearrange his life and take the twins on."

"He's a good man, I take it?"

"I suppose you probably have pictures of the day he went to the front of the church with Xander."

"Not quite, but I did get some of the story from their pastor." He tipped his head to one side to study her. Joan had a hard time keeping her face calm and meeting his eyes. "You realize, I've been concerned about anyone you spend a great deal of time with. And I admit, I'm relieved that your close friends are well off."

"Matt could buy his own country if he wanted. That doesn't mean he wouldn't want more and try to horn in and take over things when I take the reins of Arc. If I do," she hurried to add. She knew she didn't fool Carter, because that little smile tipped toward a smirk for just a few heartbeats. "Besides, Xander is poorer than a church mouse, with that legal clinic of his."

"He has high ideals, and I would venture to say the Lord is supporting him in many tangible ways."

"Yeah, I guess. If only some of the nasty Bible-thumpers in his church wouldn't give him such a hard time. How come Christians fight so hard against each other? It seems to me like, with all the work you have to do, all the things you say you believe, you'd be more of a team."

"We're a family, and families tend to be made of individuals who don't like to consider the idea that their way *isn't* the *only* way to do something. Or that they might even be wrong." Carter shrugged and his face lit up when Elizabeth came over, holding out a jacket. Joan waited, watching the warm, unspoken love in the byplay between them, as she helped him put on his jacket against the slight chill slipping across the grassy slope.

"Such a serious discussion," Elizabeth said as she settled down on Carter's other side. "We're here to have fun tonight, you know."

"Philosophy, my dear." Carter reached down and caught hold of her hand, bringing it up to rest on his knee with his hand over it. Something about the gesture, so simple and casual, made Joan's throat close up and brought a stinging to the back of her eyes. She wanted that simple intimacy that spoke of long experience and knowledge and caring.

"Joan brought up an interesting point, about how we Christians tend to use our energy and battle skills against each other, rather than the enemy."

"Ah, yes, the legalists versus the 'anything goes' brand of Christianity, and both sides looking with scorn on those who just want everyone to get along." Elizabeth nodded, a rueful smile twisting her lips. "What people on the outside—and unfortunately, quite a few on the inside—don't seem to realize is that the basic rules Christ gave us are simple and concrete. The rest of it is cultural, and quite a bit is situational. The problem comes when those who want to impose their cultural bias on people claim that it's God's sovereign word and it applies to everyone. Sorting out what is required and what is voluntary… that wastes quite a bit of energy, and only makes the devil's job easier, I'm afraid."

Chapter Eighteen

"Which is why cold-hearted creeps condemn good guys like Xander to Hell, just because he won't knuckle under and live according to the laws of St. Montgomery, the only lawyer God loves." Joan nearly laughed as the last words spilled from her lips. Where had that come from? Not that she hadn't thought along those lines a few times, especially during a few encounters she had witnessed between Xander and the older lawyer.

"You're rather passionate in defense of your friend," Carter said.

"I learned a long time ago, money and houses and fancy clothes and even political power, it doesn't mean diddly if people get hurt. Friends are the most important things in the world. So when you find a good one, you take care of him. Or her," she added, thinking again about bringing Sophie to nest at Quarry Hall. The dangerous, powerful people who wanted to commandeer Sophie's programming talents would find her trail eventually, no matter what Joan and Sophie did to fuddle their paths. It was just a matter of time and resources. Joan had played with the idea of using Col. Sidarkis to deflect attention away from her and Sophie when things got hot and uncomfortable for them. She didn't know if she dared risk that now, considering how easily Sidarkis had turned her over to her father. Although, she had to admit, she wasn't quite as angry anymore.

Even if her father wasn't actively the Oracle any longer, he still had to have connections and information and feelers out in the Information Underground. The resources of Quarry Hall would protect Sophie far longer, and more securely, than anything she and Joan could cobble together, living on the fringes of society as they did.

Streamers of music came from the stage as the sound technicians tested the system. Joan glanced away, expecting to see someone working there, but the gleaming wooden interior of the band shell was still empty of all but a few microphone and instrument stands. When she looked back, she found Elizabeth had gotten up and walked over to the cooler, and Carter watched her with a far away expression in his eyes.

"Do you believe in God intervening in people's lives?" he surprised her by asking.

"I might not be part of the army, but... things have happened to me when Sophie gets praying. And I had good evidence a month or so ago that praying works..." She shrugged to cover the automatic shudder through her body. "Why?"

"You've already had some evidence of Kathryn's gift. Not that I make any claim it runs in the family, but sometimes... well, about six weeks ago, I had a dream. You were in a dark pit, tied up so your wrists bled. And your friend Matt was there with you."

"What did you do?" she whispered, all the sound she could produce as her throat closed, choking her with memories of those hot, sweaty hours in darkness.

"There wasn't anything I could do, except get down on my knees and pray. Hard. For quite a long time." Carter's hand trembled just enough to be noticeable as he reached out to touch the side of Joan's face.

He waited, and Joan knew he wanted her to tell him how much of his dream was truth and how much was just... what? She wanted to make a joke, to offer a flip remark about how he should have checked on what Kathryn had dreamed that night, but the words clogged on her tongue. When her father shook his head, his mouth quirking up in that bitterly amused little smile again, and he took his hand away, she felt oddly abandoned. She had gone nearly thirty years without a father's touch, so why did it hurt so much to have the first be so brief?

"Vincent went to your place the next day and you weren't home. He waited, asking questions in town, and saw you come back late in the afternoon, looking very much worse for wear. He couldn't find out anything. Your friends are very close-mouthed."

"Matt was in trouble. I went with him to investigate someone." Joan's throat hurt as she forced the words out. "We got caught and captured. They were getting ready to burn the warehouse down around us when some of Sidarkis' people found us."

"I'm glad that you have such a strong sense of loyalty, of giving, after the way you were raised." He sighed. "Joan, I know it doesn't do much good now, but if I could have gotten you away from your mother when you were younger, I would have. Most of Oracle's power lay in knowledge, not in actions."

"Like a guy in a watchtower. He knows everything that's going on," she murmured, "but it doesn't do a whole heck of a lot of good if he can't use it for anything."

"And that's why Arc exists now. To make up for all those years when I thought I was rich in knowledge and influence but didn't do anything worthwhile with my riches."

Joan nodded, caught in his gaze. She could guess at all the hundreds of things her father wanted to say to her, the questions he wanted to ask, and she appreciated his restraint. If he asked her for more details on that day she and Matt came close to dying, could she keep silent? The thought of spilling the events that had ended with clinging to Matt, hungry for something sweet and good, the need to be held and not feel alone for the first time in years—it made her dizzy. And through her relief that Carter didn't ask her, Joan felt an odd thread of disappointment.

Maybe confession was good for the soul. And maybe out of everyone on the hillside tonight, waiting for the concert to start, Carter was one of the few who could understand what had driven her to follow her hungers and needs instead of letting her intellect rule. But Joan couldn't let the words out. Certainly not here, where people she liked would hear of her stupidity and selfishness and think less of her.

"I think we should offer your friend the lawyer some support," Carter said, the same moment Joan rubbed her eyes and found them hot and wet.

"Xander? He could really use a chunk of money to help get his clinic on steady footing." She knew he had seen her incipient tears, and she appreciated his restraint in saying nothing about them. Having a father, she decided then, was a good thing.

"I'm thinking of annual support. He charges depending on what people can pay. I think Arc can afford to provide base salaries for his people and rent on his storefront. And better furniture," he added, one corner of his mouth going up higher.

"That would be... great. Umm—"

"Yes, it's somewhat of a bribe." He snorted when Joan sat up straighter and frowned. "I'm not above buying as much of your good will as I can. But Finley is a good man and deserves help, and I wouldn't have known about him if I hadn't been investigating you. He gets the help whether you decide to become involved in Arc or not."

"That's not much of a bribe. A bribe should have some sort of conditional part to it."

"Yes, well, there's the world's way of doing business, and God's way, which often doesn't make sense to the world. But I think it's the right way."

"You and Sophie are going to get along great."

"I think so, too. We have you in common." He sighed. "You can't imagine how grateful I was, when I realized that your closest friend was a believer."

Joan laughed, the sound surprising her as much as Carter, and Elizabeth, who had returned with a plate full of the goodies Brooklyn had packed.

"Sophie would argue with you about that. She always says she passed over from believing to knowing a long time ago," she explained.

~~~~~

Saturday, Joan slept in. It amused her a little, to realize that she felt comfortable enough at Quarry Hall to sleep late, listening to her body rather than her self-preservation instincts. Maybe the presence of Ulysses, lying on the foot of her bed, made her feel secure. She was amused to realize she didn't need the chimes of her white noise machine to block out the sounds of the house and help her sleep, either.

Before breakfast, she pulled on sweats and a t-shirt and took Ulysses for a walk, which ended up as a jog through several of the theme gardens
~~~~~

in the lower levels of the estate. Her abdomen didn't give her a single twinge, and that added to her bright spirits. She met Anne coming back from the opposite direction with Argus, her green t-shirt dark with sweat. They exchanged understanding grins. It just felt like a natural thing to take care of her new companion before taking care of herself, and what made more sense than to go for a long walk? Anne suggested she wash up in the third-floor bathroom and go to breakfast with her, instead of going halfway through the house to the bathroom attached to her guest room.

"This was the servants' quarters," Anne explained, as they reached the top of the staircase and a long hallway with plain plaster walls and dark-stained hardwood floor stretched out ahead of them. The evenly spaced doors on either side reminded Joan of the older dormitories at BWU. "I think it's appropriate," she added with a breathless little laugh.

"Appropriate?"

"Bathroom." She tapped the first door they passed.

It swung open, obviously not latched, revealing the bathroom took up the next two bedroom spaces. Three shower stalls, three stall toilets, three washbasins and a long, high tub with jets in the sides. Everything was in pale green ceramic with dark green towels, soap and other toiletries filling a floor-to-ceiling open cabinet.

"Kathryn and Jennifer and I live here. There are some other girls who work mostly on the west coast, helping with investigations, and they have rooms when they come to report. It's kind of like dorm living. We can decorate our rooms any way we want. We share in the cleaning and help Brooklyn with the cooking when we're home between assignments."

"Appropriate?" Joan asked again.

"Oh, yeah." Anne grinned and settled on the edge of the tub. "Being servants. Uncle Harrison says we should consider ourselves daughters of the house, family, but living in this part of the house where things aren't so fancy sort of reminds us that we're servants in the Kingdom, first. Royalty, second."

"Royalty." She snorted but returned Anne's grin. Sophie talked that way quite often, and Joan missed it.

Thinking of Sophie made her wonder just how her soul-sister was doing. Had she tracked down the threat coming at them through Sidarkis' system, or was their enemy more clever and persistent than usual? How close was Sophie to feeling free to come down to Quarry Hall? The sooner she could join them here, the sooner Joan would feel secure about Sophie's safety. She couldn't repress the nagging, aching feeling of impending doom that made her want to run, find Sophie, and drag her away to safety right now.

Vincent sauntered into the morning room while Joan and Anne were halfway through breakfast. Without him saying a word, she knew he wanted to give her another self-defense lesson. She considered coming downstairs to the gymnasium in the clothes she had sweated into earlier. The thought of silently joking around with him, and the ease she felt in his company, startled her.

Joan threw herself into the lesson, just to pull her mind away from the disturbing self-revelations that came at the oddest moments. She was almost relieved when the lesson was over. She limped upstairs to wash, took some aspirin for her bruises, and settled into the office with Elizabeth for another lesson on the inner workings of the Arc Foundation.

When they emerged after another working lunch into the early Saturday afternoon sunshine, Joan found Carter waiting for them, basking on the long, flagstone patio. She learned then that every other morning, a specialist in alternative medicine came in for an experimental treatment involving massage and herbal preparations, to help ease toxins from his tissues. The procedure interested her. Anything that might buy her more time to get to know her father had her approval.

Had she started to care about Carter already? Joan wasn't sure. Just knowing the disease was eating away at Kathryn, too, because she had been used as the delivery method, made her more anxious for a cure. She liked Kathryn. She admired her, because Joan knew she wouldn't have gone on quite so calmly with her life if she had a ticking bomb in her body.

"You know what I think?" she told Ulysses, when a business call took both Carter and Elizabeth back into the office. "I think this place is like a field hospital. The walking wounded, getting patched up and heading back out into battle. Kind of scary. But you gotta admire them."

"At least their armor is in place," a vaguely familiar voice said from behind her. "Do you even have any armor?"

Joan turned and found the gardener, Messenger, standing by the steps up to the patio. She wore cleaner jeans and a blue work shirt. Today, her eyes seemed more green than blue.

"I'm not even part of the army." She flashed back to what Elizabeth had told her earlier, about fighting a resistance action and nothing more.

"But you are. There're only two sides to the war going on. If you're not on one side, then you're on the other." She put a foot up on the top step and leaned forward, as if she were a runner doing warm-up stretches.

"But what if I don't want anything to do with it?"

"Sitting out of a battle can affect the outcome just as much as fighting on either side."

"Just one person can't make that much of a difference," she retorted.

"It does in tug-of-war." She winked at her and turned to leave.

"Isn't the outcome already pre-determined? Sophie told me the good guys win," she called after her.

"Don't you want to be on the winning side?" Messenger didn't even look back as she made a right turn around the corner of the house and vanished from sight.

"Weird." Joan snorted, but grinned. "Reminds me of Maggie." She laughed, envisioning the resident eccentric of Tabor wandering the extensive gardens of Quarry Hall, talking to invisible people and always coming up with observations and bits of advice that could make someone believe she could read minds. "Is she a friend of yours? You liked Maggie a lot too, didn't you?" She ruffled up Ulysses' fur, following his spine. He groaned in obvious pleasure and settled down, leaning against her. "Just shows how smart you are, I guess."

"That's the whole reason why these dogs are here." Vincent stepped out through the big French doors to join her. He walked over to the stone half-wall and leaned back against it, his elbows resting on it, one hip cocked like he would sit on the top. "What you can't handle with self-defense, the dogs are there to take up the slack. We need them to be smart. Part of their job is reading the people around them, not just the environment. Starting when they pick their owners."

"Kind of sounds like the *dogs* are the owners." She gestured down at Ulysses, thinking of the day she first saw him and how nothing, not even closed doors, kept him away from her. It had been spooky, but now she liked it.

"Might be." Vincent just gave her that superior little smirk that didn't irritate her, though she couldn't understand why. "Notice most of our dogs are the bigger breeds? We train them not to bite, but to knock down aggressors. Or knock down the people they're protecting, if necessary. If the dogs never bite, we don't have to worry about false allegations from people who want to separate dog from person."

"Smart." Joan thought of a situation where false accusations of dogs biting had removed guard dogs from someone's estate. By the time everything got straightened out and the stories of dog attacks were revealed as false, the enemy had infiltrated and stolen priceless prototype computer chips and programs. "Does Messenger have a dog friend, too?"

"Who?"

"Messenger. The gardener. Shaggy blonde, tanned, talks like she swallowed Sun Tzu's *The Art of War*." Joan grinned at him, but the expression froze when Vincent just shook his head.

"We don't have a woman gardener."

"Can anybody get into the grounds who doesn't belong?"

"Not with Ulysses and his brothers and sisters running around." Vincent held out his hand. Two fingers twitched and Ulysses got up and ran over to him. A few more hand signals Joan couldn't make out, both from subtlety and swiftness, and the big dog ran around the perimeter of the patio before settling down next to her again. "You need to learn how to communicate with your friend."

"That's assuming I take him back to my apartment to stay. And that's assuming my landlord lets me." Joan thought of big, cheerful, caftan-clad

Mandy Gordon, and knew she would only grumble for form's sake, then give in. That wasn't the problem. "What about Messenger?"

"I don't know who you're talking about or you've been talking to. Next time she shows up, call me, don't let her get away."

"Ulysses and Bea both like her. Does that mean anything?"

"Considering how hard it is to bribe these big mutts?" Vincent shook his head, smiling. "I'm going to send the dogs out to check the estate, just in case. Want to come along? Your first lesson in dog-talk."

"If it keeps you from using me as a punching bag, sure." She had to grin at him when he broke out in low, rumbling laughter.

~~~~~

Joan couldn't make sense of the hand signals Vincent used to get the attention of all the dogs wandering the estate, even though he showed them to her five times. The finger movements and flat-palm twists were beyond her, most likely because she was hungry and tired and her brain felt stretched from working in the office with Elizabeth so long. She wanted to accuse him of teasing her, that he had a dog whistle hidden in his pocket. Joan refrained. If Vincent was having fun at her expense, then she would just let him keep the joke going a little longer and deflate him by pretending to believe. She watched as he sent un-partnered dogs out to different sections of the estate. Then she and Ulysses wandered back to the house.

Anne and Kathryn were helping Brooklyn in the kitchen when Joan walked by, so she volunteered to help with dinner, too. Ulysses settled down on the floor in the hall with the other two dogs. She enjoyed the chatter, ranging from books to the latest movies to the progress of the vegetable garden and Brooklyn's plans for preserving the abundance produced by the estate.

"Quarry Hall was self-sufficient when the original builders lived here, and so are we," Brooklyn said, with a nod for emphasis. "You never know when the world will turn against believers and we'll have to guard the ramparts."

"Preparing for siege?" Joan asked quietly. She hadn't meant it mockingly, but she still flinched as the words slipped off her tongue.

"Something like that." Kathryn nodded, a glint of humor in her eyes. "Christians are aliens in an alien world, when you really think about it."

Joan bit her lip against retorting that she didn't need to think about it. That felt like childish, bratty defiance. Then her phone buzzed silently in her pocket, feeling like an attack of bees and making her jump.

She pulled it out of her pocket, half-turned to leave. The screen showed Sophie's number, but she wasn't supposed to call until that evening. Joan's knuckles went white as she flipped the phone open.

"I'm here," she said, as soon as the connection opened. "What's wrong?" She headed for the door into the hallway. She found all three dogs blocking her path, only two steps out of the kitchen. She stopped and didn't care who
~~~~~

heard. "Where are you?"

"Ithaca. Nowhere near the safe house. Don't know if it's safe. Have to check it out."

"Sophie!"

"It's *her*. She knows my name. My real name. She's playing a cat-and-mouse game right now, trying to scare me into being stupid. She knows about that sleazoid who wants me, brain and bod." Sophie took a long, rattling indrawn breath. "With the money she gets for selling me to him, she's financing a major hit on you."

"Who the heck cares? I'm coming for you."

"No." Her voice suddenly went quiet and calm. "She doesn't know where you are. That's what's got her psycho, why she's so hot to tear me apart. She doesn't know. You're safe."

"Then she won't know I'm coming after her." Joan heard the phone case creak, threatening to crack. "If she hurts you, she'll wish I had never been born."

"Don't, Joanie-gal. I've got my insurance paid up. You're still on the wrong side of the door. God'll take care of me."

"Did you ever think God put me here to take care of you?"

A hand on her bare arm made her flinch. Joan turned to see Brooklyn, Kathryn and Anne standing around her. Kathryn gripped her arm. It helped, but not enough. Joan wanted to fling herself into someone's arms and cry until the world fixed itself.

The world never fixed itself. The best she could do was give it a good swift kick and then run fast and hard and hide until things calmed down.

Sophie was in trouble because of her. How long would she have to pay, and keep paying, until she could make up for all the damage and danger that followed her steps?

"You get to that safe house and you put your head down and you stay there until I come get you," she growled. "Understand?"

"I understand. But it's not safe for you, so don't come. Love you, sister-mine."

The connection broke with a soft beep.

Chapter Nineteen

"Sophie!" Joan stared at her phone for two long seconds. "Sophie!" She raised her hand, ready to throw the phone down and shatter it on the floor as useless.

Ulysses reared up on his hind legs and came down with his huge paws resting on Joan's stomach. She stumbled backward, straight into Kathryn's supporting arms. She tucked the phone into her pocket. If Sophie felt safe, she would call. Until Sophie was safe, Joan didn't dare call, either distracting her or causing any sound or vibration that could attract the enemy's attention. Niobe had the best stealth technology at her beck and call. She could trace phone signals and know if they were incoming or outgoing. That meant silence until Sophie instigated communication. They had agreed on that protocol long ago, against a day like today. Joan couldn't break her phone, though it might temporarily feel good. She would need that phone. Joan had to believe Sophie would call.

"Who's Sophie, and what kind of trouble is she in?" Kathryn asked, her voice quiet.

"Nothing you can do about it." Joan let herself stay for one heartbeat longer in the comfort of Kathryn's arm around her shoulders. Then she gently twisted herself free.

"There's always something we can all do," Brooklyn said.

Joan swallowed down a stinging rebuke. The woman sounded too much like Sophie when she was at her most aggravatingly spiritual. That realization made her pause.

"Sophie believes like you do. If you could pray …" She shook her head, swallowing words she wanted to say without knowing why she wanted to say them. "I have to go help her."

When she fled upstairs, Ulysses followed. Joan didn't bother closing the guest room door as she gathered up her purse and her few clothes.

Vincent waited, leaning against her car, when she reached the carriage house and the parking lot behind it. A dark green Cherokee blocked Joan's car in, so she couldn't even maneuver to get around it and make her escape. Ulysses trotted over to Vincent, sat down at the man's feet, and waited for her to join them.

"So, I hear we're going to Ithaca," Vincent said slowly, a thin, irritating, smug smile lighting his face. "Brooklyn has the sharpest ears God ever made." He tugged down his dark glasses so they rested on the tip of his nose and looked over the tops of them at her. "I assume it's Ithaca, New York, rather than Greece."

"It could be Ithaca in Ohio." She crossed her arms and glared back at him.

"Nice town. I've been there. I have connections there."

"Inside or outside the law?" That train-out-of-control feeling slowed, and the crushing sensation decreased for a moment. He wasn't suggesting what she thought he was suggesting…was he?

"A little of both." He slid his glasses off, snapped them closed, and gestured with them at the Cherokee. "I'll drive. You get down in the back and don't come up for air until we're on the highway."

"So if the gates are being watched, no one suspects I've left." She nodded, understanding his thinking, and grateful. Just because Sophie said Niobe didn't know her location didn't mean it was true. Everything had changed in the last half hour. If Niobe was on Sophie's heels, then she could have accessed other information, and she knew where the Oracle was. Seeing Joan drive out of those gates now could change the entire landscape in this battle. "I can't get you involved," she said, pushing away the rush of relief.

"Kiddo, you're the old man's only kid. Your folks gave me my life back. I owe them."

"They asked you—"

"We don't work that way here. Kathryn came and got me first, and now she's filling them in. I want to be out of here before they come looking for us. They'll have ideas and advice. Just a waste of time, right?"

"Right." Joan looked with longing at her car. He was right. If someone watched the gates or her movements, no matter who the enemy was, her departure would alert them that something was wrong. Vincent driving out alone would mean nothing to them.

"I'm not getting out of the way, and there's not a thing you can do to move me." He grinned, his teeth a white slash of mixed menace and humor. "Maybe after you've had a few lessons, but not now."

"Time's wasting," she whispered, and nodded. Just because she let Vincent drive her to Ithaca didn't mean she had to lead him to the safe house.

Ulysses sat in the front seat, his head hanging out the open window, as the Cherokee slid out the front gates. Joan lay flat on her back, covered first by a silver thermal sheet and then by a dirty cotton throw, with cardboard boxes stacked all around her. Someone looking through the lightly tinted windows would assume Vincent was making a delivery, with his dog for company. The silver sheet would temporarily deflect heat sensors, if the enemy was present and prepared for many eventualities.

Joan had a long time to think, to sweat, to get bounced around, and to plan. Vincent didn't pull over until they reached the first rest stop on the highway heading for New York. She didn't move until he opened the hatch in the back and tugged the two sheets off her, first.

"You know how to be quiet, you follow instructions and you don't complain." A smile crooked up one corner of his mouth. "School of hard knocks?"

"Survival." She let him give her a hand sliding out of the back. Joan raked sweaty hair out of her face and walked around to the front of the vehicle. Ulysses sat in the back seat now. A bottle of cold water waited in the cup holder built into the door. She pulled up on the stopper on the top and drank slowly, letting the water warm for the first few mouthfuls before swallowing. "Thanks."

"First rule. Always take good care of your equipment." He gestured at the cooler sitting in the back seat next to Ulysses. "Plenty where that came from, so don't be sparing."

"I hope Brooklyn packed us a good dinner to make up for what we're missing." Joan slid into the front seat and slammed the door.

"And breakfast. And enough snacks to get us through a long stakeout." He put the vehicle into gear, made a shallow turn, and headed out of the empty parking area.

"Stakeout? What makes you think there'll be one?" She concentrated on watching the road ahead of them as Vincent drove down the access lane, back onto the highway.

"Brooklyn has perfect recall. I filled in the pieces from your half of the conversation. Tell me about Sophie."

"Computer geek. Genius." Joan sighed and closed her eyes, fighting the burn of tears. She hardly ever cried, and certainly never in the middle of a crisis. Why now?

"Who's after her and why's she in trouble?"

"Niobe." She sighed, feeling slightly nauseous from the words that needed to come out. "You know about my mother? That's what I call her. And I think that answers many questions."

"Tracking Sophie to get to you?"

"What other answer is there? She can't control me, so she's out to destroy anybody who helps me, anybody I care about."

"What other trouble is Sophie in?"

"What makes you think—" Joan opened her eyes. Vincent didn't look upset or worried. If anything, he looked as relaxed as if they were heading off on a short errand.

"Sidarkis gave your folks some idea that you two teamed up to keep each other safe."

"He needs a nuke stuffed in his pants and his big mouth nailed shut," she growled.

"It's been tried."

"What happened? The nuke ran away because it was scared?"

"No. The guy's from Krypton."

Joan glanced sideways at Vincent and caught him watching her, mischief in his eyes, fighting not to grin. Despite herself, she smiled.

"Despite what you think, he's an okay guy. For G.I. Joe."

"Yeah, that's what my—what my father says." Her mouth felt strange, saying the word out loud.

"So, what's the trouble with Sophie?"

"She writes programs and unravels problems in her sleep. An artist, like other people write music or... or weave cloth or bake or whatever. It's what she was made to do. Well, some very powerful, really sick-minded, rich sub-human creep decided he didn't want to just buy her services. He wanted to own her. Body and soul. It doesn't help that she's gorgeous. When she said no, he didn't even warn her, just started destroying her life. Blew up her car, torched the place where she worked—" Joan remembered her disbelief when she heard the story. "Followed her to church, tried to set fire to the sanctuary with everybody inside, and then called her on her cell phone to demand she come out and surrender. Well, Sophie keeps her phone turned off when she's in church. He had to call on the church phone, which alerted a lot of people. And some members of her church were cops and firemen. The fire didn't take, and the creep had gas and incendiary gizmos the police found later. Nothing worked."

She shivered, remembering the envy that had followed close on the heels of her disbelief when Sophie first related the story to her. Joan ached to have that kind of assurance of support and protection wrapped around her. And ached more to know it was beyond her reach.

"Makes sense."

"Yeah, it would to you," she muttered.

That earned a chuckle from Vincent.

"What else?" he prompted, when she didn't speak for a few minutes.

"He killed her dog and mailed it back to her in pieces. And told her all the things he was going to do to the people around her, family, friends and just neighbors who didn't even know her name, if she didn't do what he wanted. And all the things he wanted from her when she wasn't working on the computer. Sophie decided right then, she'd rather die. So she took off running. She figured she could at least protect the people she still had left if she was on the run, keeping the creeps busy."

"How'd you two meet?"

"We were both doing the migrant farm worker thing and got assigned the same cabin. She was having trouble with her notebook. I fixed it. We talked computers the next few days. Then the next few after that, we talked about our problems. She tried to save my soul but settled for saving my sanity." Joan slouched a little more and closed her eyes. "Sisters ever since."

"And now she's in trouble and you're racing off to save her."

"My fault. My problem to fix."

"How'd they find her?" Vincent listened as she explained their phone conversation her first night at Quarry Hall and then this afternoon, constantly interrupting to ask questions that Joan had no answers to. He frowned at the road ahead of him and shook his head when she finished. "Not your fault, kiddo. Blame the mole selling information."

"All that matters is getting Sophie out of there."

"Hmm. Maybe." He held up a hand, cutting her off when Joan opened her mouth to retort. "How good are you with computers?"

"Sophie does software, I do hardware, we both invent and search."

"Uh huh. Flip up the center console and see what you can do."

A thin silver case held a streamlined computer. She turned it on, speculating it was a custom job, which said something about Vincent. He gave her the passwords, and in moments she had connected with the Internet. He walked her through how to access the printing function on the ultra-slim fax hidden in the compartment with the computer, so she could print out whatever she came up with.

Joan curled up in the Cherokee's bucket seat with her back to the door, three-quarters profile to Vincent, and searched all the information he suggested, and anything that came to mind. Police department information; local offices of federal agencies; street maps; demographics of crime for the last year; newspaper stories that hinted at criminal organization activities in the area; economic demographics; and more. She had a vague idea how some of the information was useful and didn't look forward to asking him about the rest. Still, as the miles sped by under their wheels and they forged a working alliance, she relaxed. Just a little. Enough to enjoy the sensation of having someone besides Sophie to rely on, someone who might know more about the situation than she did.

During a lull, while Vincent used his headset and made a phone call to someone he called "Tiger," Joan called up information on the safe house. A nice two-story house built in the thirties, in a formerly middle-class area, it was slowly being surrounded by businesses. The heavier the traffic around the house, the harder it would be to spot unusual activity. She and Sophie made a little money renting it out, but they had quarters hidden in the basement, behind a false wall, and another hiding hole in the attic, to use even when the house was occupied. Right now, the house was unoccupied. Joan accessed the security cameras that downloaded everything they recorded into a secure cyberspace "hideout" Col. Sidarkis had given her and Sophie as the price for their last major job for him. According to the cameras, there had been no activity in or within ten feet of the house in the last four hours.

Sophie hadn't come near the safe house. Neither had any enemies, trying to track her down. Was that good, or bad?

There was plenty of cover traffic through Ithaca, thanks to the lakes in the area, the patchwork of state parks, and the transient traffic of students at Cornell University and Ithaca College. Joan and Sophie had felt safe there, able to blend in and be invisible, and had bought the house using one of their many false identities. In the six years since they had bought it, they had never needed to use it as a safe house. Until now.

"Something's going down," Vincent said, yanking her out of her thoughts.

Joan downloaded the information she had called up and put a security lock on it. Even though it was his computer, he wouldn't be able to access it. She hoped.

"Going down?"

"Tiger is a friend, somebody I met when I was on the other side and he *wasn't* a friend." He grimaced, expressing so much, yet leaving so much more for her to guess. "There's a lot of federal activity, several different agencies all converging, working together. Not a good sign."

"Big trouble when they stop bickering long enough to hunt something or someone?"

"We don't want to get spotted by anybody with a hair trigger, okay?" He glanced away from the road long enough to meet her gaze. "On either side. Some of these guys will shoot first and think up lots of nasty questions while you're recovering in the hospital. The other ones will write your confession and get you to sign it while you're soaring on meds. Let's just stick to the shadows, not draw anybody's attention, find Sophie and get out of there. Sound good to you?"

"That's how I always work."

"Yeah, I'll just bet you do. Remind me to give you a couple self-defense lessons when we have some free time."

"I thought the plan was to go in, grab Sophie and get out."

"Nothing ever works out the way we planned. That's lesson number two." He nodded at the computer. "Close up and get some sleep. We're driving up to the northern end of Cayuga Lake and taking a ferry in to Ithaca. It's going to be a long night."

Joan complied. She knew how to get into his computer again. If she had to, she would steal it and empty it of all the information she had downloaded. Besides, Vincent was right. It was going to be a long night. She had no intention of taking him within ten miles of the safe house, no matter how much help he gave her.

<div align="center">~~~~~</div>

They ate at a rest stop outside Elmira, before they turned north toward Ithaca. Joan concentrated on enjoying the ten-layer sandwiches Brooklyn had sent along, rather than asking questions. For instance: Why was Vincent so willing to help her without demanding an hour's worth of answers before he put the key in the ignition? What did he and her father expect in exchange for this help?

Joan didn't want to owe anyone anything. How much of her time, her cooperation, her life, would Carter expect in exchange for using his

150

connections to help Sophie? She didn't want to face the question, even from a rhetorical standpoint. If she didn't choose to ally with the Arc Foundation of her own free will, with no strings attached, she would always feel a little resentment, a little trapped. What fun was paradise if she didn't have the freedom to walk away?

Working with the Arc Foundation would be paradise. Security and resources. People who believed in helping the little guys, the battered, downtrodden, and helpless. People who worked in the shadows, staying away from spotlights and publicity. She could work with people like that, but not because she owed them.

She barely knew them, hadn't worked with them. Hadn't shed blood with them like she had with Sophie. How could she commit her life to these relative strangers? Especially when there was every chance they would eject her from their company the moment they learned about the person behind the mask she wore.

Vincent was on the headset phone when she got back from tossing out the trash. He nodded to her and continued listening to the person on the other end, making "mm hmm" noises that didn't give her a clue who he talked to, or the topic.

"All set?" He didn't wait for her to answer as he took off the headset, the call finished.

He opened up the back of the Cherokee and flipped a seat forward, revealing a storage compartment that Joan doubted was standard equipment. Just like the phone hookup and the computer and the special console weren't standard equipment. She nearly laughed when he extracted a collar and leash. The laughter died in her throat when Ulysses walked over to Vincent, sat down and tipped his head back, offering his neck for easy access.

Was this a normal dog?

"You're going on foot," Vincent said, standing up. He slapped Ulysses' side, barely making a sound against all that fur. He held out the loop end of the long, thick leather leash. "The less we're seen together, the safer we'll be."

"It's easier for one to become invisible than for two, you mean."

"Exactly." He nodded slowly, his gaze roving over her as if she had physically changed with that one statement. Joan wondered if she had impressed him, or made him worry. "The plan is, I'll let you off half a mile from the ferry. You'll walk up, buy a ticket, and ride to the Ithaca end of the lake. I'll be on the ferry, but we won't know each other."

"Ignore you. Got it. Can he?" She slid her finger between the studded black leather collar and Ulysses' neck. There seemed to be plenty of room, but she felt sorry for the big dog. He was still little more than an overgrown puppy.

"Once that collar is on, he knows he's on duty. You're the only person in the world, as far as he's concerned. You show any stress in your voice, or fear in your scent, all you have to do is point to the ones giving you a hard time, and he's on them."

"That could be a problem."

"On them. Not biting them. Just... on them." He grinned.

That didn't mean Ulysses couldn't break a couple ribs with his weight, or claw somebody pretty bad, or bruise them at the very least. Who wouldn't be scared into a heart attack with a bear-like dog glaring at them from a secure seat in the middle of their chest?

"Four blocks down from the docks is an IHOP. You keep going on foot. I'll drive. Tiger'll meet us there." Vincent reached back into the compartment and brought out a cell phone, smaller than the one Joan had in her bag. He flipped it open and punched a series of numbers into it. "It's programmed to connect directly to me. In case we get separated. This green button on the side is a GPS and SOS, if you can't make a call. Got it?" He handed it to her when she nodded.

Joan climbed back into the Cherokee with the phone in her pocket and her head whirling through plans. Four blocks, after dark, was a lot of room and plenty of time in which to lose Vincent. Not for good. Just long enough to get to the safe house and figure things out. With luck, she would find Sophie and get back to Vincent before he had time to move from worry to anger. He wasn't someone she wanted to anger. Not when she still needed his help.

The maneuver went smoothly, as if they had practiced it a hundred times. They reached the last ferry of the day to cross the lake going south. Sunset splashed crimson and gold across the sky at eye-level, making her wince. Joan took her change when she paid for her ticket, glanced around, and ducked into the little souvenir shop on the near side of the fence that separated the docks from the mainland. She bought a billed cap in dark blue with a gull stitched on it. She could tuck her hair up underneath it.

Vincent drove up and got in line, just as the dock workers started loading the cars. Joan pretended to be bored, leaning against the fence that kept the waiting passengers in line, but she kept the Cherokee within sight the entire time. Would it be that easy to escape Vincent and reach the safe house?

Chapter Twenty

Everything depended on the ferry reaching the docks just at that misty time when it wasn't dark enough for the streetlights to come on, but not light enough to see anything clearly. The time when all colors seemed to go gray and nobody looked familiar. She went down on one knee and pretended to fuss with Ulysses' collar and leash, and with one hand rearranged the clothes in her bag so her jacket was on top. Joan figured in the time it would take to duck around a corner, she could have the cap on, her hair tucked up and the jacket on, sufficiently changing her appearance. Ulysses was dark enough, he might just turn invisible in the twilight. If there were too many lights illuminating the street... she supposed she could tie him to a bench or traffic sign and make a run for it. But would he let her?

Vincent looked right through her as the passengers trooped onto the ferry and up the stairs to the upper two decks. Joan fussed with the leash, wrapping it twice around her hand. Ulysses turned his head once and met her gaze, and she could have sworn he gave her a "What's your problem?" look. A little boy squealed delight when they reached the observation deck and came toddling over. Before she could warn the child away, Ulysses licked his face, knocking him over and making the boy laugh.

"Some watch dog," a tenor voice commented, accompanied by breath reeking of beer, floating over her left shoulder.

Joan turned around from her place at the railing and silently scolded her stomach. She never got seasick, and she refused to let some fumes knock her off balance. She met the green gaze of a sunburned, sandy-haired, wide-shouldered man with *college student on summer break* stamped all over him. From his sandals and shorts to his three-day growth of beard and the bottle in his hand, he was visibly looking for a good time. At everyone else's expense.

No way in the world was she going to let him make her his current toy, even if only for the duration of the ride across the lake.

"Bodyguard." She released one loop of the leash. As if her irritation had flipped a switch, Ulysses turned his back on the child and placed his body like a thick, furry, fanged barrier between her and the entire world.

Good-time Man took one look at Ulysses, swallowed hard, and struggled to prop up his sagging smile. He offered her the bottle. Joan's upper lip curled back at the wash of fumes thrown at her by the slight breeze off the water. He shrugged, tipped it back, and emptied it with two swallows.

"That's so juvenile," she said, when he raised his hand, preparing to toss it in the water. A crewmember ten feet away was just turning to look at them.

"Juvenile?" He stopped, mouth dropping open. Then his crooked grin returned. "You like the harder stuff? There's this great place down by —"

Ulysses took one step forward and bared his teeth. Not a sound issued from him, but Joan sensed the growl waiting to be born.

"Alcohol is a crutch used by the weak-minded and undisciplined." She injected a tinge of British accent, borrowing from Brooklyn. "My friend doesn't like you. I don't like you. Go find someone with a single-digit I.Q. to pick on."

He goggled at her for a moment, hand still raised in the air to throw the bottle. Joan caught movement from the corner of her eye. The crewmember stepped up behind Good-time Man, took the bottle with one hand and caught hold of his arm with the other. In moments, they were gone. Joan sighed and turned around to look at the water again.

"Good job," Vincent said under his breath as he slid up to the railing three feet away.

"So glad you approve." She fought not to grin when he responded with a snort. They ignored each other for the entire ride. Ulysses slept at her feet.

At the docks, pedestrians were allowed off first. Joan walked slowly. By the prickling in her back, she knew Vincent watched her. She knew better than to make any effort to vanish right away. For all she knew, he could take a running leap over the railing of the ferry, land on the dock and tackle her in ten seconds flat. Or worse, he could simply shout an order and Ulysses would take her down and keep her pinned until he showed up. That wouldn't be good for staying unnoticed and nondescript.

At the first intersection, Joan slowed down so the red light caught her and she couldn't cross the street. It gave her time to study her surroundings and adjust her nebulous plan. These were long blocks, with lots of businesses and traffic and side streets between each major intersection. That worked to her advantage.

At the second intersection, she had the timing down and eyeballed the distance accurately enough to choose her pace. The pedestrian sign started flashing four steps before she reached the curb. Joan tugged on Ulysses' leash and dashed across the street. She didn't let herself look behind, to see if Vincent had been caught by the red light. No green Cherokee passed her, and she picked up the pace.

Her chance came when a long cargo truck started to back down the driveway ahead of her. The woman guiding the driver motioned for Joan to cross the driveway before the truck got up to the sidewalk. She thanked the woman with a nod and counted her steps. At ten, she looked back. The truck blocked her view of the street, with its bumper sticking more than a foot out over the curb, causing some of the more cautious drivers to swerve outward a little. If she couldn't see Vincent, he couldn't see her.

"Come on." She wrapped the leash once more around her hand and darted right, into the gap between a bait and tackle shop and a drive-through beverage store. Ulysses loped along beside her, never hesitating. Joan felt a twinge of guilt for bringing him on this little side trip. Ridiculous. Was she answerable to a dog?

Out the other side, she paused in the shadows and put on the hat and jacket. For good measure, she slung the strap of her bag over her neck and put the jacket on over it.

"Come on, boy. Want to see my nice little safe house?"

Joan jogged down the street. She wondered if Vincent swore, and how angry he would get when he realized she had ditched him.

She saw the lighted tower of the campus the same moment the phone in her pocket rang. She jumped, nearly tripping over Ulysses. Slapping her hand over the phone to muffle the generic high-pitched cheeping, she glanced around to see if anyone watched her. She saw three other human-and-dog couples. No one glanced in her direction. Scowling, she yanked the phone from her pocket and thumbed the tiny green button that she guessed would open the connection. The phone stopped chirping at her.

"It's not that I don't trust you—"

"You don't trust anyone," Vincent interrupted.

"I'm going to scope out the safe house. It's better if you don't know where it is."

"Better for who?"

"I'll call you in half an hour, no matter what I find. Swear." Joan thumbed the red button, cutting the connection.

A quick study of the case revealed the switch that let her change from audio ring to vibrate. Joan thought of Vincent getting angry, stuck her tongue out at the phone, and jammed it back into her pocket. Almost before her fingers let go, it buzzed. She shifted it to her bag and kept walking. The safe house was only half an hour of walking away.

This section of town had neighborhoods built in the thirties, with a common alley running behind all the houses and no driveways leading onto the street. The buzzing under her fingertips finally died when she turned down the alley half a block from the safe house. Vincent was probably planning some dire punishment, but he would have to catch up with her, first. When she was sure Sophie was safe, then they could work together to convince him she had done the right thing.

It bothered her a little, to realize she wanted Vincent's approval.

The house's most attractive feature, in terms of security, was the cellar entrance. It took a month of working at night to rig the door so it would open on special hinges in the side, completely bypassing the enormous padlock and bar that ordinarily kept it closed. When Joan reached the shadowy, handkerchief-sized backyard, she got down on her knees next to the cellar door and tugged out the loose brick that hid the touch pad. The mechanism hesitated on stiff hinges for a few seconds, once she pressed the key sequence in. She glanced around in the deepening shadows and tugged off her cap, just in case Sophie watched.

Ulysses was reluctant to go down the steep steps into the cellar, and Joan didn't blame him. He whined a few times, edging toward the steps to the back door, then returning to her. Finally, she let go of the leash and started down the steps without him.

She heard his claws on the wooden boards before she was halfway down. Her trailing fingers found the switch hidden in the pebbly cinderblock wall. The door swung closed and latched. The second it clicked into place, the dim green ghost light came on. Joan grimaced at the damp on the raw cement floor. The basement had flooded since the last tenants had left and the rental agent had checked the place over.

Now wasn't the time to worry about the condition of the house. She stepped over to the rickety shelves that covered the false wall, lifted up on the third shelf and pulled. The entire wall slid out without a sound, releasing a wave of plastic-tinged fumes. The ghost light came on in the storage room. Visual inspection showed nothing had been disturbed. She slit three plastic cases with her thumbnail and extracted house keys, packets of bills and pepper spray. The rest of the supplies would have to wait until she had inspected the house. She turned on the regular lights, making the ghost lights shut off automatically. It was a matter of moments to close up the secret room and put the shelving back in place.

The wail of a police siren passing by in front of the house froze her with her foot on the second step of the stairs up to the kitchen. Joan gripped the splintery banister and waited until the sound faded away. Instead, it died abruptly. She swallowed hard and continued up the steps.

Ulysses growled and pushed her aside to go ahead of her when she was halfway up the steps. He pawed at the door, then turned and nudged her with his head, almost shoving her backwards.

"What is wrong with you?" Joan pulled down on the antique latch and shoved the door open.

The coppery smell of blood flooded over her, carried on the warm summer air.

Lights. She needed lights. The basement light didn't reach beyond the top step. Joan shoved aside Ulysses and headed to the right, reaching for the bank of switches for the kitchen, right next to the back door.

Her eyes adjusted to the semi-dark just in time to show her the rectangle of lighter twilight where the closed door should have been. Joan continued reaching for the lights on the wall by the door, even as it registered that the door hung halfway open. Her foot connected with something soft and solid as she took a step. She lost her balance and went down, sprawled across whatever it was.

Her hands landed in something tepid and sticky, coating the floor, and slid a few inches.

The stink of drying blood filled her nose.

Joan screamed and threw herself backward, off the still-warm body lying on her kitchen floor. She refused to believe that was Sophie. *Please, God, don't let them kill Sophie!*

"Police!" a man barked.

A flashlight blinded her and feet pounded on the back steps. Glass crashed and wood splintered as her front door slammed open. More running feet brought another man through from the front of the house.

The kitchen lights came on. Joan knelt on the floor, staring at her bloody hands. She stole a glance at the body and nearly wept when she saw it was a man. Not Sophie.

The policeman at the back door was huge, sunburned, what Sophie had always laughingly referred to as "Godzilla with a shave." He lowered the hand that had flipped on the lights and brought the gun back to bear on Joan while he thumbed off his flashlight and hooked it back on his belt. Ulysses stayed standing, leaning close against Joan, so she felt the silent rumble of a snarl just waiting to erupt.

What had Vincent and Kathryn told her about Ulysses being ready to defend her?

Joan pushed that thought aside. There was no way she could make a run for it with two policemen blocking her only exits, and guns in their hands. She wouldn't risk Ulysses, and there was nowhere to go if she stumbled down to the cellar again. They would follow and catch her, and probably shoot her before she could get the door open.

"I've got her," the man at the back door said. "You check out the rest of the place.

Joan swallowed a gasp but couldn't hide her shiver at the sudden mental image of someone else with a gun hiding in her house. The body had felt warm when she sprawled across it those few seconds, but not warm enough. There was an odd clay-like feeling through the clothes, as if consciousness gave flesh a different density.

The second policeman was Asian, with a buzz cut and a scar across his nose. His eyes were kind as he looked at Joan. His gaze lingered on her hands. She started to open her mouth to ask if she could wash her hands, but the first officer repeated his order, and he left.

"You're in a heap of trouble, aren't you?" Officer Godzilla's eyes glittered maliciously and his voice held a growl like a pit bull begging someone to step within his reach.

Joan swallowed down the urge to blurt that she hadn't done anything. It wasn't her fault someone had left a dead body in her house.

She hoped Sophie hadn't been here when this happened. Where was Sophie right now?

"Well, well, well, what do we have here?" He stepped through the door and reached with the toe of his boot under the baseboard of the cabinets on the other side of the kitchen. Something heavy scraped and slid out into the light.

Joan gaped at the sight of a gun, lying there on the spotted white linoleum. She felt as if she sat a very long way away from the kitchen, watching everything through a telescope. It was just a bad dream. Wasn't it?

"What'd you do? Panic when you heard the siren, and trip over him on your way out the door? Dropped your gun and got squeamish?" He shook his head and made a *tsk* noise. "Well, pick it up."

The distant feeling shattered, bringing Joan back into reality with a jolt. Her brain spun dizzily, calculating everything that was intensely wrong with this scene. This wasn't a TV police show, after all.

Shouldn't he be handcuffing her and leading her away? Shouldn't he leave the scene for the lab people to investigate? Moving the gun had to be against orders.

Telling the supposed killer to pick up a gun was just plain stupid. What if it was still loaded?

Picking it up would put her fingerprints on the gun. How would she prove to them that it wasn't hers and she hadn't fired it? Besides, her hands were sticky with drying blood. Joan clenched her hands into fists and stared down at them.

She knew what would happen next. If she picked up the gun, she would put her fingerprints on it, and Officer Godzilla would shoot her. He would claim she had lunged for the gun, threatened him and made a break for it. She would be dead and he would be a hero, and nobody would speak up for her.

"Pick it up!" he barked.

"It's not mine."

He swore and repeated the order. Joan scooted backward to put as much room as possible between her and that body. And the gun. The click of the gun cocking stopped her. Cold sweat trickled down her back. Ulysses growled.

"That dog makes one move, he's dead."

"Ulysses," she whispered, her throat dry as sand. "Be quiet. Please."

"Pick up the gun."

"No." She flinched as he took a step toward her and raised his fist.

"Hold it," another male voice snapped.

"Agent Holt." Godzilla transformed into a grinning Good Old Boy. His fist unclenched and he slid his gun back into his holster. "Moshi is checking out the rest of the house."

"And you're threatening an innocent bystander." Agent Holt stepped into the kitchen and into the light.

He had the lean look of a former athlete who hadn't let himself go to seed quite yet. Dark blue suit, white shirt without a tie, telltale bulge under his jacket from a shoulder holster. Definitely federal. Joan thought she would have known what he was even without Godzilla's response. His short, dark, sweaty hair looked like he had just raked his fingers through it. Lines around his mouth and eyes didn't come from laughter, and furrows made inroads on his forehead. Joan guessed he was in his mid-thirties, but by the time he reached forty he would look sixty.

"Innocent?" Godzilla attempted a chuckle. "We caught her with the gun, sir."

"I saw you kick the gun out into view and I heard you order her to pick it up. Sounds like tampering with evidence." Holt took a step back, leaning one hip against the counter next to the blocky old white enameled gas range. "Seems I've heard that charge made about you before."

"But—"

"You're on suspension, Wilkes."

"You don't have the authority," Godzilla-Wilkes growled.

"That's right. But your captain already knows what happened. Heard it and saw it." Holt brought a cell phone from behind his back. "As of now, you're suspended, and you'll be tied to a desk when you go back to work. If you go back. Out, Wilkes." He waited, calm, even looking slightly bored, while Wilkes turned and stomped out the back door and down the steps.

"I didn't kill him," Joan whispered. She unclenched her hands. Her fingers didn't want to unbend. "Can I wash my hands, please?"

"Can you promise me Cujo won't go after my throat?" Agent Holt attempted a smile and gestured at Ulysses with the cell phone.

"He didn't attack Godzilla, did he?" slipped out before she could stop to think.

Holt laughed, just two soft, tired barks, but Joan felt better about being alone with him. When she couldn't seem to maneuver off her knees, he reached down and helped her stand. Ulysses stepped back, giving them room to move, but then he pressed against Joan's side as she tottered across the kitchen to the sink.

"I know you didn't kill this guy," Holt said, when Joan managed to bang on the faucet knob with her fists until it turned. "I was outside when the gunshots went off, and I called for police backup. I saw you come through the back. Interesting trick with the cellar door, by the way."

"It's my house," was the only response she offered to the questions in his eyes.

"That doesn't answer many questions."

Joan shrugged and soaped her hands for the third time. She reached under the sink and brought out the scrubber pad and worked at her fingernails. Even though she couldn't see a speck of red, she could feel the blood clogging the pores of her skin.

"This is rental property," he said after several moments of quiet, broken only by splashing and the far-off sounds of a police radio squawking.

"McClosky Realtors handles it. Adrienne is my agent. I can give you her cell phone number if you want to check it out." Joan reached for the paper towels and bit back a growl when she saw the roller was empty. "Tenants always empty the place out." She turned to look in the storage cupboard, but the sight of the body lying on the floor froze her again.

"Why are you here, at this time of night, and why go through the cellar?"

"I have problems. I came without my keys and had to get them out of storage downstairs. This is a getaway place, that's all."

"Getaway from what? Where are you from? Why no luggage but that bag, if you're here for a getaway?"

"My luggage is in the car." Joan sighed, crossed her arms, and leaned back against the cabinet. She could just dry her hands on her jacket. "Ulysses was restless and my friend wanted to stop to get gas and something to eat, so I decided to walk the rest of the way."

"Shouldn't your friend be here by now?"

Joan shrugged, fighting the sickening drop in her stomach. If Vincent had come with her, what would have happened? She felt dizzy with the longing for someone to stand between her and this Fed. What was wrong with her, that she wanted someone to depend on?

Why had she been so stupid, and run away from Vincent? She almost looked forward to the scolding she would get from him once they met up again. Better that Vincent punish her now than to see disappointment or disgust on her father's face.

And wasn't that frightening, that only after a few days, she cared very much what this stranger with a blood bond to her thought about her?

Officer Moshi and two more plainclothes men came into the kitchen from the front of the house, saving Joan from having to answer Holt's question. They looked curiously at Joan but deferred to his leadership. One man took down her basic information: name, address, driver's license. Joan thought about her precious, thoroughly legal identity, and wondered if she would have to abandon it after this. The temptation to use one of her false identities, to provide a smoke screen and distract these people if she tried to make a break for it nearly overwhelmed her. That knowledge frightened her. She stayed quiet, torn between her options, while Agent Holt took the reports from the other three, gave them more instructions, then looked at Joan and gestured at the back door.

"Time to leave the crime scene. Anything you want to take with you before we go?"

Chapter Twenty-One

"Go where?" Joan thought of Sophie, hopefully hiding in the darkness somewhere. What would her soul-sister think of police cars, lights flashing, and guns everywhere?

Holt simply stood there, a hand out, waiting patiently for her to move. Nobody was going in through the open back door until she moved. Joan looked at Ulysses. He didn't seem to vibrate with protective anger, as he had when Officer Godzilla was around. Was that a good sign?

She would have to learn to pay better attention to him and study the world through his senses. He hadn't wanted to go into the house, hadn't wanted her to open the door from the cellar. If she had listened, if she had stayed hidden, if she had detoured around the house, things might be very different now.

"You'll need these." Joan dug into her pocket, brought out the house keys, and handed them to Holt. He passed them along to the taller of the plainclothes officers.

At Holt's car, he let her sit in the front seat, once they got Ulysses situated in the back. Joan leaned against the door and didn't miss the discrete click when the automatic locks went down the moment the agent put the car into gear. She looked around, wishing for a glimpse of the Cherokee. Just her luck. When she wanted Vincent's help, he wasn't anywhere around. And just whose fault was that, after all?

Why had someone been shot inside her house? The place had been emptied of its last tenants a little more than two weeks ago. There was no reason for anyone to be inside. Adrienne was a good caretaker, stopping by at intervals to check out the place, look for signs of tampering, and to make sure nothing happened, like the basement drains backing up again.

"Were you meeting someone at that house?" Holt asked out of the darkness.

"I don't know who that was on my floor."

"You know, I used to think it was irritating when people answered my questions with more questions." He flashed her a thin smile. "You go completely away from the subject."

"Who are you with, then? FBI? DEA? Black Ops?" Joan flinched, wondering why that slid out, why she had even been thinking that. Maybe her wish for Vincent to come running to the rescue was a little stronger than she guessed.

"I'm guessing whoever got killed was left as a warning for whoever you came here to meet." He glanced once more at her and finally started the engine.

There was a reason, Joan knew, why she preferred working through computers, holding people at a distance, communicating in writing, never face-to-face. In-person encounters denied her time to weigh options, to guess how someone would react, to read between the lines.

"I have a friend who's in trouble," she began slowly, once Holt had pulled out of the alley onto the side street. "People are after her. We were supposed to meet, and I was going to get her to a better hiding place."

"What kind of people?"

"We don't know. All we can do is guess." She took a deep breath. In for a penny, in for a pound, as she had read in a book once. "She's good at computers, and the people tracking us — her, were following her trail from her latest job."

"She must be very good with computers," he muttered.

Joan tugged her jacket closer around herself, feeling cold despite the warm night. She thought of the dead man, still warm. If she had been a little faster getting away from Vincent, she might have walked in on the shooting.

Holt had been there, outside, heard the shooting, and saw her go in.

"Why were you at the house? Did you follow the man who got shot?"

"I'm the one asking the questions." He shifted into the turn lane and stopped at a red light. "If the people looking for your friend are the same ones I'm trying to track down..." He shrugged. "She's in a heap of trouble. Could cost her life, if she's not careful. And if you don't cooperate."

Joan shook her head. She refused to retort that she was cooperating, because she very much feared she would whine when she said it. Then she remembered what Vincent had said when he contacted his friend or accomplice or whatever Tiger could be called.

"It's big, isn't it?" Her stomach turned over. "It's a whole bunch of different agencies, all working together. National and international. Lots of trouble."

Holt gave her a look hard to read in the darkness of the car and didn't answer. Maybe that was all the answer she needed. Joan wished she had the right to pray.

Her head hurt. She blinked hard to fight tears. Shifting around on the seat, she dug into her bag and pulled out the cell phone. Time to admit she couldn't do it on her own and ask for help. There was no reason for God to listen to her, but if she could get Vincent to listen, he could work on God. She turned the phone on and thumbed through the directory. The only phone number in the memory was Vincent's.

The phone still rang when Holt pulled into a parking lot surrounded by bushes, in front of a squat office building that blazed with lights. Joan held onto the phone and left it ringing, waiting for Vincent to answer, almost eager to hear him chew her out. But Vincent didn't answer, even after she got out of the car and let Holt escort her and Ulysses up four steps and into the building.

"Stone wants to see you and your guest yesterday," a woman in a security guard uniform said, as Holt led Joan toward the elevator.

"Great." He caught hold of Joan's arm. Ulysses growled and slid between them, knocking the agent off balance. "He's going to get himself or you killed if that keeps up. Can't you control him?"

"I wouldn't be here if *I'd* listened to *him*." Joan considered letting Ulysses off his leash. Then she thought of an entire building full of agents, all carrying guns, all ready to shoot anything that looked threatening. Ulysses in protective mode could be very threatening, even if he never opened his mouth.

Holt led her down another hallway to the right of the elevator. It opened into a massive room, studded with support pillars. Joan guessed all the walls had been taken out, reducing a series of office suites into one large room. A corner had been sectioned off with floor-to-ceiling deep amber glass partitions. Holt headed for it and its half-open doorway. Ulysses whined and strained at the leash when they were still five steps away. Joan hesitated, but Holt gestured for her to go through first.

Vincent perched on the edge of a massive L-shaped desk, arms crossed, watching the doorway. He never took his gaze off Joan, even when Ulysses tugged the leash out of her limp hand, sat down at his feet, and put a paw on his knee.

"You," Holt growled. He shoved the door closed, hard enough to slam. "Chief—"

The lean, ginger-haired man sitting behind the desk stopped him with an upraised hand. "Extenuating circumstances, Holt."

"Extenuating circumstances?"

"You okay, Joan?" Vincent ignored Holt, who glowered at him from only three steps away.

"Have a seat, Miss Archer." Stone gestured at the area of the office behind her.

"Am I going to get my head handed back to me?" She took a step back toward the low, brown leather sofa pushed against the far wall.

"If you don't turn off that phone, you might." Vincent dug in his back pocket, brought out his phone, and slapped it down on the desk. It rattled and buzzed against the surface.

"Sorry," she said, her voice dropping to a whisper. She pressed the red button and closed the phone, then offered it to him.

The air got a little easier to breathe when one corner of Vincent's mouth twitched upward. He shook his head and gestured for her to keep the phone. She put it back in her pocket.

Holt swore and jammed his fists into his hips. He jerked his chin in Vincent's direction. "Is he your friend? The one holding your luggage?" The sneer in his voice made Joan wince, then bristle deep inside.

"You don't know what's going on," she began.

"You know, I really believed you were innocent, despite your —" He gestured at her, then shook his head. "That you just got caught in the wrong place at the wrong time. Finding out you're mixed up with Javelin here makes me rethink everything."

"That's enough, Holt," Stone snapped.

Joan met Vincent's steady gaze. She mouthed, *Javelin?* but he didn't even blink, gave no indication that he had any idea what she was talking about. Joan supposed she deserved that.

"Sir, do you know what this man has done?" Holt jammed his clenched fists down on the edge of Stone's desk.

"I do. And I know what you and other good men have had to do for the sake of this country." Stone leaned back in his chair, visibly making an effort to relax. "That was a long time ago, when we were all very different people."

"Javelin and his gang don't change. They're programmed to be what they are."

"God can change the best and the worst kind of programming," Vincent said, his tone mild. He shrugged and met Holt's burning gaze with a cool calm that Joan envied. "I'm out of that game, for good."

"Going religious is the oldest trick in the book. I don't buy it."

"That's enough, Holt," Stone repeated.

At the same time, Vincent said, "You don't have to. God is the one I'm answerable to now. He's a lot better at looking inside people's heads and seeing their true motivation. How about you?"

"Can it." Stone stood up, bracing his arms on the desk and giving Holt a look that made Joan feel a little scorched, and he wasn't even looking at her. "Javelin is dead, as far as I'm concerned. Vincent is a friend and an ally, and it looks like he and Miss Archer here might be able to give us a few breaks in the Salamander case. I suggest you shut up and put your past and your vendettas on the back burner."

"Look," Joan said. "I don't know what all you're referring to, but I can guess. Vincent isn't the one who tripped over a dead body. He's supposed to be watching out for me, and I screwed up, okay?" She looked away from both men, who had good reason to be angry with her, and met Stone's blue-eyed gaze as it turned amused. Instinct took a leap. "Are you Tiger?"

Holt's mouth dropped open, Vincent bowed his head and shook it, and Chief Stone laughed quietly. He gestured for them all to sit down. Joan settled on the edge of the sofa. Ulysses came back to her and curled up at her feet. Vincent slid off the desk and moved over to lean against the wall, where he could see everyone. Holt pulled a folding chair away from the wall, unfolded it, and straddled it backwards.

"Chief, are you going to let me know what's going on here?" Holt asked, his voice a little less tense now.

"First, tell us what happened." Stone held out his hand. "Pictures?"

"Ought to be good." Holt pulled a slim digital camera from his pocket and handed it over as he related the events of that evening.

Stone took a memory card from the camera and inserted it in one of a dozen slots in his computer. Vincent stood still, barely moving. Joan watched him until he blinked, to be sure he hadn't turned to stone.

Holt and his team had been following two men who were suspected assistants to a freelance terrorist, code named Salamander. Halfway through the day, they realized the two men tailed someone else, so intently they didn't realize they had been identified and were being trailed. At sunset, the quarry led the two men to the house.

"Sophie?" Vincent asked,

"Probably. I hope not." Joan shrugged. She wasn't quite sure if she wanted to know where Sophie was. On the loose, she was free and safe.

"Sir?" Holt stepped around the desk and turned the computer monitor so they could all see. He flipped through several screens until an index of pictures came up. He clicked on one and it enlarged to fill the screen.

Joan held her breath and refused to blink, even though her eyes burned wet. She knew the three men watched her, and she didn't care what she looked like or what they thought of her.

Sophie stood under the big, ugly, droopy willow in the side yard between the safe house and the enormous, cat-filled house next door. She had a sling bag hanging across her chest, resting low on her hip. Her computer carrying case rested on her other hip, its strap crossing her chest, giving her a bandito look of bandoleers. Sophie looked hot and sweaty, her eyes big, like they became when she was exhausted.

All the colors were odd, and Joan guessed the photo had been taken at dusk, artificially enhanced to take in as much light as possible. The beads in Sophie's dozens of narrow braids looked garish. She stood with her arms reaching above her head to the lowest branches. Her head tipped back, slightly turned, as if she heard or saw something.

"Right after I got this picture, the subject stepped behind that tree and vanished." Holt clicked, minimizing the photo, and brought up another one, with two men in it.

Joan flinched, recognizing the dead man she had fallen over in the kitchen. He was thick and scowly, and looked like he was ready to punch someone. His mouth was open, twisted in what was probably argument. His lean, shaggy blond friend looked just as irritated. It wasn't a stretch of the imagination to picture the two men arguing, until one shot the other. The question was: why?

"What do you mean, she vanished?" Vincent said.

"These two ducked behind the tree right after we lost sight of her. A few seconds later, they came out the other side of the tree, guns out, looking worse than they do here." Holt actually smiled for a moment. "As far as we could tell, the woman just vanished."

A smile inched onto Joan's face as hope sprouted a tiny root deep inside.

"You okay?" Vincent said.

"Sophie is okay. At least," she hurried to correct herself, "there's a chance she's okay. If nobody else was in the house. If the other guy got scared away."

"Oh, that tells us a lot," Stone said. "What happened to her?"

"She climbed the tree. We have a secret entrance into the attic, right under the eaves where the tree branches hide everything."

"She's inside?" Vincent asked.

"I hope so. Take me back to the house—"

"No," Holt and Stone said in chorus. The agent stepped back, deferring to his superior.

"After what just went down, that house is probably under observation from twenty different sides. Salamander will kill her own people to send a message to her enemies. That man was left for either you or your friend to find. Or one of my men, if they weren't as good at keeping undetected as they think," Stone added with a sideways glance at Holt. "Will your friend be all right if we don't go back for a day or two? To let things calm down."

"We have food stored there. And she can get water and use the toilet. But she'll worry about me… especially if she saw me leaving with Inspector Detector."

To her surprise, Holt grinned at her jibe. She wondered if he understood the reference to the old *Speed Racer* cartoons.

"We'll keep an eye on the house, then, and make sure nobody else gets inside," Stone said, nodding. "If we make it obvious we're watching the place, waiting for someone to return, Salamander and her people will probably steer a wide course around it."

"Who's this Salamander?" Vincent asked. He ignored the sharp look Holt cast him.

Joan wondered if she dared ask him eventually about his dark past. It was obvious Vincent had been involved in something pretty shady, and Holt knew about it. Why was Stone so calm and ready to believe Vincent had changed, when his underling wasn't?

"Now that's the big news of the night," Holt said. He stepped in and manipulated the mouse again. Before he clicked on the second photo from the top in the index, he gave Joan a long, searching look.

"What?" she asked.

"Just wondering what your reaction will be, that's all." He glanced at his superior and Vincent. "Four days ago, we got a good, clear shot of Salamander. No more relying on composite sketches and blurred photos. Too bad we couldn't have got a clear shot with a rifle."

"Holt," Stone said softly.

The younger agent nodded, accepting the rebuke. He turned the monitor a little more so they all had a better view, and clicked on the photo. Holt watched Joan, rather than the screen.

She saw a woman holding a limp, wide-brimmed straw hat in her hand. Her other hand raked through her medium brown hair and held sunglasses between two fingers. Her square face drooped with a scowl, and her eyes were wide with anger. Hazel eyes. Stubby nose. Squarish chin. If she lost maybe thirty pounds, she would …

Joan took a deep breath. Something was definitely wrong with her tonight, slowing down her brain. The woman looked a lot like Nikki had last Easter, when she had let her foster sisters dress her up with a big, floppy hat and dangling earrings and ribbons and bows. But a Nikki with a lot of years on her and an extra fifty pounds. A Nikki who looked like she was ready to chop somebody's head off.

And Nikki James looked like her.

"That's Salamander?" Joan whispered and leaned against the desk when she wanted to back away.

"Something going on here, Holt?" Stone asked.

"Maybe. You know her by another name?" Holt watched Joan.

By this time, Stone and Vincent were both watching her, only taking momentary glances at the image on the screen.

"I knew her by a lot of names." Nausea threatened to close her throat. "My—" She swallowed and tried again. "Carter knew her as Elaine."

"It's okay." Vincent came around the side of the desk and rested a hand on Joan's shoulder. She welcomed his touch, the comfort and support offered. Then Ulysses whined and leaned hard against her, and she nearly lost it.

Something was definitely wrong, that she welcomed the comfort of a big dog, and the sympathy of a man she hadn't trusted only a few hours ago.

"Carter?" Stone said. "Your boss? What exactly do you have to do with the Arc Foundation, Miss Archer?"

"I have no idea yet." Joan met his frowning gaze. "But this is all starting to make some really nasty sense. You guys are after Salamander. That's why you brought me here, instead of letting the police handle the whole thing. Because I look like her. Because you think there's some connection, and the whole coincidence with the house and Sophie and the dead guy and my …" A choked laugh escaped her. It was either laugh or scream. "And my gizmos and secret entrances. Well, there is a connection."

She glanced once more at Vincent, aching for the support, needing it, grateful for it. What overwhelmed her was the surprised realization that she wished her father was there. But he didn't need to see this ugliness, and she didn't want him to see it. Joan nodded and took a deep breath.

"I escaped her when I was a kid. So she wants me dead. I'm a traitor. Salamander is after Sophie, to get to me." She swallowed hard. "I call her Niobe, and she's my mother."

~~~~~

Stone sent Holt off on a long series of errands that Joan suspected were to keep the younger agent as far from Vincent as possible. She was grateful. She curled up on the couch on the far side of the office, stroked Ulysses' fur, and listened half-heartedly to Vincent and Stone go over maps and strategies. Some time during the long night, someone brought food; sandwiches, apples, glasses of milk, and a big carafe of coffee. Joan thought it odd that the agency used glassware and decent stoneware, rather than paper plates and cups. She supposed she had seen too many police movies and TV shows, and assumed it was a rule to only drink from paper cups and eat stale food out of dispensing machines.

Eventually, Stone sent her and Vincent, without the expected escort, to a hotel close by. Joan waited for the lecture to start, as soon as they got in the Cherokee. Vincent didn't even look at her, said nothing, just turned the key and drove away. She noticed him checking the rearview mirrors constantly, almost more than he looked ahead of them. That started other thoughts.

"You followed me to the house, didn't you? You recognized Holt and you knew what he was doing, where he would take me."

"How could I follow you to the house? You lost me." Vincent gave her one sharp glance. "You're good, kiddo. Just might keep your skin in one piece. For a while, anyway."

"Okay, so I lost you on the street, but you still found me at the house." She inhaled sharply, furious at both him and herself when the answer jumped into her head. "The homing signal in the phone."

"Doesn't do a whole heck of a lot of good if you're injured or you can't turn on your phone, and you need help. Ulysses sure can't do it." His shoulders hunched and she watched him grip the wheel a little tighter. "You have a big problem with trust, Joan Archer. You didn't trust me with your little safe house, and it nearly cost you."

"I know," she whispered, when he paused to take a breath. "If I had been a few minutes earlier, that could have been me dead on the floor."

"No. They would have caught you and used you to lure Sophie out of hiding and then you'd both be up Schist Creek without a dang boat, much less a paddle." He thumped hard on the steering wheel. That surprised Joan. Usually Vincent was so elegantly controlled.
~~~~~

Chapter Twenty-Two

"I'm sorry." The words caught in her throat. She couldn't remember the last time she had apologized. Joan avoided entanglements, so she would never need to apologize for anything.

"Your old man warned me you'd fight. Should have known you were a little too quiet." He glanced at her, just before pulling into the parking lot of the little hotel.

It was a horseshoe, three stories tall, with outside doors and walkways looking out over an inner courtyard and swimming pool. Joan thought she could point out a dozen weaknesses that would make this place dangerous to stay in. A dozen places where she and Vincent could be ambushed.

At the same time, she could imagine slipping out through the shadows, vanishing easily if someone came after her. She had no assurance that Niobe's people hadn't been able to follow her from the safe house to the agency's office building to here. No matter how good Stone's people were, nothing was sure. Nothing except what she could do for herself. And tonight had certainly proved how fallible she was.

Maybe she had been fooling herself all along. Maybe Niobe had been able to find her as easily as Carter had. She had left her alone, to get complacent, watching from the shadows, waiting for the perfect moment to swoop down and destroy everything precious to her. And everyone. Joan thought of Nikki. Had she spent too much time with her half-sister, enough to draw attention to her? She hoped not.

Please, God, Nikki belongs to You even if I don't. Take care of her. Don't let anything happen to her because I'm stupid. And Sophie, she's —

"You okay?" Vincent stood in the open passenger door and grasped her shoulder to shake her a little.

They had parked by the open stairway in the gap between two wings of the building. Ulysses stood on the pavement behind Vincent, waiting.

"Fine." Joan turned to slide out of the seat. She ached all over. A faint glimmer of light along the horizon threatened an early dawn. She felt old, suddenly. Old and useless and taken down about a dozen pegs in her estimation of her abilities and intelligence.

She could still feel the sticky, cooling blood on her hands.

That could have been her. Or Sophie.

Why had Niobe killed one of her own people? It didn't make any sense. Of course, very little that her mother had done had ever made any sense. The woman had lived by her own code, in a seething, cold fury because the world didn't move as she demanded.

"You're not fine." Vincent hooked his arm through hers, to pull her out of the seat and lead her up the stairs. "But you will be. Hot bath, good long sleep, decent food."

"Sophie."

"We'll get her out of there. Stone's right, though. As long as we don't go near that house and she doesn't make a move or a sound, she'll be fine. Let them concentrate on tracking down Salamander. You and I will work on getting to Sophie without anyone knowing what happened."

"Easier said than done." Joan blinked and found herself on the second floor, waiting while Vincent pulled out the rectangular, dark green plastic key chains Stone had given him.

Jumping from a second-floor window was easy and relatively safe. Would anyone expect her to do it?

"You'd better learn to pray, that's all I can say." Vincent unlocked the first door and stepped in, dragging her in after him. The moment Ulysses stepped into the room, he shut the door. He went immediately to the connecting door and opened it.

"Not that easy." Hadn't she been doing more praying in the last few days, unintentionally, than she had done in several years?

"Nothing is ever easy. Stay here." He didn't wait for her response but went into the connecting room and looked around. Joan waited, not taking a step. She couldn't help a tiny smile when Vincent came back, saw she hadn't moved, and rolled his eyes in exasperation. "Your room. Get some sleep."

"Bath, first." She rubbed at her hands.

"First dead guy you ever saw?" His voice was soft.

"Touched." Joan shuddered. "I saw a lot of things before I got away from… why do they call her Salamander?"

"Probably because she has a gift for walking through fire without getting burned." Vincent dropped down heavily on the end of the first bed. "You saw her kill people?"

"She put my baby sister in a stolen car and left her in the middle of a river in a storm. Just walked away." She wrapped her arms around herself and retreated into the room.

"Sorry, kiddo."

The sympathy in his voice relaxed something cold and hard and tight, deep inside her. Joan hurried into the bathroom, in case she started crying. She didn't bother trying to close the connecting door. She knew Vincent would demand that it stay open.

~~~~~

Vincent woke her just before noon. Holt brought a bag of burgers and escorted them back to the safe house. The agents watching the house had determined that no one was inside, but they still wanted Joan to go inside
~~~~~

and look around. With protection.

"They don't mean just Ulysses, do they?" she murmured, when she and Vincent were alone in the windowless van the agency used for transport. Holt had climbed out of the driver's seat to confer with the two agents set up as a lawn care company three houses down from the house.

Joan wondered if the agency realized what a stereotype it was to use a dark, windowless van for any kind of government activity. It was always the first thing people suspected. Then again, maybe they figured since everyone expected it, no one would believe it when they saw it.

Maybe the strain of all this affected her mind? What happened to her ability to focus and let nothing sidetrack her until "mission accomplished"?

Joan decided not to tell any of them that Sophie could still be in the house, despite what all the high-tech scanning instruments might say. That was why they had considered the house safe. Lots of hiding places, and metallic screens to bounce signals and sound waves and heat. Sophie could very well be tucked up safe and quiet in the attic, reading or working on her computer, and chewing her fingernails down to the quick, worrying about Joan.

Holt came back and took the van around the block, to come up on the alley behind the houses from the opposite direction. His watchers claimed all was still clear and no one had approached the house since the police left last night. With noon traffic on the surrounding streets, anyone going into the house would have a good chance of being unnoticed.

Joan knew if she had a good chance of being unseen in all the traffic and bustle, the enemy had just as good a chance of invisibility. Were they using her as bait, or testing her? That was all right. She didn't trust these people any more than they trusted her.

Holt had brought a costume for her: short cotton sundress, glittery clips for her hair, big sunglasses, a flowered purse that clashed with the pattern of the dress, and sandals. She considered protesting that she needed to shave her legs, then decided the agent was still in a bad mood and wouldn't react well. Whatever grudge Holt had against Vincent, he wasn't mature enough to keep it from spilling over on others.

On the other hand, she supposed that if Vincent was her bodyguard or keeper, that tarred her with the same brush of whatever past sins Holt still held against him.

Joan walked down the street ten minutes later, in costume and amused to find she liked being placed firmly on Vincent's team. He hadn't let her down yet. He supported her, teased her, listened when she shared one of her secret pains, and chewed her out when she needed it.

Kind of like a father would, maybe?

"I have a father. Or could have a father," she muttered. "Deal with it when all this is over. Sophie is the priority."

Ulysses stopped and looked at her over the gleaming, slicked-down fur on his shoulder. It was hard to disguise a big dog like him, but Vincent had controlled him long enough to brush something like gel into his fur to make it smooth, so he didn't look quite like a dark gray bear. That glittery leash and prissy, decorative collar with all sorts of jangling tags added to the impression of a useless dog that had been bought for show and nothing else.

"Sorry," she muttered. Ulysses' dignity meant something to her.

Maybe all this soul-searching was a result of not enough sleep, with worry and guilt piled on. Why was she thinking about Ulysses' feelings and Vincent being a friend and ally, and making plans to get to know her father?

Her musings stopped as she reached the gravel path between the old houses. Now was the test of Ulysses' training and her faith in Vincent's promises. She tugged three times on the leash and dropped it to the right, trying to make it look like the glittery leather slipped from her fingers. Ulysses took off like a shot, dashing down the path, his paws crunching on the stones. Joan followed. She bit her lip against a grin, grateful she had refused the high-heeled sandals Holt had brought for her disguise, and insisted on low, plain white ones. The soles were still slippery, but much easier for running. And climbing, if necessary.

In the shadows between the houses, where the thick trees kept even the noonday sun from penetrating, she pulled out her keys and darted up the back steps. The hairs prickled on the back of her neck as she unlocked the door. Joan fought not to look behind herself, half-expecting to see someone emerge from the peonies in the neighbor's yard, with an Uzi pointed at her.

Chalk and bloodstains still marked the floor where the body had lain last night. Joan carefully stepped around it and eased through the house, with Ulysses beside her. Before going through each doorway, she paused and watched the dog. He didn't stop, didn't growl, and showed nothing but interest in the new territory.

There was something to be said for having another set of senses to trust.

The stairs to the attic were hidden in the back of a closet, with shelving jury-rigged on the right side of the steps. The closet was still locked, and from first glance, the canned goods, paper supplies, and dry food like oatmeal and pasta had been untouched by the last set of tenants. Joan climbed the steps easily and tried not to pause when she reached the fake wall. She didn't want any watchers with their motion and heat detectors and ultra-sensitive microphones to figure out how she opened the panel and got into the secret room.

A can of sirloin burger soup sat upside down on the little two-seater table, the label facing Joan, in the twelve o'clock position on the circle pattern inlaid in the wood. That was all she needed to know.

Sophie had been there and left. The type of soup indicated the situation, and the position chose the time she would come back to the house to meet Joan.

Red meat rhymed with dead meat, meaning the situation was bad. The upside down can meant night, versus a right side up can for day, meaning midnight instead of noon.

Joan wouldn't tell any of Holt's people, but she would tell Vincent. He had bailed her out of what could have been a tough situation, just by being friendly with Stone. She supposed it had been a mistake to confess that Salamander was her mother. She had been doing a lot of stupid things lately, though. Maybe she was losing her mind.

She nodded as she closed and locked the door to the stairs. Yes, she would definitely trust Vincent and ask for his advice and backup when she went to meet Sophie tonight. After all, he had advised her not to trust Holt's people with any of the security tricks hidden in the house. He had argued to let her go in alone, so no one could see the hidden room.

"Ready to go?" she asked Ulysses. He looked up and down the hallway, then turned and trotted back to the kitchen. Joan noticed the dog went around the place where the body had lain, on his way to the back door. He stepped outside and down the steps, his fur standing up despite the goo used to smooth it.

Ulysses paused, his front feet on the ground and his back feet still on the steps. Joan felt the tension cut through him and stumbled backwards almost the second the dog did a 180-degree turn and charged at her. She went down, catching a flash of dark blue, then a glint of sunlight on metal. And then heard the gunshot.

Her back hit the door and Ulysses' weight left her with the impact of a rocket launching. Joan grabbed for the leash that dangled out behind him like a comet's tail. Her line of sight followed him, his feet never seeming to touch the ground. Officer Godzilla emerged from the peonies next door and squeezed off another shot.

Joan screamed, imagining Ulysses running straight into that bullet and going down. The next instant, dog and man collided. She thought she heard the crunch of bones breaking as they went down. Or was that just the snapping of peony stalks? She flung herself forward, nearly going on hands and knees for the first two steps before she got upright. Two men in lawn care uniform polo shirts and shorts converged from one side, Vincent from another. Holt followed him, gun out but in no hurry. Joan hated him.

"Ulysses!" She stretched out a hand to the dog and choked as he leaped off the gasping, red-faced, prone officer and ran to her, wriggling like a puppy. She dropped to her knees and wrapped her arms around him. "Good boy. Thank you. What a smart boy." She ran her hands over his flanks, searching for blood.

The sound of flesh and bone colliding with flesh and bone startled her. Joan looked up to see Officer Godzilla fly backwards, and Vincent standing there with one arm stretched out. He reminded her of a vengeful wizard that had flung his enemy away with a burst of power.

"That's enough," Holt said, stepping into the scene. His two men went down on their knees to restrain the officer with blood on his face.

Vincent had punched him. Maybe he liked her? Enough to get angry on her behalf? Joan shook her head, trying to drive the thought away. She definitely needed some sleep.

"What are you doing in uniform?" Holt asked, when his two agents had Godzilla on his feet, his hands cuffed behind his back.

"All the better to blend in during a police operation," Vincent offered. Holt glared at him but didn't contradict him. "You okay?" he continued, turning to Joan.

"Fine. A little bruised, but I don't mind." She stood up, feeling a little shaky, hating it that everyone watched her, including the crooked cop who had just tried to kill her. "This is exactly why I don't like dresses. Something always goes wrong when I put one on."

"Nobody could see up your skirt, if that's what you're worried about." He winked at her.

Even Holt grinned at that one. Just for a few seconds. Then he turned back to the prisoner. Vincent wrapped an arm around her and led her down the alley, to the van that pulled up on the street and waited for them. Ulysses ran ahead.

"He saved my life," she said.

"That's what he's there for."

"Thanks. For him."

"That's what I'm here for, too."

"My own mother wants me dead."

"You know," he drawled, as they reached the van, "I just can't imagine you being such a bad kid she'd go crazy like that. Must be change of life or something."

Joan choked on something that felt like a giggle and a sob mixed together. She took the bench seat in the middle of the van and wrapped her arms around Ulysses when he climbed up next to her.

"They didn't get Sophie. At least, not yet," she whispered, when Vincent settled down onto the bench seat, putting the dog between them.

He held a finger up to his lips, signaling her to silence, and glanced at the agent driving the van. He waited until Holt came up to the van and gave the driver instructions.

"Here?" he murmured. She nodded. "When?"

"Midnight."

"It's a date." He watched Holt. "You know, you came pretty close to biting the bullet. Literally."

"I know." Joan wished she had her jeans on, so she could curl into a little ball.

"Do you know where you'd go, if you had died?"

"Oh, yeah." She closed her eyes. "But I figure, the way my entire life has been, I'm already in Hell, so what's the difference?"

"A big difference." Vincent startled her, touching her face, two fingers under her chin and his thumb stroking the line of her cheekbone. His hands were warm and gentle. "The thing you gotta remember is that you still have time to get out of Hell permanently."

She nodded and closed her eyes before she cried. She definitely needed some sleep.

And she definitely couldn't tell Vincent he was wrong. It wasn't a matter of avoiding Hell, but being refused entrance into Heaven.

~~~~~

Joan rolled over on the hotel bed and her outstretched hand encountered fur. She smiled, rising from the depths of dream-free sleep. She had to keep Ulysses, no matter what she decided to do with her life. Weirdly enough, knowing the big dog was there, lying on the bed, ready to guard her or offer a sympathetic whine when she needed it comforted her, helped her relax. So, he couldn't talk—what difference did that make? He kept her nightmare away. He could still communicate with his eyes, his body language, his actions. Once she learned to pay attention and trust him, Joan knew her life could only be better.

Vincent had told her she needed to learn to trust.

She heard him speaking in the room next door. Joan raised her head and looked at the connecting door, surprised to see it was closed. Why would Vincent close it? The sound of the door closing and latching had awakened her. What was going on?

Ulysses followed her, dropping down to the floor without a sound, when Joan got up and crossed the room to the door. She tugged on the panel just enough to glimpse around it. There was darkness on the other side, meaning the panel on Vincent's side was closed, too. She pulled her half of the door open and pressed her ear against the thin gap.

"I don't know what kind of game you're playing, Holt, but it's not funny," Vincent said.

"No game." Holt paced, almost stomping on the hotel carpeting. "The records don't lie. Joan Archer is Natalia Benidetto, a computer hacker wanted by the International Courts and InterPol, among others."

"You're wrong." Vincent sounded almost bored. Joan wondered how many times he had repeated himself.

"Fingerprints don't lie."

"Records can be tampered with. She told us how her mother's out to destroy her. Why not play with the records and frame her, hang an identity on her that'll get her locked up? You know how many assassinations happen every year in prisons? We're helping the crooks clean house."

"We?" Holt's voice lowered the temperature in the room, sending chills
~~~~~

down Joan's back. "Don't you dare put yourself on the same team with me. Javelin."

"Like it or not, we are on the same side, so just relax, Dick Tracy."

Joan muffled a snort of laughter. She didn't think Vincent was the sarcastic type. Or was he deliberately ruffling Holt's feathers? If so, why? And why shut the connecting doors between their rooms, after they had hung open all morning and afternoon?

Joan wished she had a long history of working with Vincent, so she could know what he wanted her to do.

She knew what she wanted to do, however.

Run. As fast and as far as she could. Immediately. If Agent Holt thought she was an international criminal, then he was here to take her in. From the tone of his voice, Joan suspected he'd like to take Vincent in, too. She wondered what stopped him. Maybe Stone protected him?

Stone wouldn't protect her, because he didn't know her. Even Vincent vouching for her didn't seem to be enough. For all she knew, Stone had sent Holt out here to pick her up.

Joan pulled on her shoes, hooked the strap of her purse over her neck and across her chest, and went to the balcony that looked out over the back of the hotel. Someone had put a mini-golf course in there, but it had failed. The pitiful remains of the putting greens, a dry waterfall, a crumpled windmill and other cheesy obstacles offered some hiding places. Still, there was an awful lot of open ground to traverse. She wished it were full dark instead of just late afternoon. If she got down to the ground fast enough and away before Holt got into her room, she might just make it to the thick border of trees and beyond that fence. Then she would be beyond his sight, beyond his reach, and on her own.

Why didn't that feel good? Wasn't it her normal state? Alone and on her own and depending on no one.

She had to think. She had to stop feeling. She had to work only with facts.

Chapter Twenty-Three

Holt had her fingerprints. How did he get them? Joan nearly groaned aloud as she remembered the glass of milk with her dinner last night. She should have realized there was an ulterior motive for feeding her and Vincent and avoiding cardboard cups and plates.

So, someone had fiddled with the records to put her name and face on an international criminal. She supposed she should be grateful she hadn't been labeled a murdering psychopath. Like mother, like daughter. Likely Officer Godzilla had been part of it, but Joan couldn't quite figure out how or why yet, or how she would even convince anyone.

She had to stay free, even if it was only long enough to get Sophie to safety. Joan stepped up to the balcony and leaned over the edge, pretending to admire the view, just in case someone was watching. The argument in the other room got louder. From the few words she caught, Holt threw Vincent's past crimes back in his face, mocking his new religious life. Did Vincent goad him, driving him to more volume, to warn her, maybe to buy her time to react? Joan hoped so.

Any second now, Holt would realize his mistake and come barging through the connecting door after her.

Joan fought the urge to lock the connecting door. Instead, she picked up the thin pad of hotel stationery and scribbled a note, putting the time for nearly half an hour earlier, and promising to be back in another fifteen minutes. Any longer, Holt might decide to go looking for her, rather than wait for her to return.

She slipped the cell phone into her purse, and prayed Vincent wouldn't use the homing device. Or if he did, he wouldn't tell Holt.

All that mattered was getting Sophie to safety.

"Please, God," she whispered, and couldn't finish as she swung her leg over the railing and perched there. Ulysses whined. She turned to look at him. He backed up into the room and ran. Before Joan could try to stop him, he sailed right at her and over the railing. She watched with her heart in her throat, until the dog landed and rolled and got back to his feet.

She was definitely in trouble, worrying about a dog of all things.

Correction: She was in trouble if she tried to go back to her normal life without Ulysses.

Joan slid down the balcony railing support post, letting her legs dangle, and hung onto the cement pad. She swung her legs forward and back, and pushed off when her legs were on the outward swing. She landed with a thud and crashed into some rusty-looking bushes planted around the foundation of the hotel. No one seemed to hear, or at least no one was in a hurry to come investigate the noise. Joan didn't wait for them but got to her feet and ran.

Would they expect her to head for the neighborhood around the safe house, or would they think she was too smart for that? Joan knew she could work herself into a headache, trying to predict what the agents would decide and do, and what they might think she would do. She compromised by walking as fast as she could at a ninety-degree angle to where she wanted to be. She had only a vague idea of the neighborhood, but there had to be some place where she could waste time, hide in plain sight, until it was time to head back for Sophie. She couldn't even try to raise Sophie on her cell phone. Joan gritted her teeth and vowed she would think of some better way to protect them both in the future.

What did it matter that her enemies couldn't find her, if she let her closest friend, her almost-sister, get captured, hurt, even killed?

She stopped after an hour and went into a McDonald's for air conditioning, to get off the street, and to get something to drink. Ulysses caught hold of the side seam of her jeans in his teeth, effectively stopping her as she reached for the door handle. He wasn't growling and didn't look alert or upset, so it took her a minute to figure out what he wanted. Joan almost laughed when she remembered how the dogs stayed out of the kitchen at Quarry Hall.

"You can't go in there, can you? Vincent trained you really well, didn't he?" She went down on one knee and ruffled the dog's neck fur. Ulysses closed his eyes and leaned into the pressure of her hand. In another minute, his tail would start thudding. Joan stopped and stood up again. "Promise to stay out here and wait for me and not get into trouble?" She did laugh, when he gave her a look that would have clearly said, "Who are you kidding?" in a person.

Ulysses, she decided as she went into the restaurant, was a person. It didn't matter that he was wrapped in fur and couldn't speak English. He communicated quite well.

She bought four cheeseburgers and an iced tea and asked for a waxed cardboard tray to fill with water. The girl at the counter started to give her a strange look, but laughed when Joan explained she had a dog outside.

"You deserve steak," Joan said, as she took the tray, filled from the water fountain, outside to where Ulysses waited patiently. She set it down on the grass, and ached when the dog nearly attacked the water. "You deserve a whole lot more than steak, but this is the best I can give you right now."

While he drank, she peeled the meat out of the cheeseburgers and put them on one wrapper on the ground, saving the bread, cheese, and pickles for herself. The sandwiches would be greasy when they got cold, but she would have something to eat and keep her awake while she waited for midnight to come around.

She thought about Vincent, about trying to make arrangements with him to meet. When she reached into her purse, her phone was buzzing. How long had he been trying to call her, but she hadn't noticed? Joan took a deep breath to brace herself before she pressed the button.

"I'm sorry," she said immediately.

Total silence. Joan cringed, wondering if she had made a mistake bringing the phone at all. Then she heard the low gusting sound of Vincent sighing. She had the feeling he had been doing that a lot lately.

"Glad I finally got hold of you, Frankie," he said. "Got a little bit of a problem. The boss-man's kid has taken off on her own again. She's gonna get herself killed, either some crooked cops or one totally hacked Fed, take your pick."

She hadn't been working with Vincent very long, but Joan could guess the subtext. Holt was nearby, listening.

"I want to go home," she said, putting emphasis on the last word. Would he understand?

"Nope, no way in the world I can track her down. Sometimes I feel like putting a bell around her neck, but the old man won't put up with her being treated like a criminal."

Was that a warning? If she showed up, she would get thrown in jail?

"Can they prove those aren't my prints?" She wished she hadn't asked, the moment the question left her lips. Waste of time and worry.

"You know what I say in these situations." Vincent sighed again. "Find yourself a church, doesn't matter who it belongs to. Find yourself a church, hunker down and pray. That's what I'm going to be doing. No matter what Dudley Do-Right thinks about me."

Joan heard a snarl and what were probably a few muffled curses in the background.

"Get to work from your end, will you?" he continued. "Her old man wants her home safe and sound by this time tomorrow. I don't care what sort of eleventh hour miracles you have to pull off," he said slowly, enunciating each word.

She guessed, hoped, that meant he would be waiting near the house after eleven.

"I'm depending on you," she said. "The fur ball says hi."

That earned a snort of laughter from Vincent. "Yeah, thanks, Frankie. You take care. Hope you have good news the next time I call. And keep your phone at hand, would you?"

"I swear." Joan closed her eyes as she pressed the red button. She gasped when Ulysses put a paw on her knee, startling her. "What is it with you guys?" A glance down showed he had eaten everything. "Ready to get going?"

Joan used the tallest building of the college campus as her line of sight guide, to keep her going in a straight line. Vincent's words spun through her thoughts. She knew she would understand all the hidden messages if they had worked together more. She did want to work with him more. For a long time.

"Since when have I started thinking about the future?" she asked Ulysses, when they were relatively alone on a side street. "Figures, that the moment I might not have a future anymore, I want one. I want to get to know my father. I want to… yeah, I want to help with the foundation. I want to keep you. I want to be more than just friends with my sister."

A splash of bright yellow and green caught her attention. The colors stood out in marked contrast to the long shadows as sunset sprawled across the landscape. It was a playground full of equipment painted in bright, basic colors, surrounded by a vinyl-clad chain link fence. Joan followed the lines of the shadows to the long building beyond the playground, assuming it was a school. Then she saw the steeple and the cross. Vincent's words echoed through her mind again.

A church would be a good place to hide, to rest, to wait until full dark. By now, Holt's men were probably combing the city, stopping every brown-haired woman with a big gray dog. What was it they had called it in the Middle Ages? Sanctuary?

But in this day and age, would the door be open?

She tried the front door. Locked. She wasn't surprised. The door would probably open for anyone else, but never for her.

The church was golden brick, built around a central hub, with wings extending out on four sides, parking lots tucked into two quarters of the property, green lawn stretching to the street in the third, and the playground in the last quarter. Joan followed the sidewalk around the church, letting it take her back behind the building, into the deepening shadows, out of the line of sight from the street. The next door was at the end of the first wing; also locked. She turned the corner and saw cars sitting in the parking lot. More than janitorial staff, probably some church business meeting.

Joan seriously doubted these people would appreciate a stranger with a dog showing up at their church, just wanting to sit in the dark for a while. A few weeks ago, she wouldn't have hesitated to sneak in and find a place to curl up and try to stay invisible, but now, something inside of her had changed.

"Please, God," she whispered. And again, she couldn't go any further.

Following the hub of the building, she studied the windows. Most of them had shades pulled down or curtains drawn. Joan saw a big double door, metal, and guessed it was a utility door. Probably to let maintenance equipment or furniture deliveries into the building. She imagined a janitor's office or storage room close at hand. That would be a good place to hide.

Ulysses broke away from her side. Joan reached for him, wishing she hadn't removed that ridiculous collar and leash. Then she saw the tall, thin man with the shoulder-length blond hair, who walked around the next wing of the building and headed for them. He wore jeans and a blue work shirt, and his smooth, long-legged, and leisurely stride seemed strangely familiar. She opened her mouth to call out a warning, expecting Ulysses to attack. Instead, the man went down on one knee, and Ulysses wriggled like an overgrown puppy. No, that was a woman. How had she mistaken her for a man? Joan fought a sickened, sharp feeling of betrayal, when the dog tucked his head under the woman's arm and begged for petting.

"You look like you could use some help," Messenger said, raising her head so the last streaks of the sunset illuminated her features.

Joan stopped short and stared. "What are you doing here?"

"I'm wherever I'm needed. Do you want to go inside?"

"Can we?" She shook off the dozens of other questions poised on her lips, and the queasy certainty she didn't want to know what was going on. If Messenger worked for the Arc Foundation, even just as a gardener, she could be trusted. Couldn't she?

But wait, Vincent had said no woman gardener worked at Quarry Hall. Joan wished she had pursued the matter more when she had the chance. It wasn't a question of whether she could trust Messenger right now. She had to.

"The door is always open, and no one is turned away, no matter what you might think. All you need is to ask." Messenger stood up, giving Ulysses one last rub, and reached for the maintenance door. She pulled on the handle and pushed down on the latch. It opened easily, without a sound. Joan let her lead the way into the darkened building.

They were in a storage room, with the door on the other side of the room hanging open so light from the hall spilled in. Joan waited until Messenger pulled the outer door closed, then followed Ulysses out into the hall. Glass filled the opposite wall, letting her see into the round sanctuary beyond. Skylights in the dome ceiling let fading scarlet and gold light into the sanctuary. The colors, the angle of light, gave a surreal feeling to the rows of golden oak pews and dark blue carpeting. Joan wanted to go in, but stepping into the light meant being seen.

"Sometimes the best place to hide is in the light," Messenger said. She strode past her, around the curve of the hallway, heading for the glass doors into the sanctuary that hung open.

"What about the people who belong here?" Joan had to follow, because Ulysses did, and she didn't want to be left alone.

"You belong, if you want."

"I'm not—I'm not ready for that kind of step." That dropping sensation in her stomach nearly rooted her to the floor. Echoes of loving, sometimes teasing, sometimes exasperated lectures from Sophie flooded her thoughts, and invitations from Xander to come visit his church. Both of them talked about the belonging that came from a higher sense of unity, of family, of bonds that went beyond the building and documents and membership duties.

"When will you be ready?"

"Sophie says—" She swallowed the sob that wanted to erupt at the mere mention of her friend's name. What was wrong with her?

"Who do you think you are, to keep God waiting?" Messenger smiled as she said it. She slid into the back row pew and made room for her. Ulysses lay down in the aisle.

Joan stopped short again, her hand on the back of the next pew. Funny, how she had never looked at the question from that angle.

"Is He waiting? How can He want me?" She felt as if someone had reached deep inside the darkest part of her and pulled the words out.

"If you can't let yourself trust God, how can you trust anybody?"

She nearly snapped at her, hating how Messenger answered her questions with more questions, but wasn't that what she did to people? Joan sat down, crossing her arms on the back of the pew in front of her.

"If God will get me out of this one..." She sighed and closed her eyes and rested her forehead on her arms. "Sophie told me to never make bargains with God."

"God doesn't need or want anything you can offer Him."

"Oh, thanks, that's really good for my ego."

"He wants everything that you are."

Joan had heard that from Sophie before, too. All her secrets and shame and pain, her anger, her dreams, everything she was good at, everything she was bad at, her discipline and passions and her weakness for chocolate and peanut butter, any way she could get it. He wanted that terrifying, glorious, sad night she and Matt had shared.

God wanted Nikki, and Joan's fear and hatred for Niobe. He wanted everything, until there was nothing left.

"He can't. There's nothing in me for Him to want."

"Who are you to tell Him He's wrong?"

"I just can't," she whispered.

"You can. You just won't."

"You can't read my mind, you don't know what's inside me!" Joan flinched when her voice rang off the ceiling. She jerked to her feet and found herself taking three steps down the aisle, toward the front platform. She stared at the podium, the table with the words, *Do this in remembrance of me*, carved into the golden oak.

"Maybe. Maybe not," Messenger said. "But I do know that you were followed here. You only have two options. Die when they catch up with you or ask for help."

Joan turned around, scalding words on her lips.

Messenger was gone. Ulysses just lay there, watching her.

She couldn't hear footsteps. More than two-thirds of the sanctuary walls were glass, but she saw no movement to tell her which way the strange woman had gone.

"Okay, now I'm getting scared." Her cracking voice echoed back to her, vibrating in the glass. Suddenly, the church felt very empty. Cold. Dark, in the blink of an eye.

She could run, or she could stay here.

No. Hadn't Messenger said her two choices were to die or ask for help?

She pulled out the phone and fumbled the button, almost immediately hearing a muffled, "Yo," on the other end.

"They followed me."

"Where are you?" The calm and strength in Vincent's voice drove away the chill trying to sink into her bones. He made her repeat the directions and description of the church three times. "How'd you get inside? Are there other people in there with you?"

"Messenger was here, but she just took off." Joan wasn't about to say the woman vanished into thin air, lacking even the chiming whine of a *Star Trek* transporter beam.

"Who?"

"Messenger. The woman I thought was a gardener. We don't have a gardener, do we?"

A loud thud, followed by a scream of warping metal and a crash, echoed through the building. With the hallway circling the sanctuary, Joan had no idea where the sound came from.

"Vincent—"

"We're on our way. Stay hidden, hear me? Let Ulysses take care of you. That's what I trained him for."

"Okay." Joan hated to push the button to turn off the phone. She stared up at the skylight, the fading twilight spilling through. She didn't want to be alone here in the growing dark. She'd never minded being alone, she preferred it, most of the time, but the sense of abandonment was too strong here in the darkened sanctuary. Even God wasn't here anymore.

Since when had she ever expected Him to be there?

Ulysses rubbed against her leg and whined and nuzzled her hand. Joan took a deep breath and rested her hand on his head. Her back protested the hunched-over position, but she wasn't going to lose this small bit of contact and guidance until she absolutely had to. Ulysses led her down the aisle, around the bend in the hallway, away from the janitor's closet and the door she had come in through.

That made sense. Her enemy would try to get in the way she had.

Another thud and crash made her jump. Out in the hallway now, Joan could tell where the sound came from. Someone tried to break down the double doors, but they held fast. She hadn't seen Messenger use a key or do anything to lock the doors. Maybe that was what she had gone to do when she left so suddenly. But if so, where was she now? Why hadn't she come back to help her?

Darkness would protect her, but it was *too* dark inside the church. Where could she go, in unfamiliar territory? One wrong turn, into a classroom with no second door, and she would be trapped. She had an image of running around the circular hall like a hamster in its wheel, on and on forever. Joan thought of innocent church members, in some classroom, taking care of church business, suddenly having federal agents and terrorists racing down the halls, shooting at each other. She had to get outside again, where she could move, where there would be light, where she could run away and keep running in a straight line, as long as it took.

A glimmer of twilight beckoned from around the next bend. Joan sped up the pace, Ulysses only a few steps ahead of her. She choked on something that could have been a laugh or a sob as she saw the wide bank of glass doors, at the front of the church. There was a reason they called the opening mechanisms *panic bars*. She understood, more than she ever had before.

The danger she had sensed all her life had been far away. She had been able to put false identities and research and her tenuous connection with legal and military authorities between her and the threats in her life. Just like she had kept most friends at long distance or put masks between them and her. Now, however, all the masks and walls had been pulled apart. Her father knew the truth, Vincent, everybody at Arc. Probably now Stone and Holt knew. Niobe, obviously, knew about her, too. The distance of a few miles meant nothing when there were men with guns trying to break into the same building.

"Please, God, whatever You want from me—" Joan stopped herself when she would have slammed both hands into the panic bar of the first door she came to. That would make too much noise. She took a deep breath, silently repeated the partial prayer—even unfinished, it was a prayer, wasn't it?—and reached out both hands to push the bar.

She expected an alarm to go off somewhere in the church's shadowy depths.

Nothing. Not even another crash from the janitor's doorway. Did that mean the men had broken in and were sliding through the shadows, catching up with her?

Joan pushed the door open barely enough to get through and slid out, holding it open for Ulysses to follow. Then she took off, across the front of the church, with a vague idea of heading for the parking lot and the tree-filled lot in back. She could hide there. She hoped.

Chapter Twenty-Four

Most of the cars she had seen earlier had left the parking lot. That was one worry reduced, if not eliminated. Joan glanced at the passing traffic on the street, wondering if anybody turned to look at the church as they drove by. If they noticed her and Ulysses walking around the perimeter of the building, would they care? She remembered how Niobe had amused herself vandalizing and bombing churches and Christian schools, even summer camps. In this day and age, with scandals among the religious and self-righteous, would anybody care if someone did damage to a church? This church in particular?

If the members of this church were as giving and truly good as Xander and Sophie, and the people in the Arc Foundation, Joan thought the community would care. They would be protective. Who would want to lose a resource like that?

"If I get out of this..." Joan shook her head. Was she trying to make deals with God? Sophie said never to do that, because whenever anybody challenged God, they got turned around and upside down and shaken until their brains rattled.

Joan supposed if that person had any brains left, she'd straighten out her life and make things right with Him.

Right now, she wondered if she had ever had any brains, much less if she would have any left.

All that mattered was staying alive long enough to find Sophie and get her to safety.

Her musing took her around the back of the church. Joan flinched every time she saw a window or thought she heard a footstep, or a door creak open. She tried not to run, knowing movement attracted attention, but it was hard when her heart thudded faster and louder, and with every step she took the safety of the trees seemed to retreat.

Finally, the thicker darkness enclosed her. She breathed easier. The hunching of her shoulders loosened when she lost that itchy feeling like a premonition of a bullet slicing through her back.

As her eyes adjusted to the deeper darkness below the trees, she saw a cleared area in the middle. She spotted a square shape that resolved into a picnic shelter, with a roof and three walls and a small fireplace in the left-hand wall.

It would make the perfect place to sit and hide until someone came to get her.

Problem: it could be the *wrong* people coming to get her. And probably the first place someone would look for her. Joan turned her back on the picnic shelter. Even in a storm, she wouldn't go in there. She knew she had made a lot of bad decisions lately, but that didn't mean she was stupid.

Ulysses moved out ahead of her, away from the shelter. Joan took a deep breath and followed. Vincent had said the dog was there to take care of her, wasn't he?

"Taking more self-defense lessons, when this is over," she vowed on a whisper. Ulysses' ears twitched, but he never looked back at her.

He led her to a spot where several sky-scraping trees had fallen, probably toppled in a storm, and caught against a fourth tree, all leaning into and tangled with each other. One broad trunk was wide enough and lay at an angle that allowed walking up. Joan was glad her eyes had adjusted to the shadows, because she wouldn't have believed what she saw otherwise, when Ulysses walked up the trunk to the tangle of limbs at the top, where the trees intersected.

It gave her an advantage, she realized, of looking out over the grove, and above the trees toward the church and parking lot. Joan scrambled up the tree trunk, hunched over with her hands reaching out to grasp the rough bark that still clung to the forest giant. The spot where the branches intersected didn't make the most comfortable perch, but leaves clinging to the limbs helped hide her. She couldn't quite sit, and she didn't trust her full weight to any one branch. Right now, shelter was more important than comfort. Ulysses waited until she'd somewhat stretched out along one limb, leaning against another upright, with her arms braced on two almost parallel branches to take some of her weight. Then the dog went nose-first down the trunk four steps and lay down. Joan envied his ease and comfort. She wished she dared lie down, but right now, she needed to see, more than she needed to be invisible.

From her vantage point, she saw three men in dark clothes, wearing ball caps and jackets, walking around the outside perimeter of the church. Two went clockwise, the other counterclockwise, once they came out of the janitor's double door entrance. That was a telling clue.

A dark van with no side windows pulled into the back of the parking lot, just as the lone man came around the wing of the building. He ducked backward into the shadows, around the corner. Two men jumped out of the van almost before it stopped. One was blond. The other was dark-haired, probably Holt. Should she be relieved he had come to her rescue? Or had he just come to put handcuffs on her as soon as he could?

Gunshots pierced the night quiet. Holt and the blond agent ducked behind the van, which rolled forward and gave them shelter crossing the parking lot. They headed into the trees.

"No way it can be this easy," Joan muttered, watching them head straight toward her.

She turned back to find the lone man. He had a shorter path to the trees. The other two men who followed her into the church came running, back the way they had come. More gunshots rang through the thickening night.

Ulysses whined and stood up, looking out through the trees to the back of the property, away from the church. Joan could hardly tear her gaze off the five figures moving through the trees and the strange game of hide'n'seek taking place below her, but she did turn. A dark green Cherokee rolled slowly up along a trail through an empty lot, around a pond, heading for a ragged gap in a chain link fence at the back of the church property.

"Thank You, God," she whispered. Vincent was coming for her, just like he promised.

Joan understood now. Holt and the others were drawing the attention of the men hunting for her, while Vincent snuck in the back way and got her out of there. She pulled out her phone and punched the button to dial.

"I can see you," she said, when she heard the connection open, before Vincent had a chance to speak.

"Stay down," he ordered.

"Can't. I have an eagle's eye view." She fought the urge to laugh. Joan suspected if she started laughing, she wouldn't be able to stop, until it had turned into tears or even screams. She had years of tears and screams to make up for, and that debt felt like it was coming due.

"Nobody looks up anymore. Stay there, hear me? It's getting bad down here. I think I can see where you are."

Joan jerked, nearly losing her balance in her precarious perch, as a crashing sound echoed through the forest directly below her. She leaned over and looked down. One of her pursuers stumbled through the underbrush, heading straight for the fallen tree Ulysses had climbed. If he had the same idea of getting a vantage point, she was in trouble.

"Freeze!" Holt's voice echoed off every tree and stone. The man didn't even slow.

"Joan?" Vincent asked.

"They're close," she whispered. "Can't talk." She closed the connection and shoved the phone into her pocket.

Holt fired. Three times. She thought she heard the wet squelch and crunch as one bullet struck the man directly below her. She did hear his choked scream, the scuffle and crunch as he fell and staggered back to his feet. More running feet, as someone caught up with him.

Joan knelt on a branch that tipped dangerously under her and looked through gaps in the branches. She saw the other two men scoop up their staggering friend and open fire. Holt lunged backward, rolling through the underbrush. The three men vanished into the deeper darkness beyond the edge of the grove. Joan watched them run into the picnic shelter.

Silence seeped through the trees, taking over, and the smell of blood and gunpowder faded. Her ears still rang with the sound of gunfire. Joan couldn't feel her hands. She gripped the branches around her so hard her knuckles were white.

A branch crunched. Down below, Holt had regained his feet. She heard his voice, a harsh whisper, and looked down to see him holding something to his mouth. Probably a phone. He had backup of some kind.

It wasn't going to do him any good.

From her vantage point, Joan saw his path led him in a straight line toward the picnic shelter, and the end with the little window. The three men would see him before he could see them. What use was one gun against three?

The next thing she knew, she had left her safe nest and half-walked, half-slid down the tree trunk. Somehow, she made it without a sound.

"Holt." She winced when her whisper seemed to boom through the trees. Joan heard no echoes, so she couldn't have been too loud. Dangerously loud. Here-I-am-please-shoot-me loud.

The agent turned so quickly she thought he would fall over. Joan stared at the gun pointed straight at her. She swallowed hard. Tried to speak. Swallowed again. Ulysses joined her and pressed hard against her leg. His fur was the only warmth in the entire dark mini-forest.

"Come here." She beckoned. He just stood there, still pointing that gun. Joan felt a scream rising in her throat. "Come with me."

Holt shook his head and held out his hand, gesturing for her to come to him. And follow him straight into the ambush. It would be a slaughter.

"Come here." Joan took a step back. He raised his gun higher, and she could have sworn she heard the click of his trigger. Did she smell the warm metal of his gun, or was that the stink of fear in her sweat? "Would I give myself up if it wasn't important?"

Holt glared at her, looked around, looked at her again. Then he finally took a step toward her. Joan took another step back. He took three quick steps. Ulysses moved between them when he reached out to grab hold of her arm.

"Follow me," she whispered.

Holt sighed when they reached the tangle of fallen trees and started climbing, but he did follow her. Joan settled gingerly on one thick limb that dipped dangerously under her weight and gave him the better spot in the lookout. She pointed to the picnic shelter.

"They're in there. All three of them."

"Are you sure?" He pulled out his phone.

"They were when I climbed down to warn you."

He paused, met her eyes, and that stern look softened a little. "Yeah, you did." He settled into a more comfortable position and talked softly into his phone.

The shivers started then. Joan clung to her tree limb and closed her eyes. His words were gibberish to her. If he spoke in some kind of secret agent verbal shorthand or if she had finally started falling apart, she neither knew nor cared.

Her phone buzzed in her pocket and Joan almost fell off her perch before she could pull it out. When Vincent demanded to know what was going on and what she was doing and if she had obeyed him, she handed the phone to Holt.

Holt stayed up there in the tree nest, watching the picnic shelter, while he directed the other two agents. They came at the shelter from two different angles, with Vincent for backup.

"What kind of backup can he be without a gun?" Holt wanted to know. Joan didn't answer, because she was pretty sure he wasn't talking to her.

The capture was a definite anti-climax, using gas to knock the three men unconscious. Joan stayed up in her tree after Holt went down, until Vincent stood below and called her.

"Right on time," he said, and bent to give Ulysses a heavy-handed stroke of approval.

"Time?" Joan knew she probably looked as dazed and stupid as she sounded. She couldn't seem to break through the thick shell around her that put the entire world at a distance.

"Eleventh hour. Just like I promised."

"Eleventh? Sophie'll be waiting at midnight." Joan felt icy shards fill her. "Can we—we have to go meet her."

"Meet her where?" Holt said, coming back to join them. He didn't scowl at her or Vincent. That had to be an improvement.

"Look, I don't have time to argue with you. I'm not this international computer hacker criminal terrorist. Somebody played with the records and put her name on my fingerprints."

"We know." Holt gave her a vicious grin when Joan shook her head, not quite sure she heard right. "Guess what? The agency can figure these things out without your help."

"Just takes some time, that's all," Vincent muttered.

"You're meeting your friend, right?" he continued, without giving Vincent the expected, killer glare. When Joan nodded, he finally slid his gun back into his shoulder holster. "Then let's go. A smart man is always early for this kind of thing."

Joan knew she should argue but couldn't think of a single reason why.

Holt let them take the Cherokee. Joan curled up in the back with Ulysses and listened to the two men go over options, then confer with Stone and someone else back at the office by phone. She wondered if they realized how well they worked together. They both knew what they were doing, and when they had a common goal, all differences fell away. Should she point that out to them?

Holt swore and yanked from his ear the plug that had let him communicate so quietly. He flipped a switch and the radio crackled and hissed and voices came through it, distorted.

"Something's going down at the house," Vincent said.

"Sophie," Joan whispered. She met his gaze in the rearview mirror. His sympathy and worry didn't help.

Holt explained the new development as they tore down the last few side streets and around corners. When Joan fled the hotel, Stone had authorized a continual watch at the safe house, on the chance she decided to go there. They had all believed Sophie would try to return, and it seemed that Salamander's people believed the same thing.

Vincent pulled up five doors down from the house, around a bend in the street where they had some shielding from view.

"We have two holed up inside," a woman reported, coming out to meet them. She wore jeans, dark boots, a black turtleneck despite the heat, and had night-vision goggles pushed up on her forehead like some weird kind of hair ornament. "Neighbors have been evacuated on all sides. They shot at the first agent who approached the house. When we used gas, it had no effect."

"Masks," Vincent grunted. Holt nodded, his frown deepening by the second.

"Why would they go inside?" Holt mused, frowning up at the house.

"Heat scan shows just the two in the center of the house." The woman agent bit her lip, glanced at the house, then back to Holt. "There's some anomaly in the attic ..."

Everyone turned to Joan.

"We have some insulation around a secret room," she offered.

"Could Sophie be up there right now?" Vincent said.

"Impossible," the woman agent said, shaking her head. "Nobody has gotten in or out since we set up watch last night."

"Sophie got past you after that man got killed," Joan said. "A safe house isn't much good if people see you coming in or going out."

"Can you get in and get her out, without anyone seeing you?" Vincent said.

"No." Holt got out of the passenger side and leaned against the door, glaring through the window at Joan. "There is no way I am endangering a civilian, on the off chance someone is inside there."

"They haven't found the secret room yet, but that doesn't mean they won't. What else do they have to do while they're waiting for their reinforcements to show up?" Joan thought of the path up through the overgrown tree, the little window into the attic, the emergency ladder stashed between the rafters, under layers of pink insulation.

"Can we provide a distraction for her to get in unseen?" Vincent said.

"There's no 'we' in this operation," Holt snarled.

"You're sure they're working for Salamander?" Joan asked.

"With Salamander, who can be sure of anything?"

"Sir?" The woman agent gave Joan and Vincent askance looks, meaning this wasn't something usually discussed with non-agency personnel.

"They're in deep, Sawyers," Holt said.

"How badly do you want her?" Joan shook her head and raised a hand to stop them from responding, while a plan whirled through her mind. "How badly do you think she wants me?"

That got silence from all three. Granted, the silence was all confusion from the woman agent. Vincent went icy quiet, his gaze unreadable. Holt got that look of a man thinking hard and not liking what he thought.

"Do you guys have any equipment to track their cell phones?" Joan asked, while her mind raced through scenarios. Which one wouldn't get her killed, and yet rescue Sophie?

"I like how she thinks," Sawyers said, nodding. She graced Joan with a tight smile.

"Get to work on it," was all Holt would say before he turned away and stomped across the street to the van being used as a control booth.

"I wasn't lying, when I said I promised to get you back to your father in one piece." Vincent took a tight hold on Joan's arm just above the elbow.

"It'll distract them, won't it? It'll let Sophie know we're here, so she can slip out."

"What if your mother has decided she just wants you dead?"

"Sophie would do the same for me."

"I won't fight you on that." Vincent shook his head. "But Sophie knows where she'll wake up if she gets a bullet between the eyes. How about you?"

Joan couldn't think of a comeback worth using. She tried to smile, gently tugged free of his grip, and went to find Holt. Maybe she could con a bulletproof vest out of him.

Holt was busy, getting reports from his people, talking on the radio, studying diagrams of the house, the neighborhood, and several screens inside the van that looked like something straight out of a high-tech spy movie. He met Joan's gaze a few times while she stood there and waited, but otherwise ignored her presence.

What was she to him now, she wondered. Civilian, or still a suspect, or just someone he didn't want to deal with because of her ties to Vincent?

"Archer?" Sawyers approached her the moment Joan turned to go back to the Cherokee and get comfortable. "I need you to fill me in on the setup in the basement."

"Setup?"

"Our equipment is having trouble with a few parts of it. We know the area is much larger than we're getting on a clear scan. More hidden rooms, just like in the attic?"

"What use is a safe house if you don't have secret rooms?" Joan offered with a shrug.

"You ought to come work for us." She tipped her head toward Holt. "If you don't get your head handed back to you, first."

"I think I want to get out of the cloak and dagger business, thanks very much."

Sawyers led Joan down the driveway of the next house and into the backyard, where equipment had been set up in the shelter of a little brick arbor laced with grapevines. It gave a perfect view of the backyard of Joan's house and the cellar door.

"Movement," the man sitting in front of a flat screen murmured. The picture looked like a photo negative. Joan guessed it was infrared.

A lone figure picked its way through the peonies next door. Joan itched, just thinking of all the ants living among those flowers, crawling all over whoever moved through their thick, fragrant shelter. She studied the image, wishing the person would come out just enough to give them an idea.

"Female," Sawyers said after a moment.

"How can you tell?" Joan whispered.

For answer, the agent tapped the little display panel full of numbers. Joan had no idea what they meant, but she assumed they dealt with height, weight, density, something that differentiated between male and female. That was one bit of expertise she hadn't gained and didn't want to.

Then a bit of movement, dark against the warmth radiating in streaks from the partially hidden body, struck her as familiar. Joan leaned closer to the screen. The movement came again.

It looked like the way Sophie's beaded hair swung when she pushed it back, raking it out of her face with both hands. Joan could almost hear the soft, chiming clatter.

"It's Sophie."

Sawyers dashed up the driveway, probably to report to Holt. Joan went down on one knee, trying to put herself where she could see the screen and the mass of peonies in the far yard. The neighbors' yards had never seemed so huge and far apart before.

All it would take to get Sophie to safety was a short walk down the alley that ran behind these half-dozen houses. But that walk meant going through moonlight, in direct view of whoever was inside Joan's house. Detouring around the block would take too long. Sophie would be out in plain view for just a crucial minute or two as she tried to get to the tree on the other side of the house. Long enough for someone to shoot her. Joan couldn't go through the houses on the other side of the alley because of the high wooden fence.

The night grew incredibly still, so Joan thought she could hear the whirring buzz of firefly wings in the next yard. No wind. No traffic. No sound of TVs or people talking anywhere on the street. For a few seconds, the entire world seemed to hold its breath and focus on that thick, overgrown clump of peonies in the far yard.

Chapter Twenty-Five

A shadow changed. Joan started to stand as the round balls of flowers shuddered and swayed and something dark emerged from among them. Moonlight hit the multi-colored beads in Sophie's hair.

"Please, God," she whispered. "I know I don't belong to You, but Sophie does."

A hand on her shoulder wrung a gasp from her. She turned and stared into Messenger's eyes.

"What are you doing here?" She let the woman guide her backward, away from the brick arbor and the technician, who never glanced at them.

"Protecting you."

"I don't care about me." She shrugged off her hand and took a step away, glaring.

"Many people are praying for you, for your protection. Don't grieve them, Joan. Don't make foolish sacrifices that won't do any good."

She opened her mouth to scald her with her anger but stopped. There was no time, and this certainly wasn't the place to shriek and demand answers. Giving in to fury had always been Niobe's territory.

And those were Niobe's henchmen waiting inside the house.

Joan heard the distinct click of a gun cocking, ready to fire. Her breath caught in her chest as Sophie stepped over the decorative little knee-high fence between the two yards.

"Stop!" she shouted, waving her arms, and darted into the yard, heading for the back door. All she could hope was that her resemblance to Niobe would make the people inside the house pause, confused, and not shoot first.

Sophie stared at her. Joan waved for her to go back. Shadows moved behind the curtains in the kitchen.

A gunshot shattered glass, spraying Joan with dozens of fine razors and heat. She twisted aside, trying to dodge.

"Joanie!" Sophie ran to her, arms outstretched, her beads streaking out behind her like a comet's tail.

"Go back!"

More gunfire. Sophie went down, spinning from the impact, her back arching. Red spattered the air in a spiral, glittering dark ruby shards in the moonlight.

Answering gunfire filled the air, streaking over Joan's head as she went down. An explosion answered from inside the house.

Sophie lay gasping in the grass, shuddering, eyes wide. Joan knelt over her, feeling blood and tears mingle on her face.

"It's all right." Messenger put herself between them and the house. She rested a hand on Joan's arm and reached to cup Sophie's cheek.

"I know you," Sophie whispered. Then she shuddered and clenched her eyes tight shut.

"My fault." Joan felt as if she had her gut ripped open. She crumpled over Sophie, ignoring the sounds of men shouting, feet thudding on pavement and gravel and grass. The gunfire had stopped, but she didn't care.

She was too late. She had failed.

"Please, God," she sobbed. A feeling like a fist clutched at her throat, trying to crush the words before they erupted from inside her. "Don't kill Sophie. She's the only one who loves me. Don't hurt her for it." The words were like shards of glass spewed from deep inside her.

~~~~~

Joan let Vincent make all the arrangements, handle the questions with the agency and the police, make all the promises. Whatever he agreed to, she would abide by. Hadn't she brought all this on them, by trying to do things her way? It was her fault Sophie lay in a hospital bed now, bristling with tubes and wires, her spine shattered.

Why hadn't God let her die, to buy Sophie's safety? Did He hate her so much He had to destroy the only person who loved her?

She stayed by Sophie, tucked into the corner of her hospital room when the doctors and nurses periodically checked on her, sitting by the side of the bed and holding her hand the rest of the time. Nothing could get her to leave. Fortunately, no one tried.

Joan had a lot to think about. Some things she didn't want to consider. Such as the mystery of Messenger.

The blonde gardener had stayed with her and Sophie, blocking them from the activity in the house, until Sawyers and another man got to them. Vincent was only two steps behind. He held Joan back when panic fried her common sense and she interfered with the paramedics working on Sophie. He shook her and tried to drag her away and gave her the strangest look when she asked him where Messenger had gone.

Vincent had seen no one, even though Messenger hadn't moved until he knelt down next to Joan. Messenger looked right at Vincent and he looked right through her.

No one, as far as Joan could tell, had seen Messenger.

Except Sophie. She had spoken to her. She had recognized her.

Joan tried not to think about the mystery woman, just like she tried not to think about the holes in the dirt all around where she and Sophie had been. Holes from bullets that should have hit them. Except for the first bullets that knocked Sophie down and shattered her spine, they had been
~~~~~

untouched. That made no sense, in the firestorm that had raged around them.

In self-defense, for the sake of her sanity, Joan made plans. She made phone calls. She made promises, to Sophie and to God and to the future. Vincent agreed with all the things she wanted to do and set off to make the arrangements. Now, all there was to do was wait. And try to anticipate the fallout, the punishment for everything that had happened.

When Sophie opened her eyes nineteen hours later, Joan was there to see it, alone with her, aching and stiff and bleary-eyed. She felt like dancing. The only thing that could have made the moment more perfect was if Ulysses was there with her. No matter how the hospital rules stretched for her, they wouldn't stretch enough to allow dogs in the rooms.

"You look like you got run over," Sophie whispered, after they had grinned wearily at each other for several minutes.

"Yeah? Stay away from the mirror for a while." Joan blinked away a gush of hot tears. "How are you feeling?"

"These are really great drugs. Can't feel a thing." She managed a shaky grin. "So, who won? The cowboys or the Indians?"

"Doesn't matter. We're not playing anymore."

"From what I could see, there was a lot of tech. Sidarkis to the rescue?"

"My father. The Feds." She swallowed hard, thinking of Messenger and the mystery she didn't want to consciously acknowledge. The word slipped out anyway. "God."

"Uh huh. Tell me everything, sister-mine. Chronological order, with no foreshadowing. You spoil every story, y'know?"

Despite her teasing, Joan knew Sophie wasn't as bright and chipper and pain-free as she pretended. Talking would distract her, at the very least. She got a little more comfortable in the hospital chair, if that was actually possible, took a more secure grip on Sophie's hand, and started with Sophie's phone call two days before. Joan included everything she had guessed and everything Vincent and Holt had told her during the long hours while they waited for the doctors to finish working on Sophie's shattered spine.

Vincent came into the room at the point in the story when Joan climbed over the balcony to get away from Holt, after the fake fingerprint report. He leaned against the wall, arms crossed, looking tired but satisfied. He didn't move until Joan reached the point where she saw Sophie emerge from hiding at the house and fell silent.

"So, what do the doctors say about me?" Sophie asked.

"They're willing to let you go home with us," Vincent said, finally moving away from his post against the wall. He braced both hands on the rail on the other side of the bed.

"Home?" Sophie tried to smile, but weariness and tears eroded her brave front. "What does that mean?"

"All the arrangements are set?" Joan felt as if a huge weight had slid off her shoulders, but only for a moment. She would carry the weight of her bad choices and her pride for the rest of her life. Every time she looked at Sophie.

"What arrangements?"

"It's too early to tell yet how lasting the damage will be." She reached for Sophie's hand and held it, gently, because of the tubes taped to the back of it. "That bullet hit your spine dead on and shattered three vertebrae. Did a lot of damage to the spinal cord. An inch to either side, you might have bled to death before anyone could get to you. An inch or two higher, you could be paralyzed from the neck down, instead — "

"That isn't drugs, is it?" The tears seemed to instantly dry from Sophie's eyes. "I'm dead from the waist down."

"Like she said, it's too early to tell." Vincent leaned down, commanding her attention. "We're getting you transferred to the Cleveland Clinic, the best doctors, the best equipment, the best therapy."

"Cleveland? Why?"

"Because it's close to Akron, and Quarry Hall. And as soon as you're able, you're coming home with us. To stay." Joan blinked to fight the hot wet trying to break through her control. "Like you've quoted at me a few dozen times, in my father's house are many rooms, and one of them is prepared for you." She tried to shrug. All her movements felt jerky stiff, painful. "What's the use of all that money, all that power and connections, if I don't use it?"

"We need you at the Arc Foundation," Vincent added. "With Joan on board, we can start expanding operations, but we need someone at home to coordinate, to handle our security programs and communications, to watch over everybody who's out on the road, doing the Lord's work."

"And me like a big fat spider in the center of the web," Sophie whispered. Her eyes glimmered with tears she couldn't quite repress. "It's a little fast, isn't it?"

"Sometimes it's like a tornado. You'll get used to it." Joan squeezed her hand and tried to smile.

~~~~~

"Messenger, huh?" Sophie looked out the window of her private room at the Cleveland Clinic. There was nothing to see but lights, this late at night.

"You said you knew her," Joan said. Her throat hurt from talking, but sometimes talking was the only defense she had against thoughts that tried to overwhelm her.

She knew she should leave and head down to Akron and Quarry Hall and the long-overdue reckoning with her father. But she didn't want to leave Sophie. She wanted to stay with her friend through all the operations, all the therapy, all the rehabilitation. However long it took.

"The guy who was with us after I got shot, yeah, I knew him."
~~~~~

"Her." Joan fought down the flicker of panic. It was just the pain medication messing up Sophie's memory. It had to be.

"You saw a blonde woman. I saw a man." She looked at the notebook computer sitting neglected on the bed table. "The guy I saw had eyes like stars and skin darker than midnight," she whispered. "Wearing gleaming armor."

"Sophie? What kind of drugs do they have you on?" Joan tried to smile.

"I've seen him, out of the corner of my eye, when I've been in a jam or four. Or maybe it's just been someone who looked like him. I'm not sure they really have bodies, y'know?"

"What are you talking about?"

"You know what word means 'messenger,' in the Bible?"

"No." Joan shook her head, even as a chill raced up her back.

"He said he was there because people were praying for you, remember?"

"Sophie—"

"You met your guardian angel. Or maybe Messenger is assigned to Quarry Hall. Who knows how these things really work? What's biblical, what's folklore, what's a lot of myth and wish-tales made up by people hungry for answers?" Sophie's eyes sparkled. "We were protected by God's warriors. That's all that matters."

"All that matters." Joan leaped from her chair. She needed to move, or she would start screaming. This late at night, that wasn't a smart move. The hospital staff was already bending the rules so hard they should have snapped long ago. She didn't want to find out what the breaking point was. She needed to be with Sophie.

"You're blaming yourself again, aren't you?"

"It's my fault." She swept her arm around the room, taking in Sophie's condition, the equipment monitoring her, the past and the future.

"Hmm. Maybe. And a lot of it is my own fault. We're the product of the choices we make, and we choose to look on the bright side, or to wallow in grief and guilt and complaining. I choose to look for the good. A lot of good came from this."

"Such as?"

"I'm officially dead, thanks to your new friend, Agent Holt. Doctor's certificate and everything. Not my fault nobody recorded that I was revived on the operating table."

"Twice!"

"Those jerks looking for me will stop now," Sophie continued with a shrug. "I'm safe. And with all that money you want to throw around, I can play with the best and newest toys on the market, design programs to my heart's content and do something worthwhile with this talent God gave me. You know how much time and energy we use up, just keeping safe and free? Think of all the things we can do now, with the Arc Foundation to protect us and support us."

"Yeah. Just think. All the things you can do. Maybe stuck in a wheelchair for the rest of your life."

"Joanie-gal, that just means I'm a genuine article holy roller."

Joan laughed because Sophie expected it. The only alternative was to break down crying and keep crying until there was nothing left.

She had fought tears of any kind for so long because Niobe had hated them. She mocked them as weakness, immaturity, foolishness, sentimentality. Joan nearly laughed, choking on the sound caught in her throat, when it occurred to her that Niobe was nothing but emotion and immaturity, letting hatred, pride, and hunger for revenge guide everything she did. Maybe it wasn't healthy to keep making choices that were opposite of what that woman wanted, but she suspected it was a good start in figuring out what really mattered.

"You're wrong, you know," Sophie said, when the room had fallen so quiet Joan heard the humming of the various monitors keeping track of her vitals.

"There are so many things, which is it?"

"I'm not the only one who loves you."

Joan shook her head, not sure what Sophie was referring to for a moment. Then she remembered the poison and pain that had gushed from deep inside her after Sophie was shot.

"I can tell, Vincent cares about you. And from all those messages he passed on before he headed back to Akron, there are a lot of other people in Quarry Hall who do. Your father, Elizabeth. And what about Xander and Matt, and his cousins, and your sister?"

"They don't know me. The real me. It's a miracle you can stand to be around me, with all you know. People like me don't get more than one of that kind of miracle in a lifetime." Joan curled up in her chair, shivering from a cold core that settled deep inside. She was too tired to guard her words. Too tired to care.

"People like you?" Sophie's voice rose a little. "Sometimes, Joanie-gal, you are just so smart you're stupid. Did you actually accuse God of hurting me because I loved you?" A long, exasperated sigh escaped her. "So help me, if I could sit up, I'd come over there and slap you silly. Do you actually think God hates you?"

"Everything I've done—"

"Yeah, everything you've done. All the good things you've done, think about that. You've made up a thousand times over for all the crimes your mother made you commit when you were too young, too weak to fight her."

"It's not enough." Joan rubbed at her eyes. They felt hot and dry, and she wondered if she had fought tears so long, she would never be able to cry again.

"That's exactly right. That's just what I've been trying to tell you all these years. You're trying to earn your ticket to Heaven. You can't."

"God doesn't want me, anyway." A bubble of laughter escaped her. Had she actually said that?

"What part of 'whoever believes' don't you get? Where in the Bible does it say that you have to clean up your act before God will save your soul?" Sophie glared, and the heart rate monitor flashed a little faster. Joan watched the twitching line, fascinated. "Do you believe in what Jesus did to pay for our sins? Everybody's sins?"

"Yeah." The word escaped her.

"Even yours?"

"Yeah."

"Do you want to go to Heaven?"

Joan could only nod.

"Do you think there's anything in this entire world you could do that's so bad it's impossible for God to forgive?" Fire almost shot from Sophie's eyes. "Name one that's too big for God."

Joan shook her head.

"You know who's keeping you out of Heaven, you stubborn idiot?" She grasped the bed rail and pulled herself up a few inches.

"Sophie, don't—"

"How long have you been there, at the door, wanting into Heaven, thinking you'd get your sorry butt kicked if you knocked?"

"All my life, seems like," she whispered.

"What would you call someone who wants something, but is so sure she'll be told no, she doesn't ask?"

"Wimp." Her mouth ached as one side inched up.

"Stop being a wimp."

~~~~~

"What do I call you?"

Carter raised his head slowly from studying the papers on his desk. He didn't look surprised to see Joan in the doorway of his office. She suspected he had known the minute she drove through the gates, the second she climbed the stairs and exactly how long she had stood in the doorway, watching him work, trying to find the right words to say.

"That isn't the first question I expected from you." He smiled and gestured for her to take a seat in the chair to one side of the desk.

Her father was having a good day. His color looked good, like he had been spending some time in the sun. No dark shadows under his eyes. His voice sounded strong, no hesitation or straining for breath. No cane leaning against the desk or a walker tucked into the corner. He wore a dark blue button-down shirt with the collar open. No robe today. A good sign.

"Everything's all right with Sophie now? You feel comfortable leaving her alone for a while?" he asked, when she had settled down and he had turned his chair to face her.
~~~~~

"The best of everything. I owe you so much—"

"No." He raised a hand sharply to stop her. "I owe both of you. My sins, my choices, contributed to the situation both of you were in." Carter shook his head. "Even if I had nothing to do with it, I would help because I'm able. And because she's your friend, and you're my daughter."

"Whatever you want from me, I'm ready."

"Joan…" His face crumpled, twisting between a rueful smile and grief. He took a deep breath, glanced out the side window, then back to her. "Is that why you're here? To pay your debt? You're getting involved in the foundation to pay for my help with Sophie's needs?"

"It's the right thing to do." She couldn't meet his eyes any longer.

"Hmm. Maybe. But I want you here, working with me, eventually running the entire foundation, because it's right for *you*. Because this is what you want to do with your talents. Not because you think you owe me. Someday, you'll resent the bargain you made. I don't want that." He sighed. "I don't know if we can ever be father and daughter, and feel for each other what God and nature intended, but we can at least be friends and respect and like each other."

"So." Her voice cracked. She forced herself to meet his gaze. "What do I call you? I mean, Father is too formal. And Daddy isn't… respectful. Kind of immature. Nikki called—" Joan choked, wanting to tell him about the wall she had finally broken through in her life. The problem was that she felt as if the wall had fallen down on her.

On the other hand, what were a few bruises when she knew God didn't hate her?

"Nikki. Your professor's foster-daughter." He sat back in his chair. "What about her?"

Joan suspected he knew, or at least had enough clues to guess, her convoluted relationship with Nikki. If Holt could see her resemblance to her mother, then Carter could see the resemblance between her and her sister.

"Did you know my mother had another child? I was twelve when my sister was born. My mother went crazy when her lover died and then after she couldn't track you down here, she… she left my baby sister in a stolen car in the middle of a flooding river. In Tabor."

"So that was your reason for settling there. Logical."

"To find out what happened, and to be near my sister. She was saved. We're friends." Joan shuddered. "I have to tell her, don't I?"

Chapter Twenty-Six

"Are you trying to decide if the truth will hurt Nikki or help her? Or if it will destroy your friendship?"

"I need to protect her. I was researching this guy she's been hanging around with. He looks good on the surface, but I just know he's trouble." Joan shrugged. "I wonder sometimes, maybe some things are genetic. Messing up with men. Like mother, like daughters."

"I don't think so. She had many advantages. I'm sure in the end, Nikki will be all right."

"She's a Christian. Doesn't she know any better?"

"I was a Christian when I slept with Elaine. Knowing better doesn't mean we do better."

"So no guarantee I'll be smarter and make better choices, now that I finally have my soul straightened out, huh?" Joan forced a shaky smile.

She shuddered and that hot, aching pressure returned to her eyes, when her father's eyes widened, then brightened, and he reached out to grasp her hands.

"Being a Christian is a continual process of changing to become like Christ. It's a lifelong effort, and even when we die, we're nowhere near the end of it."

"That's encouraging." She tried to look out the window, but the angle of the sun and the glare of light on glass and through the sheer curtains made that impossible. "The thing is… I don't want to screw up anymore. I've been on my own for so long, and it took me this long to figure out that I need someone to teach me. Despite the hundreds of books I've read, all my studying, I don't know anything worth knowing." She met his gaze again. "Will you?"

"That's what fathers are for, Joan."

Carter's hands shook, clasping hers, but Joan suspected it didn't have anything to do with his illness. The warmth that spread through her from his touch soothed beyond the flesh.

"I'm somewhat old-fashioned, you know." He nodded, managing a more normal smile when she gave him a confused look. "I'm not one of those modern fathers who can have his daughter call him by his first name. Why don't we try 'Dad,' and see how it works?"

"Dad. Yeah. The only other alternative is 'Pop,' and that's just not you."

They shared wide smiles, both of them too drained, suddenly, to indulge in laughter. But Joan felt it vibrating through the office, just waiting for another chance to come out.

She would spend a lot of her time in this office, she knew. And she liked the idea.

~~~~~

"Joan Archer." Dr. Holwood smiled wearily and stepped back from the doorway, beckoning for her to come inside his home. She had been a guest here several times, but now Joan felt like an intruder.

She wanted nothing more than to flee back to her apartment and hide for the rest of the day, but she was already over the threshold. She glanced back at Ulysses, who obediently sat down on the top step of the shadowy, wrap-around porch.

"I see you have a new friend," Dr. Holwood said. "He's welcome inside, too, if he promises not to chew anything."

"Or anyone," Joan muttered, earning a bark of his famous, deep, rumbling laughter. His resemblance to James Earl Jones had never been stronger. She held out her hand in the signal Vincent had taught her. Ulysses jumped to his feet and trotted over to her side.

Doria Holwood joined them before they had reached the sprawling front room, full of couches and floor pillows, that always seemed to be open for university students to drop by to socialize and ask for advice. The Holwoods' foster children were conspicuously absent, neither playing in the side room designated as their playroom or running around upstairs. Joan had always liked coming to the Holwoods' house because there were always at least three children, always making noise. She hadn't seen them in the backyard as she walked up the side street from Main. Maybe Nikki had taken them to the municipal pool.

A few knots in her gut relaxed when she considered that she could tell the Holwoods the truth first and get their help in talking to Nikki. Her father had convinced her that while Nikki might be furious to learn the truth now, after all these years, she wouldn't hate her. And maybe Joan would be able to break through to her and free her from Brock Pierson's influence before something bad happened.

"I'm here for Nikki, actually." Joan took a deep breath. Tried to smile. "In more ways than one. I know who put her—" She stopped short when she saw the pained look the Holwoods exchanged, then the tears that filled Doria's eyes. "What's wrong?"

"Nikki's gone." Dr. Holwood huffed out a breath and seemed to deflate, collapsing into the big leather armchair that was his sole domain.

"Gone?"

"She ran away." Doria settled on the wide arm of the chair and her husband took hold of her hand in his. "Just four days ago. We have police looking for her, but she went with Brock and he seems to have a talent for..." She shrugged, struggling for a moment for the words.

"Falling off the radar?" Joan filled in. Her gut regained those knots and
~~~~~

added a few more. Something sharp, like shattered glass, churned inside her. "It's my fault."

"Of course not."

"No. She was asking me for advice—I told her about my psychotic mother—I asked Xander about getting a restraining order, registering a complaint against Brock, and I didn't follow through. I had information. She asked me for advice and I told her how I ran away because I couldn't take it anymore." Joan slapped both hands over her mouth to keep more words from spilling out. Her eyes ached and burned, but the tears didn't come yet.

"Joan, I hardly think—"

"No, there's more, isn't there?" Dr. Holwood held up a hand to quiet his wife. "You know more, don't you?" He waited, no condemnation on his face, as Joan nodded and lowered her hands. That lack of blame helped her, though a weight in her chest grew with every word.

"I know who left Nikki in the car, when she was a baby, when the police found her and brought her to you. I was just a kid." Joan gasped when Ulysses sat up and rested both paws on her thigh and nuzzled her. She wrapped her arms around his thick, furry neck. "My mother. Our mother."

Doria let out a soft, pitying sound, and settled down on the couch next to Joan, putting an arm around her. Her comforting touch made Joan want to fly from the house and never come back.

How different would things be if she had told Nikki, even a few months ago, that they were sisters?

"You came back to find her," Dr. Holwood said, his words slow, as if he worked through the parameters as he spoke. "Now that we know, the resemblance—" He stopped, his frown deepening, when Joan choked on ironic laughter. If only he knew how much trouble her resemblance to Niobe had caused her. Would it harm Nikki someday, too? "All this time you've been here, why didn't you ever tell her?"

"Scared to," Joan admitted, her voice small.

"Rance, please," Doria gently scolded.

"I should have told her. When we met at the gym and I told her how I ran away from my—our mother, I should have told her then. She might have listened when I told her Brock was trouble."

"I seriously doubt that," Dr. Holwood said. "Nikki has a lot of problems, a lot of grief and complaints. Some, she's brought on herself. Some... well, let's just say hormones are interfering with her thinking. Everyone thought Rich was her knight in shining armor, and then he went off to college and betrayed everything he stood for at our church and broke her heart. Then along comes someone much older, exciting, gallant..."

"I have connections." Joan rubbed at her eyes, wishing for just a few tears, something to ease the aching pressure. "I'll have people looking for her. I'll bring her home, I promise."

"No." Doria hugged her a little harder. "Nobody will bring her home except God. We haven't quite worked it through to leave this in God's hands, but we're sure the only way Nikki will come home is by His grace, and His timing."

Joan bit her tongue to keep from objecting. What was the use of all the connections and influence and knowledge available to her, if it wasn't put to good use?

~~~~~

Joan blinked and found herself crossing the street heading toward Heinke's Grocery. The sanctuary of her apartment lay behind her. She had no clear memory of what she had been thinking in the twenty minutes since she left the Holwoods' house, let alone what route she had taken. Ulysses whined and nudged her hip when she paused. She continued across the street.

Stepping up on the curb, Joan turned to look behind herself, back toward her apartment. She would climb those steps and go through a security check of her apartment, just like she always did when she had been gone more than two days. What would she do after that? A surge of panic threatened to choke her when she couldn't push her mind to the next step. Ulysses reared back on his hind legs and rested his big paws on her chest, knocking her off balance. Joan gasped, partly laughter, and went back a step.

"Hey, monster, give me a break." Tears burned her eyes as she thought of having to go through the last week without him.

The thought of Ulysses sitting next to her desk while she checked her newsgroups and investment reports comforted her. She swallowed back the aching in her throat that just aggravated the ache in her chest and her head and went down on one knee. Ulysses nuzzled her and pressed close, clearly begging for petting.

"You're probably wondering what the heck I'm doing, aren't you? We just came back here to get some things, tie up a couple loose ends. You want to go home, don't you?" Joan exhaled loudly, fighting a giddy sensation at the realization that she did indeed consider Quarry Hall home now. It fought with the aching, heavy feeling that squeezed her and stole her breath, every time she let her thoughts even turn in the direction of Nikki.

Ulysses licked her cheek. She sputtered laughter, when it occurred to her to be grateful he hadn't licked her mouth, like she had seen too many dogs do to other people who got within tongue's reach. That just proved what an intelligent dog Ulysses was. Her dog. Her bodyguard. Her guardian angel, watching out for her.

That thought seemed to jolt the logjam of thoughts in her head. Joan smiled shakily at the slightly stunned realization that she had responsibilities. It would take a while to decide what to move to Quarry Hall. It was a given her apartment, however long or short a time she stayed there, needed to be more dog-friendly, for starters.
~~~~~

"You hungry?" she said, getting back to her feet. Joan looked over her shoulder at Heinke's. "Whatever I have in my 'fridge is probably green and fuzzy. Let's get some chow, okay? We'll goof off tonight, go for a walk in the Metroparks, watch a movie. Leave the work for tomorrow."

When she reached the automatic doors of Heinke's, Joan almost motioned for Ulysses to follow her inside the grocery store. He saved them, settling down in the shade between the cart rack and the box that took grocery bags for recycling. Joan sighed, smiled at the intelligence and training of her companion, and went inside.

Nothing in the produce section attracted her. She put that aside for later in her shopping trip. Joan decided to look at dog food, first, then doubled back to get a cart. She should have driven her car, just in case she ended up with more than two bags' worth of supplies.

"Going up in the world?" Susan Reichman's syrupy coo jolted Joan from chill into instant heat.

She turned, the handlebar of the shopping cart caught in a white-knuckle grip. The main reason for not attending Tabor Christian with Matt faced her with her usual smug, self-righteous look. What was Saint Susan's justification for dressing for a garden party to go to the grocery store? All she lacked was a wide-brimmed straw hat, decked with silk flowers and trailing multi-colored ribbons, to go with that poofy floral sundress and pale pink strappy sandals. Who wore mascara and painted their nails to match her dress to go grocery shopping?

Joan bit back a dozen acid retorts poised on her tongue. Knowing Matt wouldn't ask Saint Susan out on a date to save his life didn't offer much comfort. Susan had convinced the interfering old biddies in the front row at church to play matchmaker because she was such a demure shrinking violet, she would never dream of chasing a man. But digging her claws into every female whom Matt willingly spent time with didn't fall under the heading of "chasing a man," did it?

"I have no idea what you mean, nor do I care." Joan turned her back on Susan, even as a prickling sensation traveled down her spine. The overdressed twit had lasers in her eyes. If looks could kill, rigor mortis would have set in two years ago.

"Then you must be hard up for money. Shopping in the dog food aisle." Susan raised her voice to compete with the announcement coming over the PA system about half cakes on sale in the bakery.

Joan picked up the first can of dog food she saw and checked the price on the shelf. How could people on a budget afford to feed a dog this stuff? She would be better off buying steak for Ulysses, at these prices. And the food would be more natural.

"This one says it'll make your coat shiny and guard your immune system," she said, turning back to find Susan had pulled into the aisle behind her. "I wonder if there's one that's guaranteed to increase your intelligence or balance your temper?" Batting her eyelashes, she forced a wide smile, teeth bared, and turned her back on Susan as her nemesis gasped and huffed.

Joan heard the clatter of shopping cart wheels head away from her. She took a few deep breaths and gripped the handle of the cart to steady her trembling hands and fight the weakness in her knees.

Just hungry. Haven't eaten since last night, and I didn't eat much at the hospital, period.

She hadn't stayed for lunch at Quarry Hall, and her vague plan for confronting Nikki had included convincing her sister to come with her to Stay-A-While for a late lunch, or maybe Perk & Perch for one of their decadent desserts.

Joan chose a small bag of dry dog food, a dish with food and water compartments, a bottle of shampoo, and four large cans of wet food, and headed for the bakery. She definitely needed something greasy, fried, and full of sugar and chocolate. Her run-in with Saint Susan shouldn't have shaken her like it did. Blaming it on low blood sugar and lack of junk food was the easiest explanation.

Nothing tempted her, not even her favorite comfort food: apple fritters bigger than her outstretched hand, glistening with sugary glaze. Joan gave up and headed for the produce section. Maybe she would just get something from the salad bar, load up her container with pasta salad and marinated artichoke hearts and all the goodies she ordinarily didn't buy for herself.

"Just give up," Susan hissed, as Joan reached for the round aluminum pan provided at the end of the long, refrigerated salad bar.

Joan fumbled the pan and glimpsed Susan's smirk as she went down on one knee in her attempt to catch it. She failed, and the nine-inch round pan banged hollowly to the floor.

"You're not his type," her nemesis continued.

Joan ignored her, though she couldn't resist slapping the pan down onto the stack she got it from. Her appetite had definitely vanished.

"Walk away now before you get hurt."

"Are you threatening me?" Joan flinched, hearing Niobe's cold rasp in her voice. She had seen grown men go pale and back away, sweating, when her mother used that tone. Susan obviously heard nothing, because she kept talking.

"I don't know what he sees in you. He's wasting his time. You don't even go to church."

"Yeah, and you're an advertisement to make people want to go? I'm surprised Matt even stepped foot inside your church, if he knew you were waiting to pop out of your web and try to suck him dry."

"Suck him—" Susan let out a little squeal that made a few blue-haired women in jogging suits stop and stare. "You're the leech! Vicious little tramp looking for a sugar daddy—"

"Wrong on both counts," Matt said, coming around the deli display case, with three sub sandwiches in his hands. "Joan has more money than me. She's a silent partner in my business, by the way." He nodded to Joan, nothing but a pleasant smile on his face. Until she looked closer and saw the sparks in his eyes. The same sparks had burned when he realized someone was not only stealing his invention but trying to frame him for espionage and treason. "Hey, Rocky, should I be flattered or insulted that Miss Reichman here thinks I'm a sugar daddy?"

"Insulted, definitely." Matt's teenage cousin sauntered into view from the other side of the department, holding a plastic pie container. His name was Peter, but he had been nicknamed Rocky during summer camp, after hearing the story of how Jesus called Peter a rock.

Joan wished a big rock the size of the Terminal Tower would fall down out of the sky and clobber Saint Susan right then. She wanted to run, but her feet felt like they were nailed to the tile floor.

"Now, Matt," Susan said, her voice going sweet and soft. She tipped her head to one side and fluttered her eyelashes. "How many times do I have to ask you to use my first name? Aren't we good enough friends for that? Hmm?"

"No. And that's *Mr. Cameron* to anyone who makes false accusations against my friends. I've known Joan a lot longer than I've known you, or anyone at our church."

"I've known her for a long time," Rocky said. "Take it from me, you've just seen the tip of the iceberg. Told you she was the biggest man-hunter in the whole church."

"Now Peter—" Susan began.

"You can call my cousin *Mr. Cameron*, too," Matt said.

"Better yet, don't call any of us at all," Tris, Rocky's twin sister, announced as she joined them with a tub of potato salad in one hand and a carton of lemonade in another.

Joan suspected they were stocking up for a picnic dinner at Blossom. The intensity of her longing to be invited to go along, to laugh and lounge on the grass, made her sick to her stomach.

"Excuse me. I have to—" Joan shook her head, spun her cart around, and headed for the checkout lines.

Ulysses appeared from nowhere as she put her few items on the conveyor belt of the self-serve checkout. Joan felt a nudge on her thigh and looked down. He didn't make a sound, just pressed against her and looked at her with his unnaturally intelligent, big eyes. She swallowed down a sob that tried to suffocate her, and looked around, waiting for store security or a manager to come after her. Dogs weren't allowed in the store, unless they were Seeing Eye dogs, and even then someone always complained. Usually the same people who felt that giving disabled drivers special parking spots close to the door was unfair.

No one came after her and Ulysses. The lack of reaction frightened Joan more than if alarms had sounded and police spilled through the door with guns drawn.

"Joan." Matt appeared at the end of the checkout line, four people and their carts between him and her. She fought not to look at him as she signed the checkout screen.

The wisest course of action was to just ignore him and get out of there as quickly as possible. Would Ulysses attack if he thought she was in danger, or just frightened enough? She didn't want that. Despite all the frustration she had given him over the last few weeks, Matt would never hurt her. She knew that, just like she knew the best thing she could do for Matt Cameron was to stay out of his life.

Joan gathered up her two bags and headed for the automatic doors. Ulysses ran ahead of her, opening the doors and then standing aside, as if he held the doors open for her. She started to laugh, but the sound caught in her throat. Matt didn't call her name again, and her eyes filled with heat and wet when she realized that.

Had he finally given up?

Joan got halfway up the street to the bridge over the river, to Main, and she had to stop. She went to her knees in the grass, dropped her bags, and wrapped her arms around Ulysses. The tears came, silent sobs that shook her body.

Please, God, it hurts!

Arms wrapped around her, and she nearly leaped to her feet before she realized Ulysses hadn't growled.

"It's okay," Maggie half-crooned, half-growled. The town eccentric smelled like lemonade, carnations, and peppermints. "It's about time you just gave up, y'know? Just let go. It ain't against the law. Stop trying to be Superman."

Joan leaned back, just enough to glimpse Maggie's sun-browned, smiling face and the baggy blue, long-sleeved cotton shirt she wore. Then a ragged wail escaped before the pain rose up in her throat and choked her. Maggie turned Joan around to face her, as much as she could without letting go of Ulysses and guided her head down onto her shoulder.

"You ain't alone anymore, y'know? Stop trying to do it all by yourself. You got nothing to prove anymore."

"It's all so wrong." Joan choked, feeling she might drown in her tears.

Chapter Twenty-Seven

Maggie's arms slipped away for a moment, making her panic, then came around her stronger and tighter again. Joan pressed her face into the spicy-scented cotton and let the tears come, her arms still tight around Ulysses, until the pressure faded and she felt empty, light, as if she would float away. Those big, strong arms still held her, while the flood reached its crest and then the pressure finally released and began to fade.

That was when the differences struck her conscious mind. Joan inhaled sharply and tried to push free. Those strong, *bared* arms tightened. She felt muscle and crisp hair pressed against her bare arms, not the baggy, faded blue long sleeves of Maggie's overshirt. That was aftershave she smelled. The expensive, spicy kind that reminded her of the forest. The Bulgari she had helped Tris find for Matt for Christmas last year, just because Stephanie Plum loved how it smelled on Ranger.

"You take one step to try to run away from me, and I'll put you over my shoulder so fast your head will swim," Matt growled.

"Been there, done that." Joan felt justifiably proud that her voice didn't shake, even if it was barely two steps above a whisper.

"I don't know what you've been up to. You don't have to tell me if you don't want to."

Joan stiffened with the shock of realizing she *wanted* to tell him. But where could she start? Where was it safe? She lifted her head and could barely make out his face through her tears. Where had Maggie gone?

"But I gotta tell you, you look awful," Matt finished.

"You should see the other guy." She thought maybe he smiled.

"You guys are making a spectacle of yourselves," Tris said, her voice coming from a good twenty feet away.

Joan looked up and blinked away tears to see Tris and Rocky sitting on the hood of Matt's SUV, arms crossed, looking bored as only two recent high school graduates could look.

"If you're trying to make sure Susan the Snake leaves you alone, that's the wrong way," Rocky added. "Now she's going to get all the grannies in church to help her save you from yourself."

"Maybe we should take it inside," Joan said. Funny, how much easier it was to talk now.

"You willing to come home with us?" Matt got to his feet and held out a hand to her, to help her up. "You really look like you need somebody looking after you. No offense."

"How about..." Joan swallowed hard. "How about you guys come home with me, instead?" She sputtered laughter and finished wiping the last tears off her cheeks with the back of her hand, when Matt, Tris and Rocky all gaped at her. It was a joke among them that Joan never invited anyone inside her sanctuary. "What do you say, Ulysses? Are we up for company?"

"Gee, if we'd known a dog would soften you up," Rocky began, to break off with a grunt and his twin's elbow in his gut.

"I've got a better idea," Tris said. "How about Tactless and I take the groceries home while you two talk? We can come back for you in an hour or so, okay?"

Joan suspected all she had to say to Matt would take considerably more than an hour, but she agreed. It was easier to breathe, she discovered, once Matt tossed the keys to his cousin. He took the heavier bag, with the canned food in it, and started up the street before Tris got into the driver's seat. Rocky was still standing there, looking confused, caught between pouting and laughing, when Joan turned to head up the street to her apartment.

Matt didn't say anything for the entire walk, and she was grateful. Ulysses walked between them. She wondered if maybe he was the reason Matt waited for her to start talking. He followed her up the stairs and took the other bag from her while she dug in her purse for her remote control, finally remembering it was in her pocket. He followed her inside and only raised an eyebrow when she checked the security system. Matt let her take the bags from him, and wandered around the small main room, looking at her bookshelves and racks of CDs. Joan filled Ulysses' new dish with water and stepped out of the tiny kitchen to see Matt standing on front of her painting of Joan of Arc.

That was a good place to begin, she realized.

"Joan Archer isn't my real name. I took on a new identity when I came to Tabor," she said. Part of her expected a *Yeah, right,* reaction. She was pleased when he just nodded and waited for her to continue.

"I'm not even sure what my real name is, or if I even have one. My mother is a... let's just say she's psychotic and leave it at that. I ran away from her when I was fourteen. I'm still pretty much hiding from her."

"What about your father?"

"That's where I've been. Meeting my father." Joan sank down into her computer chair, leaving the futon couch for Matt. Ulysses walked over to her, dripping water from his muzzle, and pressed his wet fur against her leg. She smiled and buried her fingers in his fur. What would she have done without Ulysses to go through all that with her?

"Rough time?"

"Only if you consider tripping over a corpse in my other house, getting arrested by the FBI and shot at, my best friend almost dying, and finding out my mother is an international terrorist 'rough.' Yeah, it was."

"You don't joke around enough, Joan." Matt slouched a little, tipping his head back on the couch so he nearly touched the edge of the painting with the top of his head. "I have the feeling you're not joking around here. You don't cry, either. What brought that on, after a stupid run-in with Susan?"

"Everything." She took a deep breath. Telling those details to Matt had been easy, compared to what pressed against her tongue, demanding release. "You know Nikki James? How she was found and all that?"

"The Holwoods go to my church."

"She ran away from home with that creep, Brock Pierson."

"Hadn't heard that." Matt sat up a little. "Why would Nikki matter..." He narrowed his eyes and it felt for a few moments as if his gaze bored into her. "I just had the craziest idea."

"It's not crazy." Joan tried to smile, but it made her face hurt.

"You do look alike."

"We look like our mother." She took a deep, quick breath, and hurried on before she lost her nerve. "I originally came to Tabor to find out what happened to the baby. My baby sister." Joan wrapped her arms around herself. "Our mother tried to kill her. Weird, isn't it, how even after all this time, I'm still fighting to accept what happened?"

"You shouldn't have to accept any of it."

"I've been here four years, and never told Nikki we were sisters. Then, when I finally get up the guts, God keeps knocking my feet out from under me, and Nikki is gone when I come to tell her."

Ulysses whined and got up on his hind legs, to press his face against Joan's and lick her cheek. She gasped a little laugh and wrapped her arms around him.

"Where'd you get him?"

"He adopted me the minute I stepped out of the car at my father's house."

"Must have been a rough couple of days. You look like you've been run over and half-drowned and hung up to dry upside down."

"That's about how I feel." She closed her eyes, hating this recurring breathless, helpless feeling, along with the words that kept pressing at her tongue, demanding the right to be heard. "I've needed to let that out, for a really, really long time."

"Glad to be here, then."

Joan wondered if he really was. He spoke so calmly, with his usual warm, pleasant expression, just a few flickers of concern in his eyes and voice. Was he just in shock over what she had told him, and needed time to digest it before he could let himself react? Or had she pushed him too far when she gave her ultimatum? Matt was here, listening to her, but she could blame a lot of that on curiosity more than caring.

"He wants me to work with him. My father. He runs a foundation."

Joan took a deep breath. In for a penny, and all that. "He was involved in… well, information brokering would be a nice way of putting it. Powerful and rich and playing with international politics. And he's dying. So he finally made contact with me, to set things right, I guess."

"Only it's not really safe for you to be in contact?"

"I've never felt safe in my entire life, so what difference does it make?" She flinched when Ulysses whined and nudged her hand, reminding her he was there. "Until Ulysses adopted me, of course."

"Of course." The corner of his mouth flicked into a brief smile.

"He's a Christian. The entire foundation is."

"You can't seem to escape us, can you?"

"Like Sophie said, God won't give up, so I might as well." She took a deep breath, and realized she felt a little calmer after that confession.

Joan braced herself and met his gaze. Every bit of information would just bring on more questions. Her own fault, she supposed. If she had been open with Xander and Matt from the beginning of their friendship, trusted them not to toss her like hazardous waste, she wouldn't have so much to cover and backtrack now.

"Sophie is in the Clinic right now, with a broken spine. She took a bullet meant for me. And if that isn't bad enough, she's got a big, powerful creep on her tail, trying to make her use her computer genius for his profit." A groan escaped her. "That sounds so melodramatic."

"You've had a busy week, all right." Matt crossed his arms over his chest. "So should I be worried or flattered that you're opening up like this?"

"Both?" Her smile trembled and she gave up trying to be flip. "I'm just a breath away from shattering. I owe you so many explanations." Her indrawn breath hitched, a sob muted just barely in time. There was no way she could tell him about that emergency trip to the clinic on Col. Sidarkis' tab. Not yet. Maybe in a few years. If ever. How could she admit that their one night of death-defying passion had resulted in a baby that miscarried before she even realized she was pregnant?

"Sounds like God has been piling it on to get you to listen to Him," Matt said, when they just sat and looked at each other for a few more minutes.

"Right now, I can't even hear myself think, let alone God."

"Maybe the person you should be talking to about this is your father. He knows where you're coming from."

"Yeah. I guess." She took another hitching breath. "Want to meet him?" she blurted, knowing she had to speak before she swallowed her words and lost her courage.

"Where is he?"

"Akron. Quarry Hall. He owns it."

"We sold them a security system about a year ago." He stood up and crossed the room to her. "The Arc Foundation is pretty impressive."

"My father has a lot of crimes to make up for." Joan took a deep breath.

"Just like me."

"Depends on how you look at it." Matt held out a hand, to pull her out of her seat. Joan stared at his outstretched hand, unable to push her brain into gear and figure out just what the gesture could mean or what taking it would imply for her. "I guess I'd better drive, huh?"

"Drive?" She finally decided she had to move, or they would still be in their positions long after Tris and Rocky showed up. It jolted her, to feel Matt's hand holding hers. She remembered how safe she had felt when he held her in the darkness.

"You're going to tell me everything that happened the last few days. I figure you'd better be free to concentrate on that."

"Everything?" Joan started to tug her hand free, before it shook and betrayed her. Matt let go and wrapped his arm around her shoulders. "You won't like a lot of it. Might make you run for the hills."

"Just try me."

Rocky muttered something about "meeting the parents," when Matt told them what he and Joan were doing, and that the twins weren't invited to come along. Tris quelled her twin before he got more vocal, and the two of them were remarkably quiet, sitting in the back seat of the SUV all the ride back to their house in Stoughton. Joan let herself feel a little smug when Ulysses ignored everyone and huddled at her feet in the front, refusing to let anyone but her touch him, despite Tris's attempts to make friends. Considering how well Tris got along with animals, an almost magical touch, it was rather odd, and satisfying, to see Ulysses refuse to be charmed. Her smugness turned to laughter when he leaped into the back seat the moment the twins got out, and stretched out, claiming the entire expanse for himself.

"Smart boy," Matt said. He waited until they were on I-71 before he demanded her story.

Joan began with the package waiting for her in front of her door. She had to backtrack several times, explaining the significance of Fuppy Bear and her sneakers, and give him glimpses of her nomadic, fugitive life with Niobe. His deepening frowns, some muttered comments she didn't quite catch, comforted her. Matt was angry on her behalf.

He asked more questions about her father's past as Oracle, and about the setup of the Arc Foundation, and caught on quickly to the origination for the name. Joan appreciated his tact when his only reaction was a grin before he asked more questions. Matt jerked the wheel a little when she narrated how she tripped over the body in the dark in her kitchen. A few more mutters came when she related, with as few details as possible, the hard time Agent Holt gave her.

They turned off Market Street onto Portage Trail by the time she wrapped up the tale, with her pursuers caught and Sophie in the hospital. Joan left out all mention of Messenger. She wasn't quite sure what to make of the woman and would have passed her off as a stress-induced hallucination, except that Sophie had seen her. And seen her as a Black man, in armor.

Joan was in no condition to doubt anything. If Sophie wanted to believe Messenger was an angel, sent to look after them, give them guidance with cryptic remarks, she would try to believe, too.

"Anything Sophie needs, you just tell me," he said, when she got to the doctor's report, delivered that morning before she left the Clinic.

"Arc is covering all her bills," Joan reminded him.

"Well, yeah, that, but I've been brainstorming a few things. Not quite virtual reality, but I know someone who's been playing with tapping directly into the brain... We could make her a lot more mobile, no matter how extensive the damage is." He glanced sideways at her, offering that endearing, eager smile that had drawn her in from the day they met, paralyzing her instinctive flight reaction whenever people tried to get close to her.

"Let's see what the doctor says. After everything that's happened, and especially where Sophie is involved, I'm willing to believe in miracles." Joan shuddered a little, shaken by how easily those words slipped from her lips.

"Me, too." Matt reached over to grip her hand.

"We're here." She pointed at the gates of Quarry Hall, pulling her hand out of his range.

He mock-glared at her. Joan blinked hard at sudden tears, choking on the wave of gratitude that things seemed to be healing between her and Matt.

He pulled the SUV into the wide apron, stopping in front of the closed gates of Quarry Hall. Joan wasn't surprised to see Vincent step out of the stone cottage by the gates, with three of the house's dogs at his heels. She opened the window and waved to him. Vincent gave her a knowing smile, and the gates opened without him signaling anyone or even taking his hands out of his pockets. She guessed he had a gate control in his pocket.

"Cameron, right?" Vincent leaned on the edge of Joan's open window when Matt paused by the cottage, and nodded to him. "Any upgrades coming to that security system you designed for us?" He winked at Joan. She hoped that meant Vincent approved of her bringing Matt here.

"A few ideas. Nothing proven beyond the initial testing phase yet."

"Keep us in mind." He gestured up the long drive, toward the sprawling lawn in front of the house. "Perfect timing. Your dad's got a guest who came into town early, just to meet you. Go on up."

Joan decided now was not the time for resisting or trying to make things go the way she had envisioned when she asked Matt to come to Quarry Hall with her. If she had learned one thing, it was to follow Vincent's directions. Matt parked by the carriage house and they started down the flagstone path to the front of the house. Then she wondered who her father's guest could be, and why this person wanted to meet her. It couldn't be Col.

Sidarkis, so who?

"You know who that is?" Matt said, when they had crossed maybe twenty yards of lawn and two men came out of the shadows of the trees on the far side. "Allen Michaels," he said, when Joan only squinted at the tall, broad-shouldered figure standing beside the man leaning on a cane. She could make out nothing of either man except they wore light-colored clothes.

She said nothing but shuddered a little when Ulysses whined and pushed against the back of her thigh with his nose, urging her forward. Matt didn't even look at her, all his attention on the men who now looked up and watched them approach from across the lawn. Joan wished she could have Matt's clean conscience and look forward to meeting one of the foremost evangelists in the world. A man with an impeccable reputation and history, respected even by his enemies because of his humble ability to admit when he was wrong, and apologize.

Memory brought to Joan the smell of the chemicals in the explosive device her mother made her carry to the front of the arena, during the children's story time portion of one of Michaels' early crusades. She had tucked it under the platform, behind the canvass covering, as ordered, too terrified of her mother's acid disappointment to hear much the smiling preacher said. She wondered now if things might have been different if she had listened that day, and told someone about the box inside her backpack, instead of fleeing the arena as ordered. Would she have resisted her longing to surrender to God for so long, with fewer crimes on her conscience?

Okay, God, do You have to keep smacking me between the eyes?

"There you are," Carter said, smiling. Joan was glad to note the absence of so many pain lines around his eyes today. Something twisted inside her chest, when it struck her afresh how good it felt to be not only welcomed, but wanted. How glad would her father be to have her here, when she told him about her first encounter with the revered Dr. Allen Michaels?

"Dad—" She choked when her father's eyes lit up at the address. Suddenly, nothing else much mattered.

"This is Joan. At last," Carter said, turning to Dr. Michaels.

"It's nice to finally meet you, Joan. Your father and I have been praying for you for years." Allen Michaels held out his hand, and Joan grasped and shook it without thinking. She barely heard as Matt introduced himself and the three men exchanged pleasantries.

"The Arc Foundation has been a valued partner of my ministry for many years," Michaels said, turning back to Joan. "Your father's experience and advice have helped me avoid some sticky situations and provided security that saved quite a few lives. I'm looking forward to working with you, in the future."

"Maybe you shouldn't," Joan almost whispered. She forced herself to meet his gaze. "When I was thirteen, I tried to kill you."

"No, your mother used you to try to kill me. There's a difference," he responded without even blinking.

"You knew." Joan was glad for Matt's arm going tight and firm around her shoulders. There was no place to sit, and she didn't fancy ending up sprawled on the grass at their feet.

"That's how we met," Carter said. "I was following Elaine's trail. God used me to save Allen's life that day, and we have been friends, praying together for this moment, ever since."

~~~~~

Joan looked around her room and smiled. It was pretty bare right now, with just the basic furniture and plain bedding. There would be time later to personalize it.

Like the other daughters of Quarry Hall, Joan had chosen a room in the servants' quarters of the house. It made sense, it felt right. Luxury wasn't for her. Maybe she didn't quite grasp the whole philosophy of what drove the members of her new family, but she was coming to understand.

Right now, the thing to grasp was the telephone. Ulysses' ears twitched as Joan tapped through her phone to bring up the number for Common Grounds Legal Clinic.

"Hey, Mr. Big-Time Lawyer Finley," she said, when Xander answered. She laughed when he exclaimed over her abrupt disappearance and started demanding answers. "You'll hear the whole story soon. I'm actually calling to make an appointment to meet with you. Remember when I told you I'd give you a million dollars? I'm putting my money where my mouth is."

THE END
~~~~~

THANK YOU!

Thank you for reading this book from Mt. Zion Ridge Press.

If you enjoyed the experience, learned something, gained a new perspective, or made new friends through story, could you do us a favor and write a review on Goodreads or wherever you bought the book?

Thanks! We and our authors appreciate it.

We invite you to visit our website, MtZionRidgePress.com, and explore other titles in fiction and non-fiction. We always have something coming up that's new and off the beaten path.

And please check out our podcast, **Books on the Ridge,** where we chat with our authors and give them a chance to share what was in their hearts while they wrote their book, as well as fun anecdotes and glimpses into their lives and experiences and the writing process. And we always discuss a very important topic: *Tea!*

You can listen to the podcast on our website or find it at most of the usual places where podcasts are available online. Please subscribe so you don't miss a single episode!

Thanks for reading. We hope to see you again soon!

About the Author

On the road to publication, Michelle fell into fandom in college and has 40+ stories in various SF and fantasy universes. She has a bunch of useless degrees in theater, English, film/communication, and writing. Even worse, she has over 100 books and novellas with multiple small presses, in science fiction and fantasy, YA, suspense, women's fiction, and sub-genres of romance.

Her official launch into publishing came with winning first place in the Writers of the Future contest in 1990. She was a finalist in the EPIC Awards competition multiple times, winning with *Lorien* in 2006 and *The Meruk Episodes, I-V,* in 2010, and was a finalist in the Realm Awards competition, in conjunction with the Realm Makers convention.

Her training includes the Institute for Children's Literature; proofreading at an advertising agency; and working at a community newspaper. She is a tea snob and freelance edits for a living (MichelleLevigne@gmail.com for info/rates), but only enough to give her time to write. Her newest crime against the literary world is to be co-managing editor at Mt. Zion Ridge Press and launching the publishing co-op, Ye Olde Dragon Books. Be afraid … be very afraid.

And please check out her newest venture: Ye Olde Dragon's Library, the storytelling podcast. Each week, listeners are invited to join Michelle on her blog to ask questions and give feedback and suggestions. Interspersed between the chapters will be interviews with authors of fantastical fiction. Listen to the podcast on your favorite podcast app or listen on the website: www.YeOldeDragonBooks.com, and click on the Ye Olde Dragon's Library link. Then go to her blog to interact: www.MichelleLevigne.blogspot.com

www.Mlevigne.com
www.MichelleLevigne.blogspot.com
www.YeOldeDragonBooks.com
www.MtZionRidgePress.com

Look for Michelle's Goodreads groups:
Guardians of Neighborlee
Voyages of the AFV Defender

NEWSLETTER:
Want to learn about upcoming books, book launch parties, inside information, and cover reveals?
Go to Michelle's website or blog to sign up.

Thanks for reading!
If you enjoyed this book, would you help Michelle by posting a review on Goodreads?

Are you a member of Book Bub? If so, please follow Michelle on Book Bub, and you'll get alerts when new books are coming out.

As a way of saying thanks, Michelle invites you to the Goodies page on her website. It will change regularly, offering you a free short story, a sample audiobook chapter, sneak peeks at new cover art, inside information on discounts and new release dates, etc.

Please go to: Mlevigne.com/good-stuff.html

Also by Michelle L. Levigne

Guardians of the Time Stream: 4-book Steampunk series
The Match Girls: Humorous inspirational romance series starting with **A Match (Not) Made in Heaven**
Sarai's Journey: A 2-book biblical fiction series
Tabor Heights: 18-book inspirational small town romance series.
Quarry Hall: 11-book women's fiction/suspense series
For Sale: Wedding Dress. Never Used: inspirational romance
Crooked Creek: Fun Fables About Critters and Kids: Children's short stories.
Do Yourself a Favor: Tips and Quips on the Writing Life. A book of writing advice.
To Eternity (and beyond): *Writing Spec Fic Good for Your Soul.* A book defending speculative fiction.
Killing His Alter-Ego: contemporary romance/suspense, taking place in fandom.
The Commonwealth Universe: SF series, 25 books and growing
The Hunt: 5-book YA fantasy series
Faxinor: Fantasy series, 4 books and growing
Wildvine: Fantasy series, 14 books when all released
Neighborlee: Humorous fantasy series

Zygradon: 5-book Arthurian fantasy series
AFV Defender: SF adventure series
Young Defenders: Middle Grade SF series, spin-off of *AFV Defender*
Magic to Spare: Fantasy series
Book & Mug Mysteries: cozy mystery series
Quest for the Crescent Moon: fantasy series starting in 2023
Steward's World: fantasy series reboot and expansion
The Enchanted Castle Archives: fantasy series, Liars' Quest, 1st book in the Ye Olde Dragon's Library podcast

9 781955 838740